Semishigure

SHUHEI FUJISAWA

Translated by Thomas Harper

This translation first published by Honford Star 2025

Honford Star Ltd.
Profolk, Bank Chambers
Stockport
SK1 1AR
honfordstar.com

SEMISHIGURE by Shuhei Fujisawa
Copyright © 1988 Nobuko Endo. All rights reserved.
English translation copyright © 2025 Thomas Harper

Original Japanese edition published by Bungeishunju Ltd., in 1988.
English translation rights reserved by Honford Star, under the license granted by Nobuko Endo, Japan, arranged with Bungeishunju Ltd., Japan through Japan UNI Agency, Japan.

ISBN (paperback): 978-1-915829-29-0
ISBN (ebook): 978-1-915829-30-6
A catalogue record for this book is available from the British Library.

The extracts from *The Book of Songs* and the *Analects* are slightly adapted translations by James Legge (1815-1897).

Printed and bound in Paju, South Korea
Original cover art by Toru Kageyama
Design by Bumpei Kii
Typeset by Honford Star
Cover paper: 250 gsm Vent Nouveau by TAKEO, Japan
Endleaves: 116 gsm NT Rasha by TAKEO, Japan

1 3 5 7 9 10 8 6 4 2

Contents

One Morning a Snake …	5
The Night Festival	25
The Storm	40
Beneath the Clouds	53
Savage Wind, Sudden Downpour	76
Like an Ant	99
The Sound of Falling Leaves	121
The Elder's Mansion	141
Summer Rains, Cloudy Skies	162
One Hot Night	185
Somekawa-chō	196
A Single Blow, Heaven-sent	218
Cloudburst	238
Early Spring	256
Flowing Waters	273
An Invitation	290
Hidden Strife	317
A Trap	329

Reversal	343
The Assassin	373
Cicada Showers	394

One Morning a Snake …

1

In the domain of Unasaka, the residential quarter assigned to samurai of the Defense Works Unit was favored in a way that neither the homes of other samurai nor the barracks of the foot soldiers were. Along the rear of the quarter flowed a rivulet, which, though less than six feet broad, the residents regarded as their supreme treasure.

Not far from the castle town, off to the southwest, lay a range of rolling hills. Down from the depths of those hills flowed a network of little streams, of which this was one. It flowed out across a broad expanse of rice land until it came up to this quarter, at the northwest corner of the town, then turned sharply and wound its way off to the northeast.

Eventually, it emptied into the Goken River, downstream from the town. But along the way, the residents of the Defense Works quarter could wash their clothes in it and dip into it to water their gardens or clean their houses. The shallow stream flowed constantly, so that the faint trickle of its current was always to be heard, while the sandy patches and small stones beneath the water, and sometimes even the dark backs of little fish swimming upstream, were clearly visible. In the warmer seasons it was not at all unusual to see people on the banks of the stream washing their faces in the morning.

The Goken River that flowed through town was large enough to accommodate the traffic of small freight boats. At the water's edge, wherever the river was deep enough, stone-paved cargo landings had been constructed, which people from the merchant houses could use to wash their clothes. But the water there, whether from the nature of the soil or because it had passed through the town, was always murky. No one ever came to wash their face in this water.

By comparison then, at least so far as water was concerned, members of the Defense Works Unit having a stream just behind their homes so clean they could wash their faces in it, enjoyed, one might say, a heaven-sent blessing. It was nothing they boasted about to others; but inwardly and secretly, they were quite pleased to be the beneficiaries of Heaven. Maki Bunshirō was one of those who felt this way.

When Bunshirō stepped out of the vestibule, towel in hand, he circled around to the rear of the house. His mother, always so strict and proper, said it was uncouth to wash one's face in the stream rather than at the well. It would not please her, he knew, but it was a beautiful day, and he was drawn instead to the bank of the rivulet. Even his father would occasionally wash his face in the stream, exchanging greetings with one of the neighbors in a loud voice, so Bunshirō told himself it was all right.

Bunshirō had been adopted into the Maki family. His adoptive mother was the younger sister of his real father—actually his aunt. But Bunshirō felt much greater affection and respect for his father, with whom he shared no blood relationship, than for his painfully proper mother. His father, Sukezaemon, was a man of few words, but very manly.

Semishigure

The residential quarter of the Defense Works Unit was where the lower ranking samurai lived—those paid thirty koku per year or less—so the houses themselves were small. But they were on the outskirts of town, and so the lots upon which they were built were large, from 250 to 300 tsubo, more land than anyone would need even if they kept a vegetable garden. And between the houses, as well as at the rear, large trees grew here and there: zelkovas, oaks, maples, magnolias, cypress, damsons. In winter, when the zelkovas and oaks had lost their leaves, it did not seem such a thicket; but in summer it was transformed into a forest so dark one could hardly even see the house on the far side of the hedge.

When Bunshirō reached the bank of the stream, Fuku, the girl who lived next door, was there washing clothes.

"Good morning," Bunshirō said.

Fuku turned and glanced toward him, then rose and nodded her head, but said nothing. Then she turned away, crouching again, so as to hide her face from him. Now, in place of her pale visage, it was the soft curve of her bottom that faced him.

"Hmm!" Bunshirō smiled. Even when she was much younger, the daughter of their neighbor Koyanagi Jinbei had always been a quiet child. But whenever Fuku would see Bunshirō, morning or evening, she would always greet him properly. When was it, Bunshirō wondered, that she had begun to be so short with him? A year or so ago, it must have been. It was about then he began to feel that Fuku might be trying to avoid him; but he hadn't the slightest idea why.

"No need to wonder about *that*!" his good friend Owada Ippei had told him. "Just a girl becoming a woman." Ippei had spoken in his mock know-it-all manner; but their deadly serious friend Shimazaki Yonosuke had been with them, and he just couldn't understand what "becoming a woman" meant. Bunshirō could remember what a sweat he and Ippei had been in trying to explain. But even now Bunshirō had his doubts about Ippei's conclusion. Fuku was still only twelve.

His mother, Toyo, had been thirteen when she was married to Sukezaemon; it was perfectly normal in those days, people said, for girls to marry at that age. But things were different now. Bunshirō knew that nowadays, so long as a girl was married before she was twenty, that was fine. In fact his own elder sister Kie had not been married to Ishizuka Hannojō until the autumn of last year, when she was eighteen. Fuku was still too young to be "becoming a woman."

Bunshirō washed his face with a great deal of noisy splashing. If his mother had been there, he would have been scolded for his bad manners. But it was not his mother who was there; it was only Fuku, whose recent reticence, according to Owada Ippei, meant she was "becoming a woman."

After Bunshirō had washed his face, he sponged himself with the wet towel from his neck down to his chest and arms. Now he felt refreshed, the sweat of the hot, humid night cleansed from his skin. Filled with a wonderful sense of liberation, he gazed across the stream at the rice fields spread out beyond its banks. That broad expanse of green was tinged a pale pink in the morning sun, but out where the fields met the dark green of a grove around a distant village, a bank of mist still lingered from the night. And then that motionless bank of mist too was tinged by the sun. Even at that early hour, someone was out inspecting the crop. The dark shadow of a man, sunk up to his thighs in the rice, slowly receded into the distance. Above, in the leafy shade of the zelkovas, the cicadas were shrilling. For a moment, the pleasure of it all engulfed Bunshirō in a reverie. Then suddenly, his reverie was shattered by a scream of pain.

Semishigure

Behind every house, at the water's edge, there was a little dam, built to make a place where they could launder their clothes. Beginning from the bank and out toward the middle of the stream, they would hammer in three or four stakes, then place planks against those stakes reaching down to the bed of the stream and damming the flow. Then, in front of the dam, they would lay down planking or sink a large flat stone there. The members of the Defense Works Unit were very skilled at this sort of work.

There was one of these washing platforms behind each and every house; and the water in front of them, that had grown deep over the years, made a pleasant trickling sound the whole day through as it spilled over the dams. But every family seemed to have had a different idea where they would place their dam; some stood midway along their stretch of stream, some near a corner of the property. Bunshirō's family had built their dam at the right-hand corner of their lot, immediately adjacent to that of their neighbors the Koyanagi, from which it was separated by a simple fence.

It was Fuku who screamed. Bunshirō immediately leapt the fence between them. No sooner had he landed on the Koyanagi side than he spied a snake, slithering away from the place where Fuku stood, frozen with fright. It looked to be a tiger snake, about two feet, four or five inches long. Fuku, blue in the face, was squeezing a finger.

"What happened? Did it bite you?"

"Yes."

"Where?"

He reached for her hands and saw that the tip of the middle finger on her right hand had gone bright red, and a very small drop of blood welled up from it. Bunshirō did not hesitate. He took her finger in his mouth and sucked hard at the wound. The faint scent of blood filled his mouth. Fuku had yielded her hand to him unconsciously, but now began softly to cry. Thoughts of poison and the snake must have filled her with fear.

"Don't cry!" Bunshirō spat. His saliva was red. "A tiger snake is not as dangerous as a viper. There's no need to worry. Besides, no child of a warrior house should cry about anything this slight."

After he had sucked enough blood from the wound to make her finger turn whitish again, Bunshirō released Fuku.

"I think you're safe now," Bunshirō said. "But be sure to tell them you've been bitten by a snake when you go home." Fuku bowed but said nothing, then went trotting off toward her house. She seemed still to be upset.

Bunshirō knelt down amongst the scattered bits of washing Fuku had just begun to launder, scooped up some water, and rinsed out his mouth. Then he stood and started looking for the snake. A tiger snake is harmless, they said; but one mustn't take a chance. If he could find it, he meant to kill it. And finally he did find it, in a dark clump of bamboo by their border with the Yamagishi family, their neighbors on the other side of the house. He grabbed it by the tail and dragged it out of the thicket. The snake curled back, its fangs bared, but Bunshirō beat it upon the surface of the earth, and lastly bashed its head with a stone to ensure it was dead. He had been taught he must never leave a creature to die in agony.

When he returned to the house, however, Bunshirō said nothing to his mother about meeting Fuku out back or killing the snake. He ate his breakfast in silence. His mother, he reckoned, would not be pleased to hear that he had been sucking Fuku's finger or that he had put a snake out of its misery by smashing its head.

In recent years Bunshirō's thoughts had become burdened

with matters he could not mention to his father and mother. Now he felt that one more secret had been added to that burden. Any number of times he had washed the hand with which he had grabbed that snake, but to his disgust, all the while he was eating, it seemed to him that it smelt foul.

Shortly after breakfast, his father left the house to go to the castle. Bunshirō went to the vestibule with his mother to see him off as he left through their humble gate.

When the Works Unit was busy with a construction project, his father, Sukezaemon, usually would not report to the castle but would go directly to the work site. For which he would wear travel trousers or breeches and sometimes leggings with tied straw sandals. But today there must have been no works in progress as he was dressed in a worn suit of formal linens. Sukezaemon was of middling height, but his back was broad and he looked to be a strong man.

Bunshirō followed his mother back into the kitchen, where he asked her to prepare some rice balls to take with him for lunch.

"Couldn't you come back and eat here?" she asked.

In the morning, Bunshirō would be going to Ikoma Reisuke's academy, where he was studying the Chinese Classics; and in the afternoon he would go to the Ishiguri Dojo in Kaji-machi, where he was practicing swordsmanship of the Kūdon school. That was his daily routine; so sometimes his mother would make rice balls and he would not return home. But Bunshirō's home stood between the Ikoma Academy in Aoyagi-chō and the dojo in Kaji-machi. It was not that his mother begrudged the time and effort it took to make rice balls, it was just that she worried for Bunshirō's sake when he had to be away from home all day, so she would always voice a brief protest. But Bunshirō had plans of his own.

"I promised Ippei and the others I'd eat outdoors with them, if the weather was good."

"You mean you're still friendly with *that* boy?" His mother's distaste showed quite plainly on her face. Half a year earlier, a young maid in Ippei's household had quit and returned to her village; after which a rumor spread that Ippei had been dallying with her. Owada Ippei was sixteen, a year older than Bunshirō. He had already come of age and physically was very big. His beard was growing, and he looked in every way an adult. Bunshirō thought his appearance alone might have given rise to the rumor; Ippei himself claimed it was totally false.

"You're known by the company you keep. You had better watch your step." Bunshirō's mother spoke sharply, but still made the rice balls for him. With the bundle containing his lunch and a woodblock copy of his text under his arm, his bamboo sword and practice gear over his shoulder, Bunshirō left the house.

2

When they clashed, Yada Sakunojō's bamboo sword struck Bunshirō's shoulder, and Bunshirō struck Yada square on the forehead. Bunshirō's bamboo sword had struck a mere instant earlier and struck hard. "Arh!" Yada blurted, leapt back, then pressed his hand against the spot where he had been hit, just above his headband. At the Ishiguri Dojo, when they practiced with bamboo swords, they wore gauntlets to protect their wrists and headbands of silk floss wrapped in tanned leather. Bunshirō's blow seemed to have reverberated even below Yada's headband.

"Good. That will do for now," Yada said, lowering his sword and removing his gauntlets and headband. His forehead glowed red.

Semishigure

"I'm sorry about that," Bunshirō said apologetically. Yada Sakunojō was a samurai serving as a personal attendant to their lord; he ranked fifth among the top disciples at the school.

"What? That's nothing to apologize for." Yada was a mild and affable man. As he spoke he adjusted his grip on his gauntlets and headband, narrowed his eyes, and looked straight at Bunshirō as if to praise him for that fine blow he'd been dealt.

"You won that one, you know!"

"No. That …"

"You needn't be modest. I hadn't noticed before, but you've really improved."

Bunshirō looked down, struggling not to let the joy of being praised show on his face.

"How old are you, Bunshirō?"

"Fifteen."

"You haven't come of age yet?"

"Not yet. Not until next spring, my father says. He'll find a sponsor for me sometime this year.

"Fifteen? Frightening, this new generation." Yada smiled. "I'd better watch out, too."

Ishiguri Yazaemon, the master of the school, had already announced the end of practice for that day and gone within. A few people still continued to practice. Outside, at the well, some were washing the sweat away; most of the others had gone back to the changing room or were changing in a corner of the instruction hall. One of them had long since finished changing and was sitting cross-legged on the floor, chatting to the others in a loud voice. Ippei had come late to practice and was the first to quit. Even so, he was a solid swordsman.

Yada bowed, and Bunshirō, too, removed his gauntlets and headband. Whereupon, from the far end of the hall, a violently angry shout erupted. Everyone turned and looked that way, as did Bunshirō. It was Satake Kinjūrō, assistant to the master, who was angry; before him, his head hanging, stood Shimazaki Yonosuke.

"Got that? We *both* strike!" the assistant yelled. "You *don't* run away—just because you think you'll be hit! If you don't get the rhythm of it you'll never learn!"

"Yes," Yonosuke said, in a voice so faint it sounded like the murmur of a mosquito.

Someone in the crowd heard him and began sniggering.

"Who was that laughing just now?" Satake glared at them, and everyone in that corner of the hall went dead silent. Even Owada Ippei, who had been lounging there self-importantly, chattering away, hastened to sit up properly.

Satake Kinjūrō served the domain as a trainer of His Lordship's horses, an insignificant post for which he was rewarded less than ten koku per year. But in the Kūdon school of swordsmanship, at the Ishiguri Dojo, there was no one who could challenge him. Some years earlier, they say, before he became assistant to the master, at the annual competition sponsored by the Kumano Shrine, Satake defeated all five swordsmen of the Ittō school from the Matsukawa Dojo. That story lived on as a legend at the Ishiguri Dojo. But most likely because he drove himself so hard, he demanded the same of others, and at times his harsh nature revealed itself in the cruel lessons he inflicted upon his students, all of whom feared him. Now it was Yonosuke who had come up against the merciless Satake Kinjūrō.

"You understand that?" Satake's eyes flashed back at Yonosuke. "If being hit doesn't hurt, you can't expect to make any progress."

In the Kūdon school, one attacks from the figure eight position—left foot forward, arms raised to the right, blade pointing upward—then moves in and strikes. Everything depends upon the speed with which one strikes. That, one is taught, is the very essence of it. First one learns the basic movements with a wooden sword; and once one has mastered those, one moves on to practice with bamboo swords. To show fear of the opponent's bamboo sword violates the most basic principle of the school. This was a point Satake was particularly peevish about; so much so, apparently, that he raised his bamboo sword, and faster than the eye could follow, brought it down with a crack upon Yonosuke's shoulder. Then he stalked off at a great pace and went within.

Yonosuke tottered under the blow. The buzz of gossip arose again as the others began to leave. Yonosuke just stood there, still grasping his bamboo sword.

"Shimazaki, what's the matter?" Bunshirō called to him as he began walking to the exit that led out to the well. Finally Yonosuke raised his face, removed his gauntlets and headband, and walked slowly toward Bunshirō. He was blue in the face.

From the dojo in Kaji-machi, they walked a little way down a side street until they came to the broad thoroughfare along the bank of the Goken River. Before they left, Bunshirō, Owada Ippei, and Shimazaki Yonosuke had secured the bundles of their practice gear to their bamboo swords. Ippei, though, lazy as he was, couldn't be bothered tying his gear together with a cord. He just threaded his things onto the sword, so that he looked like he was carrying a skewered block of roast tofu on his shoulder as they walked south along the riverbank. The townspeople heading in the opposite direction were finding it difficult to suppress their laughter as they passed, but Ippei just strolled along, roast tofu over his shoulder, without the least sign of concern on his face. Even when they veered west, the hot sun still bathed the riverbank thoroughfare, but they found some relief in the shade of the green willows.

"I'm just not suited to learn sword fighting," Yonosuke said, then grimaced as he twisted the shoulder where Satake had struck him.

"Does it still hurt?" Bunshirō asked.

"Here; let's have a look," Ippei said, grabbing his shoulder. Yonosuke let out a shriek of pain and tried to pull away; that big hand must have grasped him right where it hurt most. But Ippei was big and Yonosuke was slight and weak. Ippei forcefully restrained him, then pulled his collar down and exposed his shoulder.

"Yaa! He really whacked you!"

"Oh, my!" Bunshirō peered at it too.

A narrow welt had risen on Yonosuke's shoulder, and all around it the skin had turned bright red.

"Satake-san must have been deadly serious when he did *that*," said Ippei.

"Certainly seems so," Bunshirō responded.

"Don't make such a fuss over it," Yonosuke protested. "I mean, let go of me. It's indecent to be carrying on like this out here."

When Bunshirō looked up, he saw that passers-by were eyeing the three of them strangely. True, they were only youths; but with one of them standing there bare shouldered, and the other two staring at him as if something were amiss, it was bound to excite people's curiosity. Ippei noticed, too, and took his hands off Yonosuke.

"Is it bad?" Yonosuke asked in a worried voice, as he adjusted his clothing.

"It's nothing," Ippei said. "If it were me, I'd just ignore it. But you're such a weakling. You could go home and cool it with water."

Semishigure

"Is that all?"

"If it worries you, you could rub some ointment into it."

"Well then, that settles it," Yonosuke said. "I'm going to quit taking lessons at Kaji-machi."

"Just because Satake-san thrashed you? That's ridiculous." Bunshirō smiled as he spoke. "You'll never find a school that pats you on the head while they teach you, no matter where you go."

"No, that's not what I mean." Yonosuke shifted the load that rested on the shoulder that wasn't sore. He was so frail he looked as if the bamboo sword and his bundle of practice gear were as great a load as he could ever carry. "I've been wondering lately whether I shouldn't quit trying to learn sword fighting and devote my full time to scholarship."

"What?!" Bunshirō and Ippei exchanged knowing glances. In that case, Bunshirō thought, he could understand. Ever since Yonosuke enrolled in the Ikoma Academy, they had said he was brilliant. Sometimes he would even take the place of their mentor Reisuke and lecture the students on the Confucian *Analects*. It was not as if there were no future in this.

Then leaping ahead, Yonosuke told them: "I may even get to go to Edo. Not right away, of course, but …"

"Well, well, now! Really?" Bunshirō said. The three of them turned in at the stone storage yard just upstream from the Ayame Bridge and sat down. There, hidden behind the branches of the willows, they should be able to talk this over without being observed by the passing throng.

3

Yonosuke sat down on a big square-cut block of stone, grabbed the head of a stalk of grass sprouting up between his legs, yanked it loose, and started chewing on the stem. The sun was sinking in the sky and before long would settle amongst the merchant houses on the far shore and the roofs of the adjacent fish markets, where great numbers of people still bustled about beneath the eaves. The sun was tinged a doleful shade of red, and its intense glow cast shadows on Yonosuke that gave his gaunt face an aura of wisdom, as if he were an adult.

Yonosuke took the long stalk of grass that he held, flipped the head to the rear and the stem to the front, and tossed it onto the water.

"Ikoma Sensei has long since told me this," he said. "If I would like to make my living as a scholar, I could go to Edo, and he would recommend me to the Kasai Academy."

"Really? That's extraordinary," Bunshirō said, while Ippei gave out a deep rumble of approval. Kasai Randō was a renowned scholar of Zhu Xi Confucianism whose name was well known even in the rural domain of Unasaka. Ippei was one of the poorer students at the Ikoma Academy, but even Ippei would have known that not only their mentor Ikoma Reisuke but also the dean of the domain academy, Shibahara Kenjirō; Junior Elder Tōyama Ushinosuke; and Samurai Commander Komoda Shōbei had all studied at the Kasai Academy.

"When will you go to Edo?" Ippei asked.

"That's not decided yet," Yonosuke said, "but if I do go it will be in the autumn."

"This year?"

"Mmm."

"That's very sudden," Bunshirō said, but Ippei and Yonosuke said nothing. Edo was 210 leagues from the castle town of Unasaka. Like Bunshirō, the two silent youths may also have been entertaining fancies of that city they had never seen.

Yonosuke, looking down at the ground, grabbed the head of another stalk of grass and pulled it up.

"But I'm not like you," Yonosuke said, "I'm not the heir to a household." Perhaps he had been thinking about this for some time, but Yonosuke was sounding very mature. He was the second son of a minor official who made the rounds of rural villages checking the condition of the lacquer trees from which candle wax was tapped. "I have to decide for myself what I'll do with my life."

"But you could be adopted as an heir," Bunshirō said. "There are several families in the Corps of Vassals who have only daughters and are keen to find a husband to adopt." When he said that, Bunshirō was recalling the Koyanagi family next door. Their daughter Fuku was the eldest of three daughters.

But Yonosuke just cast a weak smile at Bunshirō. "An adopted husband?" he said. "That's a form of lottery. Draw the short straw and you're stuck for life."

"No!" Ippei boomed. "Yonosuke must go to Edo." Ippei was firm. Bunshirō and Yonosuke both looked him in the face, but Ippei confirmed his verdict with a grave nod of his head.

"Yonosuke is no swordsman."

"Oh, come now!" Bunshirō said reproachfully. Yonosuke smiled bitterly; but Ippei went on, his face still deadly serious.

"I heard everything Satake-san said this morning, and once you've been told that, you haven't a hope."

"That's what I thought, too; and that's why I said I would quit Kaji-machi." Yonosuke was no longer smiling; he wore a dejected look.

"That's good. You should put all your energy into scholarship. With your brains, you're certain to succeed, even if you go to Edo."

"I'm not so sure about that," Yonosuke said. "But I'll never know if I never go."

"No," Bunshirō said. "If even Sensei is willing to recommend you, everything will go exactly as Ippei says. So make up your mind: You're going to Edo, and you're going to strive to become a scholar."

"That is how I feel," Yonosuke said. "Especially today since Satake-san told me off, I've felt that's the only way open to me."

"That's all right, isn't it?"

"But you need money to go to Edo."

When Yonosuke said that, Bunshirō had to shut his mouth. He had absolutely no idea what it cost to go away and study. Ippei seemed the same. For a time they said nothing, but then Ippei spoke up, as if something had just occurred to him.

"Travel expenses? We'll go around to all our friends and collect a going-away gift for him. Right?" Ippei was looking at Bunshirō when he said this; but Bunshirō shook his head.

"No. What Yonosuke is talking about isn't just the cost of travelling. When you go off to another province, it costs a lot of money to pay for food, clothing, and a place to live. It's not like living and eating at home."

"Yes, I suppose so."

"What I'm saying is, my parents don't have that kind of money; we're a poor family," said Yonosuke, but without a hint of gloom on his face. His voice sounded almost as if he was finding their poverty amusing. "Ikoma Sensei knows all about this. He said he would ask the school to take me on as their employee so I could study there."

Semishigure

"So you would work for the school *and* study at the same time? That would be exhausting," Ippei said.

"Grueling, to be sure," Bunshirō said, "but if you could manage it, you'd have no worries about eating or a place to sleep."

"True. But the way Sensei was talking, it isn't as if I'd never need a single copper. I'd need a certain amount in addition every month for clothing and food. And then there would be the cost of books."

"There would indeed," Bunshirō said. "And having gone to so much trouble to get to Edo, you'll want to see all the sights. It would never do to shut yourself in at the school and never set foot outside, just because you have no spending money."

"A monthly allowance of spending money …" Yonosuke began. "Sensei was saying he would send me enough for that. But Sensei himself must be just as poor as we are. It would make me feel terrible to accept that sort of kindness from him."

"Yonosuke! You are …" Ippei burst in again with his great voice. "Ikoma Sensei is saying this because he has great expectations of you. You are a lucky man!"

"Why don't you just do as Sensei says?" Bunshirō urged. "Won't it do to pay back your debt after you've completed your studies?"

Yonosuke was deep in thought. The sun had sunk below the roofs of the houses on the far shore. Only a pale reddish tinge lingered on the fields upstream overlooking the Goken River. To the southwest, rising darkly into view behind the rows of houses, stood the grove of trees surrounding the castle. And though separated from it by some distance, the Goken River that flowed before their eyes served as the outer moat of the castle. Along the dark waters of the river, flowing as though through a deep valley, freight boats could be seen gliding slowly downstream, both boats and the boatmen poling them now but blurs of black. The town was beginning to be shrouded in dusk.

Yonosuke raised his head. "You're right. But I'll think about it just a bit more." As if Yonosuke's words were their signal, the three of them rose, returned to the street, and began sauntering south again.

"Hey, don't you head back from here?" Ippei said. The most direct route to Bunshirō's home was across Ayame Bridge to the west. But Bunshirō was in no mood to return home. Even if he were to return, his father would not yet be home from the castle; only his mother would be there. It wasn't that he was avoiding his mother, only that he thought it would be more interesting to stay with Ippei and Yonosuke than to be alone with his mother.

"That's all right. I'll go along with you."

To which Ippei replied only, "Oh?"

The three of them hadn't as much to talk about now as before. They just wandered through the town, at times as if they had no particular destination in mind. The streets were now completely dark, and the passers-by had vanished.

"But it'll be lonely when Yonosuke leaves," Ippei said. Bunshirō felt the same. They discussed when he might return home again, once he had left for his studies, but none of them knew anything for certain.

As they drew near the Gyōja Bridge, upstream from Ayame Bridge, they spied several samurai in formal linens crossing the dusky bridge, heading for the near shore. Probably men returning from the castle. Once they had crossed the bridge, most of them disappeared into the residential quarter straight ahead, but one of them turned onto the riverside thoroughfare and came walking toward them. As he came abreast of them, they could see that he was a well-dressed samurai in his forties. When the three of them bowed to him, he stopped and called out to them.

Semishigure

"Whose sons are you?"

"I am Owada Ippei of Urushibara-chō." Ippei identified himself. Having lost his father when he was ten years old, he had already succeeded him. He had not yet been assigned a position in the castle, but his status was different from that of Bunshirō and Yonosuke; he was head of the Owada house with a stipend of one hundred koku per year. The man stared at Ippei's face as if to verify what he had just been told.

"On your way home from the dojo?" the man asked, his sharp eyes fastened upon the three youths. Ippei, as their representative, told him that was so. "Well, it's not good for young men to be wandering about in the dark streets. So get yourselves on home, quickly." Having said which, the man walked off with broad strides. The three bowed but said nothing as they saw him off.

"Angry wasn't he? Who do you suppose he was?" Yonosuke said, but neither Ippei nor Bunshirō knew his name. But that had put a stop to their stroll. Bunshirō decided he would cross at the Gyōja Bridge and go home. When they reached the bridge, he raised his hand to bid them farewell; but then, as if he had just remembered something, he called back to them.

"Oh!" he said suddenly. "Is a tiger snake poisonous?"

"If it bites you, of course it's poisonous," Ippei said.

"Even if you suck the blood out?"

"You sucked it out?"

"Mmm."

"No problem, then. Who was bitten?"

"Oh, no one," Bunshirō muttered.

When he arrived home the sun had completely set. Bunshirō apologized to his mother for being late.

"Yonosuke said he may be going to Edo, so we talked about that for a while."

"That boy? To Edo …?" His mother sounded surprised. He thought she might have more to say, but she said only that Sukezaemon would be late, so he should have his dinner first. Bunshirō wanted to ask if anything untoward had happened at the Koyanagi house next door, but he controlled himself.

The next morning, when the cicadas were shrilling above his head and he went out to the little stream, Fuku was there doing her washing. When she saw Bunshirō, she undid her sleeve tie, stood up, and thanked him for yesterday, just like a grown woman. Fuku's cheeks were just as white as ever.

"Have you been all right?" Bunshirō asked; but then her cheeks flushed, and he could sense that shyness had suffused her whole body. Bunshirō, too, felt flustered and averted his eyes.

The Night Festival

1

Bunshirō was barefoot, watering the eggplants in their vegetable garden. The eggplants occupied only three rows in a corner of the garden, but they were still putting out purple flowers and were covered with glossy fruit. For a family of three, a plot of three rows not only produced enough eggplants for pickles and soup every morning but also filled a cask to be preserved in salt in readiness for winter. But there was no plot of earth that drank up more water, Bunshirō thought, than that eggplant patch. If you don't give eggplants enough water, it was said, their skin will be thin and tough and their flesh won't taste good. And so every morning and every evening he would water them, and the eggplants would soak up the water as if they had been planted in sand. Bunshirō had to carry the bucket down to the stream and back to the garden at least four or five times.

Bunshirō set his dipper down in the bucket and mopped the sweat from his brow. As the sun continued its circuit west, half the garden was already shaded by the trees at the rear; but at the front of the house, the hedge and their humble gate were still being punished by the powerful rays of summer sun. The air was so hot it seemed it might even catch fire, while the cicadas in the trees shrilled as if to stir that air to still greater heat. Bunshirō was sweating from head to toe. Only the bottoms of his bare feet were cool enough to feel good.

That will do, he thought. Bunshirō looked at the eggplant patch with satisfaction. He had watered it well, and the surface of the rows shone with a thin coat of moisture. The water that remained in his bucket he would spread over the adjacent patch. Tonight was the festival at the Kumano Shrine, so practice at the dojo had been called off.

As Bunshirō picked up the dipper again, he heard his mother calling him. She seemed to be in the vestibule. Bunshirō hurried around to the front of the house, where he found his mother standing with their neighbors, Koyanagi Fuku and her mother.

"Ah! Bunshirō-san, watering the eggplants?" Koyanagi's wife greeted him with a smile on her gaunt, flat face. "You do work hard." She went on flattering Bunshirō, but his mother said nothing, so she came directly to the point.

"It's a great deal of trouble for you, I'm sure, but ... might I ask you again this year to look after Fuku at the festival?"

Bunshirō looked at his mother. Toyo did not like Koyanagi's wife. She was always pestering her—"lend me some soy sauce, lend me some miso, lend me some rice." Sometimes even "lend me some money." And never once had she paid any of it back of her own volition. The money could not be ignored, and his mother had to demand it to get it back.

"The most slipshod woman I've ever known," Bunshirō's mother would grumble.

Even so, when Koyanagi's wife would come demanding that Toyo lend her something or teach her how to cut the material for kimono, she found it too difficult to refuse, so she would always end up accommodating her. This time, too, when Bunshirō looked her way, his mother, though sullen and silent, was nodding her head slightly in assent.

"Yes, I'll do it," Bunshirō said. What he was agreeing to do was take Fuku to the Night Festival at the Kumano Shrine.

It was said that Ukyō-no-Daibu Masatake, lord of the domain two generations earlier, was the one who changed the Summer Festival at Kumano Shrine into the boisterous affair it had now become. It was a three-day festival. But in the past, on the first day, commoners were not even allowed to enter the precincts of the shrine; the entire day was devoted to the most solemn rituals in honor of the gods. From the second day forward, vendors had been allowed to set up their stalls within the shrine, and ceremonial sumo matches were held, which attracted crowds from the villages surrounding the castle town. Even so, they say, the festivities had not been at all uproarious. But from the time of His Lordship two generations earlier, on the third night, wheeled floats and bands of dancers began to weave their way through the streets of the town, and the festival at the Kumano Shrine was transformed. They began calling it the Night Festival, and it became the liveliest event in the whole domain.

A parade of three hundred or so colorfully costumed men and women dancing through the streets would be followed by fifteen wheeled floats from the commoners' wards, as well as two more which His Lordship commanded be drawn by his musketeers, archers, and lancers—seventeen floats in all. By the Fifth Hour (8 p.m.), the men pulling the floats would be fully under the influence of the saké with which they had been plied before they set out and thus prone to riotous ructions at every intersection. It was nothing unusual for two floats, propelled by an excess of energy, to collide, ending in a brawl between their crews. "Wild floats" they called them, for they were constantly running up against one another. And with not the slightest gap between one person and the next at the side of the street, the crowds of spectators, too, suffered the consequences. The Night Festival was a dangerous festival; yet the proximity of danger had itself become one of its attractions.

But it was not just because of the danger that Koyanagi's wife asked Bunshirō to look after Fuku. She had other worries.

The lord of the domain, two generations earlier, maintained a residence outside the castle walls—the White Bush Clover Mansion—as a place of respite for his household. And being a lover of festivals, he commanded that the dancers and the floats pass before him, prior to parading through the town. Nor had he any objection to the samurai in his Corps of Vassals, his foot soldiers, and even his liveried menials joining him there to enjoy the festival, in the course of which everyone was permitted to eat and drink as much as he pleased. In short, all formalities were dropped, and that custom continued to the present day.

In like manner, the higher ranking officers of the domain would hire the second stories of merchant houses on the main streets of town, where they and their families could view the parade while they ate and drank their fill of saké. Those of less exalted station just stood at the roadside, passing flasks of saké around amongst themselves. Inevitably, as the saké took effect, fights would break out, but the domain did not go out of its way to punish these altercations. Most often it would be younger samurai of low rank or foot soldiers who would start the fights. Recognizing this, the domain, just this once, would allow them to dispel their pent-up grievances. At the Night Festival—and only then—they would turn a blind eye to this brawling.

But this policy of the domain could not have been more

troublesome for the children of their vassals or the wives and daughters of the townsmen. It encouraged drunken men to harass these women in public. Some women were so appalled they refused even to go out and watch the festival. This was the reason Koyanagi's wife had come to ask Bunshirō to take Fuku to the festival. Not that her request came as a surprise. Bunshirō had accompanied Fuku to the Night Festival for the past four or five years in a row.

Even so, Bunshirō felt he understood why his mother now looked so sullen. Yet again, Toyo would surely have been thinking, here comes Koyanagi's wife with another presumptuous request. But that would not have been her only thought. Toyo no longer regarded the twelve-year-old Fuku as a child. That Koyanagi's wife could be so insensitive as to demand that he take Fuku to the Night Festival must have aroused her anger.

Yet when Bunshirō said he would take her, Fuku looked up at him and Toyo, and the delight that filled her face was entirely innocent. Not just her face, her whole being bespoke her joy. Bunshirō was glad he had agreed.

After Fuku and her mother had thanked them profusely, and they had seen them off at the gate, Bunshirō's mother said, "What ever can she be up to, that woman?"

Bunshirō said nothing. It was only too obvious that his mother was in a foul mood. He had to take care that an ill-judged response did not make her forbid him to go to the festival. But his mother said nothing more except to warn him not to draw attention to himself when he went with Fuku.

When they went in the house, his mother asked if he would need any money. Bunshirō was lost in thought, so she gave him ten copper coins—the ones with the hole in the middle.

At the dojo, after a hard practice session when they would

sponge away the sweat and set out for home in the evening, their hunger would be unbearable. And having perceived the hunger of these youths, someone had set up a sweets shop just opposite the Ishiguri Dojo, which in winter sold rice cakes and bean-paste balls, and in summer bean-paste balls and leaf-wrapped rice sweets.

It didn't happen every day, of course; but every now and again the boys would make a run for the sweets shop and, doing their best to avoid the gaze of their elders, crowd into the rear or sneak around back and gobble down their sweets as greedily as hungry ghosts. Then, with their hunger temporarily allayed, they would make their way home.

But not everyone could afford to buy sweets. Whoever happened to have spending money would be the one to pay. In Bunshirō's group that would be Owada Ippei, and Bunshirō and Yonosuke would be his guests. It was three years ago that his parents first learnt of this, whereupon Toyo stared at Bunshirō as if she were quite beside herself.

"What kind of upbringing can Owada-sama have given that boy?" Toyo muttered. But finally she pulled herself together. "Can't you bear a bit of hunger until you get home? The son of a warrior should have more endurance than that." She chastised him severely, but Bunshirō could see that it wasn't so much buying sweets and eating away from home that troubled her, it was his shameless acceptance of a friend's largesse.

2

After that incident, Toyo from time to time told Bunshirō that if ever he needed money he should tell her.

"That doesn't mean it's all right to throw money around out

there," Toyo said, "but if by some chance you should need it to avoid being shamed, then ask." Then she lectured him yet again on how ashamed he should be to eat sweets at Owada Ippei's expense.

Her gift of ten coppers, too, Toyo had given him because she knew there were vendors at the Night Festival, and even the sons of samurai, claiming relaxed formalities as their excuse, could buy sweets and roast squid. For last year's Night Festival, too, she had given him ten coppers.

"I'm not saying you should buy something with this," she would tell him. "It's just in case." That was his mother's mantra, repeated whenever she mentioned money. But Bunshirō himself had no intention of spending any money he was given. Now that he was fifteen, Bunshirō no longer ate at the sweets shop, and thus was seldom given spending money. But when he tucked those ten coppers his mother had given him into the fold of his kimono, it did make him feel that now festival time really had come. Bunshirō had no idea whether his father, Sukezaemon, knew he had been getting money from his mother this way.

Fuku came while Bunshirō was still eating. He hurried to finish his meal while she waited in the vestibule. Then they left the quarter together, his mother reminding him they should not stay out too late.

The parade of dancers and floats would set out from the Kumano Shrine at the Sixth Hour (6 p.m.), and midway along their route they would rest for an hour at a teahouse in Ariake-chō. That would be the only break in their circuit of the castle town, which would continue until daybreak. But their route and their timing were scheduled, so spectators could know where and when they should go to see them.

Bunshirō and Fuku crossed the Goken River to the corner

of Yoshizumi-chō. This was not one of the main streets; it was a neighborhood of merchant houses, but the parade would pass that way. People were already gathering along the street.

The intersection was illuminated by torchlight, and shops that normally would be shut by now had left their doors open, lit their lamps, and hung lanterns from their eaves. The street through Yoshizumi-chō was as bright as at noonday. Bunshirō had promised to meet Ippei and Yonosuke here, but when he looked about, he could see neither of them.

"Let's wait here," he said to Fuku. Just then Bunshirō heard the flute and drums of the dancers, still a long way off, but carried this way, perhaps, on a faint breeze. Then it stopped; and then he could hear what sounded like cries of excitement. The parade must be approaching.

Suddenly, just as he heard the sound of someone running up behind him, a hand grasped Bunshirō's shoulder. It was Ippei.

"You haven't seen Yonosuke?" Ippei asked. His face was contorted.

"No, I haven't seen him. What's the matter?"

When Bunshirō said that, Ippei heaved a great sigh. Then he stared fixedly at Fuku.

"Who's she?"

"The Koyanagi daughter, O-Fuku."

"Aah! Next door ... A pretty girl, she's become, eh?"

Fuku quietly hid herself behind Bunshirō. It would have frightened her to be leered at by Ippei, who was even bigger than Bunshirō.

Ippei seemed then to recall Yonosuke and made an angry face. "I came straight here," he said, "but I've heard something strange."

"Something strange?"

Semishigure

"That Yonosuke has been dragged away somewhere."

"By whom?"

"By a gang. Five or six of them, apparently. But I know who put them up to it."

"Wait! You mean Yamane?"

"Right. Mizoguchi says he saw the rat's face."

Mizoguchi was a younger student at the Ikoma Academy. Bunshirō understood immediately what Ippei was saying.

"Ugly. Beating up on Yonosuke."

Yamane Seijirō had for years been a rival of Yonosuke at the academy. But their rank had by now been firmly established, for a considerable difference in academic ability had arisen between them.

Seijirō was heir to the house of the vanguard commander, enfeoffed at 230 koku per year. Nor was he only academically inclined; as a student of swordsmanship at the Matsukawa Dojo in O-Yumi-chō, it was said he had gradually risen to the head of the class. He was a very proud young man, but academically he had never been able to surpass Yonosuke, and ultimately he had been left behind. And ever since this had become obvious, Seijirō had neglected his studies at the Ikoma Academy. If he so disliked studying with Yonosuke, he could have enrolled instead at the domain academy. But he didn't, and half-a-year or so ago, rumor began to whisper that Yamane might just abandon his studies. Yet to the son of a high-ranking vassal, for whom roads to advancement were always open, it seemed intolerable that he should be deprived of academic distinction. Yamane Seijirō was seventeen, two years older than Bunshirō.

It was this background that led Bunshirō to say, "Beating up on Yonosuke." Yamane, by nature, was a quiet but determined young man. It may well have been that he blamed his own unanticipated failure on Yonosuke. Or he had heard that Ikoma Reisuke was to sponsor Yonosuke at the Kasai Academy in Edo—and he could not stomach that thought.

"The rats. They probably planned it for tonight."

"The rats" would be Yamane and his gang. Yamane always had four or five men who stuck close to him. They would have waited to punish Yonosuke until the night of the festival, Bunshirō thought, when the domain turned a blind eye to all the fights and quarrels.

"No doubt about it," said Ippei. What Bunshirō had said rang completely true to him. "Filthy scum. All right then. I'll go looking for him again."

"I'll go, too," Bunshirō said. But Ippei held up his hand to deter him.

"You stay here," Ippei said. "Yonosuke may come back. But if not, and I find Yonosuke, I won't be able to handle them alone. I'll come back and get you."

"All right," Bunshirō said. "Agreed." Ippei turned his back and before long his large body had vanished into the throng.

In the meantime, more and more spectators were crowding in. There were townsmen and there were samurai. And rosy-cheeked young men, obviously just in from the nearby villages. When they could hear the parade approaching through the adjacent neighborhood, excitement began to show on the faces of the spectators and echo in their talk and laughter. Bunshirō was surrounded by an incessant buzz. And then the parade did indeed reach them. The music of flute and drums, and the cries of the men pulling the floats, so faint and distant before, could now clearly be distinguished.

Wandering up and down the street before the rows of spectators were all sorts of vendors—candy peddlers in red kerchiefs;

stewed devil's tongue peddlers, their wares in tubs suspended from bars over their shoulders; roast squid peddlers—adults and children alike calling out to stop them. Bunshirō seemed temporarily distracted from his thoughts of Yonosuke's abduction as he gazed at all these people around him. Then suddenly he came to his senses and looked around at Fuku.

Fuku had gone nowhere. She was still right behind Bunshirō. When their eyes met, she smiled shyly.

"Would you like some candy?" he asked. Fuku opened her eyes wide in excitement but shook her head vigorously.

"No need to hesitate. I've got money." He stopped one of the peddlers who had just passed, bought a lollypop, and gave it to her. Even at night he could see how flushed Fuku's face had become. Then she hid behind Bunshirō again and began licking her candy.

"Still a child," Bunshirō thought, a feeling that for some reason put his mind at rest.

Just then he saw Ippei running back, pushing his way through the crowd.

"I found him!" When he came up to them, Ippei cast a quick glance at Fuku licking her lollypop, then whispered in a deep, ominous voice, "To the riverbank; that's where they've taken him."

"Don't go anywhere," Bunshirō told Fuku. "Wait right here." And he ran off straightaway with Ippei.

3

As they ran down the alleyway, it was so dark and quiet it was as if all the jollity on the main street did not even exist. Not a sound could they hear, nor did they encounter a single person there in those back streets. At first Bunshirō could hardly make out the ups and downs in the surface of the street he ran down, and several times he almost stumbled, but before long his eyes grew accustomed to the dark. They said nothing as they ran. Emerging from the alleyway, they raced down a side street, then through another alley so narrow they could only pass one at a time, and finally came out on the riverside thoroughfare. There they both stopped. In the distance they could see a group of men.

"Look! That's where those rats have gone," Ippei said. The sky was clouded, but a faint glimmer illuminated the thoroughfare. The glow of the river, it seemed. Against which stood the shadows of that gathering. That would be Yamane and his gang. But what had become of Yonosuke, they could not tell.

"Don't draw your sword," Ippei said. "If you draw, there'll be trouble afterwards. So, shall we go?" he whispered.

The two advanced at a normal pace, and as they drew nearer they saw what had become of Yonosuke. Their approach had been noticed; and there, about six yards away from the men who stood stock still watching them, lay what looked like a black log.

Bunshirō and Ippei withdrew their short swords from their waists and left them at the foot of a willow tree. When their opponents saw this, even though they could not see their faces, they seemed to know who these two were. Immediately they began mumbling to each other, then turned their backs.

"You there! Wait!" Ippei shouted, and they stopped. "So have you finished roasting Yonosuke? We know who put you up to this. Yamane must be there with you."

"And what if he is?" A cold voice answered. It was Yamane Seijirō, without a doubt.

"I want ask why you've done this to Yonosuke."

Semishigure

"He got too full of himself," the expressionless voice answered. "So we had to teach him his proper place."

"His proper place? Very well. Then it's up to us to thank you for what you've been good enough to teach him, isn't it?" Saying this, Ippei stamped the earth and broke into a run. Bunshirō followed him. With the exception of one of them, the others all threw down their swords. These were men who were accustomed to fighting. Yamane had quickly stepped aside, where he could look on as a spectator. That made it a fight of two against four.

Bunshirō pivoted deftly and thrust a hip into the gut of his first opponent, then rolled him over his back, and slammed him to the ground. But the second man struck him in the face with such force that he felt fire flash from his eyes. In contrast to his previous encounter, he himself was thrown hard against the ground. But as he fell, Bunshirō knocked his opponent's legs out from under him, and the two of them fell almost simultaneously. Each tried to pin the other to the earth, and they ended up in a sand-smeared brawl. The other man was bigger than Bunshirō, and several times almost succeeded in pinning him. But every time, Bunshirō would somehow manage to grasp an arm or a leg and squirm out of his grip. And finally, after countless rounds of this, it was Bunshirō who ended up on top.

But then, suddenly from behind someone grabbed his neck and began strangling him. It must have been the man Bunshirō had previously sent flying. He had come around behind, scissored Bunshirō's neck in the crook of his arm, and was pressing with all his might. Bunshirō tried to dislodge the arm, but when inadvertently he rose up, the man beneath him rolled free, stood, and kicked him in the side. Bunshirō felt he might faint. In that state of vague consciousness, he could hear Ippei raging. Then the pressure on his neck relaxed, and he could hear the footsteps of his assailant running away. When Bunshirō regained consciousness, he was lying flat, his face pressed to the earth.

"Are you all right?" Ippei was peering down at him as he spoke. Bunshirō pushed himself up and sat cross-legged.

"I'm all right," he said. His side where he had been kicked was painful, and his nose must have been bleeding because his face was soaked, but at least he was fully conscious.

"Look at Yonosuke," Bunshirō said.

"He's all right. He's standing up now."

Yonosuke had been bashed and kicked, and although he was able to stand, his body was swaying. Bunshirō went over to him, and Yonosuke spoke in a voice as faint as the hum of a mosquito. "That was horrid," he said.

"What did those rats say to you?"

"That it was impertinent of me to go to the Kasai Academy."

"Just what I thought." Bunshirō and Ippei exchanged glances in the dark.

"So now, if only for the sake of pride, you've got to go to Edo to study. You've got to show them, Yonosuke," Bunshirō said.

"So do it!" Ippei, too, urged him on.

"Can you walk?"

"Not alone," Yonosuke said in a pitiful voice.

"All right, then. I'll take you home," Ippei said. "And Bunshirō, don't forget Koyanagi's daughter."

"Oh, that's right."

"Don't worry about Yonosuke. I'll be all right alone. Leave him to me," Ippei said.

Occasionally suppressing the pain in his side, Bunshirō hurried back to Yoshizumi-chō. The parade had passed and only a scattering of people remained. The lamps were still lit, but they

Semishigure

cast their light upon a deserted street. Fuku was still there waiting at the corner. She stared at Bunshirō's blood-smeared face, but when he said, "Let's go home," Fuku followed him silently.

The Storm

1

As autumn deepened, the days grew markedly shorter; but on that day, Bunshirō returned home before dark. About a month earlier, Yonosuke had left for Edo, ever since which Bunshirō and Ippei had not been loitering on their way home from the dojo as often as before.

Dark, low hanging clouds shrouded the sky, and the pale light of evening lingered only in a tiny patch of white cloud still barely visible in the northwest. The dark clouds, especially those stretching across the western sky and on to the south, were thickening ominously; in that sector, the sky was almost as dark as night, and the clouds were roiling about tempestuously.

And the wind was up. The warmish wind that had been blowing that morning had suddenly grown since midday so strong that, if it struck you square on the chest, you would have to lean sharply into it just to move forward. The rain that had fallen intermittently throughout the morning had let up, but the wind was still heavy with moisture.

The trees in Yaba-machi, where the Defense Works quarter was located, were waving about wildly. The deciduous zelkovas and oaks were casting off dried leaves as if they were flinging small birds into the dark sky. Although occasionally, high in the swaying treetops, from a corner of the sky in the northwest, a faint gleam of light would peep through, the neighborhood was so dusky that anyone walking down the street could hardly be seen. A storm was coming, Bunshirō could see. It reminded him of the violent wind that was blowing that day they had seen off Yonosuke to the border of the domain.

As luck would have it, when autumn came two samurai who were stationed in Edo had just completed their mission in the domain and were about to return. One of them, a man named Sonomura, had studied at the Ikoma Academy and thus was a fellow disciple with Yonosuke. And so when his former teacher Ikoma Reisuke asked him, he gladly agreed to escort Yonosuke to Edo.

Bunshirō and Ippei walked with them the five leagues to the checkpoint at the border and saw Yonosuke off from there. For days thereafter, Bunshirō could not banish from his mind the image of Yonosuke squeezed in between those two burly samurai.

That day, too, the wind had been blowing, and Bunshirō recalled how Yonosuke, a valiant smile on his face, had frantically held down his hat to prevent it blowing away. But on the morrow, the violent wind and rain were followed by a bright, tranquil autumn day, the sun shining from corner to corner of the heavens, as if to wish Yonosuke a brilliant future.

By the time his home quarter hove into view, the sky was growing steadily darker, and the white clouds in the northwest were losing their glow. Then Bunshirō spied two men standing on the dark road in front of his house. Both men were wearing breeches and tied straw sandals. They were samurai dressed for travel, in rain hats and rain capes. He could see the tip of a sword protruding from a vent in the cape of one, but his face was not visible beneath his broad hat. The other had a small bundle slung crosswise over his back. They looked as if they had come from afar. But those two men, just standing there, their raincapes fluttering in the wind, seemed somehow ominous to Bunshirō. They were looking straight at him as he approached.

He nodded to them as he was about to enter the gate, whereupon the taller of the two men called to him.

"I beg your pardon, but … is this the home of Maki Sukezaemon-dono?"

"Yes, it is," Bunshirō said. The two men turned to face him, then stopped still. Bunshirō felt he should be on his guard, for neither man had introduced himself or removed his hat, and though he could now see them clearly, he had no recollection of having seen them before. Yet the impression they gave was not at all threatening. On the contrary they seemed friendly and warm. Sensing this, Bunshirō altered his tone.

"I am the son of Sukezaemon."

"Oh, are you?" The tall man spoke as if for some reason he was relieved to hear this. Even in the dusk, Bunshirō could see that he was a dark-complected man of a fearless mien. The smaller man, who had said nothing, was a bit portly and pale.

"Is Maki-dono at home?"

"Well …" Bunshirō again felt a bit defensive. His father, Sukezaemon, had gone to the castle as usual this morning, but he did not know whether he had returned home yet. More than that, however, Bunshirō could not but wonder: If these two men standing here had already ascertained that this was the Maki residence, why had they not gone in and inquired whether Sukezaemon was at home or not?

Semishigure

"I've just returned from the dojo. I don't know if my father is at home." Bunshirō spoke cautiously, but then, as if moved by a premonition, he looked to his rear. And there he saw Sukezaemon himself, walking along the road Bunshirō had just returned on, his clothes blowing in the wind. Sukezaemon was alone, carrying a closed umbrella.

"Ah! He's just come back," Bunshirō said. The two men looked fixedly at Sukezaemon. Their gaze gave the impression that they did not know him, which made Bunshirō uneasy. But both of them then put their hands to their hats, thanked him for his trouble, and strode off in the direction of the approaching Sukezaemon. Sukezaemon and the two men met midway, and nothing of the sort Bunshirō had worried might happen took place. They greeted each other and exchanged hurried pleasantries. But the men still had not removed their hats.

As Bunshirō watched all of this from in front of the gate, Sukezaemon left the two men, strode back to Bunshirō, and told him that something urgent had come up.

"I won't be coming home until late," he said, "so tell Toyo you can have dinner and then go to bed." Saying nothing more, Sukezaemon left. As the three men turned their backs and walked away, heavy rain began to fall.

2

That night, Bunshirō awoke to find the house engulfed in the roar of violent wind and rain. But that was not what awakened him; between the bursts of wind and rain, he could hear the boom of a drum. The drum was in the district deputies' turret, in the third perimeter of the castle. Sounded in the night, it signaled an emergency. Bunshirō stiffened and strained his ears, and as soon as he had counted the beats, he leapt out of bed. He prepared himself swiftly and left his room.

In the sitting room, the lamp was lit and his mother, Toyo, still sat there. She appeared never even to have undone her obi.

"It's a flood," Bunshirō said. There had been three beats of the drum followed by a rest, then two more beats and another rest. Then repeated. That was the signal for a flood, which meant that everyone in the Defense Works Unit, as well as all the Works Unit laborers in the Kitsune-chō barracks, were to rush to the castle immediately.

"And father?"

"Not yet."

"Then I'll go."

Bunshirō returned to his room to fetch his short sword. When he went to the vestibule, it was lit with a lantern, below which he found a pair of leggings and sandals. As he hurried to prepare himself, his mother lit a hand lantern and brought it to him.

"Here, take this." And once he had finished, Toyo pointed to the boarded wall. There hung a straw rain cape and rain hat. He stepped down onto the earthen floor and donned the cape and hat. Both were a bit big for Bunshirō, and the hat was still a loose fit even after he had tied it snugly. The wind and rain were still roaring.

"Go over to Jinbei-dono and ask him to let you go with him," Toyo raised her voice and told him over the roar. Jinbei was the name of Fuku's father. "And when you get to the river, watch your footing. You could slip."

"Don't worry," Bunshirō said, whereupon the wind and rain grew even stronger, and the house began to creak. "What time is it, mother?"

Semishigure

"It will soon be the Eighth Hour (2 a.m.)."

"Eight?" Wherever had his father gone with those two men? Bunshirō wondered. And who were those men?

When he bade his mother farewell and opened the door, a blast of wind and rain blew into the earthen-floored vestibule, causing the flame in his hand lantern to waver wildly.

As he leapt out the door, Bunshirō could hear the faint voice of his mother calling out, "Take care, now." but the instant he turned to look her way, the wind nearly ripped the hat from his head and the lantern from his hand. Pressing the hat down with one hand and sheltering the flame in the lantern with the other, Bunshirō bent forward so far it seemed he might fall and pressed on. Even before he reached the gate, his clothing was soaked.

Outside the gate, he could see others here and there moving about with lanterns in hand. Bunshirō set off at a run and slipped through the gate of the Koyanagi house next door. The door to the vestibule was open, and he could see light within. He could tell that Jinbei was preparing himself.

Jinbei was just then donning his rain cape, as his wife and Fuku and Fuku's younger sister, Yasu, came out to see him off. When Bunshirō appeared, they all turned toward him.

"Where's your father?" Jinbei shouted as he tied the cord on his rain cape. The noise of the wind and rain was so loud he could not have made himself heard in a normal voice.

"Father is at a family gathering and hasn't come back yet. Please, take me with you."

"All right." His rain cape secured, Jinbei tied on his hat. Jinbei was a plump man and not very tall. In his cape and hat, he looked much like Bunshirō. "If you're fifteen, you can do a man's work. So, let's go."

The two of them rushed out into the rain, left their own

quarter, made their way through a deserted merchants' neighborhood, and, choosing the most direct route, ran on to the castle. Both before and behind them, they could see the swaying lanterns of others running. At the wooden gate in Motoyui-chō, they crossed the bridge over the moat into the castle, where they could see lights moving about in a corner of the third perimeter. When they came closer, they saw that the men working in the front garden of the district deputies' residence were handing out mattocks from the tool shed to the assembled samurai and laborers.

Bunshirō and Jinbei, too, moved forward and took a mattock; whereupon the deafening beat of the drum in the turret just next to them suddenly stopped, and a man standing beside a huge lantern began shouting.

"Listen up everyone! I am Aiba Sōroku, assistant to the officer in charge. I'll be directing the works tonight." Aiba announced himself in a voice so powerful that even the wind and rain could not drown him out. "Three wards have already been flooded: Yoriki-chō, Tenjin-chō, and Kyokushi-chō. If we fail to act, the damage will spread through the whole area around Takajō-chō, Somemono-chō, Hyōe Michikuchi, and Ōmi no Kōji, and possibly, we fear, inundate half the whole castle town. The only way to prevent this is to do as we've done before, and breach the dike of the Goken River upstream."

Aiba's voice was forceful and clear—so much so that some suspected it was just for the power of his voice that he was appointed to supervise that night. But there was nothing nonsensical in what he said.

"Now, I'll tell you what we have to do. We'll make the cut in the dike at Willow Bend, which is in Sameguchi in the village of Kanai. If we cut the dike there, the flow downstream will be reduced by half, and the flood waters in town should drain away. I've already sent men to two villages, Kanai and Aohata, to assemble laborers. With their help, I expect we'll have sufficient numbers." Aiba then turned to the men at his side and said, "Well then, let's get going."

Whereupon one of the many men on that side stepped forward, faced everyone else, brandished his mattock, and shouted, "Give it your best; we're depending on you!"

"That's Akiyoshi-sama, the duty elder," Jinbei whispered to Bunshirō. Akiyoshi Genba's mansion was in the third perimeter.

"And the officer in charge?" Bunshirō asked.

"That's the man standing next to the elder," Jinbei replied. The man Jinbei referred to was an old man and was wearing neither a rain cape nor a hat. "He's too old to take charge in a storm like this tonight."

While Jinbei was whispering, Aiba again raised his voice. He was dividing the men into squads, and when he finished, he said, "Squad One will go first."

"We're in Squad Three," Jinbei said, grabbing Bunshirō's sleeve. "Come with me."

"This is Maki's son," Jinbei told the squad leader. "Sukezaemon had to go to a family gathering and hadn't come back yet. He'll be coming along soon, I'm sure. But until then his son will serve in his place."

Jinbei handled the situation beautifully, and the squad leader raised no objection. He just clapped Bunshirō on the shoulder and said, "Give it your best!"

Beginning with Squad One, the six squads made up of the Defense Works Unit and their laborers moved out from the third perimeter. Bunshirō only now noticed that the rain had raised the water in the moat almost to the level of the cross beams on the bridge. But those waters were reflected only briefly in the light of the lanterns at the head of the column, and then vanished again into the darkness.

After crossing the moat, the Works Unit cut across Cavalcade Square at a trot and entered the town. The wind and rain showed no sign of abating but continued as wild as ever. The lanterns they carried reflected the white spray the rain threw up as it struck the streets and the roofs of the houses in the town; and the rising waters of the Goken River were lapping over the planks of the Gyōja Bridge as they crossed.

The Works Unit cut diagonally through the several wards and finally reached the bank of the Goken River out beyond the town. From there they went on upstream to the southeast for another half a league to a place called Willow Bend—so called because the banks there were thick with willows—and that was where the river took a sharp turn.

"Run now!" Aiba Sōroku shouted from the head of the column. "Full speed to Willow Bend!"

To which some of the men responded with cries of "Ooh, Ooh!"

Out in the countryside the wind and rain seemed so much stronger that one felt one could be swept up in the flood or blown away.

If one slipped, one would fall into the river, and so the Works Unit descended from the dike and ran along the paths at the edge of the rice fields. Even so, Bunshirō, trying hard to keep up with Jinbei, was twice struck by a blast of wind and ended up running in the paddy. But when they reached Willow Bend, they found that no one had come to help them from the villages of Kanai or Aohata.

"Let's get to work!" Aiba Sōroku shouted, holding up one of

the only two lanterns that remained lit after their run through the wind and rain.

Then another voice, every bit as powerful as Aiba's, shouted. "No, *wait*—please!"

3

Bunshirō could not believe his ears. It was the voice of his father, Sukezaemon.

"Aiba-dono, are you taking charge tonight?" the voice said.

"That's right."

Bunshirō could not see them, but Aiba seemed to recognize Sukezaemon.

"Is that you Sukeza? We're terribly busy. What's the problem?"

"I have an urgent request."

"Tell us, and be quick about it."

"I'd like you to move the cut upstream, to Duck Bend."

"You're talking nonsense. We don't have time."

"No! I beg you!"

Sukezaemon's booming voice overpowered even the raging wind and rain. Aiba spoke as if it had subdued him as well.

"So state your reason."

"If we cut the dike here, as you can see, it will flood all these rice fields that haven't yet been harvested."

"How great an area will be flooded if we cut here?"

"Roughly ten chōbu."

"But it's too late."

"No, it's *not* too late." Again Sukezaemon's voice overwhelmed the area. "Duck Bend is only three chō from here. So please, change your mind! If we cut here and flood these fields, we'll get no help from the village of Kanai."

"You're right. Well said." Aiba was quick to make up his mind. "We're changing the location of the cut to Duck Bend. Now hurry!"

Aiba's voice set the Works Unit running again, but not a one of them complained. Bunshirō was running along with them.

Duck Bend, like Willow Bend, was a place where the Goken River took a sharp turn. As its name suggests, there was a broad pool there where wild ducks would gather in their migratory season. Beyond the banks, Sukezaemon told them, lay a stretch of marsh land filled with reeds and wild growth. Any water drained there could cause only minimal damage to the nearby rice fields.

Father's amazing, Bunshirō thought as he ran. At home, Sukezaemon was a man of few words. When he spoke to Toyo or Bunshirō, he did so in a soft, kindly voice. Bunshirō was fired with emotion to see that this same Sukezaemon was capable of a speech so powerful and impassioned that he prevented a cut at Willow Bend that would have flooded ten chōbu of rice. I've got a lot to learn from father, Bunshirō thought. His respect for the man now rose to new heights.

"That was unusually powerful for Sukeza." Koyanagi Jinbei was still breathing hard as he came up to Bunshirō, chuckling as he spoke. "Our great talker Sōroku sure lost that bout."

Sōroku and the several squad leaders climbed to the top of the dike and began looking for the best place to make the breach. And while they were scurrying about up there, one of the men shouted.

"Help has come from the villages!"

Bunshirō looked up and saw lights coming closer across a dark field upstream. Those would be peasants from the villages of Kanai and Aohata, whose help they had sought. There was a vast number of lanterns.

Semishigure

"Squads One, Two, and Three," Aiba called. "Come up on the dike. The rest of you, Squads Four, Five, and Six, will dig away the lower half. I'll tell you where in a moment. Don't get flustered; just do as your squad leader tells you."

Bunshirō and the others climbed up the dike. In the pale light of the lanterns, he could see that the normally calm pool at Duck Bend was churning like a whirlpool.

"The breach will be as broad as between the lanterns," Aiba said. Hearing which, the two squad leaders atop the dike, one on the left and one on the right, raised their lanterns and waved them.

"Now you know how the work will proceed, don't you? As always, we'll dig the earth away from the outside, in such a way as to leave an inner layer intact. Then finally, we'll cut away that layer from its two edges. That's the procedure. But wait, wait—not yet." One man had already raised his mattock, but Aiba restrained him with his hand.

"Help is coming. We'll start work as soon as everyone is here. And needless to say, you have to keep an eye on those to your right and left, and move forward at the same rate. If anyone pushes ahead and breaks through the dike, people are going to get hurt. We've got to work carefully."

While Aiba was explaining this, twenty or thirty helpers arrived. Aiba explained the procedure to them and then gave the order to begin. The laborers from the villages had brought several lanterns with them, which could now be used to illumine the site and enliven the workers. But Sukezaemon was nowhere to be seen, and there was no time to look for him, so Bunshirō and Jinbei set to work swinging their mattocks.

The dike had been reinforced at the bend; it was about twice as thick there as elsewhere along the river, and the soil was thick with roots and stones. It was hard digging. But at least the wind and rain seemed to have abated a bit in the interim.

When the breach had been cleared to the point that only a quarter of its thickness remained, Aiba called a halt to the work and made everyone come to the top of the dike. The final cuts at the edges he assigned to the most experienced of the unit's laborers.

They began digging on both sides of the breach, and water began to fall. Then suddenly the thin remaining layer of the dike collapsed, and an incredible surge of dark water gushed out into the wasteland. The force of it instantly caused the dike where Bunshirō was standing to crack, and when he attempted to escape, he slipped on the earth and was beginning to teeter. Then a powerful hand grabbed him by the arm. It was Sukezaemon.

Beneath the Clouds

1

Bunshirō had shut himself in his room and was reading a book. On his bookstand lay the "Selected Airs of the States" from the *Classic of Poetry*. At the Ikoma Academy, the year-end recess had begun on the twenty-fifth of the Twelfth Month; and tomorrow, the third day of the First Month, they would celebrate the New Year with their first lecture. After the lecture they would be treated to mochi soup, the traditional New Year's dish, homemade by the wife of their mentor. *That* the students were looking forward to. But before then, Ikoma told them, they must read the "Selected Airs of the States."

The skies were clouded and his room was dark. Bunshirō had pushed his bookstand directly below the window to gather as much light as he could on the words he was reading. Now and again he would rub his hands together. When one sits perfectly still, one's hands and feet become unbearably cold.

Sleet and hail had already fallen several times. They had seen very little sunlight; most days the skies over the domain had been shrouded in ashen cloud. Sometimes those ashen clouds hung so low it was as if they could no longer bear the weight they held, and they would pour down cold sleet or dry hail. This year, though, the snow was late.

But on those rare days when the clouds would lift and the sky would clear, you could see that the mountains that surrounded the domain on three sides were already capped with snow down to the seventh station on the paths to the top. Within a few days, they were saying, snow would be falling down on the plain. And this creeping advance of the snow seemed to bring insufferable cold along with it.

Bunshirō was again unconsciously rubbing his hands together when he heard the sounds of someone in the vestibule. It was a man's voice, but not his father's. Since yesterday, his father, Sukezaemon, had been making his round of New Year's calls at the homes of his superiors—the superintendent of works, the assistant superintendent, the section leaders—as well as the homes of some of their relatives. His father had gone out this morning properly dressed in formal linens. It was too early for him to be returning, Bunshirō thought.

This New Year the lord of the domain would be away in Edo. Two years or so earlier, Bunshirō had heard, a directive had ruled that, when His Lordship was absent from the domain, all New Year's observances were to be curtailed. Yet this New Year's season remained as hectic as ever. If this were a visitor, who might it be? Bunshirō wondered. Then he heard his mother outside his room calling to him. Bunshirō quickly closed his book and stood up.

"You have a visitor," his mother said. "His name is Komiya-sama, he says, and he has brought a letter from Yonosuke-san in Edo. You should be the one to accept it and thank him."

"I'll do that," Bunshirō said.

In the vestibule stood a young samurai wrapped in a traveler's rain cape, who, when he saw Bunshirō, spoke to him in a friendly manner.

"I understand you're a friend of Shimazaki Yonosuke?"

"That's right. I am Maki Bunshirō."

"I've come at the request of Yonosuke." From a packet in his hand, the young samurai produced a letter wrapped in oiled paper and handed it to Bunshirō. Both he and his mother thanked Komiya and saw him off from outside the house. Bunshirō then returned to his room and opened Yonosuke's letter.

"You're well, I presume," Yonosuke wrote. "I, too, am well." As Ikoma Reisuke promised, Yonosuke was enrolled as a student at the Kasai Academy. As a live-in student he had expected he would have to clean house, run errands, stand door watch, and anything else asked of him. But there was a maid to do all the cleaning. Yonosuke, at most, would sweep up the leaves that fell in front of the entryway, accompany Kasai Randō when he went out, and attend to dealings with bookshops. Randō held no official position as a Confucianist, but he was patronized by three daimyo houses, and several times per month he would go to their mansions to lecture on the classics. One of those patrons was the Unasaka daimyo house, and so twice a month, in attendance upon his mentor, Yonosuke would visit the Edo mansion of his own domain. And thus, he wrote, he was nowhere near as lonely as he expected he might be.

Thereafter Yonosuke described in detail his studies at the Kasai Academy, and how he hadn't enough money to hire a courier but that he hoped to send this letter in the care of someone who would be returning to the domain from Edo. And finally, he mused, the year would soon end, but how many more years would pass before he could return home? Just thinking of Bunshirō and Ippei left him feeling oppressed with loneliness, Yonosuke said in a strangely sentimental ending to his letter.

"Hmm. Looks like he's lonely, too." Bunshirō smiled. But then the image of Yonosuke floated up before his eyes, so much more timid than anyone else, yet bravely holding his own in Edo—pitiful, to be sure, Bunshirō felt, and yet promising, too.

And Yonosuke's written hand had grown remarkably more skilled. Yonosuke's writing had always been better than that of most, but now, Bunshirō had to admit, it was polished and truly mature.

Bunshirō stood and prepared to go out. From mid-Fourth Hour (11 a.m.) the celebration of the first match of the New Year with bamboo swords would begin at the Ishiguri Dojo. There would be no general practice session. The master's assistant, Satake Kinjūrō, and one of the senior disciples would give the traditional demonstration of the school's techniques, after which everyone would be served sweet saké and then disperse.

Before he left, Bunshirō greeted his mother in the sitting room and told her about Yonosuke's letter.

"Yonosuke says he's really working hard."

"That's wonderful," Toyo said. As Toyo saw it, Owada Ippei was rough and rude, for which she disliked him, but Yonosuke, the talented scholar, she thought well of.

"That boy will amount to something."

"He's grown quite skilled at calligraphy," Bunshirō said. "He has a very mature hand now. It has real character. I'll show you later."

"You have to work hard, too, you know," Toyo said, and then went with him to the vestibule to see him off.

"I'll have lunch ready, so don't be late coming home."

Semishigure

2

Bunshirō did not respond to his mother's admonishment. He just said goodbye and left the house.

Once outside, the cold penetrated his entire body. Probably because it was so cold, the only others to be seen, even off into the distance, were a few children playing shuttlecock. The street through their quarter was all but deserted. The clouds that hung low over his head stretched far off into the distance, distinguished only by faint differences in their shades of gray, and so dark it seemed snow might begin to fall at any moment.

"Well, I simply won't be able to come straight home," Bunshirō muttered to himself. Feelings of rebellion against his mother's inflexible pronouncements began to well up in his breast. Just to walk straight to and from the dojo in Kaji-machi would take an hour. And then there was all that was to go on there. Nor was he now bound for Kaji-machi. He was headed for Ippei's home. He hadn't talked with Ippei since the end of last year, and there was much they must discuss, Bunshirō felt. He would probably be so deep in conversation with Ippei that he would return by a circuitous route as well. Which meant there was no way he could be home by the Eighth Hour (2 p.m.), and if their discussion were to grow lively, it could be mid-Eighth Hour (3 p.m.). Which suddenly reminded him how he would be scolded for that. "But the kitchen is still a mess," his mother would say. Yet surely, Bunshirō thought, one should not have to give up seeing one's friends just to keep the kitchen tidy? His mother was astonishingly ignorant of such considerations.

But for Bunshirō, these strangely contrary feelings toward his mother never lasted and he quickly calmed down. This time was no exception. As he walked, he began to think perhaps he should return home as quickly as he could. It was hard for his mother, too, being as attentive as she was to every little detail. Thinking of it in these terms, he felt steadily more sorry for his mother having to manage a household containing two men who could never be convinced to do as she wished.

When he arrived at Ippei's home in Urushibara-chō, Ippei came out immediately and told him, "It's been decided. Starting this spring, I'll be working at the castle."

"This spring? You mean immediately?"

"No, starting in the Third Month."

"Doing what?"

"I'll be in the Bodyguard."

"So you'll be quite busy," Bunshirō said. "No more sword fighting? And no more academy?"

"No, at first I'll just be in training. I won't be all that busy, they tell me. So I'll still go to the dojo. *That* I've already requested of the Bodyguard commander." Whereupon Ippei smiled mischievously at Bunshirō. "But I will quit the academy. Even if I were to insist upon continuing, it's not likely I'd learn a lot more. And to be perfectly honest, I'm sick of 'Thus spake Confucius …'"

"That's the spirit!" Bunshirō said. "Ikoma Sensei will be delighted to be rid of one more troublesome student."

The two looked at each other and chuckled.

"Right you are! I'm doing it for the good of our mentor."

Bunshirō looked squarely into the face of Ippei, who had thrown himself into the jest so willingly. "I'm too flippant today," he said. "I expect you're very pleased that you've been assigned a position."

"You're right, of course," Ippei said, looking as if it were only proper he should feel that way. "As you know, my family have been receiving a stipend that I've done nothing to earn. That troubles me terribly."

Semishigure

"Does it? Well, now you'll be a fully-fledged adult."

"No, for the time being I'll only be half an adult. But at least I'm no longer a child. That's for certain. Half an adult, but working amongst adults. I'm just telling you what the Bodyguard commander said, though …"

"When was this decided?"

"Last night. With no notice, I was summoned to come to the mansion of the Bodyguard commander accompanied by a kinsman. There were other ranking people there. And there the command was issued."

"That's just splendid!" Bunshirō said.

"Nothing new with you?" Ippei replied.

"I had a letter from Yonosuke."

"Oh? When?"

"Just a little while ago. A fellow named Komiya was returning from Edo. He brought it."

"You don't say? Crying with loneliness, I'd imagine."

"He did sound a bit that way. But for the most part it was about how hard he is working. For Yonosuke, at least. I should have brought it with me so I could show you."

"No. Rather than read it, you can tell me," Ippei said, and so Bunshirō gave him a detailed rundown of everything in the letter.

The two of them walked along the north side of the Goken River in a northerly direction, but there were very few people out and about in any of the neighborhoods they passed through. Only in the merchant districts did they see a few children, the boys spinning tops, the girls playing shuttlecock.

"That's what he says," Bunshirō said, "so it seems there's no chance he'll be used like a servant."

"So he was right, after all, to make up his mind and go."

"And his calligraphy has really improved."

"His calligraphy?"

"Mmm. How shall I put it? His writing looks like an adult's now."

"That's because we took that cute little boy and made him travel, Bunshirō." Ippei was deadly serious when he spoke, but Bunshirō could not resist making a joke of what he said.

"Yonosuke? A cute little boy?" Both of them burst out laughing—and then looked nervously about. But they could see only one woman crossing the street off in the distance. Closer by, there were only a few children and no one else in sight.

"Now then, Bunshirō." Ippei cast his eyes about, then turned to Bunshirō and lowered his voice. "Have you heard anything more about that incident in Yamabuki-chō?"

"No." Bunshirō shook his head.

Yamabuki-chō was the residential quarter to the west of His Lordship's respite, the White Bush Clover Mansion. There, on the fifth night of the Twelfth Month of the previous year, a samurai had been cut down and left lying dead on the street. He had been found early on the morning of the sixth. The inspector general's report said he appeared to have been killed late the night before.

This was the "incident in Yamabuki-chō" that Owada Ippei referred to; there were aspects of this incident that were causing people to shake their heads in wonderment and that those investigating the case found perplexing.

The victim was Yoshimura Shinzō, a samurai employed in the finance section. In the first place, it was not clear why Yoshimura should be walking the streets of Yamabuki-chō late at night.

Yamabuki-chō was the quarter where middle-ranking samurai, enfeoffed at one hundred to two hundred koku, lived and not where Yoshimura resided. Yoshimura was on a small stipend of only twenty koku and lived on the opposite side of town, to the east of the Goken River, in Obune-chō. Nor had he any kinsmen, acquaintances, or superiors who lived in Yamabuki-chō. Moreover, the inspector general had questioned the commissioner of finance and found that on the fifth of the Twelfth Month, when Yoshimura had been killed, he had been given no assignment that would have taken him to Yamabuki-chō.

With so little evidence to go on, there were those who speculated that Yoshimura Shinzō may have had business elsewhere and had been passing through Yamabuki-chō on his way to or from some other destination. But to the west of Yamabuki-chō there were only rice fields belonging to the rural villages, and to the south, extending as far as the castle moat, was the quarter called Babasaki, where the mansions of the samurai commanders and the domain elders stood. To the north was Daikan-machi, another quarter for middle-ranking samurai. Having investigated all of these neighborhoods, the inspector general still could find no clue to the death of Yoshimura. And of course, no one in Yoshimura's own family could offer any explanation why Shinzō, the head of their house, should have been walking on the far side of town in Yamabuki-chō, late on the night of the fifth of the Twelfth Month. All anyone questioned could do was shake his head in puzzlement.

And then, the circumstances of his murder, too, were mysterious. For one thing, nothing was stolen. Neither his sword nor his money nor anything else was taken from him. It may have been that Yoshimura was on his way to deliver something to someone, and that had been stolen. In that case he would have been killed intentionally, and not incidentally in the course of a robbery.

There was one more thing the inspector general's men found surprising. The murderer struck down Yoshimura Shinzō with a single blow from behind. In the course of the investigation, it was discovered that Yoshimura was a highly skilled swordsman who had been awarded a certificate by the Matsukawa Dojo in O-Yumi-chō, which drew the attention of the Inspector General's men to the murdered man's own abilities. The inspector general concluded that the murderer must intentionally have set out to kill Yoshimura.

3

That was all that was known, and the inspector general's investigation had reached an impasse, as just about everyone in the Corps of Vassals knew. And since the incident was so recent, and the details of it so puzzling, it was still being whispered about amongst the vassals.

"Someone must have had it in for Yoshimura-san," Bunshirō said. "Even if no one held a particular grudge against him, there could have been someone who had never got on well with him …" Bunshirō, for his own part, had been pondering Yoshimura's death at odd moments all the while he was studying "Airs of the States" from the *Classic of Poetry*. "But the inspector general must have looked into that, too."

"Ogata-sama is not likely to have overlooked anything of that sort," Ippei said. The Ogata-sama of whom Ippei spoke was Inspector General Ogata Kumaki, a man of high repute for his competence. "They say he investigated everyone—the finance department, Yoshimura's family in Obune-chō, the Matsukawa Dojo—and found nothing that seemed linked to the crime."

"Very thorough!"

"Mmm. In fact he even eavesdropped on what people in the neighborhood were saying in their houses." Ippei was rubbing his face with his palms, obviously uncomfortable. His rather full face, from the bridge of his nose and across his cheek bones, had turned purple in the cold.

"Even so, though, it must have been someone of considerable skill," Bunshirō said. "Even if he did attack from the rear, don't they say it looked as if Yoshimura-san never got his hand near the hilt of his sword?"

"He probably closed with him in an instant," Ippei said. "Yoshimura Shinzō never even heard his footsteps, I'd guess."

The two looked each other in the face; in the distance the Chidori Bridge hove into view. Just across that bridge was where Kaji-machi began, and from there they could see the gate to the dojo. They were arriving right on time.

The first match of the year at the Ishiguri Dojo was a grand affair. Except for three who were absent having caught colds, all fifty-some disciples had gathered there.

At the appointed hour, once they had welcomed their master, Ishiguri Yazaemon, to the dojo, the ceremonies began immediately. First of all, the master's assistant, Satake Kinjūrō, made a congratulatory speech on behalf of the disciples, following which Ishiguri delivered his customary brief admonition. Thereafter, this year's rankings, as determined by Ishiguri and based upon the results of their final matches, were announced. The rankings were read by the second-ranking disciple Maruoka Shunsaku. Bunshirō had risen from twenty-second to fifteenth, and Owada Ippei from twenty-fifth to eighteenth.

The hall was abuzz with voices after the announcement of the rankings, but once Ishiguri had commanded that Satake and the third-ranking disciple Ōhashi Ichinoshin tie back their sleeves, fit their headbands, take up their wooden swords, and advance to the center of the floor, total silence suddenly returned. The demonstration of the school's techniques would now begin.

A "demonstration" they called it. But performed by two of the highest ranking disciples, this was a breathtaking exhibition of true skill, the intensity of which had every year overwhelmed everyone who saw it. This year, too, those techniques were exhibited with such drive and skill that even an instant's misjudgment could have caused broken bones. And when it was over, everyone watching was gripping palms soaked with sweat, and the performers themselves were dripping sweat from head to toe.

Once the demonstration was finished, Ishiguri, the old master, went within, and sweet saké that had been warming in a vat was brought in and ladled out to the disciples, sitting in a circle around the vat. With an endless buzz of conversation filling their ears, Bunshirō and Ippei sat sipping saké. Their rise in the rankings pleased both of them. Most of the talk that swirled about them concerned the demonstration they had just seen or the rankings that had been announced. Some were happy, some angry that they hadn't risen as much as they had expected. Their sense of liberation had loosened the tongues of these young men, and they grew more talkative than usual.

Then someone stood and tried to silence the chatter. "Everyone listen!" he said. It was Satake Kinjūrō.

"Some of you may think it inauspicious of me to mention this so early in the New Year; but this is something I cannot pass over in silence, so I will say it." As he spoke, Kinjūrō thrust out the narrow shoulders on his tall, thin frame. "I expect you all know that last month a man was cut down in Yamabuki-chō. The dead man is Yoshimura Shinzō of the Matsukawa Dojo. Which some of you, I expect, are aware of as well. But the question remains: *Who* cut him down?"

Once everyone had turned their attention to Kinjūrō, he nodded their way.

"I have seen Yoshimura's body." Kinjūrō stared fixedly at everyone, from one end of the circle to the other. Then he spoke more sharply. "The person who killed Yoshimura is one of you."

"Impossible!" said Hashimoto, his fellow demonstrator of the school's techniques. A strange, brief stir ran through the hall, then immediately quietened down. In its place an uneasy silence ruled the scene. Bunshirō, still holding his sweet saké cup, remained stock still, gazing at Satake Kinjūrō.

"No, they showed me the wound," Kinjūrō said in reply to Hashimoto, then turned his eyes back to everyone else. "That wound was not made by anyone of the Ittō school, or the Mugai school. It was made by someone of this school."

Kinjūrō seemed to have found strong evidence and stated his conclusion with complete confidence. There were three schools of sword fighting in the castle town: the Ittō school at the Matsukawa Dojo, the Mugai school at the Ono Dojo, and the Kūdon school at the Ishiguri Dojo. That each had its own particular traits was commonly recognized.

4

Satake Kinjūrō must have seen unmistakable signs of a particular technique on the body of Yoshimura, Bunshirō thought.

"I've told no one other than the master about this," Kinjūro said, in a softer voice. "What I've said here today is to be a secret of this dojo. If possible, I would like to keep it a secret, but at some point it will probably leak out. The inspector general's people will hear of it, and I shall probably be summoned, but I've no intention of telling them anything. Though, as I've said, I've seen evidence. I'm keeping that to myself. There are any number of ways I can avoid telling what I know. But ..." and here Kinjūrō again spoke with force. "But—I'll not condone a cover-up. Whoever you are that did this to Yoshimura, come and tell me! If you don't want to tell me why you did it, I won't presume to ask. But this I'll say once more: I will not condone a cover-up. I've discussed this with the master, and that is what we have decided. Understood?"

When Kinjūrō concluded his address, the group gathered for the first match of the year broke up, the hall still suffused with an atmosphere of mystery. Everyone hurried, backs hunched, to the front gate and there dispersed in all directions.

Bunshirō and Ippei, as always, crossed the Chidori Bridge to the riverside thoroughfare. The clouds were unchanged, still hanging dark and low as if about to sleet or hail, the distant mountains obscured down to the fifth or sixth stations. They watched several large birds take off heading for the mountains, but what sort of birds they had no idea.

There were more people out and about than before midday when they had set out for the dojo, many of them, of course, in festive garb, making their round of New Year's calls. There were even a few samurai in full formal linens followed by their trains of attendants. Would his father have returned home by now? Bunshirō wondered.

"That was horrific, what Satake-san was saying," Ippei said. Then he cast his eyes all around them, and lowered his voice. "Who do you think did in Yoshimura Shinzō?"

"Wasn't it you?" Bunshirō made a joke of it. But his joke so shocked Ippei that his face flushed, and he waved his hands about in a panic.

Semishigure

"Don't say things like that; people could take it the wrong way. We don't know who might be listening."

"Don't worry." Bunshirō smiled wryly. "No one will ever suspect you. There are others with far more skill. The master's assistant would have to know it's one of them."

"Surely not Ōhashi-san? But if not him, Maruoka-san. He ranks second." Maruoka-san didn't say a word all the while the master's assistant was talking.

"But that doesn't mean you can say Maruoka-san did it," Bunshirō said. "There's Tsukahara-san, too, and Yada-san."

"No, not Yada-san," Ippei said. "He did just rise a rank above Tsukahara-san, but he's not the type."

"A placid nature is no proof of innocence," Bunshirō said.

The shock of what Satake Kinjūrō had said was powerful, and the two of them ended up discussing it heatedly all the way along their walk to Urushibara-chō. When Ippei's home came into view, they halted.

"Won't you come in? Mother would be delighted."

Ippei's family consisted only of his mother and her two children. But they were of higher rank than Bunshirō's family, so there were servants as well. Ippei's mother was always pleased when Bunshirō, Yonosuke, or any of her son's friends came to visit. Like Ippei, his mother was a large woman of an easy-going nature and not at all withdrawn. But Bunshirō was already a bit late returning home, besides which he was at a loss how he could tell his mother he had stopped in at Ippei's house.

"No, I can't," Bunshirō said. "But do give my regards to your mother."

"Oh?"

"And don't forget. Tomorrow we go to the academy."

"Me forget? I'll be going to eat the mochi," Ippei said.

Bunshirō continued up the street that led to the south side of the castle, then turned toward his own quarter at the northern edge of town. The cold did not relent even slightly. It permeated the withered vistas of one neighborhood after another, but at least there was no wind, and that made his walk a bit more bearable.

And indeed, Bunshirō realized, it was nearly midway through the Eighth Hour (3 p.m.) by the time he neared home. He had heard the Eighth Hour bell at the temple Shōenji as they were walking toward Ippei's house. At that point he had felt no qualms, but the closer to home he came, the more the extent of his tardiness began to trouble him. His mother had told him she would prepare their midday meal and await him. Perhaps he should have parted with Ippei along the way and come straight home.

But then there was what the master's assistant had told them, and so their gathering had lasted longer than expected. That was a fact, but how could he offer that as an excuse to his mother? What could he say if pressed to tell her what they had been talking about? Lost in thought as he was arriving home, Bunshirō almost collided with the neighbor girl Fuku as she emerged from their gate.

"Happy New Year." Fuku was hiding something she held in her sleeve, and her face flushed as she greeted him. When Bunshirō returned her greeting, she hastily turned her back and trotted off into the gate of her own home.

Bunshirō stopped and gazed absently after her; and then he realized that what he was watching was the sway of her bottom and the white of her ankles as they fluttered into view beneath her kimono. In that instant he returned to his senses.

Haven't I ... haven't I just been looking at her in an indecent way? he asked himself. No, that's all right, isn't it? a faint, slightly unconfident voice from within replied.

It was sometime last year, Bunshirō thought, that Fuku's body, once straight as a stick, had begun to round out. Yesterday he had noticed the curve of her shoulders; today he had been surprised to see how translucently beautiful her skin had become. In short, Fuku had reached that age when, day by day, she was growing to be more of an adult. The femininity she had just revealed in only an instant's movement, Bunshirō now realized, had the power to transfix him.

Fuku, too …? Becoming an adult? The thought left Bunshirō with a vague sense of sorrow as he turned his back on the street and went in through the gate.

When he entered the house, his father was not at home. "Awfully late, aren't you?" his mother grumbled. Bunshirō offered no excuse, only apologizing, and then told her he had risen in rank.

"This year, I'm fifteenth."

"That's because you've worked so hard. Last year you were twenty-second." Toyo remembered well. She praised him for his efforts, but then, as if she still hadn't grumbled enough, she went on to say, "But that's no excuse for coming home so late."

"No, of course not," Bunshirō said. "I'm very sorry about that."

When their meal was served, he was suddenly overwhelmed by an unbearable sense of hunger. He wanted only to be done with his mother's grumbling and eat. After he had finished and felt more relaxed, he said, "I met Fuku at the gate. What did she want?"

"She came to borrow rice," Toyo said. "It must have been painful for her, so early in the New Year. She said her mother had caught a cold. But now that she's grown up, there's no reason she can't run errands of that sort, is there?"

Suddenly Bunshirō recalled that when he met her, the New

Year's season notwithstanding, Fuku was wearing an everyday kimono. The Koyanagi were paid five koku per year less than Bunshirō's family. Bunshirō tended to forget that, but the poverty of the Koyanagi was severe. Bunshirō's family were poor. He and his father most often dressed in clothing that Toyo had repaired. But they never borrowed rice from anyone. Yet with two more children and five koku less, he could see how much worse off the Koyanagi were.

Yet if you borrow … then you must pay back. So what about that rice? What would they do about the rice Fuku was hiding in her sleeve? Bunshirō wondered as her image rose anew in his mind. And again, a vague sense of sorrow tinged his feelings.

Toyo had nothing good to say about Koyanagi's wife, but Bunshirō was pleased that she seemed kindly disposed toward Fuku. Bunshirō stood up, and on the way to his room, he called to his mother in the kitchen.

"Mother, I'll give your shoulders a rub tonight."

5

There were about twenty students at the Ikoma Academy. Ikoma Reisuke, in a soft, calm voice, was reading out a poem from the "Airs of the States.":

"Fair, fair," cry the ospreys
On the islet in the river.
The modest, retiring, virtuous, young lady:
For our prince a good mate she.

Here long, there short, is the duckweed,
To the left, to the right, borne about by the current.

Semishigure

The modest, retiring, virtuous, young lady:
Waking and sleeping, he sought her.

He sought her and found her not,
And waking and sleeping he thought about her.
Long he thought; oh! long and anxiously;
On his side, on his back, he turned, and back again.

When he finished, Ikoma went on to explicate the poem carefully. This poem, he said, describes the feelings of a man in quest of a beautiful woman. But in the end she does not respond, and this distresses him, even as he lies abed. Throughout the long, long night, he tosses and turns, unable to sleep. At the rear of the room, one of the students was sniggering.

"Emori, was that you laughing?"

"Yes, I'm sorry." It was one of Yamane Seijirō's followers who spoke, a boy whose face was covered with pimples.

"Apology accepted. You may leave now and go home." Ikoma, normally a placid man, rebuked the boy harshly, in a voice quite unlike his own. Emori left the academy in a state of fright, after which Ikoma continued his explication.

"Confucius says, 'The Odes serve to stimulate the mind. They may be used for purposes of self-contemplation. They teach the art of sociability. They show how to regulate feelings of resentment.' Emori seems to have disparaged this poem as a mere song of dalliance between man and woman; but that it is not. This poem is a prayer for the happy marriage of the lord of the land. Indeed, Zhu Xi speculates that it may be a poem in honor of King Wen of Zhou and his wife, Tai Si. In any case, it expresses the unadorned human desire for a happy marriage. And it is essential for those who rule over the four classes of people to cultivate an understanding of these simple feelings of the common folk, their joys and anger, their sadness and pleasures. This is a matter of great importance. Then, too, as a samurai, one must maintain control over oneself. One must never disparage the *Poems*."

The modest, retiring, virtuous, young lady: For our prince a good mate she? Bunshirō repeated to himself, thinking vaguely of Fuku.

"No mochi for you yet?" Ippei said, nudging Bunshirō's knee.

There was soup enough for second helpings, so most of the students had two bowls, and the two large pots were quickly emptied. But Ikoma and his wife were actually quite pleased by the hearty appetites of the young men.

"I had four bowls," Owada Ippei boasted, as they were leaving the academy after their meal. "That made Sensei very happy."

"You just think that because you're a glutton," Bunshirō teased him. "Whether that would have made Sensei happy, I'm not so sure."

"What?" Ippei struck back against Bunshirō's raillery. "Of course he was happy. Sensei was all smiles. 'Your fourth bowl, Owada? Eat up! And if that's not enough, I'll share mine with you.' That's what he said."

"Oh, did he …?"

"But compared to me, what about that Yamane? He eats one bowl, then makes a nasty face, as if to say, 'I should eat this foul tasting stuff?' Arrogant fool!"

Suddenly Ippei broke off speaking and slowed his pace. Bunshirō noticed immediately and slowed with him. At the next corner stood Emori, the boy who had just been expelled, and surrounding him were Yamane and his gang. Yamane and the rest of them were staring intently at Bunshirō and Ippei as they approached. But as the distance between them narrowed, they suddenly turned their backs and streamed around the wall at the corner.

"Hmmph," Ippei snorted. "Thought they'd ambush us and start a fight, maybe? Then changed their mind?"

"Too cowardly to try that, the rats," Bunshirō said. As they crossed at the corner, they could see the backs of Yamane and the others dwindling into the distance.

"This year we may get to compete in the cherry blossom matches at the Matsukawa Dojo."

"No, it's too soon for us."

"Just once, I'd like to have it out with Yamane," Ippei said. Then, as if his thoughts had taken a sudden leap: "The soup was delicious, but Sensei's lecture was interesting, too. 'The modest, retiring, virtuous, young lady: For our prince a good mate she,' was it? Last year's was good, too: 'When a crane cries at the Nine Swamps / Its voice is heard in the wild.' That was it, wasn't it?"

Ikoma only taught poetry at his first lecture of the New Year. Normally he lectured on the *Analects* and *Doctrine of the Mean*. What Ippei was talking about was "The Crane's Cry," a poem from the *Lesser Elegant Odes* that had been the subject of the previous year's first lecture.

"'The fish lies in the deep. / And now is by the islet.' Remembered it pretty well, haven't I?" Bunshirō said.

Ippei didn't reply; he just continued his recitation. Perhaps he had come to enjoy poetry? "'Pleasant is that man's garden / Where the hardwood trees are planted / But beneath them …' And then, uh …?" Ippei faltered.

"'But beneath them, only litter,'" Bunshirō filled in for him. Then the two of them went on reciting in unison.

"'There are other hills whose stones / Are good for grinding tools.'"

They were walking through a corner of Yamabuki-chō. It was a quiet spot in a samurai neighborhood, where one rarely saw anyone out walking just after midday. And on the two of them went, still chanting in unison:

The crane cries in the ninth pool of the marsh,
And her voice is heard in the wilds.
The fish lies in the deep.
And now is by the islet.

A samurai woman and her attendants, the only others on the street, passed them from the opposite direction. It was a woman about the age of Bunshirō's mother, and she turned and smiled at the two of them chanting their poem as she passed.

When they had finished reciting "The Crane's Cry," Ippei turned and faced Bunshirō. "You know, I may be getting married."

"Married?" Bunshirō was shocked. "Right away?"

"No, not right away. We have to find someone first."

Ippei seemed a bit embarrassed and rubbed his palm against his face. Ippei's face was purple in spots from the cold, but now the purple took on a rosy tinge and his face was dappled with color.

"My mother was saying she would start looking now, and if possible she hopes we can hold the ceremony in the autumn."

"Hmm." Bunshirō felt as if Ippei had suddenly been transformed into an adult, quite beyond his reach. He looked blankly into Ippei's dappled face.

"Married? What does that feel like?"

"What does it feel like, you ask? How would I know? I don't have a wife yet."

"Then did Sensei's lecture today really hit home for you?

Semishigure

"But is there any 'virtuous young lady' out there for me?"

"She'll be out there, somewhere." As he said this, Bunshirō glimpsed an image of Fuku as it flashed through his mind.

"'Fair, fair,' cry the ospreys / On the islet in the river. / The modest, retiring, virtuous, young lady: / For our prince a good mate she …"

Ippei seemed quite taken with the poem he had learnt just today and repeated it again aloud. Then in a strong voice he said, "I'm not the sort to be anyone's lord, but …" It looked as if Ippei, having decided to quit the academy this spring, was now developing a fondness for scholarship.

Today, too, the skies above the castle town were shrouded in thick winter cloud, within which the peaks of the mountains on all three sides were hidden. Tomorrow, perhaps, snow would fall, and then they would be isolated in a world beneath ashen clouds. Yet even within that ashen world, Bunshirō felt he could detect the faint fragrance of springtime. Perhaps because of the poem he had been taught at the Ikoma Academy, he wondered, or because Ippei had told him he was to be married this autumn?

"I'll write to Yonosuke tonight," he said to Ippei. "May I tell him about your marriage?"

Savage Wind, Sudden Downpour

1

The announcement made by Satake Kinjūro, the master's assistant, on the day of the first match had shaken everyone at the Ishiguri Dojo. But nothing had been heard since then about anyone coming forward; none of the name tags of the higher ranking disciples had been removed, nor had any of the inspector general's men extended their reach to the school, as Satake had said they might. On the surface, at least, there had been no change whatsoever throughout the long winter and the coming of spring.

In the interim, no one gazing into the wrinkled visage of the master or the deeply etched brow of his assistant would have discovered any clue of anything being done—or not done—about what Satake had said. Neither, despite the eagerness of the Owada family, was there any word of a bride being found for Ippei. Then, in the Fifth Month, His Lordship returned to the domain.

It was not that His Lordship's presence caused such a great difference in the domain, but the merchants' quarter did become a bit livelier and busier. One more often saw merchants bustling in and out the meeting rooms of the castle than when His Lordship was in Edo. Which of course meant that orders for one thing and another would increase and that some merchants had been awaiting this moment to market their goods. In Somekawa-chō, where all the teahouses and restaurants were clustered, and the geisha played their shamisen, evenings could grow quite lively with merchants entertaining officials from the castle.

In the course of all this, the rainy season came to an end, and the heat of summer descended. On one such day, Maki Bunshirō and Sugiuchi Michizō, a younger disciple at the dojo, had just crossed the Chidori Bridge to the riverside thoroughfare. It must be about midway through the Seventh Hour (5 p.m.), they thought, for although the sun was receding to the west, it wasn't yet about to set, and the streets were still bathed in its glare.

"Satake-san gave you quite a beating today, didn't he?" Bunshirō said.

Michizō was fourteen, two years younger than Bunshirō, but he was considered one of the more promising students at the dojo.

"Yeah, he really got me," Michizō said. His voice was changing, but he still had the childlike face of a boy. "My whole body aches from it."

"Just bear up," Bunshirō said. "Satake-san must think you show potential; that's why he makes you practice so hard." But then Bunshirō recalled Yonosuke when Satake was castigating him. Satake was a harsh teacher, whether a student showed promise or not.

Bunshirō himself cleverly avoided practicing with Satake and most of the time was taught by the milder-mannered Yada Sakunojō or the second-ranking Maruoka Shunsaku. But he didn't think that proper behavior. Satake was a harsh teacher, he knew, but whenever he endured a lesson from him, he felt that his skills had improved.

"It seems cruel, but at your age a good night's sleep will cure the pain." As he spoke, Bunshirō was surprised by the sight of a company of lancers running along the far side of the river.

"What's that?" Bunshirō said. Michizō, too, seemed to have noticed and was following intently the company of men running north along the sandy path on the far bank of the river. Then the unit, the blades of their lances sparkling, turned as one away from the riverbank into Daikan-machi.

Michizō looked back at Bunshirō. "What's up?"

"Twenty men," Bunshirō said. Whereupon, on the Ayame Bridge which had just come into view, another company of lancers appeared, wearing headbands, their sleeves tied back, their blades unsheathed, just like the previous company. This group crossed the bridge from west to east, then turned immediately and ran to the south on the same street as Bunshirō and his friend. To their rear they raised a cloud of white dust.

"I know," Bunshirō said. "They're heading for the gates." Bunshirō recalled having once heard that, whenever trouble arose, the company commanders, leading their units of lancers and archers, would secure the wooden gates to the town on all four sides.

As the company of lancers ran past, people walking down the street of course looked shocked and halted to watch as the men ran on. But once they were out of sight, people went on walking just as before. It was as if the hot, slanting rays of the sun had restored the neighborhood, unchanged, to its previous state. But in Bunshirō, a strange sense of foreboding lingered on.

"Looks like trouble," Bunshirō said. Michizō's face froze in fright.

Semishigure

"What sort of trouble?"

"I have no idea." If Ippei were there, he could have talked with him about this. But not with Michizō, Bunshirō thought.

When Ippei had begun reporting for duty at the castle, he had formally withdrawn from the Ikoma Academy. He would continue to attend the dojo, he said, as he was still only a half-trained member of his unit, but things seem not to have worked out that way, and he was often absent from the dojo, too. At this point, three days had passed since Bunshirō had seen Ippei's face.

"This is where we part," Bunshirō said. "So go straight home and don't loiter along the way." When he and Michizō parted, Bunshirō crossed the Ayame Bridge to the west. The drum signaling the end of working hours at the castle should have sounded by now. But there was no drumbeat nor was anyone to be seen on the street returning from the castle. It was an eerie feeling.

By the time he arrived back in his own neighborhood, Bunshirō had seen another company of lancers rounding a corner in the distance, as well as a number of samurai hurrying toward the castle dressed in formal linens, each of them followed by one or two attendants. It was obvious these men were coming from Takumi-chō, where there were several mansions of such officials. His suspicion that trouble of some sort had arisen had not been wrong, Bunshirō thought.

But back in Yaba-machi, there was only the shrilling of the cicadas to be heard. The quarter lay in a hushed silence that seemed to belie the notion that trouble had arisen in the castle.

The name Yaba-machi came from the fact that in the past there had actually been a yaba—an archery range—there, where the archers could practice shooting.

2

The practice range for the archers' quarter, and later the practice range of the musketeers with it, had been moved to the base of a hill in the village of Sanae, to the west of the castle town, but the vacant space left by the old archery range was still there. It was a broad, empty plot, overrun with weeds, at the edge of the quarter on the far side of the street. The lot was surrounded on three sides by a grove of trees. But one knew that this had once been an archery range from the weed-covered earthen wall at the deepest extreme of the lot. In springtime, children, not only from Yaba-machi but other neighborhoods as well, came to the field and the grove to gather flowers. It was a perfect place for them to play, but in summer it was overgrown with weeds as tall as the children themselves. Occasionally some of the neighborhood children could still be seen there, collecting insects and butterflies, but most of the time it was dead silent.

As Bunshirō walked down the street, glancing to the side as he passed the field, he could see mountain lilies and day lilies in bloom there, and in the grove, the cicadas seemed to vie with one another, each of them shrilling so loud it made his ears ring. Bunshirō recalled the word "semishigure"—cicada showers.

His mother was preparing dinner when he arrived home. The western sun was shining in through the open window of the kitchen, along with the cries of the cicadas in the grove at the rear. As he watched his mother calmly preparing their evening meal, the several scenes suggesting trouble that Bunshirō had seen on his way home suddenly seemed to fade into the distance. Perhaps it had been nothing of any importance at all, he began to think.

His mother turned from her cooking to look back at Bunshirō.

Semishigure

"What's the matter?" she asked, as if concerned that he remained in the kitchen after greeting her. "A man doesn't hang about watching kitchen work."

"Yes, but . . ." Bunshirō's face flushed. "On my way home, there was something disturbing."

"What was it?"

"There were companies of lancers running to the north and to the east."

"Is that all?"

"And the drum in the castle didn't sound when the time had come; and there was no one to be seen leaving the castle. But I did see men coming from Takumi-chō, dressed in formal linens and heading toward the castle."

"Oh, my!" Toyo put the lid on her pot, laid down her chopsticks, stood up slowly, and turned to Bunshirō. "How many men were there in those companies of lancers?" she asked.

"Fifteen or twenty in each."

"And their blades were unsheathed?"

"Yes, the townsfolk were quite shocked."

"In that case, they must have been going to secure the wooden gates." She looked down and frowned. Then, as if it had just occurred to her, she said, "So your father will be late."

Even after the sun had set, there was no drumbeat from the castle, and Sukezaemon did not return. Finally, when they had grown weary of waiting, Toyo and Bunshirō at the Fifth Hour (8 p.m.) made arrowroot gruel and ate that in place of dinner. Bunshirō then returned to his room and sat down at his book stand, but his feelings remained unsettled.

The heat of the day lingered on. Even with the window open, the room was hot. Now and again a beetle or a moth would fly in and flit annoyingly about the lamp. Bunshirō could not concentrate. The words on the page just passed meaninglessly through his mind. When he gave it up and gazed out into the darkness, there was only the occasional cry—*ji-i-i, ji-i-i*—of a cicada.

Bunshirō was weary from his practice at the dojo and felt himself beginning to doze when he heard a voice out front and realized he had no idea what time it was. He recognized immediately, though, that the voice was their neighbor Koyanagi Jinbei. Bunshirō got up and hurried to the vestibule.

Jinbei was talking to his mother. When Bunshirō greeted him, Jinbei turned a worn and weary face toward him.

"I was just telling Toyo-dono, but Sukezaemon will probably be allowed to return tomorrow, so don't worry too much about it. Your father was under suspicion of some sort, they say, and was arrested by the investigators."

"Investigators?" It was an unfamiliar word. Bunshirō looked questioningly into Jinbei's face.

"It's an office they only activate in case of emergency," Jinbei said. "Five senior officers of the domain and eight heralds will assist the inspector general to clear up the suspicion."

"Suspicion? Suspicion of what?"

"That I know nothing at all about." Jinbei sounded totally bewildered when he replied. Jinbei must only now have returned from the castle; he was still wearing his formal linens. "They summoned everyone in our Defense Works Unit, one by one, and questioned us about one thing and another. It was just a little while ago that they told me I could go."

"Was father the only one arrested by the investigators?"

"No, there were three people from the Defense Works Unit. How many others there were, I don't know, but I've heard they'll be sent to the temple Ryūkōji sometime tonight. But

Semishigure

that's only hearsay. I have no idea what it's all about. I can't imagine that Sukezaemon-dono has broken any law. I expect we'll know something more tomorrow. But things being as they are, Sukezaemon-dono probably won't be back tonight. So I've come round to let you know that much."

After they had thanked Jinbei and seen him off, Toyo and Bunshirō just looked each other in the face. They returned to the sitting room, but for a time neither of them could say anything. Then, in a quavering voice, Toyo spoke.

"There must be some mistake."

It was then that something, quite suddenly, loomed up into Bunshirō's thoughts.

3

"No," Bunshirō said. He clearly recalled that day in the autumn of the previous year, when those savage winds and rain roared through and did such dreadful damage to the crops of the domain—and outside their gate stood two men, their rain capes fluttering in the wind.

"No, Mother, it may not be so simple a matter as that."

"Is it serious?"

"It is." Bunshirō felt it would be wrong to comfort his mother with some vague explanation. It would be better to tell her exactly what had just occurred to him.

"Do you remember last autumn, that night when the Goken River was overflowing its banks?"

"I most certainly do remember. Sukezaemon-dono was not at home, and you ran to the castle to take his place."

"That's right. But did Father ever tell you where he had gone that night?"

"No," Toyo shook her head, "but hadn't he taken those two travelers who came looking for him somewhere? And wherever it was he took them, he too must have been involved in their discussions—which, I thought, must be why he was so late."

"You're absolutely right, I think. But looking back, there are two or three things that strike me as strange."

"Such as?"

"The men who came looking for Father spoke in Edo dialect."

"Edo dialect?" Toyo cast an anxious glance at Bunshirō. "Are you saying they were not men from this domain?"

"No, they could be men who have been stationed in Edo for a long time and grown accustomed to speaking that way. They may even be men who are stationed there permanently. They must be men of this domain, I think. But another thing that strikes me as strange is that they seemed not to recognize Father."

Toyo looked Bunshirō hard in the face. Two men speaking Edo dialect, who did not recognize Sukezaemon—she appeared to be pondering what all this might mean.

"And therefore …?" she asked.

"Those two men must have come from Edo to deliver a message to someone," Bunshirō said. "That 'someone,' of course, was not Father himself. Father would only have taken them to that 'someone' for whom the message was intended—would he not? Those men spoke in Edo dialect and did not know Father's face because someone in the Edo mansion would purposely have chosen to send his message with men who would not be recognized in the domain—would he not?" That was the explanation, Bunshirō thought as he articulated it, that best fit the atmosphere of events on that windy evening.

"But who was that 'someone'?"

"I don't know."

Semishigure

"And those messengers …?" Toyo asked. "Why wouldn't they have gone there directly?"

"Perhaps they thought it unwise to go there directly; or perhaps they didn't even know this 'someone'?"

"But why so much fuss?"

"Probably …" Bunshirō looked intently at his mother. "Probably because the message they came to deliver concerned something secret."

"But Sukezaemon-dono would not have been privy to that secret, would he? He would only have taken those men to the home of whomever they came to see."

"No, Father, too, is one of them," Bunshirō said. There was no point in allowing his mother to embrace some comforting fantasy. He wanted her to face up to the harsh reality of what he was now about to tell her.

"The person those two men from Edo came to see was probably a high-ranking official in the domain. That was why in Edo they chose to use Father, a member of the same group but low-ranking and inconspicuous, and then gave his name to those men and told them where he lived."

Toyo listened to what Bunshirō was saying with her head lowered. After he finished, she continued to ponder it intently for a time. Then finally she lifted her face and spoke softly. "I'm hungry. Let's have dinner."

"Yes," Bunshirō said. And then he realized that the lamp in his room was still lit. He rose to leave the sitting room, when his mother called out to him from behind.

"Bunshirō. What is your father's secret?"

"I don't know," Bunshirō said. Neither, for that matter, had he any notion what the "suspicion" that Jinbei had mentioned consisted of. Yet even though it remained a mystery what his father had been involved in, and for which he had been arrested by the investigators, he was not likely to have participated in any wrongdoing, Bunshirō believed.

A faint ray of light was cast upon that mystery at about midnight that night, when his elder brother from the family of his birth, Hattori Ichizaemon, unexpectedly came to call.

"I just left the castle," Ichizaemon told them, sipping appreciatively the tea Toyo had brought him. "I've come because I'm worried how you might be taking this."

The family of Bunshirō's birth, the Hattori, were enfeoffed at 120 koku, and served in the secretariat of the domain. Their home was in Takajō-chō. After Bunshirō's natal father died, his eldest son, Ichizaemon, succeeded to his position. He was now thirty-four, nearly twenty years older than the youngest son, Bunshirō, who felt the force of his manner and speech to be more like that of a father than a brother. In fact, Ichizaemon greatly resembled their late, rather stern-natured father. When he had finished his tea, Ichizaemon turned a sharp gaze upon Bunshirō.

"Whatever may happen, you must never lose control of yourself, Bunshirō."

"Yes, I understand that," Bunshirō replied, feeling a chill run through his breast as he spoke. He was resigned, but now he was assailed by a premonition that whatever this secret in which his father was involved was, it would not turn out to be anything mundane. His brother had only just left the castle. He must have come here knowing something of the truth of this incident. His mother seemed to have felt the same.

"Ichizaemon-dono," she said to her nephew. "Has Sukezaemon been sent to Ryūkōji?"

"Yes, just a short while ago," Ichizaemon said. "With about

twenty other men, all told. The investigator's men are still making the rounds of other homes here and there. They say they're expecting quite a number of people will end up in Ryūkōji."

"What was Sukezaemon's crime?" Toyo used the word "crime" for the first time. Ichizaemon told her he didn't know, but Bunshirō wondered whether he really didn't know or knew and was unwilling to mention it. Just then Ichizaemon lowered his voice to a whisper.

"This is strictly confidential. You must never mention it to anyone else, but for some time now, there has been a dispute within the domain over who should be the heir to His Lordship. Sukezaemon-dono seems somehow to have become involved in that."

"His Lordship's heir …" Toyo murmured, and then fell silent. This was a world beyond her reach that they were talking about, and her face revealed that it left her totally at a loss.

Ichizaemon saw the look on her face and softened his words. "What the inquiry will be like, I have no idea, but it will be some time before any conclusion is reached. You had better go to bed now. You, too, Bunshirō."

"I'll do that," Bunshirō said. "But what's the situation at Ryūkōji?"

"The gates have all been barred with bamboo fencing, and are secured by foot soldiers from the companies of lancers and musketeers. They won't let you in, so there is no point wasting your time trying. After I leave, you should go outside and have a look around. Every position of strategic importance is lit with bonfires and guarded by companies of lancers. The town looks like a sea of fire."

"Will the inquiry be held at Ryūkōji?"

"It appears so. I may hear something about that before anyone else does. If I do, I'll let you know."

When Bunshirō saw off his elder brother, he went out beyond the gate. It was just as his brother had said. Looking to the south and east from Yaba-machi there were fires here and there, as if they had set the heavens alight. But had those fires also alarmed the cicadas in the grove behind the old archery range? They were still crying.

The full reality of this irretrievable disaster now began to weigh oppressively upon Bunshirō.

4

Half a month had passed when, one hot day, Bunshirō's elder brother, Ichizaemon, came to tell him he must prepare himself and come with him, as Bunshirō would now be allowed to meet with Sukezaemon.

"His sentence has been decided, then?" Toyo asked as she helped Bunshirō don his trousers and surcoat. Ichizaemon, a look of gloom on his face, nodded in assent.

"Mmm, that's right."

"Is it seppuku?"

"Well, now …" Ichizaemon averted his eyes and evaded the question. "Nothing has been decided officially."

"When will the sentence be announced officially?"

"Tomorrow."

Those who had been detained at Ryūkōji included the former elder Hirata Tatewaki, Junior Elder Kanematsu Kumanosuke, thirty-seven samurai from the Corps of Vassals, and twelve foot soldiers. The investigation proceeded swiftly, with no mention being made of what anyone was accused of. Only the sentences were made public, and those who had been demoted, placed on "restriction" or in domiciliary confinement, or banished from the domain had already been dismissed from Ryūkōji. Only twelve samurai and one foot soldier remained. Among those twelve samurai were Bunshirō's father, Sukezaemon, and Yada Sakunojō, the high-ranking disciple at the Ishiguri Dojo.

Bunshirō's pace was labored as he headed for Ryūkōji with his brother. The outcome was so obvious that even his mother had guessed. His father and Yada-san would be sentenced to seppuku; of that he was certain. And that would be why he was allowed this meeting, provided he came in the company of a kinsman. The thought made him feel like his feet were treading thin air, and he tended to fall behind his brother. Yet on the other hand, Bunshirō felt he must now maintain strict control over his feelings. If he let his immaturity show, it could make his father uneasy.

When Ryūkōji hove into view, its gate blocked by bamboo fencing taller than the height of a man, Ichizaemon turned to Bunshirō.

"Your meeting with Sukezaemon-dono will be very short. Now is the time to think of what you want to say to him. And there'll be no time for crying." Ichizaemon spoke sharply, as if he had noticed the grave expression on Bunshirō's face. "You're to do nothing shameful like that. As a member of the Hattori family, and as heir to the House of Maki, your conduct must be exemplary, so as not to invite ridicule. Understood?"

At the gate, Ichizaemon turned to the lancer who was standing guard and said, "We are kinsmen of Maki Sukezaemon." One of the guardsmen opened a wicket from the rear of the fence and invited them to enter.

Ryūkōji was a large Sōtō Zen temple in Hyakunin-chō, in the northeastern corner of the castle town. Within the gate, the white hot afternoon sun shone down on the graveled grounds.

Stretching from the bell tower to the rear of the main hall was a dark grove—almost a forest—of cedars and various other trees, and there, too, the cicadas were shrilling.

Bunshirō and Ichizaemon mounted the stairs of the hall and entered the temple. At the entrance there were several samurai, all armed with their swords. When they saw the two men approaching, they were quick to call out and demand that they identify themselves; and having checked their names, they relieved them of their swords and guided them within. These men, as arrogantly spoken as they were, must have been in the service of the inspector general, they thought.

Once Ichizaemon had stated their names, their reception was silent and proper. But Bunshirō sensed a certain disdain in the attitude of these men, as if he were already being treated as the kin of a criminal.

Entering from that bright, sunlit expanse, the interior of the temple was dark. As they moved further into the dusk, glancing obliquely at the soft glow of golden ornamentation about the pedestal of the statue, they could see those who had arrived before them. These would of course be the kin of the remaining thirteen men, come in response to their summons, all of them sitting there dark and grim-faced.

Bunshirō and Ichizaemon took their places alongside the rest. Reed mats had been spread on the floor, but beneath them lay hard planks. This, Bunshirō felt, was yet another manifestation of their treatment at the hands of those men who had challenged them. Which for the first time brought home to him with full force the inevitability of his father's seppuku. His father would be forced to slit open his belly, the Maki family would be deprived of their income, and he and his mother would be left helpless on the roadside—or so he thought. And even if, perchance, they should be taken in by their kinsmen, must mother and son go through life as the hopeless remnants of the Maki house, now become naught but a nuisance to their relations?

Bunshirō and Ichizaemon were not the last to arrive. After them, still others came and were shown to another corner of the hall, bringing the total of those in that area of the temple to more than thirty. Diagonally to his left, Bunshirō could see some of the latecomers seated near the veranda, where he could make out their faces. Most of them were adults, but he could see one boy younger than himself. There was only one woman. She was an oval-faced beauty whom he took to be about twenty. She stared intently downward, never once raising her eyes. Out beyond the veranda stood a clump of magnolias and maples, the distant reflection from which made everyone's face look pale.

It seemed that about an hour had passed, when a middle-aged samurai, somewhat more elegantly dressed than those at the entrance to the hall, appeared from within, tucked in his trousers, and sat facing everyone.

"Well then, we shall now begin the meetings," the man said, looking calmly about the room. "So as to create no unnecessary confusion, only one person per family will be allowed in. You may talk about anything you wish. No subject of conversation is forbidden, but the meetings will be short, so you should be prepared to limit yourselves. And do please refrain from speaking in a loud or angry voice."

"May I ask a question?" someone seated in the audience suddenly asked. It was a white-haired old man. "I am the father of Sekiguchi Shinsaku. For what crime is my son being made to slit his belly? If you know, I should like to ask the reason."

The thin-faced, middle-aged samurai looked directly at the

old man who said he was the father of Sekiguchi, but immediately shook his head. "Official notification will be made to every family tomorrow morning. The reason for the sentence rendered, concerning which you ask, sir, will I believe be stated at that time. At the moment, however, we cannot say whether the sentence will be seppuku or not."

"But then …"

"Even so …" The middle-aged samurai restrained the old man. "In your meetings, I think you may, if you wish, assume the sentence of seppuku to be a possibility." Saying nothing more, the samurai quickly stood and disappeared down the hallway into the interior. Thereafter silence descended upon the assembly. Everyone appeared to be trying to digest what the samurai had said as he left.

"That was the weapons officer, Isogai Shirōta," Bunshirō's brother whispered in his ear. "He was treating us not as the kin of criminals but as members of warrior houses. It had to be that way."

Bunshirō was not listening to his brother. He was watching a black and yellow striped dragonfly, that just then had emerged from the trees, fly across the stream of sunlight then on to the veranda of the temple, where it seemed undecided whether to come into a room so unexpectedly full of people and was flying back and forth along the veranda while it made up its mind. But while he was watching the dragonfly, Bunshirō's feelings were consumed by his coming meeting with his father, the question of what he should say when they met drifting in and out of his conscious thoughts. But before any particular idea occurred to him, someone's name was called and a samurai of about thirty arose from the seat next to him and left the room. Bunshirō came to his senses again.

Semishigure

Bunshirō's name was the fifth to be called. It was one of those men who had spoken so arrogantly at the entrance that came to guide him; Bunshirō left the wooden floored room and stepped out into the sunlit corridor. As he walked down the long corridor, Bunshirō encountered the young woman who had been called just before him, returning from within. Her eyes lowered, she bowed slightly as they passed. She did not appear to have lost control of herself, but her pallid cheeks caught Bunshirō's eye.

Bunshirō turned a corner in the corridor and could feel that he had entered another building. At the direction of his guide, he opened one of the panels and entered a room. It was a large dark room of about twenty tatami mats. When he closed the panel and turned, he saw that there was a samurai in the room.

"Maki Bunshirō?" the samurai said. He was a well built man of about forty, with a conspicuous growth of beard, even after shaving. When Bunshirō told him who he was, the samurai showed him where to sit, and in a calm voice said, "Sukezaemon will come in a moment, so wait where you are." The samurai rose and left the room. Bunshirō felt as if his very breast were roaring.

<u>5</u>

One side of the room probably faced a garden, but with the panels shut tight, no light entered from outside. Only at the place from which the samurai left had one panel been left open. From the corridor there, on the opposite side of the room from which Bunshirō had entered, some light shone into the room.

Bunshirō was sitting motionless in the still, cool air of the dark room, when, unannounced, someone appeared at the entrance. With the light at the man's rear, Bunshirō could not see his face, but he knew at a glance that the shape was that of his father, Sukezaemon. He must have been talking with the man who had escorted him there, for he turned to the side, said something briefly, and came into the room alone. Then he sat facing Bunshirō at a distance of about four yards, which must have been his assigned seat. Bunshirō expected there to be a witness to their meeting; but there was no sign that anyone else would come. Father and son sat facing each other in silence.

"Everything all right?" Sukezaemon said. His voice was as calm as ever.

"Yes," Bunshirō said. Even now he was fraught with anxiety, for he had no idea what he could say that would be appropriate to their last meeting in this life. Sukezaemon came to his rescue.

"This must have come as a shock to you. I'm sorry I've caused you this worry."

"Father, please tell me what happened," Bunshirō said.

"That you'll know, sooner or later ... But I've done nothing to be ashamed of. I did it not to satisfy my own desires, but for the sake of what is right. Afterward, I shall probably bear the stigma of a traitor, and I can see that this will mean terrible hardship for you. But Bunshirō! You must never be ashamed of me. Don't ever forget that."

"Yes."

"I've heard about you from Yada Sakunojō. He says you're the most promising of all the young men at the dojo. Go to it!"

When Sukezaemon said that, the same samurai as before appeared at the one panel left open at the rear of the room.

"Maki Sukezaemon, that will be all," he said. Sukezaemon turned and bowed to him. Then he looked at Bunshirō and smiled. Bunshirō, his eyes now accustomed to the darkness, clearly saw his father's smile.

Semishigure

"Look after Toyo for me," Sukezaemon said, then stood up smartly. Bunshirō tried to say something, but the words just would not come. He could only turn toward his father as he walked out the door and bow as deeply as he could.

As Bunshirō left the temple with his brother, Ichizaemon, the midsummer sun shone down upon him, and the shrilling of the cicadas returned to assault his ears. Outside the gate, Owada Ippei was waiting.

"A friend of yours?" Ichizaemon seemed to have noticed that Ippei had bowed to him, too, as they approached. Ichizaemon stopped and turned toward Bunshirō.

"This is Owada Ippei of Urushibara-chō. We're classmates at both the dojo and the Ikoma Academy. He's now serving in the Bodyguard."

"Would you like to talk with him?"

"Yes."

Ichizaemon looked down silently, as if he were pondering something, then raised his face and said, "Good. I'll go and tell your mother that the meeting went well. And also that you conducted yourself admirably."

"I'm sorry to put you to that trouble."

"Not at all," Ichizaemon said. "I mustn't go home without seeing her myself ... But don't be too late." He bowed lightly to Ippei and left them.

Ippei immediately came over to Bunshirō. In his trousers, both swords properly placed in his sash, wearing a linen surcoat, Ippei, as tall as he was, looked fully adult.

"I hear you've been allowed a meeting."

"Mmm."

"Have you met?"

"We just met," Bunshirō said. They both fell silent and began walking along the earthen wall at the side of Ryūkōji. It felt like a long time had passed, but apparently he had been in the temple only about an hour. The sun was still high; the shadow cast by the wall was short. As they walked along the brightly glaring street, they sensed they were being watched from behind. Probably, they were being seen off by the lancers standing guard at the gate of the temple, and when they turned at the corner of the wall, their sense of being watched immediately vanished.

On one side of this street stood the long earthen wall of Ryūkōji, and along the other side stretched the shabby old barracks of the foot soldiers. Within the temple wall a dense grove could be seen all along its length, trees swaying in the wind, glinting in the sunlight. And from the grove came the cries of the cicadas, shrilling madly.

In the gardens behind the hedge around the barracks, they could see women hanging out their washing, as well as three or four children at the roadside picking hibiscus flowers from the hedge, but at the height of the heat, no one else was to be seen on the street.

"How was your father?" Ippei asked, after they had passed the end of the temple wall and hedge around the foot soldiers' barracks.

Hyakunin-chō, as its name indicates, was at first a quarter where barrack blocks meant to house one hundred foot soldiers were built. It was in the north-east corner of town, and even then a slightly rural atmosphere pervaded the quarter, which was still dotted with a few farmhouses and fields. Just beyond the end of the foot soldiers' barracks, there was a farm field and next to it a grove of trees.

"Same as always, no change," Bunshirō replied.

"Just the two of you together? They allowed that?"

Semishigure

"That's right."

"Did you talk about anything?"

"Nope," Bunshirō said, shaking his head slightly. "I told him I wanted to know what had happened, but …" But this isn't what I want to talk about, Bunshirō thought. And then, all the things he had wanted to say to his father suddenly came welling up in his breast. "I should have thanked him for raising me. Why wasn't I able to tell him frankly how much I respect him? And I should have told him he needn't worry about mother. He shouldn't have had to mention that himself. He must have thought me terribly immature for a boy of sixteen."

"Do you want to cry?" Ippei asked. They had turned into the street that intersected the one they had been walking along and which ran beside a farm field. They stopped beneath a huge zelkova tree with a massive trunk. This street was said to be a remnant of the old highway, which the zelkovas and pines that lined it made cool and shady. Here, too, the cicadas were shrilling.

"If you want to cry, cry as much as you like. It's no problem for me."

"There were so many other things I wanted to say." Bunshirō could feel the tears streaming down his cheeks, but he didn't think his voice was quavering. "But while I was with Father, I just didn't think of them."

"That's the way it is. Humans are made for regrets."

"If only I had told my father how I respect him."

"Is that it?" Ippei said. Bunshirō pressed his brow against the bark of the zelkova. With his forehead against the hard bark, the flow of tears felt good. That refreshed him and to a certain extent emptied him.

As he wiped his tears away, Bunshirō turned and faced Ippei. Ippei's eyes sparkled.

"A bit unseemly, that."

"Not at all," Ippei said. "A man's not made of wood or stone. There are times when you just have to cry."

Bunshirō looked about the place. The scene seemed somehow different now. He hadn't noticed before, but the sun had clouded over.

"Looks like rain on the way," Ippei said. "Shall we go back?" As if his words were a signal, a dusty wind blew in just then. It was a chill wind that sent a shiver through them. They turned and saw that half the sky was now covered in black cloud.

"A young woman came to the temple, you know," Ippei said, as they ran. "That was Yada-san's wife."

Large drops of rain began falling on the two running men, and thunder roared so loud it reverberated in their bellies. The storm descended upon the castle town as if it were indignant there should be men awaiting their death in Ryūkōji, and it battered the houses of the town until midnight.

Like an Ant

1

Come morning, the sun again shone down upon the houses of the town, washed clean in the storm of the previous night. By about the middle of the Sixth Hour (7 a.m.), its rays had already begun to reveal quite openly their unbearable heat. And by the Fifth Hour (8 a.m.), messengers from the castle had arrived at Bunshirō's home.

There were two messengers. Shown into the room that Toyo had swept clean for them, with Toyo and Bunshirō seated before them, they read out in their most official manner the text of the sentence. "For the crime of treason . . ." the document began.

For the crime of treason against the domain, Sukezaemon is commanded to commit seppuku. The stipend of the Maki house shall be reduced by three-quarters, they shall be dismissed from the Defense Works Unit, and their home shall be removed to a barrack block in Fukiya-chō.

And having read their text, they went on to say, still in the most official tones of course, that at dawn this morning

Inspector General Ogata Kumaki, with the duty elder of the month and the superintendent of defense works as witnesses, had conveyed the same sentence to Sukezaemon.

Bunshirō then expressed their acquiescence, as Toyo had instructed him to do; whereupon the expressions on the faces of the messengers for the first time softened a bit. But what they went on to say was nonetheless unadorned.

"After the suicides, we shall ask the individual families to take away the bodies. It will probably be more convenient for you if you can obtain a freight cart, but of course we have no objection to your using a storm door or a litter …"

"By what time should we arrive?"

"We shall begin at mid-Fourth Hour (11 a.m.). Sukezaemon-dono will probably come after midday, but it may be best to arrive at the temple by midday."

They would have to work fast. One did occasionally see freight carts in the town, but where they might find one now, they had no idea. A rice dealer would probably have one, they thought. They could ask Ise Han, to whom they normally left the disposition of the bales they received in payment from the domain—but the cart he uses to carry bales of rice, he would not likely lend to transport a dead body, Toyo said.

And so they divided the task between them, Bunshirō going to discuss the matter with his elder brother and Toyo to their neighbors, the Koyanagi. Ichizaemon was at home. He had taken half-a-day off from his duties in anticipation of today's proceedings. It would be extremely difficult to obtain a cart, he told Bunshirō. They could only transport his father on a storm door, but Bunshirō was not to worry, Ichizaemon would come with men to help carry it. Yet when he ran home to report what his brother had said, Toyo told him it looked as if they *could* get a freight cart. The Defense Works Unit had three carts, one of which was small enough to be pulled by two men, and Jinbei had already gone to borrow it.

It was nearing the Fourth Hour (10 a.m.) when Jinbei showed up, pulling the freight cart and drenched with sweat. Bunshirō apologized to him.

"I'm sorry to put you to so much trouble."

Jinbei shook his head. "I'd like to go with you, but I really must report for duty today. I'll come to the wake tonight, though."

Ichizaemon had warned them: "They're not likely to allow you a normal sort of wake and funeral, but when I get to the castle, I'll ask about that." That said, they all exchanged glances and said nothing further.

In the generation of Sukezaemon's father, the blood line of the Maki main house had died out. They did still have distant kin within the domain and in neighboring domains, but none so close that they still mourned for each other. Now there was only Bunshirō's elder brother, Ichizaemon, to stand in for the main house and direct all such matters.

Ichizaemon brought two men with him, his manservant and a lackey, one of whom he planned to send to their mortuary temple, the Hōshōin, and the other to the undertaker.

"But if I send Yasuke to the temple," Ichizaemon said, "and then I, too, go around to the Hōshōin from the castle, there will be no one to go to Ryūkōji with you. Can you go there and back by yourself?"

"Yes," Bunshirō said. "I'll be all right alone."

Ichizaemon looked fixedly at Bunshirō, as if he were weighing the distance from Ryūkōji to Yaba-machi and Bunshirō's physique on a scale. Then, with a look of worry still on his face, he said, "That's too much. I'd better ask someone to go with you."

"No. Please, brother, don't worry," Bunshirō said firmly. He and his dead father would return home together. How could that be too much? Bunshirō was feeling quite full of himself.

And so in the end, matters were to proceed as Ichizaemon had planned. He and his servants left the house in a rush, and Bunshirō, too, set out, pulling the cart Jinbei had borrowed for them.

"Bunshirō!" From in front of their gate, some distance behind him, Bunshirō's mother called out to him. He turned and saw Toyo standing before the gate. She called out only that once. Toyo was standing stock still in the glare of sunlight so bright it dazzled his eyes. Bunshirō lowered the shafts and went back to her. Toyo had raised her eyes to the sky and was staring vacantly into the distance. She had called out to stop Bunshirō, but she was not looking at him.

Then Bunshirō realized what his mother was looking at. She was looking in the direction of Ryūkōji. Sukezaemon is now still living. But when I reach the temple with the cart, he may no longer be of this world. When she came out to see me off at the gate, Mother probably could bear that thought no longer, Bunshirō realized. Toyo's face, overnight, had grown pale and worn. Worry probably had kept her from sleeping the whole night through. Bunshirō put his hand on his mother's shoulder.

"This heat is harmful to your health," he said. "Please, wait quietly in the house." Bunshirō could feel Sukezaemon's words—"Look after Toyo for me"—echoing deep in his ears. He put his arm around his mother's shoulders, embracing her as he led her back to the gate.

"I'll bring Father back with me."

Toyo nodded. Then suddenly she raised her sleeve to wipe away the tears that had begun to flow. His mother, who ever since she had first heard of the incident had seemed to accept things in a relatively calm manner, now, for the first time, lost control of herself.

After he had seen his mother, her back bent, enter the house, Bunshirō returned to the cart and walked on.

2

When Bunshirō arrived at Ryūkōji, a number of others come to carry away their dead had gathered at the temple gate. There were some who had carts and some who brought storm doors; but Bunshirō could see only a few carts, just three including his own. It made him realize how fortunate he was that Jinbei had sought out this one for him.

Neither the carts nor the storm doors were allowed within the gate, but then a palanquin arrived, which was permitted to enter. Among those commanded to commit seppuku were some of high rank, such as the former elder Hirata Tatewaki. Bunshirō reckoned that the palanquins had come to carry away people of that sort.

Those unbearable moments dragged on while the white heat of the midday sun poured down on those waiting at the temple gate. The heat, too, was unbearable, but even more so, it was what was going on within the temple that burnt so unbearably into their feelings.

"Come take away your dead, they say—at high noon …" The sudden shout came from the same man who had said he was the father of Sekiguchi Shinsaku and demanded that Isogai, the official, tell him the reason for his son's seppuku. The old man had come with three strong men and stood next to the storm door they had leant carelessly against the temple wall. "I don't know how the domain can treat the dead like this," he went on.

"Couldn't they have chosen a more appropriate time—either at dawn or at sunset?"

But no one responded to the old man's words. Instead, he had made their eyes wander uneasily, as if his use of the words "your dead" had bored painfully into their breasts. The bamboo fencing that stood at the gate until the previous day had been removed, and now only two lancers were on guard, but even the soldiers ignored the old man. Having received no reply, the old man now looked down, his shoulders drooping. Seen from the rear, his hair completely white, he looked in that instant pitifully beaten down. Bunshirō averted his eyes and gazed off at the merchants' quarter opposite the temple.

At the rear of Ryūkōji, there still remained farm fields and groves of trees, but at the front of the temple was a rundown merchants' quarter made up of small shops and plain houses. As always, people passed up and down the street that ran through the neighborhood—though not a great many of them. As Bunshirō watched aimlessly, he was straining his ears, thinking he might hear the shouts of the "seconds" from within the temple. But no voices were to be heard, only the shrilling of the cicadas.

Then suddenly the gates swung wide open and someone's name was called. It was the name of the old man who had been railing against the domain. The samurai who appeared at the gate asked whether the old man had brought a cart or a storm door, and when told it was a storm door, he instructed the old man to bring it in. A noisy stir arose among the people outside the gate.

Thereafter things moved along smartly. Name after name was called, and the corpses that were handed over were moved out from the temple. After about an hour had passed, Bunshirō's name was called.

Semishigure

Bunshirō entered the gate behind the samurai who had called his name. When he reached the graveled space before the main hall, two more samurai were there, their kimonos pulled loose, fanning themselves. When Bunshirō appeared, they snapped their fans shut, and one of them told him to wait a moment. He did not have to wait long. A group of men came around the side of the temple bearing a storm door upon which lay a body covered with a brand new rush mat. When they lowered the body, the samurai who had told him to wait checked Bunshirō's name again, then crouched by the storm door and folded back one end of the mat. He then beckoned Bunshirō, apparently asking him to identify the dead man. Bunshirō crouched and looked at his father. His eyes and his mouth were closed, and his face was calm, as if he were asleep. But from his neck down to his chest, a great, ghastly gout of blood remained. His neck had been stitched. Even though this was the first time he had seen such a thing, Bunshirō knew that his father's second had performed splendidly, leaving one flap of skin on his neck intact. His father's hands were crossed upon his chest, and his swords lay alongside his body. Already a fly had appeared out of nowhere and was crawling across the corpse.

"All right, then?" the samurai in charge of the transfer asked, his face dripping with sweat.

Bunshirō nodded. "Yes, this is Maki Sukezaemon. No doubt of it."

"I understand you've brought a cart?"

"Yes."

"Carry him out to it." the samurai said to the men who had brought the storm door. When he stood, he opened his fan, as if he could bear the heat no longer, and began fanning his chest. The other, somewhat younger, samurai followed his lead.

Bunshirō turned away, then turned back to them. Something still weighed on his mind. "There's something I'd like to ask you," he said.

"What?" The men stopped fanning themselves and looked defensively at Bunshirō.

"Who was it that served as my father's second?"

The two men looked at each other. "It's all right to tell him, isn't it?" the elder man said. The younger nodded. Then he turned an unblinking eye on Bunshirō.

"You really want to know?"

"Yes. By all means."

"It was Murakami Shichirōemon of the Bodyguard."

Bunshirō thanked him, then followed the men carrying the storm door, who had already begun to move.

The men carrying the body of Sukezaemon were astonished to learn that Bunshirō meant to pull the cart by himself.

"Sonny, that'll be too difficult by yourself." They all asked if there weren't someone who could help him, but Bunshirō assured them he could do it by himself.

3

With the help of these men, Bunshirō placed his father's body on the reed mat that lay on the cart. And when the body was moved, fresh blood spilt out on the mat. In the course of it all, the thought crossed Bunshirō's mind that he perhaps could not trust himself to manage such a task under the noonday sun.

The number of people at the main gate awaiting the handover of their dead was considerably fewer than before, but two or three of them came over and held Bunshirō's cart steady for him. Once the body had been shifted into place, Bunshirō removed the reed mat for a moment and spread out a surcoat he had brought to conceal his father's body. When he had replaced the mat atop it, he thanked the people who had helped him and began pulling his cart.

Even for a cart built to be pulled by only two men, this Defense Works Unit freight cart had strong, heavy wheels and thick shafts. When he started pulling it with a corpse loaded upon it, his body in that instant tensed against the weight of the cart. In part that may have been because the hour was now past noon and he was hungry.

Well, then ... there's nothing for it but to return by the shortest route, Bunshirō thought. Already, as he wiped away the streams of sweat with his sleeve and looked back at the cart, he could see Sukezaemon's pallid feet protruding from beneath the surcoat and reed mat. On his way to the temple, given his qualms about transporting a dead man, Bunshirō had pondered the matter of his route, thinking perhaps he should avoid the busier parts of town and return via those quarters that were little trafficked, even if it did mean taking a roundabout way. But once he began pulling this heavy cart under the scorching rays of the sun, all his discretion of that morning vanished, and he was overwhelmed by a burning desire to return home with the body of his father just as quickly as he could. And beneath this feeling lay a tenacious fear that along the way his strength might be exhausted, and that he and his father's corpse could be brought to a standstill under the blazing sun.

As he had expected, Bunshirō's cart did attract the attention of people wherever he went. Everyone in town knew what had happened today at Ryūkōji. People who had seen all the storm doors and carts that had been passing through could hardly ignore this cart that had now come, with a pair of ankles protruding from beneath a reed mat. As he moved through town, Bunshirō was painfully aware of how passersby would stop, and people standing beneath the eaves would stare at him silently, saying not a word as he passed. Their piercing gaze only intensified his weariness. Head down, stumbling along, Bunshirō pushed on. At times he likened himself to an ant, carrying a load much larger than itself under a burning sun.

In those quarters where few people walked the streets, the samurai or temple neighborhoods, he felt some relief. Bunshirō would lower the shafts to the street, wait for his breathing to calm, and look back at his father's large, pale feet pointing upward to the heavens. It was then that he had the feeling that he was all alone with his father. "Just a little more patience, Father," Bunshirō would murmur to himself as he readjusted his grip on the shafts. And having convinced himself that this was indeed so, he felt some of his strength return.

But then his route entered another of those lively merchants' quarters. Bunshirō plodded along, pulling his cart, head lowered, bearing up under the stares that focused upon him from under the eaves, to both left and right. Then suddenly he heard a voice that he recognized.

"Hey! Here comes the criminal's son, carting a dead man."

Bunshirō raised his head. He didn't have to see the face; he knew who it was: his classmate at the Ikoma Academy, Emori Toshiya.

What he then discerned, however, was that Emori was not alone. Yamane Seijirō and several of his hangers-on, arms folded, were looking sharply his way, every one of them sneering, as if they had planned this in advance. Seeing them, Bunshirō stopped his cart. Fiery rage welled up within his breast. He wanted to lower the shafts and have it out with the insolent louts there before his eyes.

Semishigure

But Bunshirō managed to suppress his anger. He felt as if Sukezaemon, lying there on the cart, his feet exposed, were saying to him, "You must not be ashamed of your father." Bunshirō thrust out his chest, glared directly at each and every one of them, then again began pulling the heavy cart.

The gang offered no further jeers, but once some distance had opened between them, he heard someone shout back at him, "Pull yourself together, Maki Bunshirō. Your legs are wobbling!" The rest of the gang began laughing, but Bunshirō did not look back.

Step by step he trod firmly forward, murmuring to himself as he went, "You must not be ashamed of your father." Sweat rolled into his eyes, and when he lifted his hand to wipe it away, he was overwhelmed by unbearable fatigue. Slowly, slowly onward, under the curious eyes of passersby, he pulled his cart, until he emerged on the riverbank road. There he turned right. This street was a shortcut to Yaba-machi.

It was a quiet place, a mixture of ordinary town houses and foot soldiers' barracks, but before it led into Yaba-machi, the road sloped slightly upward. Even though he had now turned onto the shortcut, Bunshirō still had his doubts whether he could climb that slope. It was a slope one normally wouldn't so much as notice; one could hardly even call it a hill. What made the climb so daunting was Bunshirō's utter exhaustion. Yet he knew he no longer had the strength to take a roundabout but level route. That would be too far. There was nothing for it but a do-or-die attempt to mount this slope.

When he came to the end of the foot soldiers' barracks, however, his cart suddenly felt lighter. The wheels rumbled on, but Bunshirō, still gripping the shafts, felt as if he was about to fall forward. He turned about, and there he saw a black head just behind Sukezaemon's feet. The face that then arose was that of Sugiuchi Michizō. Bunshirō halted the cart.

"Just as I was about to cross the Chidori Bridge I saw your cart," Michizō said. "I'd heard you would be alone, so I went to Ryūkōji to give you a hand, but …"

"Sugiuchi!" Bunshirō wiped the sweat from his eyes, turned toward the corpse, and gestured to it with his chin. "You're not put off by a dead man?"

"No." Michizō cast a slightly fearful look at the feet sticking out from under from the rough reed mat, but straightaway replied in a decisive voice. "He is Maki-san's father. I think nothing of it."

"Thanks," Bunshirō said. He felt he had been rescued. "If Ippei were around, I could have asked him. But now that he has duties at the castle, he's not free. You've saved me. Really."

"Not at all."

"Well then, give me a push." Bunshirō began pulling the cart. With Michizō pushing, it was easy. After they had walked a ways, Bunshirō, still facing forward, spoke.

"But Sugiuchi …"

"Yes, what?"

"You've rescued me today, helping me like this. But from now on people may avoid me, as the son of someone charged with a crime who was made to commit seppuku. You'd better not get too friendly with me."

Michizō did not reply. But when the slope Bunshirō had been worried about appeared ahead, he spoke up.

"Maki-san, are you going to quit the dojo?"

"Yes, that. What shall I do?" Bunshirō said. He would rather not quit, if that were possible. His father's words, "Go to it!" still rung in his ears. But Yada Sakunojō, one of the senior disciples,

Semishigure

had been involved in this conspiracy, so the dojo may be forced to exhibit restraint toward the domain. If it comes to that, Bunshirō thought, as one of those connected to the incident, I may be told to quit.

They had reached the foot of the slope. From the grove at the top of the gentle slope, beside the old archery range, they could hear the riotous shrilling of the cicadas. The sun still shone down directly above them, making the road and the leaves of the saplings exposed to it appear almost white.

"So! Give me a push now," Bunshirō called out to Michizō, as he threw his last remaining strength into their rush up the slope. When they had pulled the cart up past the grove into the street that ran through the quarter, both Bunshirō and Michizō had exhausted their energy. For a time they just stood there panting, neither of them saying a word. The cart had been that heavy.

Out of the corner of his eye, Bunshirō, still panting, caught sight of a girl trotting toward them from the houses. He knew even without looking that it was Fuku.

Fuku came up to them and pressed her hands together toward the body on the cart. Then as Bunshirō began moving again, Fuku, saying nothing and tears streaming from her eyes, began pulling at the shafts with all her might.

4

The wake and the funeral turned out just as Hattori Ichizaemon had feared they would. Authorities in the castle decreed that they be kept inconspicuous. This much Ichizaemon had learnt when he reported to the castle and inquired casually of his superior. That evening, however, a messenger from the castle called to inform the Maki family directly.

Those allowed to attend the wake and the funeral were Bunshirō's natal family, the Hattori, and Bunshirō's neighbors on either side from the Defense Works Unit, Koyanagi Jinbei and Yamagishi Jūsuke. Of course those connected with the dojo or the Ikoma Academy, and even Owada Ippei, who had lodged a request with the commander of the Bodyguard, were denied permission to attend. And no sooner had these paltry tokens of mourning been concluded than the day came when they were to vacate their house.

Fukiya-chō was on the southeastern outskirts of town. From the rear of the neighborhood, across an expanse of rice fields, the banks of the Goken River could be seen. To get there from Yaba-machi meant walking all the way across town, from one edge to the other. Bunshirō left his mother temporarily with her natal family. Then with Kahei, the manservant his brother sent to help him, he loaded their household goods onto yet another freight cart that Jinbei had borrowed for him. Kahei had been in the service of the Hattori since the generation of Bunshirō's grandfather. He was an old man, and his back was bent, but he still had more stamina for work of this sort than Bunshirō. So skillfully did Kahei organize everything that their preparations progressed without a hitch, and it looked as if they could get to Fukiya-chō before sunset.

Once everything was tied down securely on the freight cart, Bunshirō left Kahei to wait while he went around to the garden at the side of the house. He had had neither the time nor the inclination to water the eggplant patch or the other vegetables. The garden was rank with weeds, so much so that they had overrun the plot while the eggplants and the greens had withered.

Bunshirō went on around to the rear of the house. When he moved in under the trees, the cries of the cicadas descended upon him from above. The sunlight, faintly tinted with red, had traversed the rice fields as it moved west and now shone into the trees, so that the grove at the rear seemed to glow from within with a strange radiance that tinged even the trunks of the trees and the undersides of their leaves. The sun was still hot, but in the radiance that tinged the leaves, a hint of autumn was now visible.

Bunshirō went down to the stream and washed his face in the cool water. Then taking the towel that hung at his waist he sponged his chest as he gazed about the locale.

No one was at their family washing stone. All those bright, deserted stones somehow made the place seem lonely. There was only the trickle of the little stream, listening to which he gazed for a time at the rice fields that stretched out beyond the far bank of the stream. The rice had begun to form small blossoms, and from a village visible in the distance thin trails of smoke rose from their farm fires. This would be the last time he would see this scene, Bunshirō thought, as he started back toward the house.

It was then that he encountered the wife of the Miyaura family, who lived on the far side of the Koyanagi. She was carrying a load of washing piled high in her arms down to the bank of the stream, but when she saw Bunshirō, she instantly turned her face away and retreated to her house. The pain of that remained with Bunshirō. He hurried back to the front of the house, where he found Kahei sitting on a shaft, smoking. He put away his pipe and stood up.

"That enough, young fellow?"

"Enough for me. Let's go."

Kahei took the shafts, Bunshirō pushed from the rear, and they left the house. As they passed down the street through the quarter and approached the old archery range, the cries of the cicadas again reached them, but they seemed somehow weaker now than before. Summer, too, is slowly coming to an end, Bunshirō thought. It had been a dreadful summer.

As he pushed the freight cart, none of the passersby stared at them as they had when he was transporting the body of his father. And although the distance was great, there were no slopes along the way like those around Yaba-machi.

But Fuku didn't come out ... it suddenly occurred to him. It wasn't that he was expecting Fuku might see him off when he left the quarter. But Fuku had come to both the wake and the funeral. And since his mother had bade farewell to their neighbors on both sides that morning, even if she didn't make a point of seeing him off formally, he did somehow expect she might at some point show her face. But Fuku was not at their washing stone at the rear, nor did she hear the creak of the wheels as they passed and come out to the gate.

In his mind's eye he could still see the deserted washing stones along the bright sunlit bank of the stream. And then Miyaura's wife turning her face away the moment she saw him.

Even in Fuku's family ...? There was no way he could know what was being said inside their home, Bunshirō knew. Jinbei and Fuku had come to both the wake and the funeral, yet his wife, who so often had come demanding, "lend me some rice, lend me some salt," had not once shown her face at Bunshirō's house after the incident occurred. It could be that her mother had forbidden Fuku to go anywhere near Bunshirō's home. The attitude of Miyaura's wife was nothing unusual; that was just the way the world would be from now on, and he had better resign himself to it. It was no wonder Fuku had not come out to say goodbye.

Semishigure

The freight cart that Bunshirō and Kahei were pulling now entered a cluttered workmen's neighborhood. They passed a place where two-foot lengths of bare wood, stripped of their bark, were drying, lined up along the eaves; then a vacant lot where several stacks of old wooden casks stood, their bamboo banding falling apart; and then they arrived at their barrack block.

"Looks like this is it, young fellow."

"So it seems."

"An old wreck of a house …" Kahei summed it up. Before their eyes stood an old barracks, the siding of which was in places peeling off.

5

The barracks in Fukiya-chō, Bunshirō learnt from his elder brother, had originally been built to house the domain's crew of bird-catchers. These were men of low rank, whose task was to catch the small birds that were fed to their lord's falcons. Ten years earlier, the bird-catchers had been moved to a new barracks built for them in the falconers' quarter. Thereafter, for a time, the cooks who worked in the castle kitchens had lived here. But who lived here now? That his brother did not know.

While Bunshirō and Kahei were carrying their load into the empty rooms that the messenger from the castle had designated, a man of about thirty, looking like a menial of some sort, came out of the place next door. Later they learnt that he was the man hired by the castle kitchens to go to the seashore every morning and rush back with fresh fish. When he appeared, Bunshirō greeted him, but he only glanced back suspiciously and didn't so much as mention his name.

Around sunset, when most of their few household goods had been unloaded, a maidservant from his brother's house arrived, escorting Bunshirō's mother. His brother's wife had made a great quantity of rice balls, which she sent with the maid. They made do with these as their evening meal. Kahei and the maid, Haru, ate their share of the rice balls in the kitchen and then left.

After Kahei left, Bunshirō and Toyo made the rounds greeting their neighbors. In the course of which they learnt that there were two buildings containing seven units each, half of which were empty. When they returned to their own place and were tidying up, Owada Ippei came.

"My, it's dark," he said. "It took me a while to find you." Ippei had brought a gift box of sweets from the Tawaraya in town, which he presented to Toyo. "How are you?" he asked her. "Have your feelings begun to settle a bit?"

"Not yet," Toyo replied. "Not at all. I still feel like I'm dreaming."

"So you must. Truly, the most unexpected things can happen. It must depress you terribly. But now you'll have to accustom yourselves to a new way of life. And yet ..." As he spoke, sounding so like an adult, Ippei sat frowning at a crossbeam. "And yet to be crammed into a dilapidated barracks like this, no matter what the reason—the domain has gone too far."

"No," Toyo said, smiling at Ippei. "Sukezaemon was a criminal, in revolt against His Lordship. That we should be given a place to live, no matter how old, and still receive a stipendiary allowance—I feel we must be grateful for that ... But Owada-sama, you've grown up so since you've been going to the castle. Really, I hardly recognize you."

"No-o-o, Aunty. You're just seeing things, aren't you?" Ippei put his hand to his head in embarrassment; but immediately thereafter said, "I'm sorry I've dropped in on you so late at night, but might I have a private word with Bunshirō?" And having been given Toyo's permission, the two of them crowded into the tiny three-mat room that was to serve as Bunshirō's sitting room and bedroom.

"Hey, there's no place left to stand in here." Ippei took the wicker cases and cloth-wrapped bundles that had been tossed into the room, stacked them up briskly off to the side, and made a place for himself to sit. When the two of them sat down, placing a lantern between them, the room felt full.

"Have you been to the dojo lately?" Ippei asked.

"No, not at all."

"I suppose not. You wouldn't have had time before you moved," Ippei said. "I looked in yesterday for the first time in a long while. I went there in the morning, after I'd returned home from night duty. A rather interesting fellow seems to have turned up there at some point. Inukai Hyōma is his name, they say. Have you heard of him?"

"No."

"His father was stationed in Edo, but now he'll be serving here in the domain for the first time. He seems to have come back in the spring in the entourage of His Lordship. This Hyōma is the same age as me—and very strong."

"Kūdon school?"

"I don't know. But he knocked me for a loop, no trouble at all. And not only is he strong …" Ippei smiled. "That guy's a nasty fellow. Bunshirō— Hyōma will be a good match for you, I'd guess."

That said, Ippei seemed to have something more he wanted to talk about. With some force, he refolded his legs, and then said, "I've learnt a little something about the current situation." Ippei lowered his voice, which was probably a wise precaution.

His voice was loud and would easily penetrate the walls of this barracks.

"His Lordship has six children, and two of them are boys, Lord Kamezaburō and Lord Matsunojō. You've heard, haven't you, that there's a question which of these two is to become the heir?"

"Well, in a general way …"

"Good," Ippei said. "Kamezaburō-dono is the son of His Lordship's wife. And Matsunojō-dono is the son of a mistress, O-Fune-sama. Have you heard this much?" Ippei asked. "Kamezaburō is already nineteen. He had his first audience with the shogun four years ago and was granted the title 'Shima-no-Kami.' Matsunojō is only twelve years old. To all appearances, one would think that the succession problem had long since been settled; but in fact that is not at all the case. The truth is that for more than ten years since Matsunojō was born, behind the scenes there has been a ferocious dispute over the succession. And there is a reason." Having said that, Ippei suddenly shut his mouth, turning his ear to the window as if listening for something outside. His face was tense. But when he turned back to Bunshirō, he broke out in an embarrassed smile.

"No," he said. "There are those who give me all sorts of stupid advice—like I shouldn't even come near this place."

"Oh?" Bunshirō said, but he was not surprised. He recalled what happened only a short time ago when he saw Miyaura's wife at the bank of the stream in the Defense Works quarter. "I expect there'll be others who tell you that from now on. It doesn't worry me, but you'd better be careful."

"What? Let 'em say what they like." Ippei suddenly sneezed, then excused himself and returned to the subject. "The reason the succession problem remains unresolved is that, in the

Semishigure

women's wing, it's O-Fune-sama who wields the power, not the wife. Added to which, His Lordship himself, they say, is fonder of Matsunojō-sama than of Shima-no-Kami-sama. And with His Lordship and O-Fune-sama feeling as they do, it's only natural that a faction should arise that welcomes that idea and attempts to overturn the succession. In fact, three years ago there seems to have been a plot to disinherit Shima-no-Kami on grounds of ill health. So now you get the picture. That was what your father was involved in. In this present dispute, the balance between the two factions was upset, and it looks as if the disinheritance of Shima-no-Kami may be inevitable."

"And my father was a supporter of Shima-no-Kami-sama?"

"That's right."

"Who is the leader of the opposition faction?"

"Now, you'd best not get obsessed with who your father's enemy is," Ippei said, with a faintly sardonic smile. "From what I hear, it was a close race to see who would come out on top. Members of the defeated faction were charged with treason—that's all that they'll tell you. But it's not at all clear who's bearing the banner among the supporters of Matsunojō."

"That's not likely."

"No, it's true," Ippei said. "I've been told it must be Elder Satomura Sanai-sama. There seem to be others, though, who say Satomura is only a puppet; that the real ringleader of the plot is the retired junior elder Inagaki Chūbei."

Satomura was now the second-ranking elder of the domain. Inagaki was a gifted man. He had retired some years earlier, but was said to have been a brilliant governor when he served as a junior elder. Bunshirō finally felt a vague image of the man who had driven his father to his death beginning to take human form in his mind.

"Another matter entirely," Ippei said, "but it seems to have been Yada-san who killed Yoshimura Shinzō."

"So it *was* him, was it?"

"They say Yoshimura was the contact man for the Matsunojō faction," Ippei said, and then added, "Oh, and I'd forgotten. I've heard that Yada-san's wife will be moving in here. But can that be true? Have you heard?"

The Sound of Falling Leaves

1

When Bunshirō and Inukai Hyōma began their practice match, the clatter of bamboo swords around them gradually stilled. As always, he knew that would be because the others wanted to watch how their match would go.

Bunshirō was aware of this, but it didn't worry him. From the moment he gripped his bamboo sword and faced his opponent, his attention was riveted upon the other man's movements. As he studied the situation, he relaxed all four limbs so that he could respond even to the most minute movement, the most sudden change.

But there could hardly have been anything more difficult to read than the facial expression of Inukai Hyōma. Not only was his face pale and lean to begin with, Hyōma's eyes revealed hardly any sign of emotion, whether of joy or anger, sorrow or pleasure. Those eyes, so cold and dry, were enough to make an opponent shrink in fright, and when he took up his bamboo sword and faced off, the transformation they wrought in his expression made it impossible to grasp whatever he might be thinking.

Bunshirō, still in the figure eight position, rotated to the right, moving as though he were exploring the surface of the floor with the tips of his toes. The move was meant as an invitation to Hyōma to shift position, but Hyōma did not respond. He simply matched the turn, rotating his own body slightly to the right. Hyōma, too, was poised in the school's basic figure eight position, but certain differences from the Kūdon school were apparent in his posture—the position of his grip, the span of his stance—which made it ominously difficult to predict what his next move might be. Bunshirō did not know what school Hyōma had trained in before this, but his bearing in the figure eight position showed traces of some prior school he had practiced.

Whereupon—Hyōma silently rushed in. It was a brisk attack, and there was real power in the bamboo sword that loomed above his head. Bunshirō did not evade him but dashed forward and deflected his sword. Then, seizing upon an instant when Hyōma's stance wavered just slightly, he landed a swift blow on his gauntlet. But his opponent swiftly pulled back and nimbly withdrew six yards to the rear. It was a calm, splendidly executed retreat.

When Bunshirō again raised his sword to the figure eight position, Hyōma, too, resumed the figure eight. Both of them slowly closed the distance between them. This time it was Bunshirō who rushed in. Just an instant before they were close enough to join swords, he attacked. He rushed forward and struck Hyōma a fierce blow on the shoulder. Hyōma sidestepped the attack. Drawing back his feet and shoulders, his bamboo sword flowed smoothly into a defensive position. Then without a pause he shifted to the attack, raising his sword from the defensive to a left-hand figure eight position, one of Inukai Hyōma's uncommonly effective techniques. In an attack that raised a swirl of wind, he struck Bunshirō on the torso.

Semishigure

When Bunshirō fell back, he was certain he had been struck hard enough to break his ribs. But he had already prepared a follow-up to his first attack. From the position in which he had hit Hyōma's shoulder, he shifted in an instant into a further attack. This had brought the two of them into a position where each could strike the other simultaneously, but the speed of Bunshirō's sword in this second attack had been slightly faster. Bunshirō would be struck on the torso, but just before that, he landed a harsh blow on Hyōma's forehead. It was as sharp a blow as the one that had defeated Yada Sakunojō when he was alive. It should have had dire effects upon Hyōma, but his face showed not a hint of any change.

"Not yet!" Hyōma said immediately, and again raised his bamboo sword to the figure eight position.

Bunshirō, too, quickly assumed the figure eight position. Cautiously, he scrutinized the cast of Hyōma's eyes. His facial expression remained as impossible to read as before, but while examining Hyōma's face, Bunshirō noticed that his opponent's left shoulder was unguarded. There was no need for a second look, it was a small but obvious gap in his defenses. It would be a simple matter, he thought, to strike the gap he saw from the corner of his eye.

Bunshirō continued cautiously to explore Hyōma's expression. His opponent calmly maintained his stance. Bunshirō's eyes flashed to the gap at Hyōma's left shoulder. And in the next instant, he realized he had fallen into a trap. Before he could even see it coming, Hyōma's attack overwhelmed him, and Bunshirō himself took a hit on the shoulder. It was a blow so fierce that he almost lost his grip on his bamboo sword.

"I give up!" Bunshirō shouted as he fell back.

But Hyōma did not halt his attack. Bending his slender body

to the task, he continued to rain down blow after blow. Faced with such ferocity, Bunshirō raised his weapon to defend himself. But perhaps the angle of his defense was faulty, or perhaps Hyōma's attack was just too brutal, for with a loud crack Bunshirō's bamboo sword split in two. With no compunction whatsoever, Hyōma continued to attack. Bunshirō held up the two splintered halves of his sword in an attempt to fend him off, but he was soon driven back against the planking of the wall.

The training hall was in an uproar, but from amidst the cacophony the powerful voice of the master's assistant, Satake Kinjūrō, boomed forth:

"That's enough! Hold it! *That* is enough!"

Hyōma stopped. He retracted his bamboo sword and with that same blank look on his face stared at Bunshirō. Then he turned heel and headed for the changing room.

"What happened?" Satake asked when he came over. Satake was visibly displeased. As trainer of the domain's horses, he had much less free time than before, now that His Lordship was in residence. At most, he could come to the dojo only once in every five days. He had arrived late today, only to be greeted by this sort of nonsense. Perhaps he thought the students had been taking advantage of him while he wasn't looking. Anger was clearly visible on his face.

"Personal quarrels are not permitted here!"

"No, this was a normal practice match," Bunshirō protested. Bunshirō looked around the hall. The nearly twenty disciples had left off practicing and were staring at the two of them as they argued, no one saying a word.

"I told him 'I give up,' but ..."

"Ōhashi!" Satake called to one of the students who had been watching them, Ōhashi Ichinoshin. Maruoka Shunsaku and the fourth-ranked Tsukahara Jinnosuke were absent today, so Ōhashi was instructing the younger students.

"You heard what Bunshirō says. Is it true?"

"Yes, I think I heard him say that."

"Then why didn't you stop them?"

Ōhashi looked down at the floor, and his face flushed. He didn't come right out and say it, but students at the dojo now looked upon Bunshirō with different eyes. A sense of distance now separated them.

"All right. Back to practice. Go to it."

That said, Satake looked around at everyone, then headed off toward the master's private rooms as though there were something he had to do there. Then everyone picked a partner and began practicing again. Immediately the hall resounded with the clatter of clashing swords, spirited shouts of attack, and the stomping of feet on the wooden floor.

As Bunshirō looked about for a new partner, Ōhashi Ichinoshin called out to him.

"It's because you didn't speak up clearly enough that I caught it from Satake-san, isn't it?" There was anger in Ōhashi's voice as he grumbled at Bunshirō. So much anger that his fleshy face, already spotted with the lingering blotches of acne, had turned red.

Ōhashi was twenty-three, the son of a house enfeoffed at 120 koku. He was fairly burning with the desire to find a good family that would adopt him in as their husband and heir. But as yet there was no good match to be found for him. And so, to dispel his bitterness, it was said, the young man was spending night after night in Somekawa-chō, hanging about the questionable drinking establishments there.

There is no way he could not have heard what I said, Bunshirō thought. All the others had stopped to watch the practice match between Bunshirō and Hyōma. They must have heard quite clearly when he shouted, "I give up!"

Ōhashi was not angry because he couldn't hear me, Bunshirō thought; it was because I made the master's assistant angry with him. But the truth was, Bunshirō knew, the man's anger went well beyond that.

"I'm terribly sorry," Bunshirō said. "I'll be very careful about that from now on."

"Hmmph. I did see Inukai beating up on you after that, but there are limits to how much humiliation we can endure. I really do wonder why we spend our time teaching you, when an outsider can come in and knock you for a loop so effortlessly." Ōhashi doggedly persisted in abusing Bunshirō.

"When practice finishes today, stay here. I'll teach you a little something."

"Thank you very much," Bunshirō said, resigned to the fact that he would be completely beaten down today.

By the time he was released from his harsh lesson with Ōhashi Ichinoshin, it must have been nearly midway through the Seventh Hour (5 p.m.). Bunshirō sat on the hard floor, bearing up as best he could under the aches and pains in his shoulders and arms where Ōhashi had struck him. He was utterly exhausted; he couldn't even stand up yet.

As the last rays of sunlight streamed in through the barred window, tinting the boarded wall, he heard footsteps at the doorway, which meant that Ōhashi Ichinoshin had changed and was returning home.

Well, I landed one good blow, Bunshirō thought. Slowly he stood up. He had spotted a instant's gap and landed a clean blow on Ōhashi's forehead. Because of that blow, he had then been recklessly battered by an angry Ōhashi. But that one attack of his own gave him deep satisfaction.

2

He went out the rear door into the garden, washed his face in well water, and sponged the sweat from his torso. While he was there he could hear the coughs of the master coming from his private quarters. Ishiguri Yazaemon had caught a cold and for several days had not shown up in the training hall. As Bunshirō silently wiped himself dry, leaves were falling from the zelkova next to the well, making a faint sound as they struck the well frame.

Bunshirō replaced the lid on the well and returned to the building. In the changing room, which now reeked of sweat, he changed into his everyday clothes, checked the lock on the door, and left.

Kaji-machi—the smiths' quarter where the Ishiguri Dojo was located—was said to have been the home of a great many smiths when the house of the present line of lords had been moved here from Shimotsuke, long ago in the Genna era. Now there was no trace of them. Most of the quarter was filled with old houses falling to ruin and a few small shops near the riverbank. It was a quiet quarter. The swordsmiths, gunsmiths, and farm smiths had all been brought together in the south of town in a quarter called Shin Kaji-machi, "New Smiths' Quarter."

Bunshirō made his way out, between a small seed shop and a second-hand shop in which not a single customer was to be seen, to the street that ran along the riverbank. Previously, on his way home, he would have crossed the Chidori Bridge, which he could see from here. Now, he walked the riverbank road all the way downstream to the old wooden Kinzan Bridge and crossed there. This was a neighborhood permeated by a sense of remoteness, located on the eastern edge of the castle town. There were half-naked workmen—of what sort he knew not— their bodies gleaming with sweat this time of year, planing pillars of unfinished wood; and there were unattended roof-tile kilns, puffing up billows of smoke. A short walk further on, in empty lots between the low-roofed houses, lay discarded old tatami mats and insect-ridden building materials, barefoot children running about amongst them.

They were watching because it amused them, Bunshirō thought, recalling his practice match with Inukai Hyōma. A practice match is something two people of like mind do in a corner of the hall; it is nothing anyone need stop what he is doing to watch. Indeed, the normal thing is to pay no attention at all and concentrate on one's own match.

But when Bunshirō and Inukai would agree to a practice match, almost everyone would abandon their own matches and circle around to watch. From the look in their eyes, Bunshirō thought, you could tell they were hoping to see something brutal.

Of course, the second-ranked Maruoka Shunsuke, his younger colleague Sugiuchi Michizō, and two or three others had remained just as close to Bunshirō as before the incident that had shaken the whole town last summer. But the attitudes of the others had changed subtly. Some of them rejected Bunshirō with their eyes; others distanced themselves with their words and their manner. They were denying Bunshirō the right to approach them as he had before. Bunshirō recognized clearly that this tendency was furthest advanced in the younger students and that they found the appearance of a good match for him in Inukai Hyōma an entertaining prospect.

Semishigure

Inukai Hyōma was the second son of a man who had long been stationed in the Edo mansion as a liaison officer and was now to serve here in the domain as a herald. The family were enfeoffed at three hundred koku. He was thus a member of one of the higher-ranking houses in the domain. But Hyōma's nature, as Owada Ippei had told him, was quite unconventional. Anyone he did not care for, he would not even greet. He had little to say. But on those rare occasions when he did open his mouth, it would be to voice a curt complaint in crisp Edo dialect or to pierce someone with an stinging insult. This was not quite the same as what we usually call arrogance. In Hyōma, this attitude and this carping could be taken as his way of denigrating those he thought thick-headed, dull-witted provincials. But we've no way of peering into the mind of the man, so it may simply be that Hyōma was an eccentric.

Inukai Hyōma made no attempt to conceal his nature. No sooner had he enrolled in the Ishiguri Dojo than he earned the antipathy of everyone there. But Hyōma himself seemed to take no notice whatsoever that he was despised by everyone around him. He appeared genuinely fond of practicing swordplay, and he came to the dojo regularly.

It did not take long, once Bunshirō returned to the dojo, for Hyōma to observe his movements and discover that here, close at hand, was a good match for him. Hyōma instantly took an interest in Bunshirō; he thrust aside all his previous opponents and arranged that it should be him who came round to Bunshirō as a practice opponent. In the course of their practice, though, he seemed to have discerned that his skills fell a step short of Bunshirō's; and from that time forward, rather than simply seize the opportunity whenever one arose, he took to challenging Bunshirō to ferocious one-to-one battles.

During practice, and after practice hours had ended, the dojo did not prohibit students from having one-to-one matches. It was felt that this encouraged them to try out the techniques they had learnt during practice hours. But Bunshirō and Hyōma's matches were not of the amicable sort the dojo had in mind, and the other students soon became aware that they were exceptionally fierce. The master, his assistant Satake Kinjūrō, and the second-ranked Maruoka Shunsaku took to supervising the matches between these two very strictly. They were not quick to permit such matches, and when they did they would stand by as mediators. Depending upon the progress of the match, they would sometimes even part the two. But when none of these people were present, the violence of these practice matches would go unchecked.

What the others found so amusing, Bunshirō knew, was when he and Hyōma were battering each other with unrestrained violence. "Just one undesirable having it out with another undesirable. Let 'em go to it." That, Bunshirō could see, was the atmosphere in which their matches were immersed.

But the distance he felt was not just because he came from the family of a traitor. There had always been, within the dojo, a tacit jealousy of the son of a lowly house who had shown outstanding talent with the sword. Now, all of a sudden, it felt as if that jealousy were coming into the open. Bunshirō was well aware of this, as well.

I haven't *meant* to delight anyone, he had thought at times. It was foolish, he knew, to make a spectacle of himself and simple to refuse to become a spectacle. He need only decline Hyōma's challenges. Maruoka Shunsaku had reprimanded him sharply in precisely those same terms.

"Those are not practice matches—what you two are doing.

They're fights." Bunshirō knew it was only fair he should be taken to task for that. Yet despite all that he knew, Bunshirō had never once refused a challenge from Hyōma. If challenged, he would without fail accept. After which, when he gripped his bamboo sword, that sense of desolation so long hidden deep within his breast, that feeling of rejection that had etched itself upon him since his father's death—all of this would come violently to the fore.

Hyōma's rough challenges unquestionably had the power to call forth that sense of desolation within him, and Bunshirō would cross swords with Hyōma without ever thinking very deeply why that should be. At those times, all reason would be forgotten and he would fight as violently as a beast. Then suddenly, in the midst of the fight, it would at times occur to him that Hyōma, too, might harbor a sense of rejection and be venting his anger on him.

Bunshirō hurried through a quarter where the leaves of the trees were yellowing and the eaves of the houses hung low until he reached Fukiya-chō, where he lived. His chest and his shoulders still ached where Ōhashi Ichinoshin had struck him, but the desolation within his breast had calmed.

He entered the hedge around the barracks, opened the door to his own place, and from the earthen floor of the entrance called out, "I'm home." His mother came out to him straightaway.

"Koyanagi's daughter Fuku-san left just this minute, but …" his mother said, looking a bit upset. "She should still be nearby. Didn't you meet up with her?"

"No," Bunshirō said. He felt a bright light begin to glow within him. It had been so long since he had heard Fuku's name. "She came here?"

"Yes, because it's suddenly been decided she'll be going to Edo. She came to bid us farewell."

"To Edo? Wha …"

"She'll be leaving tomorrow, she says. She'll be serving in the women's quarters of the Edo mansion or something of that sort. But more about that later …" His mother pointed out the door. "Why don't you run after her? She must still be somewhere nearby."

"Right!" Bunshirō said, and throwing his bamboo sword and practice gear onto the floor above the entryway, he left the house.

He ran straight along the street she would have taken to go home until he ended up on the riverbank road. There was no sign of Fuku.

<u>3</u>

Bunshirō crossed the bridge to the far bank of the Goken River. Fuku was nowhere to be seen there either. Gone! Bunshirō thought. After all that, he had failed to find Fuku.

If it hadn't been for Ōhashi Ichinoshin's ruthless extra lesson, he would have been home in time. Or even before that—if he hadn't had that match with Inukai Hyōma, he'd have been home still earlier. But it was too late to lament that now.

Bunshirō walked downstream along the Goken River, until finally he had passed beyond the town and onto the levee. The sun had set and a pale glow hung over the fields. In the distance, columns of smoke rose, and at their base flickers of red flame could be seen.

She's going to Edo? Bunshirō thought. Judging from what his mother had said, Fuku would not be working in the kitchens or as a cleaning maid; she would be serving in the women's quarters. Did this mean Fuku would be serving His Lordship's wife, O-Yasu-sama? A change I could never have imagined, Bunshirō

Semishigure

thought. Suddenly, he felt, an unbridgeable gulf between him and Fuku had opened up.

Yet even so ... Fuku *had* found her own way to their barracks in the labyrinthine depths of Fukiya-chō. She must have come of her own accord, Bunshirō felt. He had seen what sort of person Fuku's mother was. After the scandal erupted, she hadn't once set foot in Bunshirō's home. Her father, Jinbei, was a good man, but no one you could call sharp-witted. It was not likely that he had told his daughter she should bid farewell to the Maki family before leaving for Edo.

Fuku probably decided on her own to come here—and to see me. The thought that Bunshirō had so far shut up within himself, he now, hesitantly, brought to the fore. He had no proof of his presumption, but it did have an unmistakable ring of truth. Fuku had left downcast because he had not been there, had she not? With that thought, Fuku's feelings seemed to transfer themselves to Bunshirō, and he felt himself growing depressed. He didn't stop to think what might have happened if he had met Fuku. He just felt hopelessly disappointed that they had not been able to meet.

When he turned and looked back, he could see the quarter where they lived. Thin mist shrouded the dark, harvested rice fields, a mist that grew a bit thicker where the barren fields and the houses ran up against each other. Within the mist, he could see the flickering light of lamps. Bunshirō retraced his steps along the levee and on the way turned off into a path that led toward the quarter.

Yonosuke and Fuku had gone to Edo; Owada Ippei had duties at the castle and could no longer spend time with him as he once had. Living on cast-offs, no prospects for the future, Bunshirō felt his sense of isolation growing ever deeper.

As he reached the street at the front of the barracks, a tall man emerged from the gap in the hedge. Just as Bunshirō caught a glimpse of him, the man turned his face away and walked off in the opposite direction.

He's come again, Bunshirō thought. That oppressive feeling returned. This smartly dressed and finely mannered young samurai had called upon the family of the late Yada Sakunojō, who lived in the same barracks as Bunshirō.

Yada was survived by two people, his mother and his wife. His mother was blind. She hardly ever ventured out of doors. After Sakunojō had been made to commit seppuku, his family line had not been abolished; their stipendiary allotment had been cut and they had been ordered to live in this barracks until otherwise decreed.

Bunshirō did not know what connection the young samurai who had come to call might have with Yada's family. But he knew from his mother's roundabout remarks that there had lately been unsettling rumors about the man's relationship with Yada's pitifully young wife—now his widow. One night, when someone from the building was returning home late, he had unexpectedly come face to face with Yada's wife and the samurai, holding hands as they emerged from a dark path.

Whether the rumor was true or false was unclear, nor did he know who the young samurai might be. It was just that Bunshirō, knowing nothing of the circumstances, had seen the young samurai calling upon the Yada family fairly often and had once caught sight of Yoshie—for that was Yada's wife's name—seeing him off out beyond the hedge.

Yet the rumors being whispered about at the barracks made Bunshirō feel vaguely uneasy. And because of his uneasiness, there were times when Bunshirō would encounter Yada's wife and he could only bow lightly and then turn his face away.

Semishigure

Yada's widow was a beautiful woman. Even when he had seen her in the temple Ryūkōji, he had thought her good looking. But under bright sunlight, her white skin flushed faintly, her cheeks were smooth, and her dark, slightly slanted eyes shone with a glow of determination; and even now, after she had lost her husband, she was radiant with all the allure of another man's young wife. Her limbs were well formed, and her bosom and hips swelled amply beneath her kimono. Seeing her, Bunshirō could not but imagine that she and Yada Sakunojō had been a well matched couple. For Yada himself was tall, handsome, and very manly.

I do hope she won't do anything too dubious, Bunshirō thought. He had only ever glimpsed the slightest bit of this world of men and women, but the abundant radiance of Yada's wife worried Bunshirō. His uneasiness aroused in him a premonition that she might yet betray the late Yada.

4

"Did you find her?" his mother asked when he returned home.

"No, but … I searched with all my might, but didn't catch sight of her anywhere."

"What a pity …" Toyo said. What did she mean by that, Bunshirō was wondering as he turned to go to his own room, whereupon his mother added, "… what's happened to Fuku. She must have come to see you, too, since she's going to Edo."

"Yes, I suppose so."

"Perhaps I should send you to the Koyanagi family with a parting gift for her?"

"Oh, I don't know about that," Bunshirō said with a smile. "She did meet you, mother. That should do, shouldn't it?"

With that casual remark, Bunshirō went into his room.

"We'll be eating soon," his mother said immediately thereafter.

Mother seems to understand, Bunshirō thought—that Fuku had actually come to see him and that it seemed she had come without letting her family know.

Bunshirō struck his flint to make a flame and lit his lamp. Then he turned up his sleeves to examine the bruises on both arms where Ōhashi Ichinoshin had hit him. The red patches where the skin had been grazed had now become dark purple bruises. These looked as if they would heal without being treated, but the places where he had taken direct hits were black and blue and still a bit swollen. These continued to ache and probably would remain painful throughout the night; it might be best to cool them with water before he went to bed.

I did want to see Fuku, Bunshirō thought listlessly. When he thought of Fuku, in a strange way it made him feel cheerful. Because Fuku was someone he could trust, without reservation—though in a way different from Ippei and Sugiuchi Michizō. Fuku was not misled by the words "traitor" or "criminal" that she was hearing from those around her; she understood the predicament Bunshirō had fallen into. In a girlish and naïve way, perhaps, but with tenderness and sincere feeling.

That she had taken the trouble to come and tell him she was going to Edo was proof of that, Bunshirō thought. Whatever those around her might think, Fuku herself would remain in the present exactly as she had been in the past; and even should she go to Edo, she would not change—that was what she wanted to say when she came to see him, was it not?

The thought made Bunshirō feel that his failure to meet Fuku was an irreparable fault. If she had come feeling as he imagined she had, would not that have amounted to Fuku's declaration of love? And leaving aside the question how he would have responded, did not that demand that he himself should be there?

On account of his failure, a dark feeling that he would never see Fuku again was beginning to take hold of him—at which moment his mother called from outside his room, telling him he must go to the entrance to greet a caller. The sudden sound of his mother's voice rescued him from the unmanly depression into which he was falling. His face flushed as he left the three-mat room.

"A caller? Who is it?"

"Now, you ..." His mother tugged at his sleeve and whispered someone's name in his ear. His mother was not her usual self, behaving in such a flustered manner; but the name she had whispered must have been quite enough to surprise Bunshirō.

Bunshirō hurried to the doorway. There was no boarded step at the entrance; and there in the dusky, earthen-floored entryway stood a large samurai. He was a man of about forty, and he must have come on his way home from the castle as he was still dressed in full formal linens. When he saw Bunshirō, he greeted him forthrightly.

"Ah, you're the son of Maki Sukezaemon?"

"I am Maki Bunshirō, and I am very pleased to meet you." Bunshirō sat with his knees properly aligned. The samurai nodded slightly in recognition.

"I've heard about you from Sukezaemon. As I told your mother, I am Fujii Munezō of Yamabuki-chō. I serve at the castle as a samurai commander."

"Yes, I do indeed know of you."

"I should have come sooner, but with one thing and another ..." Fujii suddenly looked up at the ceiling of the earthen-floored space, then seemed to peer within, and finally said, "Hmm, a much shabbier house than I'd heard it was."

"Yes, I'm afraid I'm unable to say I'd like you to come in."

"That's all right. I'm just on my way home from the castle. I can tell you right here that I've come in response to a request from the late Sukezaemon. It concerns your coming of age. We were to have celebrated your majority in the autumn of this year, and it was Sukezaemon's wish that I should be the sponsor to cap you—your eboshi-oya. I, of course, accepted with pleasure."

Bunshirō gazed at Fujii in astonishment. Fujii was enfeoffed at three hundred koku, one of those high-ranking vassals whom he thought of as a class different from his own. Finally, Bunshirō managed to tell him that this was something totally unexpected. "But how is it that Father could ask …?"

"Of course you find it strange. But what is now the Matsukawa Dojo in O-Yumi-chō, twenty years ago was the Tomura Dojo, where they taught the Jikishin school of swordsmanship." Fujii's voice seemed to ring with nostalgia for days gone by. "Sukezaemon and I were fellow students at the Tomura Dojo. When we were young, the two of us were touted as a highly promising pair," he chuckled.

Fujii was in a buoyant mood and went on to say that since this was the request of a man no longer living, he wished by all means to arrange the celebration of Bunshirō's majority and to serve as the eboshi-oya who caps him.

"Of course, owing to that incident, this year would be out of the question; but shall we do it next spring? At some point I shall discuss the matter with Hattori Ichizaemon-dono, but I should like to know that you are prepared to go ahead with it."

"But Fujii-sama …" Bunshirō's mother, who had brought the lantern and was sitting behind Bunshirō, now spoke up for the first time. "Your kind words that I've just had the honor of hearing bring tears of gratitude to my eyes. But Sukezaemon

Semishigure

was in rebellion against the domain and was punished for it. Even though you did make a promise to him when he was still alive, if you were to involve yourself with a house under censure, wouldn't that be harmful to you in your position?"

"Now, Madam!" Fujii spoke in a strong voice. "I appreciate your concern, but I must ask you not to worry about that. Speaking only of the incident last summer: I was neither Sukezaemon's enemy nor his ally; but that has nothing whatsoever to do with my long years of friendship with Sukezaemon. I am bound to do what I was asked to do by my friend of many years, and if anyone has anything to say against that, I myself, Fujii Munezō, will take him on. I'll ask you to leave that aspect of the matter to me. Now, if you ask me, it was a great error on the part of the domain to make those twelve men commit seppuku. Sukezaemon, Hitotsuyanagi Yaichirō, Yada Sakunojō; to put to death men like that who still had so much to contribute to the domain—eventually they'll be forced to pay a price for that. It is not just me; many others are saying that as well. So I'll not let anyone say anything against me for doing what I can to satisfy Sukezaemon's one small dying wish."

"But only for form's sake …"

"That I am well aware of, Madam." Fujii smiled at her. "I know it would be troublesome for me, too, if this were to be too conspicuous. But you needn't worry. Just leave everything to Hattori and me."

Bunshirō went out beyond the hedge to see off Fujii Munezō. Even after Fujii had taken his leave and was disappearing into the darkness, Bunshirō stood there in the road. He looked off at the tiny flickering lights in the villages of Kanai and Aohata, far beyond the bank of the Goken River. As Bunshirō entered the house, there seemed to have appeared a glowing sunset, and the sky was streaked with red threads of cloud while the earth was shrouded in almost total darkness. Although the lights of Kanai and Aohata could still be seen, neither the trees nor the houses could now be distinguished.

I could never have imagined such a thing. The thrill still lingered in Bunshirō's thoughts. The custom was to ask the head of one's clan or the commander of the unit in which one served to act as eboshi-oya at the celebration of a boy's majority. When his father had said, "I must ask someone to cap you," Bunshirō expected he would ask either his elder brother or a sub-commander of the Defense Works Unit. Samurai Commander Fujii Munezō lay far beyond his expectations. The appearance of Fujii restored a bit of strength to Bunshirō in the depths of his disappointment.

When he returned home, his mother had lit a lamp on the Buddhist altar and knelt there with her hands pressed together. Bunshirō knelt behind her.

The Elder's Mansion

1

Fujii Munezō had said they would celebrate Bunshirō's majority in the spring of the coming year, but in the end it was not until the autumn that they did, a full year after Fujii had come to broach the subject.

As Toyo had wished, it was not an exuberant celebration. After shaving Bunshirō's forelock, proclaiming his adult name to be Shigeyoshi, and placing the cap upon his head, Fujii gathered with Bunshirō's elder brother Ichizaemon, Owada Ippei, and Toyo in a single room of the barracks, and they exchanged only a few cups of saké accompanied by kelp and cuttlefish. In his new name, Bunshirō had been granted the character Shige from Fujii's formal name, Shigetake.

Then before long, winter had come, a winter even longer and more snowy than usual. And once it had passed, early in the Third Month, a messenger came from the mansion of the second-ranking elder, Satomura Sanai. Bunshirō and his brother, Hattori Ichizaemon, were to come to the Satomura mansion that evening at the Fifth Hour (8 p.m.), the messenger told them. And then he added that the same message would be transmitted to the Hattori family.

"What can that mean?" Toyo said, scarcely able to conceal her anxiety after the messenger left. Toyo seemed still to have it in her head that Sukezaemon's death had happened only yesterday and fear deeply that something could happen to Bunshirō as well.

"Well, I can't imagine," Bunshirō said. "But it could hardly be any worse than our present situation."

"What makes you think you know that?" Suddenly Toyo spoke with real wrath in her voice. Then she reached for a drawer in the Buddhist altar and roughly snatched up a pouch with her tobacco utensils in it. After Sukezaemon's death she had quit; now it looked as if she meant to start smoking again.

"Didn't you say that Satomura-sama is the ringleader who forced Sukezaemon-dono to slit open his belly?"

"It was Ippei who said that," Bunshirō replied, smiling wryly. "It's not certain. I won't know until I go and see. It's best not to worry too much about it until then." His mother was still visibly angry when Bunshirō left her and went outside.

There was to be a round of exegetical reading of the *Analects* tomorrow at the Ikoma Academy. Bunshirō and the other students were to read chapter fourteen, which begins with the question of Yuan Xian. He would have to prepare, but that sudden messenger from Satomura had robbed Bunshirō of the leeway he needed to face his books.

"Whatever does he want?" his mother had said; but Bunshirō's feelings, too, were sharply focused upon that point. When they sentenced Sukezaemon, the domain at the same time had cut the stipend of the Maki house to seven koku, a quarter of what it had been, and decreed that they move to this barracks. It was a hasty decision, leaving Sukezaemon's successor Bunshirō uncertain what was to become of him. At some point, though,

Semishigure

his brother Ichizaemon had told him, there should be an official decision concerning that, an understanding that Bunshirō shared. Indeed, he could imagine no other reason he should be summoned by Elder Satomura. Having learnt that he had celebrated his majority, the domain may have hastened to decide the matter, he thought.

The only problem was would that decision be for the better or for the worse? Bunshirō wondered. If for the better, that could mean that the domain, seeing that Bunshirō had reached his majority and had been capped by someone as powerful as Fujii Munezō, had decided they could not just abandon the Maki house, but must in some fashion put an end to this near-starvation treatment of them. In which case, leaving aside the matter of compensation, Bunshirō might be assigned duties of some sort. But the chances of that, he thought, seemed slim. On the contrary, it seemed far more likely the decision should be for the worse.

Twelve samurai had been made to commit seppuku, a foot soldier had been beheaded, and several others had been banished from the domain, sentenced to domiciliary confinement, or placed on "restriction." Bunshirō still could not grasp the full extent of this crime of rebellion against the domain. His only glimpse of it had been what little Owada Ippei had told him. That the final decision should be delayed this long, Bunshirō often thought, only demonstrated the magnitude of this incident, and how extraordinary were its depths. And if that decision had now been made, it was hard to imagine it could be anything he would welcome.

Bunshirō shuddered faintly. He detected the odor of bad news, he felt. The words "banished from the domain" seemed to dance about in his head. It was probably too optimistic to hope for "remanded to the custody of his kin."

Bunshirō turned back. The hour had just sounded Seven (4 p.m.). There was still time before he had to go to the mansion of the elder. He had come out intending to ponder the matter by himself, but his thoughts seemed to run only in one direction, to the worst. There was nothing more to be gained roaming about out of doors. He would return home and prepare for tomorrow's reading.

The sky was thinly clouded. Only in a small corner to the southwest did a ray of sunshine seep through to tint the clouds. Perhaps that was why the town was shrouded with a feeling that the sun was setting at a slightly earlier hour than it should. The atmosphere was dusky and silent, not a sound to be heard, nor anyone to be seen out walking.

Just as he arrived back at the hedge about the barracks, someone emerged from within. It was a slim woman wearing a hood that obscured her face, and clasping a cloth-wrapped bundle to her breast. It was Yada's widow. She was about to turn left along the hedge, but then she noticed Bunshirō walking straight down the street. She retreated two or three steps and called to him.

"Out for a walk, Bunshirō-dono?" she said in a familiar tone of voice. Yada's widow seemed to have heard from someone about the Maki family living in the same barracks and that Bunshirō had been a fellow disciple of Sakunojō at the Ishiguri Dojo. For the past year or so, whenever she would see Bunshirō she would call out to him.

"Pardon me, greeting you in this hood," she said. A strong fragrance of makeup wafted over to Bunshirō.

"Not at all," Bunshirō said bluntly. The strength of the fragrance struck him as a bit excessive. And for a samurai woman—isn't it immodest of her to be going out alone at sunset? At least, he had never seen his mother or his brother's wife do anything of that sort.

Semishigure

Whenever he would encounter Yada's widow, an ominous but inexplicable sense of anger would arise in Bunshirō's breast as he gazed at her. The fragrance of her makeup; the sunset departures; all of these things had come to seem signs of the widow's depravity. Bunshirō could see, too, that this distrust of the woman standing before him was, at root, linked to his strong antipathy toward that unidentified young samurai who was still frequenting the Yada household.

But the widow seemed totally unaware that Bunshirō harbored any such antipathy, and she spoke in a spritely manner.

"Out for a walk?"

"No, just pondering something."

"Oh, my! Pondering …" Yada's widow said, opening her eyes wide, as if in wonder. Then she laughed. Her wide-eyed face was attractively full of life and her laugh lovely. Unusually for a samurai woman, she was of an unaffectedly cheerful disposition. But to Bunshirō in his present state of mind, even that cheerfulness, so attractive to others, to him seemed only imprudent and suspect.

And the way she talks to me, isn't she just teasing me as if I were a youngster? Young I may be, but I'm no longer a child.

Bunshirō stood there, saying nothing, and the widow finally dropped her smile.

"You're in a bad mood, aren't you?"

"No, it's not that."

"Really? You don't have to keep it to yourself, you know." The mischievous look returned to her face momentarily; but then, as if she had thought better of it, she told Bunshirō, in an earnest manner, she had called out to him because she wanted to ask a favor.

"You've heard from your mother, haven't you, that I've taken up needlework as a sideline?"

"Yes."

"Since this spring, I've been sewing children's kimonos. Might I ask you to remind your mother to introduce any customers to me that she might know of?"

So that was it? But then Yada's widow brought her face close to Bunshirō's chest, smiled at him, then turned her back and left.

For a time, Bunshirō stood absently watching the widow, her shoulders and her hips somehow alluring, the white tabi on her feet fading into the last murky glow of the setting sun. Then, all of a sudden, he came to his senses and averted his eyes.

2

Was that it? That the cloth-wrapped parcel contained garments she had sewn? That the widow was just leaving to deliver the garments she had made? In that case, she could hardly avoid going out at sunset. And if her customers were merchants, perhaps it was necessary that she wear a bit of makeup. Bunshirō was reconsidering.

When she wasn't there before his eyes, Bunshirō felt generous and well disposed toward the woman. Bunshirō's inner feelings, were one to probe them, were typical of those lurking in any young man who is attracted to a beautiful woman older than himself. But not wishing to admit that, he had to find some other reason to criticize her—the unidentified samurai, the fragrance of her makeup, her too-cheerful disposition. He himself being unaware of this, he found the change in his feelings a bit puzzling.

Bunshirō shook his head. Think well of her though he did, the fragrance of her makeup really was too strong, and the strength of it, he felt, had penetrated straight to the core of his brain.

Semishigure

Perhaps I should have asked her? The thought occurred to Bunshirō suddenly as he began walking toward home. Have the surviving members of the Yada family been summoned by the elder? he wondered. The reason the beautiful young widow was even now bound to Yada's family, caring for his aged mother, could only be that the domain's final disposition of the case still was not forthcoming.

But judging from what he had just seen, it appeared no summons had arrived at the Yada household. The messenger had come only to his own home. With that thought, Bunshirō could feel his previous sense of anxiety rushing back to assail him.

After he had finished dinner, midway through the Sixth Hour (7 p.m.), Bunshirō went to his natal family's home in Takajō-chō, and from there set out with his brother for the elder's mansion in Babasaki.

"I have no idea what's up, but …" Ichizaemon had said nothing more as they walked along, but when the Satomura mansion hove into view, he turned to face Bunshirō in the light of his lantern. His manservant, Kahei, was with him.

"You're to assent to whatever you're told without the slightest hesitation. Understood?"

"I understand," Bunshirō said. But judging from his brother's tone of voice, he sensed that he, too, had strong misgivings about tonight's summons. Ichizaemon had spoken in a particularly grim voice.

The two of them entered through the wicket in the stately gatehouse to the elder's mansion. When they reached the entryway and announced themselves, a young samurai came out and guided them to a room, where he told them to wait for the moment. Shortly after the young samurai left, a middle-aged maid came in, served them tea, and invited them to drink.

They waited there for a long time. From time to time, the laugh of a man with a booming voice would leak out from within—and nothing more. But finally the young samurai returned.

"First, we'll ask Maki-sama to come in alone," he said. "Hattori-sama is requested to wait here a bit longer."

Guided by the young samurai, Bunshirō stepped out of the room where he had been waiting and proceeded within. The storm doors had been left open, so that as he walked along the corridor, the unpleasantly warm air from outside the house enveloped Bunshirō's face. Then the corridor took a turn, and there immediately before him was a lamp-lit room. When he saw the young samurai kneel, Bunshirō did the same.

"I have guided Maki Bunshirō hither," the young samurai said.

"Show him in," a deep voice from within replied.

Bunshirō entered the room. He waited until the samurai who had guided him shut the sliding panel and left, then bowed deeply.

"I am Maki Bunshirō, come in obedience to your honored summons."

"Raise your face, and be at your ease," the deep voice he had heard before said.

Bunshirō raised his face. In his nervousness, he hadn't noticed when he entered, but now he saw that not one but two men were in the room.

One was a small old man with narrow shoulders and a long, thin neck. His hair was pure white, and his dark, slender face resembled nothing so much as a sun-scorched gourd. This old man was wearing a sleeveless surcoat.

The other man sat apart from the old man, separated from him by a large desk. He was a big man, whose face and eyes were large and round. The hair at his temples was white, and he sat with his hands on his knees, staring intently at Bunshirō. He was the first to speak.

"This is Sukezaemon's son?" His voice sounded like someone blowing a battle horn made of a huge conch shell—strong and mellow. This must have been the man Bunshirō had heard laughing before. "He's grown into a strong, well-built young man."

"Children grow up fast," said the old, gourd-faced man, in a voice so low he seemed to be talking to himself. "Not like us old men, for whom the end is in sight." The old man at the desk then turned to face Bunshirō.

"I am Satomura," he said. "This man is Inspector General Ogata Kumaki."

Is this little old man the one who took my father's life? Bunshirō wondered as he looked at Satomura.

"We've summoned you here tonight because something has transpired that we wish to inform you of," Satomura said. "The inspector general is here to serve as a witness."

Satomura did not look Bunshirō directly in the face but mumbled with his eyes cast down toward his hands or the top of his desk.

"Very well. I shall read the decree," Satomura said just as Bunshirō was bracing himself. From among the clutter of papers piled upon his desk, he grasped one sheet, and turning it to face the lantern, he read:

"Maki Bunshirō shall be restored to his family's former stipend, and he is ordered to serve under the command of the district commissioner."

3

"The district commissioner is Kashimura Yasuke," Satomura said, replacing the document on his desk and turning to Bunshirō. "Actually, however, you will take up your duties in rural inspection under Kashimura two years from now. You are to wait until you reach the age of twenty. Until then, Hattori Ichizaemon will serve as your guardian. And you are not to behave in any unseemly manner in the meantime."

"This was decided by the Governing Council," Inspector General Ogata Kumaki added.

Satomura looked at the inspector general and asked, "What was said about housing?"

"This autumn a house will be vacated in the residential quarter assigned to the district commissioners," Ogata replied in his battle horn voice. "We'll put Bunshirō in there."

Bunshirō was calmly following the conversation between these two. He felt no sense of elation; his heart beat no faster. It was, to be sure, an unexpected outcome, but the domain's decision had been favorable. This he realized; and yet the dialogue between the elder and the inspector general seemed somehow far removed from any sense of reality.

Just when he wasn't expecting it, Satomura looked over at Bunshirō. His eyes were narrow, but unusually sharp.

"That's it then. Do you understand?"

"I most certainly do. And I am most grateful to you." When Bunshirō spoke, his sense of reality seemed at last to return. Which prompted him to tell the elder he wished to ask a question.

"When you say 'restored to his former stipend,' how much might my family's stipend be?"

Semishigure

"How much?" The elder and the inspector general looked suspiciously at Bunshirō, but then they seemed to realize that Bunshirō was only asking for confirmation. Ogata smiled.

"You'll be restored to your original twenty-eight koku and yearly rations for two."

"When will that take effect?"

"The date of the order …" Satomura craned his long neck and peered at the document. "It's dated today. So you'll be restored to your former stipend beginning today. You should receive notification from the person in charge very soon concerning the transfer of stipendiary rice. When you do, you should come to the castle and discuss the matter with him."

"Thank you very much indeed." The moment Bunshirō said that, he could feel his heartbeat begin to quicken. The elder's casual mention of "the person in charge" and "the castle" forced upon him a sense of the certainty that he would be restored to their former stipend.

When Bunshirō returned to the room where they had been waiting, his elder brother, Ichizaemon, was summoned to the elder's room. But they discussed only Bunshirō's orders and his brother's appointment as his guardian. Before long, Ichizaemon returned to the room. He said nothing, and his grave expression remained firmly fixed. But when they emerged from the house, the harsh lines in his brow disappeared. The two of them left the elder's mansion.

"I worried terribly what they might be going to do tonight …" Ichizaemon said after they had come some distance from the elder's mansion, to the moat at the southeast corner of the castle. "At least you can relax now."

"I'm very sorry to have caused you such distress."

"Oh, that's all right. More than that it's these next two years.

Until you're officially appointed to rural inspection duties, I'm commanded to serve as your guardian. And that leaves me a bit uneasy. You see, the Maki house haven't yet been acquitted of their crime."

"Yes."

"So in the interim, you've got to be very circumspect and do nothing that would arouse suspicion in anyone higher up."

"Yes, I'm keenly aware of that. I'll do nothing whatsoever to cause trouble for you, brother," Bunshirō promised. Needless to say, he had no intention of jeopardizing the unexpected good fortune granted him that evening.

"Once I do come under the command of Kashimura-sama, should I make a courtesy call at his home the next day?"

"You should. And to Fujii-sama as well. You should probably take gifts to both houses."

"Right. I'll discuss that with mother."

"Kashimura-dono is a good man." Ichizaemon now spoke in a more relaxed tone. "There are three district commissioners now. I've heard that Kashimura-dono is the best of them."

"Oh, is he?" Bunshirō said. It pleased him that his elder brother, usually so stern in what he said, had taken the trouble to look that far into the matter. That's a brother for you, he thought. Though Bunshirō always referred to him as his "honored brother."

"To be restored to our former stipend is a greater stroke of luck than I ever could have hoped for, but what could be the reason they decided so suddenly to do that?"

"That's something I've been wondering about, too, but I still have no idea."

"Could it be thanks to Father asking Fujii-sama to cap me?"

"I couldn't say," Ichizaemon replied. "I'll see if I can find out in a roundabout way from Fujii-sama. It might be that he himself put in a word with members of the Governing Council."

In the midst of their conversation, before they realized it, they arrived at the Gyōja Bridge.

"You'd better return home from here," Ichizaemon said. And thanking him once again, Bunshirō parted with his brother and crossed the river.

It was a moonless night. All the way downstream, as he walked along the far bank, there was only his single lantern swaying with his movement, and elsewhere naught but darkness. But the night air was warm, and something white appeared to waft up from the depths of the darkness as the river mist rose and spilled onto the land.

Mother will be so delighted, Bunshirō thought. He began to trot through the darkness.

4

The next morning, Bunshirō left for the round of exegetical reading at the Ikoma Academy. After he had finished telling his mother the day before, he had opened his books, but his mind was elsewhere, and the words never entered his head. His reading of the *Analects* had ended in disaster.

It was only to be expected, therefore, that most of the questions would be directed at the student whose preparation had been so deficient. Yamane Seijirō, in particular, he knew would fire off some satisfyingly nasty questions; but Bunshirō was not angered. He readily admitted and apologized for his own failure, which set up a stir among those who knew of the relations between him and Yamane. Bunshirō was aware of this, too, but paid it no attention. Afterward he simply explained the circumstances to his mentor Ikoma Sensei and apologized.

It was about midday when Bunshirō returned home. His new duties would be different, but his joy that the family's stipend and status had been restored had not diminished with the passing of time. If anything, it was greater than it had been last night.

"I'll be making the rounds of the villages, Mother," Bunshirō said. Under the district commissioners, he would be inspecting not only villages in the level lands but the mountain villages as well. "In the summer sun, I'll probably turn black."

"Just like the Defense Works Unit," Toyo said. "Sukezaemon-dono, too, used to turn black in midsummer."

"So he did."

"If ever you're promoted to work in the castle, you can assume your father's name." Toyo's face wore a look of good cheer for the first time in a long while. Her voice, too, was spirited. "And then you'll have to marry."

"Mother!" What Toyo had just said was not the reason, but Bunshirō now mentioned something he had been thinking about since this morning.

"After we've eaten, I'd like to go to Yaba-machi and see the Koyanagi family. What do you think?" Bunshirō would not be going for practice at the dojo this afternoon because he would be calling upon Fujii Munezō and District Commissioner Kashimura Yasuke in the evening. "The Koyanagi were very helpful to us at that time, so I thought we should let them know of this latest development."

"Oh my, I hadn't thought of that," Toyo said, smiling. "I've been so happy to hear this news, that I quite forgot about those people. Yes, we must tell the Koyanagi and also our neighbors to the north, the Yamagishi."

"Then I will go."

"And what about Owada-sama?"

Semishigure

"I stopped in and told Ippei on my way to the academy."

"So that's why you left so early this morning," Toyo said.

After their midday meal, Bunshirō set out across the river for Yaba-machi, bearing two straw wrapped packets of mountain potatoes, still feeling in high spirits.

It had been about two years since he had seen the Defense Works quarter. Walking along the street, looking nostalgically at house after house, he eventually entered the gate of the Koyanagi house and announced himself. But it was a woman he had never seen before who came out.

Bunshirō looked all around the earthen-floored entry. It had suddenly occurred to him that he must have come to the wrong house. But the earthen-floored space and the old shoji at the threshold were indeed the same that he remembered in the Koyanagi house.

Bunshirō looked back at the woman. She was kneeling at the threshold and appeared to be about thirty, far younger than Fuku's mother. And behind her Bunshirō could see a little girl of two or three who had just come out from within the house.

"I beg your pardon, but are you perchance related to Koyanagi-dono?" Bunshirō asked. The woman shook her head.

"No, this is not the Koyanagi house. My name is Matsunaga."

"Ah, Matsunaga-dono?" Bunshirō gazed at the woman in astonishment, and her round, fleshy face smiled back at him in a questioning manner.

"I beg your pardon," she said, "but your good self?"

"I'm sorry. I should have told you sooner." Bunshirō blushed and told her his name. "I used to live next door."

"Then you're a member of the Defense Works Unit?" The woman did not know the name Maki Sukezaemon. She would certainly have known of the scandal that had shaken the domain, but she might never have heard that someone involved in it had lived next door.

"That's right," Bunshirō said.

"So you've come to call upon Koyanagi-sama, have you?" The woman's face showed that she now understood, but then she shook her head slightly. "Until the end of last year, we were under the command of the superintendent of forests, but in the new year we were transferred to the Defense Works Unit. That was when we moved here. At the time, the house was empty, and Koyanagi-sama was no longer here."

"And you don't know where they've moved to?"

"We never heard. We're still only slightly acquainted with the other members of the Unit."

"Of course. And I'm terribly sorry to have disturbed you with no warning and taken so much of your time." Bunshirō apologized and hurriedly departed the house where Matsunaga So-and-so now lived. His old friends the Koyanagi and the Yamagishi were one thing, but it would never do for him to carry on a long conversation with Matsunaga's wife, whom he had only just met.

Bunshirō went out the gate and stood in the street. Far off, on the road that ran past the empty old archery range, several children were playing, but no one else was about. The sky was clouded and the sun was hidden, yet there was no sign of rain. At the edge of the grove alongside the old archery range, he could see white flowers in bloom—wild plum perhaps?

Where could the Koyanagi have gone? Bunshirō was perplexed. Unexpected though this was, he felt stymied from the very start. To tell the Koyanagi that he had been restored to their former stipend was the proper thing to do, but that was not the only reason Bunshirō had come here.

Semishigure

5

If he could just let them know, Bunshirō thought, sooner or later word of him would reach Fuku in Edo. He wanted above all to let Fuku know.

In his mind's eye indelible images remained: of Fuku helping him pull the cart that bore the dead body of his father, of Fuku softly weeping at the wake. If she knew that the Maki house had not been abolished, that he would now be serving under the district commissioners, and had become the head of his house, Bunshirō was certain it would delight her no end.

To have his high hopes so suddenly dashed was a dreadful blow to Bunshirō. He could probably learn where the Koyanagi had moved if he were to ask the Yamagishi when he called there; even so his doubts persisted. For them to have moved away from the quarter could only mean that Koyanagi Jinbei no longer served in the Defense Works Unit.

Bunshirō looked away as he passed in front of the house where they had lived. He had no desire to know how the house had changed or who was living in it now.

"Oh my! Bunshirō-san!" Yamagishi's wife was not a talkative woman, but when she saw Bunshirō a friendly smile spread over her long, dark-complected face. She was a woman two or three years older than Toyo.

"You've grown so big. At first I wondered who it could be. Is Toyo-sama well?"

"Yes, she is, thank you. I've come here today on her behalf." Bunshirō handed her a packet of mountain potatoes and told her how the family had been restored to their original stipend and that he would now be serving under the district commissioners.

"We caused you so much trouble on that occasion, but I'm

very grateful that you were so very helpful to us. Please do be so kind as to pass on my thanks to Yamagishi-sama as well."

"Now, now, no need to be so terribly formal with us," Yamagishi's wife said. "But, my, that's very good news. We, too, were worried what might have become of you; so when I tell him, he's sure to be delighted."

"Is Yamagishi-sama still as well as ever?" Bunshirō phrased his question this way, remembering that the Yamagishi family had no children. The wife told him that her husband was "still working hard."

"He'd be even happier if your family were returning to the Unit. And now Koyanagi-sama has gone, too. This place isn't what it used to be; it's lonely here now." Her mention of the Koyanagi gave Bunshirō the chance to ask about them that he had been looking for.

"Yes, Jinbei-san's family …," Bunshirō said. "When I called on them someone else was there. It quite surprised me. Where have they moved to?"

"Now, *that*, Bunshirō-san," Yamagishi's wife said. "Come sit down on the threshold. I'll give you some rice sweets." The desire to speak frankly was written all over Yamagishi's wife's face.

"Koyanagi-sama has risen in the world." Yamagishi's wife came back carrying a dish of rice sweets on a tray, which she offered to Bunshirō. She spoke to him as casually as she used to, as if she still thought of him as a youth. "We can't really call him Jinbei-san any more."

"You mean it would be impolite to call him that?" Bunshirō was watching Yamagishi's wife's expression very carefully. The suspicions he felt when he left the Koyanagi house had returned. "Then where are the Koyanagi living now?"

"He's been transferred to the storehouses and is enfeoffed at eighty koku." Then having imparted that surprising bit of news, Yamagishi's wife added, "They're living in Yoriki-chō."

"Eighty koku ..." Bunshirō didn't even reach for the sweets; he just stared at the woman's face in amazement. "That's an extraordinary rise. But how ...?"

"You know Fuku don't you? She was a little too shy, but a good-natured girl. Did you know that Fuku went to Edo?"

"Yes, I'd heard."

"There were connections of some sort, and she went to serve in the Edo mansion. Her mother Masu-dono was delighted—at the time. 'One less mouth to feed; that's a big help,' she said. They had a lot of children, that family."

Bunshirō was growing impatient, wishing she would hurry up and come to the point, whereupon Yamagishi's wife suddenly lowered her voice. "The details aren't clear yet, so please don't mention this to anyone else." Then in the same secretive tone she whispered, "I've heard that His Lordship has laid hands on Fuku."

It took a moment for him to grasp what the woman meant by those words. But in the next instant, her meaning fell easily into place. A roar began to rise within Bunshirō's head, and he felt he could see nothing but pure white emptiness before his eyes. His face suddenly flared with heat, though not simply from rage or humiliation. He was distantly aware of Yamagishi's wife saying that Koyanagi-sama would now rise even further. But once he left the Yamagishi house and returned to the street, his feeling of anger, or whatever it had been, calmed. In its place, a new emotion arose to overwhelm Bunshirō.

So that's it. It's finished. The thought came suddenly and it devastated Bunshirō, fairly swept him away. Fuku bitten by the snake; Fuku licking her lollipop at the Night Festival; Fuku hiding the borrowed rice in her sleeve. He knew now that his ties to that world were at an end. In an instant, they had vanished into the distance, far beyond Bunshirō's reach. And when he realized that, a feeling of fondness for Fuku—so intense it astonished even Bunshirō himself—welled up in his breast. It was a poignant fondness, for the Fuku from whose finger he had sucked the poison of the snake bite, for the Fuku His Lordship had now laid hands upon.

Bunshirō stopped in his tracks. He just stood there and let the flames of his anguish blaze away. He was at the far edge of the empty old archery range when he turned and looked back at the street that ran through the quarter. It stretched peacefully into the distance, not a soul anywhere in sight. Only the faint voices of children playing reached him from deep within the newly budding grove. There was no one about, either to hinder or find fault with Bunshirō's raging desolation.

But at that time …? Tortured by overpowering remorse, Bunshirō called to mind that day he had failed to meet Fuku when she came to call. But at that time, did Fuku foresee that they would one day be parted like this?

The thought enveloped Bunshirō in unbearable remorse. Yet at the same time, he could see that his present turbulent feelings, precisely because his break with Fuku was now irrevocable, were overflowing as defiance of all that was proper. It was Bunshirō himself who was defying those proprieties. Still, if this sudden parting from Fuku had not been visited upon him, his own true feelings would never have been revealed—to himself as much as to anyone else.

Bunshirō could feel himself recovering his composure, and bit by bit returning to his old ways with their countless constraints. He must now behave as if this business with Fuku had

Semishigure

been nothing at all. Doing so, Bunshirō realized, was just a way of pretending it hadn't existed in the first place; but he was well trained in bearing up under constraints of that sort. For himself, and for Fuku as well, he knew this was now essential. But of course that oppressive sense of grief remained. That he took care to hide deep down within his breast.

Once more, before he began walking again, Bunshirō turned and looked back at the Defense Works quarter. It looked different now, he thought.

When he returned home, he mentioned only that Koyanagi had risen in the world, that he had been transferred to the storehouses, and that they now lived in Yoriki-chō. He said nothing at all about Fuku.

Toyo was amazed, and after asking Bunshirō a great many questions, told him he must pay them a courtesy call in Yoriki-chō.

"Haven't we done enough already?" Bunshirō asked.

"Oh, come now. That was one thing and this is another. If you don't care to do it, then I'll go."

So now his mother would hear the reason for their rise directly from the Koyanagi, Bunshirō thought.

Summer Rains, Cloudy Skies

<u>1</u>

Bunshirō has remained behind, alone in the dojo, wielding a hardwood practice sword. He assumes the figure eight stance. Imagines an enemy about to attack. His imaginary enemy aims a vicious blow at Bunshirō's left shoulder and left fist. Sliding a foot slightly forward in response, Bunshirō in the next instant lunges forward. "E-e-i!" The wooden sword raises a swirl of wind as it strikes the enemy atop his head.

Repeating this same sequence of movements ten times, twenty times, sweat covered not only his body but welled up in his hair and streamed down his face. His arms were exhausted. The wooden sword had grown so heavy it felt as if he were swinging a bar of lead.

Bunshirō collapsed to his knees to catch his breath. He hung his head and the sweat that fell from his face dripped onto the wooden floor. Then, giving his face a quick wipe with the towel at his waist, Bunshirō stood again. This time he changed his stance, reversing the placement of his right and left feet, and in that position he awaited the attack of his enemy.

This time the enemy strikes at his torso. Bunshirō swiftly

drops back, his sword never wavering from the figure eight. Then he dashes forward, as if his feet were gliding across the floor, and as he drives deeply inward, he brings his sword crashing down. "E-e-i!" His cry of attack rends the silence of the hall. And as he relaxes his guard against counterattack and slowly rises, he retracts his wooden sword.

Whereupon Bunshirō wheeled suddenly, as if he were about to be set upon by something; he raised his sword to the ready, and fell back one or two steps. Someone was standing in a corner of the dusky hall.

"It's me." The shadow called out to him as it moved into the last bit of evening glow shining in through the barred window. It was the master, Ishiguri Yazaemon.

"Sorry to surprise you like that." Yazaemon's teeth had fallen out, and it had been a bit difficult lately to make out what he was saying. But Bunshirō could tell there was a touch of laughter in his voice, and he lowered his wooden sword. The master was in a good mood, but being stalked had left Bunshirō in a highly agitated state.

"You shouldn't play tricks on me, Sensei."

Yazaemon laughed. "Just testing you." As he came over to Bunshirō, he raised the fan he was carrying into primary position. "There was a slight flaw in that sequence you were practicing before. I'll show you. Come hit me."

"Not with this. I'll change it for a bamboo sword."

"What? That doesn't worry me. Don't hold back; just come at me."

When Yazaemon told him that, Bunshirō bowed, opened a space between them, and took up his stance. This was after all a chance to be taught directly by the master. Still, Bunshirō was concerned for the master's body. Yazaemon had often been ill of late, and for some time now had not come out to the training hall. But Yazaemon must have seen through Bunshirō's misgivings, and he reproved him severely, "I told you not to hold back. Now, come on."

Bunshirō firmed up his footing, and raised his sword to the figure eight position. Yazaemon was already in place, and of course he left not the slightest opening. He was a lean, gray-haired man, somewhat smaller than Bunshirō, and behind that single fan he seemed all but hidden, offering no place to strike.

Ishiguri Yazaemon was born the heir to a house that served the domain as company commanders, and eventually he would have succeeded to that rank. But when he was twenty he was posted to Edo, and there he determined to entrust his subsequent fate to the Kūdon school of swordsmanship. After ten years of hard training at the Kūdon Dojo, he travelled the land for five more years of practice. Then he returned to Edo and polished his skills for another three years. He had devoted a total of eighteen years exclusively to the discipline of swordsmanship. All of this was approved of by the domain, of course. And when Yazaemon returned home, the domain encouraged him to found a new dojo. The man on the other side of that fan possessed fifty years of practice in the martial arts. Bunshirō abandoned his fears for him.

Bunshirō repositioned his feet. Then he waited. Whereupon Yazaemon's body appeared suddenly to rise up and then instantly sink down and come running across the floor. The weapon coming at Bunshirō's torso seemed not a fan but the bare blade of a sword. Bunshirō stepped back to parry the blow of the fan, and as he did he moved his left pivot leg a slight bit forward. Then he pushed in deep with his right leg and struck Yazaemon on the forehead. But his wooden sword, driven with such ferocity, struck only air.

Semishigure

"That's it." Yazaemon came over to him and tapped Bunshirō's left leg lightly. "When you move that leg forward, you've got to move with the flow of your opponent's body. If you close the space carelessly, you won't get your opponent. Let's try it again," Yazaemon said.

Again Yazaemon raised his fan into position and Bunshirō attacked. This time they did it not just once; they must have repeated the same sequence ten times or more. And just before the evening glow filtering in through the barred window gave off its last glimmer, Bunshirō finally felt he had grasped the way Yazaemon's body was moving. This time his right leg drove in at an angle different from the previous times. A cry of attack burst unconsciously from his throat, and his wooden sword came down squarely upon the fan that Yazaemon held up to stop it. Yet fan though it was, Yazaemon's skill in defense was formidable, and he repelled Bunshirō's sword so powerfully that it seemed it might go flying off into space. His efforts thwarted, Bunshirō retreated. But Yazaemon, too, dropped his fan and fell backwards.

"Are you all right? You're not hurt?"

"What are you talking about? I don't get hurt." So Yazaemon said, yet when Bunshirō helped him sit up, he was in a pitiful state, gasping for breath. It had been too much just to come out to the training hall and fend off Bunshirō's attack more than ten times. Bunshirō was beset by deep regret, and he stroked his lean, bony master's back. Yazaemon's breathing soon returned to normal and he stood with no help. Then he looked at Bunshirō and spoke in a despondent voice.

"I'm glad I did that, but my eyes were spinning and I fell on my bottom. Even my body seems to have grown old and begun to crack."

"Please, you mustn't overdo it. I'm terribly sorry."

"No, it's nothing you need apologize for. I'm the one who suggested it."

Bunshirō escorted Yazaemon as far as the entrance to his private quarters and opened the thick wooden door for him. A pale light shone out from within. The lamp was already lit in the master's rooms. Yazaemon turned and spoke.

"Once you've prepared to leave, come in for a bit. There's something I want to talk to you about."

Bunshirō stepped down into the garden and was rinsing the sweat away with water from the well.

What could Master have to say to me? I've done nothing he's likely to chastise me for.

Lately, Bunshirō had been coming to the dojo every day without fail. Inukai Hyōma had noticed this and was as persistent as ever in challenging him. When challenged, Bunshirō never refused, but they no longer fought as ferociously as they had before, like two mad dogs trying to kill each other. In those days, when Hyōma would challenge him and they would fight each other with teeth bared, Bunshirō was filled with the bitterness aroused by his father's sudden death and being forced to live on leftovers in a grimy barracks. He was indignant that he could see no hope for himself in the future, while everyone around him was glowering at the criminal's son, and so Bunshirō would lose himself in violent battles with Hyōma.

It was not that his bitterness was now totally dispelled. The truth of his father's death was still shrouded in mystery, and there was no one who would tell him, loud and clear, just what had gone on. Still, Bunshirō did feel that he had found a way forward of sorts in the restoration of his family's stipend; yet when he had paid a courtesy call on Kashimura Yasuke, the district commissioner congratulated him, but also warned him: "Satomura-sama is a scheming man. Don't ever let your guard down." The man was not optimistic about the future of a house that had once been branded traitors.

Bunshirō, too, could not but think that Kashimura's observation had hit the mark. Looking back at himself, when he had gone to tell the Koyanagi and Yamagishi families of his delight at having the family stipend restored, Bunshirō now felt as if he had been doused with a bucket of cold water.

2

And speaking of bitterness: there was still another seed of despair deep within his breast that simply would not go away. Needless to say, this was Fuku, now a concubine of the lord of the domain. He was not so unmanly as to obsess over Fuku forever, now that her circumstances were changed. His feelings with regard to Fuku were firmly fixed. What had happened in the past he held dear, but all that, he knew, was now nowhere but in the past.

Still, at times there would occur to him a thought, which, like a lump of something seemed to rise from deep within his bosom and stick in his throat where he could not swallow it. He could not get over the fact that Fuku had not married into another ordinary family; she had become a concubine of the lord of the domain. He could not imagine that Fuku would have wished for this. Fuku was nothing but a flower that had been plucked. Jinbei and his wife may have risen in the world, but Fuku herself could not have been pleased to be offered up as a concubine to her lord. It was most unlikely that Fuku was happy.

Such thoughts would at times oppress Bunshirō, and at such

times would leave a faint taste of bitterness that he could never mention to anyone else. Bunshirō had unquestionably lost something on account of what had happened to Fuku.

His frequent visits to the dojo since the spring of the year were clearly inspired by this bitterness. At the dojo, when he would fix his thoughts upon the techniques of swordplay, or when he would drive his own flesh to the very limit, he could forget his concern for the future prospects of his family, or his feelings of pity for Fuku. But this bitterness that Bunshirō harbored was now hidden deep within himself. He would no longer cross bamboo swords with Inukai Hyōma as if he were a mad dog. Lately Bunshirō had developed the ability to reflect upon this world with slightly more mature eyes. He had behaved childishly, he thought. When Hyōma would challenge him, he would never flee but accept; yet never in the manner that he had before.

But this bitterness that he concealed within himself could at times seek sudden redress and spew forth. His practice match with Ōhashi Ichinoshin several days earlier may have been one such case. It was Ōhashi who had requested the match.

"We haven't practiced together in a while," Ōhashi said in that nagging manner of his. "That's because you've been avoiding me, isn't it?" he added, smiling faintly. "I hear lately that you're saying you've surpassed me. I'd be honored if you'd be so kind as to teach me."

Bunshirō replied only with a cold glance, but Ōhashi's sarcasm angered him. So kind as to teach me, he says, when clearly he means to beat me to a pulp. This was a match he must not lose, Bunshirō knew. He knew, too, that his skills had advanced to the point where he could defeat Ōhashi.

The match was held in the presence of the other students, all of whom had left off their own practice matches to watch. And Bunshirō won with two hits out of three.

But ... the way that he won may have left Bunshirō feeling uneasy. Ōhashi scored the first point with a hit squarely upon Bunshirō's gauntlet. Ōhashi was a big man, but a hit to the gauntlet was his special talent, and it was this talent that decided the first round. But Bunshirō struck back immediately with a hit to Ōhashi's shoulder, which evened the score at one to one. Ōhashi, however, refused to recognize it as a hit. It had only grazed him, he protested; he even bared his shoulder to show everyone. But Maruoka Shunsaku, who was judging the match, refused to back down from his decision to consider it a hit. So Ōhashi returned to the match with a display of discontent. It was immediately thereafter that it happened; they exchanged blows two or three times, and then Bunshirō's bamboo sword hit Ōhashi's forehead with a sharp crack. It was an indisputable hit, but Bunshirō, despite hearing Maruoka shout "Point!" continued to attack, hitting again and again, like flashes of lightning. He struck repeatedly in the same spot, until Ōhashi's forehead tore open and he fell unconscious.

Maruoka Shunsaku of course rebuked Bunshirō severely for this, and later he was admonished by the master's assistant, Satake, who happened not to be there that day. When word of what he had done reached the master, he might well be chastised again.

His head filled with thoughts of this sort as he prepared to leave, Bunshirō checked to make sure the door to the training hall was shut, then headed to the master's private quarters. Yazaemon's wife, who had heard all that was going on, came out to the hallway and led Bunshirō into the room where Yazaemon was.

Compared to Yazaemon, who was gray-haired, lean, and deeply wrinkled, his wife was young looking. This was not just because her face was childlike and full; her skin was radiant and she bustled about energetically. Which was only natural, for, as Bunshirō had heard, she was more than ten years younger than her husband.

Once Yazaemon embarked upon his training in swordsmanship, he had no time to marry, but when he reached the age of thirty, through the good offices of someone, he married the daughter of a samurai who was permanently stationed in Edo. This woman—his present wife—was only eighteen or nineteen at the time. The ceremony was held at the domain's Edo mansion, and for some time they did not return to the domain. And thus it was not until eight years later that Yazaemon's wife was to see the sights of her husband's home in the snow country.

The couple had two sons, and Yazaemon had no official duties, but the domain had maintained the emoluments of his family's enfeoffment. His heir had now inherited this and was living in his own home in the castle town, where he served as a company commander. This son's little daughter—Yazaemon's granddaughter—was from time to time to be seen when she visited the dojo. Ordinarily, though, only the old couple and a middle-aged maidservant were in residence there.

The master's wife brought tea and sweets for Bunshirō and then left the room, after which their quarters were perfectly still. No rain was falling, but the sultry summer air of the rainy season suffused the room.

"Eat your sweets," Yazaemon said to Bunshirō. Then he broke the silence with talk of an entirely different matter.

Semishigure

3

"At the Kumano Shrine Offertory Tournament this autumn …" Yazaemon began, "I've decided I'll put you up against their regular, Okitsu Shinnojō. So give it your best."

Bunshirō looked up at Yazaemon. But, saying nothing in reply, he just lifted his cup and took two or three sips of the hot tea. He could feel Yazaemon staring intently at him. He replaced the cup on its saucer and again looked at Yazaemon.

"There are others who rank above me," Bunshirō said. "Tsukahara-san, Ōhashi-san, Maruoka-san, and of course your assistant. I don't think it's my place to do this."

"Satake can't compete this year. With His Lordship here in the domain, he hasn't enough time to practice. Besides which, he says the other rising young men aren't up to it." Yazaemon smiled faintly. "I've talked this over with Satake and Maruoka before deciding to put you up against Okitsu. Tsukahara and Ōhashi could never fight off a man of his skill. And Maruoka will one day take over as head of the dojo. If by some chance he were to lose, it would be a total loss of face for us. That's how we see it."

The Kumano Shrine Offertory Tournament was held yearly on a specially chosen auspicious day in the Tenth Month. It took place in the grounds of the shrine and, ostensibly, was meant to promote friendly relations with the Matsukawa Dojo as well as foster the improvement of skills. In fact this was a hard-fought contest that had little to do with friendship. There was also the small Ono Dojo that taught the Mugai school of swordsmanship, but the Matsukawa Dojo of the Ittō school and the Ishiguri Dojo of the Kūdon school were the two main powers in town, and their matches attracted a great many samurai as spectators.

And when the lord of the domain happened to be in residence, he was likely to attend any such tournament on the pretext of promoting the martial arts—which for both sides meant that these matches must not be lost. It was in that sense that the students had come to call this the "flower of all tournaments." And yet it did have its distasteful side, with all the scheming and intriguing that went on in the background.

Bunshirō could see that putting him up against Okitsu Shinnojō of the Matsukawa Dojo was one such scheme. Okitsu was a talent who had risen to prominence like a shooting star three years or so earlier. At last year's match, Tsukahara Jinnosuke had fought Okitsu and been beaten dismally.

I understand the point of the scheme, but I doubt I'm the one to go up against Okitsu, Bunshirō thought. In the New Year's rankings, Bunshirō had risen dramatically to fifth position; but he still had no clear grasp of the level of his ability. He had no idea whether he could win against Okitsu or not. And he felt no strong urge to defeat Okitsu.

"Tsukahara-san aside, what about Ōhashi-san?" Bunshirō said. "I doubt he'd lose to Okitsu." This match that so excited everyone continued to dominate Bunshirō's thoughts. This was a flower he wished he could pass on to Ōhashi.

Ishiguro Yazaemon shook his head.

"Ōhashi has technique, but nothing more. He could never win against Okitsu. You see … when you practice the martial arts, it can happen that suddenly your skills improve sharply; you grow as strong as if you were possessed by some ferocious demon. That's what happens when the sword connects with your hidden strengths. Which is why, over and over again, I'm saying, 'Give it your all! Go to it!' If you slack, you'll never discover your own true talents."

Semishigure

"Yes, I see."

"But that doesn't mean that everyone who gives it his all is going to reach the top. There aren't many who possess true talent. But when one comes along, he can become strong very quickly. Okitsu is one of them. In our dojo, you are such a one, Bunshirō. As is Inukai Hyōma. So ... if you say you're not interested, I'll put Inukai up against Okitsu. Compared to you his technique is rough, but Inukai has the zeal that Ōhashi lacks."

"But Sensei ..." Bunshirō was still a bit hesitant. He had little desire to make a name for himself as the one who defeated Okitsu, but he had no desire whatsoever to relinquish that role to Hyōma, who ranked just behind him in seventh position. Were Bunshirō to do that, there'd be no escape; he would be accused of running from the match because he feared Okitsu's skill. And whatever the outcome, Hyōma would become the center of attention. I'll never do anything to please *him*, Bunshirō thought.

Bunshirō had lately managed to accept Hyōma's challenges with a bit more of the grace of a grown up, yet he nonetheless found him a maddening opponent. He was still determined never to give Hyōma so much as a pinch of salt.

"If refusing means letting Hyōma do it, then I'll do it. Or rather ... if you command me, I shall of course take on Okitsu."

"Good!" Yazaemon nodded with satisfaction, urged Bunshirō to eat his sweets, and waited silently until he had finished.

The master looked utterly exhausted, and so when Bunshirō had finished eating, he drew himself up properly and said, "If there is nothing further, I'll take my leave now."

"No," Yazaemon said, "there's something more I want to talk about." He grasped his teacup and slowly sipped his tea. Then he put the teacup down and suddenly said, "There are these secret techniques called 'Murasame'—Cloudburst. They are techniques that are passed down secretly and are not known to anyone in this dojo. I learnt them when I was a student of the martial arts, after which I refined them further on my own and have kept them a secret. Since then, I've taught them to only one other person, and that was a long time ago. I'm an old man now and know not whether I'll be here even tomorrow. The other man, too, is growing old."

Bunshirō, his body taut, listened intently to Yazaemon's strange tale.

"If I and the other man were to pass away, the secrets of Murasame would be lost to this world. That has been my one worry these past few years. I've been on the lookout for someone to whom I could transmit the secrets, yet so far with no success. But—if in this autumn's tournament, you should defeat Okitsu, that might be a good opportunity to pass them on. Such is what has come of my discussions with the other person. Not immediately, of course. We'll begin thinking about it after this is all over. In any case, when that time comes, I'll already be too old to make use of any secret techniques. I'll just take that opportunity to pass them on to my one successor. That was my intention earlier when I told you to 'go to it' in the match with Okitsu."

"But there is Satake-san; and there is Maruoka-san."

"No, secret teachings are an entirely different matter," Yazaemon said. "At the moment, both men are superior to you in terms of technique. But they lack character. And I can see that eventually you will surpass them in technique as well. Don't you think that's so yourself? So now ... it's just a matter of winning against Okitsu Shinnojō. What I'll teach you is a profound and invincible technique of swordsmanship, Bunshirō!" Despite the weariness of his face, there was a ring of pleasure in Yazaemon's voice.

Semishigure

After shutting the main door to the instruction hall, Bunshirō left. The soft warmth of the night air enveloped him. The sky appeared covered with rain-filled clouds, not a single point of light was to be seen. It felt like the heavy, humid darkness was hanging down from the heavens. Only the surface of the earth shone slightly white. As Bunshirō walked toward the bank of the Goken River, a night bird gave a sharp cry as it flew away over his head.

Secret techniques of swordsmanship? The excitement of hearing that tale still filled his entire being. Bunshirō's devotion to the practice of swordsmanship had not been for the purpose of winning a match against Okitsu Shinnojō, nor because he wished to learn the secrets of the Ishiguri Dojo; he had done it because the plight he had been forced into left him nothing else but to practice swordsmanship, day after day after day. Yet whatever the reason, he was now a man who for years had driven mind and body mercilessly for the sake of the sword. And when his master suggested he might be taught an invincible technique of swordplay, he found it difficult to suppress his pride.

Am I the one? Have I been chosen as the second man ever to learn these secrets? His excitement was linked to this realization. If Yazaemon's intentions were sincere, he thought, these secrets which, with the exception of only one other person, no one else in this school had ever glimpsed, I myself shall see. But it all depended upon his winning the match with Okitsu.

4

When he reached the riverbank, off to the right, beyond the Chidori Bridge, he could see the flicker of lights along the main street through town. It was still early, but some of the shops that were open seemed already to have lit their lamps. Bunshirō would not be going that way, though. He turned his back on the lamps and began walking along the river. A dark quarter, where not a glimmer of light was to be seen, stretched along one side, and on the other, he could hear the steady lap of waves washing the riverbank. Lately, low hanging clouds could often be seen shrouding the mountains that lay far upstream, which perhaps was the reason the river had been rising these past two or three days.

Against Okitsu ... can I win, or not? I don't really know, Bunshirō thought. He had of course seen last year's match, when Okitsu defeated Tsukahara Jinnosuke, but at the time Bunshirō was too busy making plans to defeat his own adversary, Yamane Seijirō. He hadn't paid sufficient attention to Okitsu Shinnojō's swordplay. He knew only that he would be a difficult opponent. Every one of Tsukahara's moves had been blocked; that his defeat was decisive was plain to see. To win against Okitsu, Bunshirō would have to get Sugiuchi Michizō, or someone, to serve as his opponent and polish the whole range of his skills.

But never mind all that ... Who might be the man to whom Master had previously imparted the secret techniques of Murasame? The question occurred to him as he arrived back in the neighborhood where he lived. The man must have been a prior disciple at the Ishiguri Dojo. Ishiguri Yazaemon had opened the present dojo at the urging of the domain when he was forty, Bunshirō had heard. That was thirty-four years ago. And given that Yazaemon had said the man was now growing old, he must have been one of the earliest disciples when he received the secret teaching. There must have been an exceptionally talented disciple at that time to whom Yazaemon entrusted the secrets without hesitation. That much Bunshirō could infer; yet never had he heard even a rumor of such a person, nor of course could he guess what his name might be. Bunshirō's interest in this mystery swordsman had begun to grow.

When he opened the door to his home, his ears were assaulted by a sudden burst of laughter from Owada Ippei. He had arrived before Bunshirō's return, and in his friend's absence was chatting with his mother. Bunshirō's mother, Toyo, made no secret of her inability to take a more tolerant view of Ippei's coarse manners, but Ippei himself appeared to be doing his best to comfort the mother of his friend who had lost her husband. Whenever he came he would always chat not only with Bunshirō but with Toyo as well. Bunshirō, who was well aware of their subtle differences, smiled wryly as he announced his return. It was Ippei who heard him and swiftly slid the panel open.

"A bit late, aren't you? I was so weary of waiting for you I was about to leave." By which he seemed to mean he had all but exhausted his supply of funny stories to tell Toyo.

Ippei said he had had his dinner before he came, so Bunshirō sent him into his three-mat room. Bunshirō ate as quickly as he could, and when he joined Ippei there, his friend had already lit the lamp and was leafing through the books stacked up against the wall.

"Hmm. This one I remember fondly: your copy of *The Book of Songs*." Then he raised his voice in a chant:

Fair, fair, cry the ospreys
On the islet in the river.
The modest, retiring, virtuous, young lady:
For our prince a good mate she.

Then he shut the book and put it back on the stack next to the wall.

"I came today to tell you something," Ippei said. Beneath the grave expression on his face, he was beginning to smile.

In response, Bunshirō grinned as he said, "Sounds like you've got some good news."

"Have you read my mind?" Ippei said, as his face broke into a smile. "Of course it's good news."

"Wait, wait! Let me guess." Bunshirō cocked his head to one side and then said, "A bride has been found for Owada Ippei. That's it, isn't it?"

"Oh, no! You depress me!" Ippei clasped his head in his hands in an exaggerated pose of distress. "If I had news *that* good, I wouldn't announce it so pompously."

"It's something else?" Bunshirō said.

It had been a long time now since Ippei's family and kinfolk had begun their search for a bride for the Owada house, and Ippei himself was keen to settle down as soon as possible. But for some reason they had yet to find a good match for him. There had been two or three attempts at negotiation, but nothing had come of them, and the matter had dragged on into the present. To Bunshirō, Ippei's impatience seemed excessive; Ippei was still only nineteen. But feelings of this sort can only be understood by the person concerned.

"It's very different from what you think," Ippei said. "It's no simple matter." Ippei lowered his voice gloomily. "No one seems to like the idea of marrying into a family consisting of only a mother and her son. So you'd better watch out, too." Then he seemed to remember what he had come to tell Bunshirō, and his voice grew lively again.

"A little while ago, on my way back from the castle, I met up with Ikoma Sensei. He said he was just coming back from the domain academy."

"Hmm. That's unusual."

"Well, yes; but he said you hadn't come to class in the last ten days or so."

"Oh?"

"Any reason?"

"No."

"Hmmph. Sounds like you don't want to tell me." Ippei snorted. "Well, all right. But that's when I heard from Sensei that Yonosuke will be coming back in the autumn."

"What? Really?" Bunshirō raised his voice in astonishment.

It had been three years since Shimazaki Yonosuke had set out to study in Edo. In the interim he had sent a letter or two every year with vassals who happened to be returning to the domain, but he himself had never been back.

"Our first meeting in three years!" Bunshirō exclaimed at this first piece of good news he had heard in some time. "I wonder if he'll have changed much." Yet he also had his doubts. "He won't have finished his studies, will he? He can't be coming back for good."

"Of course not." Ippei went on to explain what he had heard from Ikoma Sensei. "The Sanseikan Academy will invite Kasai Randō to come here from Edo in the autumn."

"Really?"

"And as an incentive to study, they will open the doors of the academy to anyone in the Corps of Vassals who is interested, even foot soldiers. Randō Sensei will lecture for twenty days on *The Middle Way*, as well as other texts, he says. It's all being arranged by Shibahara-sama, the dean of the academy, and Tōyama-sama, the junior elder. Ikoma Sensei is in on it, too."

"So that's it. And Yonosuke will come in Randō Sensei's entourage?"

"Right. But not just as an attendant." Ippei smiled. "But don't be shocked when I tell you this."

"Shocked at what?"

"During those twenty days when Randō Sensei will be lecturing, Yonosuke, too, will be giving lectures of some sort."

"Well! I *see*!" Bunshirō looked Ippei straight in the face. This was no small shock to him. "He's brilliant."

"And far more so that I ever imagined. Randō Sensei, in a letter to Ikoma Sensei, says that Yonosuke is so brilliant that in another year or two he will be top of the class at the Kasai Academy."

"It's good that he went to Edo." When he recalled Yonosuke before he went to Edo—his slight body, the timid look on his face—Bunshirō could not but smile. And still smiling, he said, "I'll bet Ikoma Sensei is bursting with pride."

"Of course he is," Ippei said, his face wrinkling alongside his nose as he, too, smiled. "The prodigy of the Ikoma Academy has become the prodigy of the world. He was so delighted that, dolt that I am, he could hardly bear to look at me."

Bunshirō laughed. "That shouldn't make you jealous. It's a pleasure to have a genius as a friend. Besides which, I'm sure Yonosuke worked twice as hard as everyone else. It's only fair that someone who works that hard should be rewarded for it."

"I've never worked hard enough," Ippei said. "That's why I still rank fifteenth at the dojo." Ippei was feeling sulky, but Bunshirō took no notice of it. He knew that arranging a marriage was all it would take to make his gloom vanish instantly, like the mist.

"So when Yonosuke gives his lectures ..." Bunshirō said, "should I go to hear him, too?"

"I'm not going. I'll take Yonosuke to Somekawa-chō and teach him about women," Ippei said, with deliberate crudity. "I'll corrupt the genius."

Semishigure

"Now, there's a good idea!" Bunshirō laughed. "But Yonosuke may enjoy that more than you think."

"Will you come with us?"

"No, I'll have to give that a miss," Bunshirō said. "I'd like to go, but I'm still under surveillance by the domain. Besides, I'm not so raging hot to have a woman as you are."

"Really, now? Maki Bunshirō!" When Ippei said that, Bunshirō raised his eyes and saw Ippei glaring straight at him. Puzzled, Bunshirō responded with a question of his own.

"What do you mean by that?"

"Well, actually I've heard a disturbing rumor; something I've been wondering about ever since," Ippei said. "It's a rumor about Koyanagi O-Fuku, who used to live next door to you. His Lordship has laid hands upon the girl, they say. Have you heard that?"

"That's no rumor; it's true," Bunshirō said. "And O-Fuku is no longer a child. She's a fine young woman."

"Oh? So you *do* know all about it then." Ippei murmured something, frowned, and then suddenly spoke again. "Forgive me if I'm wrong, but hadn't you once pledged yourself to that young lady?"

"Ridiculous!" Bunshirō said, but he was unable to prevent his face flushing with heat. Ippei had been extremely perceptive, he thought. The act had never taken place, but he could not deny that he harbored the desire within his breast. "Fuku went to Edo the year before last. As I said, she is no longer a child, but when she went to Edo, Fuku wasn't yet an adult, either. You can't pledge your future to a girl that young."

"I see. So I was mistaken, then?" Ippei cocked his head to one side. "Well, if that's so, all right. But really, you've seemed different lately, from how you were before. I wondered if that mightn't be because of O-Fuku."

"You're imagining too much. I haven't changed the least bit, in any way."

"Well, if so, that's fine," Ippei said. Then, as if to distance himself a bit, he said, "Even if it were true, that's the sort of thing even a close friend would find difficult to comment upon. I'll just have to banish that matter from my thoughts."

Thereafter the two of them talked for a while about the Ishiguri Dojo. And when Ippei finally rose to leave, Bunshirō went out with him to see him off.

5

He walked to the banks of the Goken River, and there handed over the lantern. After watching Ippei cross the bridge, lantern in hand, Bunshirō turned back; but then he noticed naked flames burning upstream and stopped to watch. Precisely at that corner where the Goken River turns to the east, there were torches moving about, as well as the shadows of two or three people. It was rather far away, but he could still see sparks from the torches falling into the water. He had no idea what sort of fish they were catching, but they appeared to be using torches to attract river fish. The whole scene was wrapped in misty, white night air. Bunshirō stood and watched for a while, then returned to the road by which he had come.

Tonight … Bunshirō thought, Tonight there were two things I avoided telling Ippei the truth about. The first, of course, concerned Fuku. Quite apart from anything that happened earlier, Fuku was now a concubine of the lord of the domain. Bunshirō saw no reason he should reveal his true feelings, given the way Ippei had questioned him.

The second concerned the dojo. He told Ippei that he had

been summoned to the master's quarters and told he would be competing against Okitsu Shinnojō in the autumn tournament against Matsukawa Dojo. But of course the secret techniques that had been discussed in that conversation he concealed. He had not lied, but he had kept two things secret from Ippei, to whom, until now, he had always revealed everything. This he was finding as oppressive as the dismally clouded skies that hung over him tonight. After wending his way back through a number of alleyways, Bunshirō came out on the street that led to the front of his barracks. Whereupon a rain that felt as if it could no longer hold off began falling from the dark night sky. It was more like mist, silently wetting his face. Bunshirō began to trot.

When he reached the gap in the hedge that served as a gate to the barracks, on the street at the front he sensed the sudden movements of someone. One person ran off, leaving behind only the sound of footsteps, and another slowly approached the place where Bunshirō stood. Out of the darkness floated the white face of Yada's widow. Bunshirō now knew who it was that had run off.

As always, Bunshirō was overcome by a mixture of anger and mild envy as he stood there. The widow came so close that they almost touched, stopped, and in a languid voice such as he had never heard from her, she said, "It's Bunshirō-san, isn't it?" Then the widow did something quite unexpected. She spread her arms and lightly embraced Bunshirō. He was taken aback, but then just as suddenly, she released him.

"It's begun to rain," Yada's widow said in that same languid voice, and then she moved off briskly toward her own home, leaving behind only the scent of her makeup and the lingering touch of her slender arms.

A loose woman, Bunshirō thought. But just as surely, he found her looseness mildly intoxicating.

One Hot Night

<u>1</u>

Bunshirō was at his desk, writing in reply to a letter from Shimazaki Yonosuke. Yonosuke's letter told him he would be coming home in the autumn and that he was looking forward to seeing him and Ippei. In his reply, Bunshirō wrote that he had heard of Yonosuke's return from Ikoma Sensei and that he too was looking forward to their reunion after these three long years. To say nothing more than that would seem brusque, he thought; but with his brush poised to tell him of recent events, Bunshirō found it difficult to organize his thoughts and decide just what to write.

It was the heat. It was that season when the hottest days of the year were beginning. The heat that by day had scorched everything and everybody lingered on into the night, and his body still felt as if it were burning. Moreover, the mosquito repellant he had lit at sundown seemed to have lost its effectiveness, and now they were flitting all about him. Distracted as he was, this was no time to be writing a letter; it was too hot even to shut the shutter on the window. Even with the window open there was no breeze; but at least the night air drifted into his room carrying with it a hint of coolness.

I can't go on like this, Bunshirō thought.

But early in the morning of the day after tomorrow, a man would be leaving for the Edo mansion on official business. "If you want to write to Yonosuke," Ippei had come to tell him, "I can ask this man to carry your letter to him." Which meant he would have to write his letter tonight and give it to Ippei tomorrow. Bunshirō pulled himself together and dipped his brush in the ink, whereupon he heard an exchange of abusive shouts outside and then the clash of metal.

A swordfight?

Bunshirō laid down his brush and in a single leap, grabbed the sword that leant against the wall and ran from his room. As he emerged from the doorway, his mother was looking out from the sitting room.

"What can that be, all that noise?"

"I'll go and see. But don't leave the room," Bunshirō said as he dashed out of doors. "Just wait here quietly."

In front of the Yada rooms in the other building of the barracks, he could see two men with drawn swords facing each other. Everyone's doors were already open to catch the cool air, so he could see the two men quite clearly in the lamplight that leaked out. One was the same young man that had been coming to call on the widow Yada. The other was much younger, a samurai who seemed about the same age as Bunshirō.

The sharp voice of a woman rang out. It was the voice of Yada's widow, who had come out in front of her doorway.

"Tsurunosuke-san! Put your sword down. What is this? This is terribly rude to Nosé-sama, can't you see? There must be something you don't understand." Then the widow took a step forward. "Now, put your sword away. If you'll just talk this over with him, you'll see. But do stop this shameful behavior."

"Don't get in my way!" the young samurai warned her. His

voice was shrill, but Bunshirō could tell from the sureness with which his sword was poised and his feet were placed that the youth was skilled beyond the ordinary. Nor did he attempt to hide the anger that his sword revealed. He was dangerous.

But his opponent, although he had drawn his sword, had positioned himself and poised his sword in such an ungainly stance, that he looked barely able to stand up. It was obvious that he had drawn his sword only because he had been challenged and could not have done otherwise.

Hmm, so that's what it is. After muttering a silent curse to himself, Bunshirō left the sword he was holding inside the door and, armed only with his short sword, walked briskly toward the other building. He crossed the open space, came under the eaves of the other barracks, and at the same pace approached the two men with drawn swords.

In the shadow of every doorway, there was someone gazing fearfully out at the duel, but when Bunshirō drew near, they all hastened to hide indoors. Bunshirō went almost as far as the home of the Yada family. The widow noticed him and was about to say something, but he put a finger to his lips and silenced her, then moved easily out into the open, behind the youth the widow had called Tsurunosuke. He covered the distance quickly until he was ten or twelve feet from the youth, then crouched and slipped up behind him at a run. When the youth noticed and made to turn, Bunshirō leapt forward and pinioned him.

"Ugh! What's this?" The youth struggled, but Bunshirō paid no attention. He was looking over his shoulder at the youth's opponent, but there was nothing to fear from that quarter. The moment he saw Bunshirō pinion the youth, the man collapsed to his knees on the ground. His shoulders rose and fell violently as he gasped for breath.

"Hey! You there!" Still pinioning the youth, Bunshirō called out in a loud voice to the man on his knees. "Why don't you sheath your sword and get out of here just as fast as you can. If you hang about, I'll not be responsible for what happens to you." Hearing that, the man moved fast. He stood, slipped his sword into its sheath, and without so much as a glance at Yada's widow, who was watching him intently, he ran off in a rush. He cut across the open space, rounded the corner of the building where Bunshirō lived, and the next instant disappeared into the darkness.

"This is a needless favor you're doing me," the youth Bunshirō had pinioned said in a low voice.

"You're from the Ono Dojo, aren't you?" Bunshirō whispered softly in his ear. He could tell from his stance. "Are you Fusé Tsurunosuke?"

"Eh?"

"I'm Maki from the Ishiguri Dojo. Maki Bunshirō. All right? I'm going to let go now." When he heard that, the youth relaxed the tension in his body. Bunshirō released him, and he replaced his sword in its sheath.

2

After sheathing his sword, the youth whirled about to face Bunshirō, as if to ascertain who this was.

"So you are Maki? Well, I'm pleased to meet you. But you've certainly seen me at my worst."

"No, no. Not to worry." Bunshirō turned and looked toward the Yada house, but the widow was no longer to be seen. She seemed to have gone in and shut the door tight. Bunshirō looked back at Fusé and asked, "But what is your connection with her?"

"You didn't know? She's my elder sister," Fusé said; and immediately added, "No, you wouldn't know. I'd rather no one knew. She's a worthless sister."

"Not at all. She's a fine sister." So Yada's widow is the elder sister of Fusé Tsurunosuke? This surprised Bunshirō.

A year or two earlier, though, he had heard of Fusé himself. The Ono Dojo had produced a brilliant student of the Mugai school of swordsmanship, Miyake Tōemon, who still served as assistant to the master there. He made such a name for himself that, at one time, it was said that even Satake of the Kūdon school could not stand up to him. Yet, perhaps because the dojo was so small, there was no one to follow in his footsteps. Then finally, about two years ago, Bunshirō began to hear talk of Ishikawa Sōroku and Fusé Tsurunosuke. But never was there any reason to connect the name Fusé with Yada's widow.

It was painfully obvious he was lying when he said she was a "fine sister." Bunshirō regretted those words.

"But never mind the incident with that fellow just now—Nosé, is that his name? Won't you come in and we can talk?"

"Well…" Fusé looked perplexed, as if he couldn't decide what to do.

"Come in and calm down a bit before you go."

Fusé smiled wryly, proof that he had already calmed down. But knowing it was Bunshirō who had intervened seemed to make him decide to go in.

As they walked toward Bunshirō's place, those figures in the doorways hastened to hide themselves indoors. Some even shut their front doors.

"Really, that was disgraceful what I did," Fusé said. The apparent madman seemed transformed into a mild-mannered gentleman.

"Did you intend to kill Nosé?"

"Nah, not really." Fusé was growling. While talking with Nosé, it seems, something had infuriated him and he drew his sword.

"Just a word of warning, then. Never draw your sword unless you *do* intend to kill."

"Yes, you're right," Fusé said.

Bunshirō greeted his mother and then led Fusé into his three-mat room; whereupon he was astonished to see how handsome the young man was. The Fusé lineage must be made up entirely of good looking men and women, Bunshirō was thinking to himself. And just then Fusé asked him how much he knew about Nosé.

"Nothing at all," Bunshirō said, shaking his head. "I didn't even know that was his name until I heard your sister call him that just now. But I've seen him around here from time to time."

"Ah, so you have seen him before?"

Bunshirō nodded. "He's often come calling in the evening or night. That much I know, but I've never been curious enough to wonder who he is or where he's from."

"Really?"

"Some of the other families may have been suspicious, but I don't suppose anyone has looked any further into it—perhaps because of difference in rank?"

"But that can't be." Again Fusé smiled wryly. "Someone came to tell us that things might not go well for Yada-sama in the future if this were to continue—meaning my sister's misbehavior."

"Someone from this barracks?"

"That's right; someone who lives here." Fusé scowled. "I was aghast. Everyone in the family felt they could die of shame. They called my sister home the other day and father warned her severely. Her misbehavior would affect not only herself, he said.

Semishigure

There's been no final settlement of that scandal yet, and this could affect the future of the Yada house."

"But couldn't you get the Yada house to break off relations with her? That would be the best solution, I should think."

"And then, there's *that*. There seem to be some among those in command who think that so long as my sister remains in the Yada family, they may be allowed to adopt an heir to marry her. She's in a delicate position. She should leave but can't."

"Hmm." Bunshirō folded his arms. As he pondered the circumstances, he began to see the dangers of the widow Yada's position. It made him shudder. He recalled that dark rainy night when she took him in her arms and embraced him. "I see. Given which, these visits from that fellow Nosé must be terribly awkward."

"Absolutely and utterly awkward." Fusé looked at a loss to do more than cluck with disapproval. "I certainly never imagined there would be any problem tonight. And when I came by to see how things were, there was nothing amiss. But then Nosé turned up and the two of them started chatting familiarly. That's what drove me crazy, so I dragged him outside and told him to draw."

"Who is this Nosé, anyhow?"

"Nosé Ikunoshin, heir to the Nosé family of protocol officers, enfeoffed at three hundred koku. But what is really despicable," Fusé said, "is that the man has a wife and children."

3

What Fusé told him shocked Bunshirō. He realized then that this couple's affair must be a clear case of adultery.

"How did this come about?" Bunshirō asked.

"That is a story that will take some time to tell," Fusé said. Ever since childhood, his sister Yoshie had been beautiful. When she grew up, people said, she was sure to be sought after as a bride by houses of high rank. Fusé's parents did not like others telling them this. But when Yoshie was seventeen, a marriage proposal came from the Nosé family of protocol officers, just as everyone had predicted. But after the betrothal had been formalized, suddenly it was broken. One of Nosé's kinsmen, it was said, was firmly opposed to a marriage with someone so inferior in rank. Fusé's parents were furious.

The Fusé were enfeoffed at seventy-five koku. They themselves had at first declined the Nosé proposal out of concern for their difference in rank. But the other party protested that the most important thing was the girl herself, that their offer was an expression of their confidence that both in looks and character she would make a wife the Nosé need never be ashamed of. And then, when finally the Fusé had been persuaded to accept, the messenger came bearing news of the Nosé's refusal. No wonder the Fusé family were furious.

"I only found out about this later, but …" Fusé smiled bitterly at Bunshirō, "the Nosé only proposed because that fellow, Ikunoshin, had seen my sister on her way to a lesson in tea or some such and was smitten by her. He persuaded his parents against their will, but they were not at all enthusiastic about the marriage. So when their kinsman opposed it, everything fell apart."

"Hmm." Bunshirō took aim at a mosquito on his arm and with a whack killed it. Whereupon Fusé Tsurunosuke, as if recalling something, began scratching his head. The night remained as hot as ever.

"But neither my sister nor my parents were deeply wounded

by the broken engagement. For within a mere three months, a match had been arranged between my sister and Yada Sakunojō. Sakunojō-dono was serving as a personal attendant to His Lordship. He was enfeoffed at one hundred koku, he was an accomplished swordsman, and in character he was far superior to Nosé. I still recall what an atmosphere of happiness prevailed with my sister and our family at that time." Fusé ceased talking, but then murmured, "No one ever imagined such a thing could happen to Sakunojō-dono."

Fusé's speech was replete with feelings of respect for his brother-in-law Sakunojō; and so Bunshirō, too, said that Sakunojō was the senior disciple he most respected at the dojo. After which he sighed and said, "So that's it. I see now what the situation is."

"No!" Fusé said, "I haven't told you everything yet." Then he lowered his voice still further. "It's not that I don't understand Nosé's feelings in approaching my sister after she'd become a widow. What I find unforgivable is that the man gives her money, 'to help make ends meet.' And my sister accepts it. Isn't that just disgraceful?"

When Fusé looked at Bunshirō and said "just disgraceful," the look on his face was flooded with shame. Bunshirō, at a loss for words, looked back at him. Fusé gave a single nod, and then said, "You warned me I should never draw my sword unless I intend to kill; but *that* is what the situation was. Can you understand now something of what I felt?"

"That's tragic," Bunshirō said.

"I hadn't intended to tell you all this on our first meeting. I should be ashamed to make such a display of my family's shame. I'd better be taking my leave now, though. I must apologize for tonight." Fusé smiled shyly. "If you hadn't been there, the results could have been disastrous. The scandal might have been noised about the whole castle town."

"Wait a moment." Bunshirō restrained Fusé as he was about to get up, and he went out into the sitting room. His mother, saying nothing, had peeled a cooled melon for them and Bunshirō carried it back to his room. The two young men ate it greedily, without a word.

After they had gone outside, Fusé suddenly turned to Bunshirō, as if he had just remembered something.

"Have you ever fought a match with Okitsu from the Matsukawa Dojo?

"No." Bunshirō shook his head. He spoke in a somewhat guarded manner, having no idea why Fusé should mention the name of Okitsu Shinnojō. "I've heard the name; but why Okitsu?"

"He paid us visit, quite unexpectedly. At the dojo."

"Oh? Wanting to sharpen up with you, was it?"

"Me and Ishikawa Sōroku." A faint smile arose on Fusé's face, illumined by the light that shone out from within the house. "He's certainly keen on practice, that man."

"So, did you fight him?" Bunshirō could sense the sharpness in his own voice. Fusé, too, seemed to notice it immediately and cast a dubious glance at Bunshirō.

"I fought him, but why do you ask?

"Before I tell you, let me ask the result."

"We were no match for him. He's much stronger than us. Sōroku was totally defeated. I just barely managed to make one hit."

"Can you remember the strokes he used?"

"Roughly."

"You see, actually …" And then Bunshirō told him that he

might be paired with Okitsu in the autumn offertory tournament. "I'd like to visit your dojo and check out the strokes he used with you; but, may I?"

"Come any time you like," Fusé said.

"Shouldn't you stop in over there before you go?" Bunshirō asked. Fusé just shook his head, glanced at the light still glowing in the Yada's place, and left.

For a time, Bunshirō stood out there and gazed at the lamplight showing through the shoji at the Yada's. As he was recalling all that Fusé Tsurunosuke had told him, the lamp went out.

Somekawa-chō

1

When he heard the time bell sound the Seventh Hour (4 p.m.), Bunshirō came out to the road at the riverside, just as they had agreed the day before, and there, downstream, Shimazaki Yonosuke appeared. He looked terribly gangling and thin as he walked toward him.

Bunshirō's first surprise, when Yonosuke returned, was to see how tall he had grown. Alongside Bunshirō and Owada Ippei, Yonosuke was now the tallest of the three. But he was still so gaunt and slender that he didn't give the impression of being a big man, the way Ippei did. Even before, Bunshirō had thought him gangling, but now, as he approached, he appeared to wander aimlessly, as if blown along by the wind. Still, the air he exuded of having somehow transcended the worldly was something new, something Yonosuke had not previously possessed. As Bunshirō stood staring at him, Yonosuke noticed, raised his hand, and called out, "Hey!"

"A little early to go to Somekawa-chō, isn't it?" Yonosuke looked off at the western sky as he spoke, and then chuckled.

On the previous day, at the Sanseikan, the domain academy,

Yonosuke had given a lecture on the *Analects* to an audience of two hundred samurai and foot soldiers. Prior to that, however, he and Bunshirō had met, and with Ippei the three of them decided they would go to Somekawa-chō today. It may have embarrassed Yonosuke to lecture on the "way of the sages," and then discuss their trip to the pleasure quarter. At least his chuckle sounded that way.

"How so? The sun is about to set," said Bunshirō. The sun was low now, shining through the great leafless zelkovas behind the houses on the far bank and reflected from the roofs in the fish market. "It gets dark in no time nowadays. By the time Ippei leaves home, it should be just the right time."

"Owada should be coming soon, shouldn't he?"

"Soon, I expect," Bunshirō said; and then, "I attended your lecture yesterday. It was splendid."

Yonosuke had lectured on Book 1, Section 4 of the *Analects*, which begins, "Zengzi said, 'I examine myself three times a day.'" This was the text from which the domain academy took its name. Yonosuke read out this passage and then explicated it with a wealth of examples in a lecture that held his audience enrapt. His words were crystal clear and his manner so imposing that he seemed an entirely different person from the Yonosuke of yore. After the lecture, Bunshirō left without meeting Yonosuke, but now he told him what he thought of it.

"I think I've heard Ikoma Sensei lecture twice on Book 1; but your lecture, I felt, opened my eyes to entirely new aspects of it."

"The *Analects*, one could say, are eternally new. It has such depths that it can give rise to any number of new interpretations."

The two of them trailed long shadows as they crossed the bridge. But no sooner had they crossed than the sun was hidden in the shadows behind the houses, and they were surrounded with chill air, while the quarter they had just walked through on the far bank, they could see, was now bathed in glowing sunlight.

"Is it all right for you to leave Randō Sensei unattended today?"

"No problem," Yonosuke said. "Until tomorrow, Sensei will be resting in the villa of Tōyama-sama. In the meantime, his disciple is free to spread his wings a little."

Kasai Randō's lectures at the Sanseikan were so overwhelmingly popular they had drawn audiences of more than three hundred for three days running. But his former disciples at the Kasai Academy—Shibahara, the dean of the academy; Tōyama, the junior elder; and Komoda, the samurai commander—were at great pains to ensure he would not be exhausted by his lecturing. This day of rest at Tōyama Ushinosuke's villa must have been scheduled by the men who invited Randō.

"Oh, really?" Bunshirō said. "Then you can enjoy yourself with no restraint." Just then the drumbeat from the castle sounded, signaling the end of the day. The two men turned, looked at each other, and said, "perfect timing." But by the time they had waited for Ippei to come from the castle and change clothes, it was well after the Sixth Hour (6 p.m.) before the three of them were crossing the bridge again, back toward the east. Ippei, who had taken the lead, was in a hurry; his lantern was dancing about and the light flickering, making it difficult to walk with him.

"Yonosuke! Have you …?" Ippei turned and looked back at Yonosuke. "Have you ever had a woman? Or are you still a virgin?"

"Well now, which would it be?" Yonosuke said, laughing.

"Hmm. If that's your answer, you're still a virgin. And there you were in Edo, with its famous pleasure quarter, Yoshiwara. What a waste!"

"And how about you?" Yonosuke asked in a teasing tone of

voice. By now he was so deeply learned that neither Bunshirō nor Ippei could compare with him as a scholar; yet he had not let scholarship make a solemn old sage of him. Yonosuke jested with them in a completely natural manner. "Have you ever had a woman?"

"Of course I have. I leave the *Analects* to Yonosuke, but if there's anything you don't know about girls, you can just ask me."

"Ippei seems to go drinking in Somekawa-chō quite regularly these days," Bunshirō said. "They haven't been able to find a wife for him, so he tends to be a bit desperate."

"I certainly *am* desperate!" Ippei bellowed. A passerby was startled and hurried to get past them. The three cut across a merchants' quarter lit by lanterns beneath the eaves.

"Is that it? You're desperate?" Yonosuke said, laughing. "Then the girls in this domain must be blind not to notice there's such a fine young man as Ippei here."

"You're the only one who's been good enough to say that, Yonosuke," Ippei said, only half in jest. "Bunshirō has been colder than I ever would have expected. I invite him to Somekawa-chō, but he just says 'Oh?' and hasn't come with me even once."

"Because I'm still on restriction," Bunshirō said. "I'm in no position to go running about drinking with you." Yonosuke looked at Bunshirō in surprise. Bunshirō had told him everything he had asked—in a general way at least—about the incident his father, Sukezaemon, had been caught up in, but he hadn't gone so far as to reveal that he was still subject to surveillance by his elder brother. Yonosuke appeared to be taken aback by Bunshirō's words.

"But why? Wasn't the incident settled when you were restored to your former stipend?"

"There are other circumstances; several sorts."

"Then you ought not to go drinking with us?"

"Oh, no. Tonight should be fine. I have a good excuse—I'm welcoming my friend who's come from afar, Shimazaki Yonosuke."

"No problem!" Ippei declared boldly. "If anyone complains, I'll deal with him." Whereupon the colorful lights of the pleasure quarter, Somekawa-chō, hove into view directly ahead of them. Ippei looked back and announced to his two friends, "First of all we'll go to Kinutaya. It's a small place; but their saké is good, and it's cheap. And their waitresses are beauties, every one of them."

"Perfect!" said Bunshirō.

"We'll leave all that to Ippei," Yonosuke added.

Once they had walked about two-thirds the length of the main street of Somekawa-chō, now crowded with pleasure seekers, they saw a small hanging lantern upon which was written KINUTAYA.

"Here it is," Ippei said. They slid open the door and the three of them entered. There were tables with kegs for seats, and in the rear a row of several small rooms—a long, dark, and narrow shop. A veritable "eel's bedroom," as such places are called. The four tables were thronged with men looking like workers and shop assistants, laughing and chatting noisily in drunken voices, while the dim light of a lamp shone down upon them as they drained their cups of saké with a quick twist of the wrist.

As the three friends moved past and into the center of the shop, a pale-faced woman approached from directly ahead and welcomed them.

"Is there a room open?" Ippei asked. The woman seemed to recognize his voice.

"Owada-sama, you're early tonight. The room at the end is open," she said, and led the way there.

Semishigure

2

"Do come in," the woman said as she lit the lamp. One after another, in they went. The room held only three tatami mats, and once the three of them were seated it felt full. Ippei ordered and the woman—she was over twenty and heavily made up—repeated their order and left. All three of them folded their legs and sat back.

"You're rather well known here, aren't you?" Bunshirō said to Ippei, who was rubbing the bluish shadow on his chin where he had shaved just before leaving home.

"So you noticed?" Ippei said, casting a slightly arrogant glance at him, as if he were chastening a witless inferior. "The shops near the entrance to this quarter are restaurants and small eating places. Then a little further on there is an intersection."

"So there is," Yonosuke said. Yonosuke seemed not to know what to do with his long legs and was lifting and lowering his knees.

"Down that cross street, whether you go right or left, is where you'll find the real pleasure quarter. Now, you mustn't denigrate these as 'whore houses' or whatnot. Some of them are positively palatial, glittering places. And the women are a bevy of beauties such as you'll never see just walking through the streets in town."

"Then, do you come here regularly?" There were heavy overtones of envy in Yonosuke's voice as he spoke. Both Ippei and Bunshirō burst out laughing.

"I wouldn't go so far as to say regularly. Entertainment of this sort costs money."

"I've heard talk of it, but ..." As he spoke, Bunshirō was gazing at the soiled walls, the scuffed tatami mats, the peeling paper on the sliding panels that separated them from the next room.

"So this is Somekawa-chō, where we are now?"

"That's right," Ippei said, "the place for saké and women. There must be quite a few of our fellow vassals here; but they don't come this far down the street. At most, as far as the intersection. They'll be drinking in the places up there that have more attractive entrances. After that, they'll move on to the brothels."

"But I prefer a place like this," Bunshirō said. "There's something nostalgic about it."

Just then, the woman they had spoken to before, together with a youngish looking girl, brought their saké and snacks.

"What's nostalgic about it?" the woman asked, as she arranged the snacks on a tray. She was obviously questioning what Bunshirō had just said.

"This guy *lives* in a three-mat room," Ippei sniggered. It's so small there's no room for anything but him and his books. This place must remind him of home."

"Hey! Will you cut that out?" Bunshirō said. Ippei's mindless chatter was annoying him. In fact he was not recalling his three-mat room in the barracks; it was an entirely different place that this room made him feel nostalgic for. But where that other place was, he did not know.

To Bunshirō, Ippei's prattle seemed but a burst of frivolity that had shattered a low moment of quiet contemplation. The sharp edge of his voice must have been felt straightaway.

"Well, later for the talk. Let's have a drink," Ippei said, raising his cup. The woman in thick makeup poured for them, and all three drank to their reunion.

"Kimi-chan, you pour now, all right?" the older woman said and left the girl in the room.

"Let's start with the snacks," Ippei said. "They're delicious here." Today they were salted flounder, caught that same day and grilled at the beach, greens in a sesame dressing, and pickled autumn eggplant.

Semishigure

"Yonosuke, grab your cup." Ippei filled Yonosuke's cup with saké. They could hardly hear the din from the tables by the doorway. There at the rear, it was as quiet as if they were in a cave. "Shouldn't we hear what Yonosuke has to say first? After all, he's been away for three years."

"That's fine with me," Bunshirō agreed.

"I had some very hard times there," Yonosuke said, then drained his cup and thrust it back to Ippei. "First of all it was language. I could understand what they were saying, but they couldn't understand what I said."

Bunshirō and Ippei laughed, but Yonosuke told them it was no laughing matter.

"There's nothing worse than when no one understands a word you say—never. I'd speak in our local dialect, and immediately they'd start making fun of me. That alone is degrading, for anyone. Silly fools, I thought; but that's the way it was until I learned to talk like they do."

"That's a sort of pain we've never experienced," Bunshirō said. The girl O-Kimi filled his cup again.

"I wrote to you, didn't I?" Yonosuke said to Bunshirō.

"A fellow named Komiya-san brought it to me. Was that your first letter?"

"That's right." Yonosuke nodded, then got another cup of saké and tossed it down. Yonosuke seemed a rather strong drinker. "When I wrote that letter, they were still teasing me about the way I talk. I wanted desperately to come home, if only there were a way."

"You don't feel that way now, do you?" Ippei asked.

"What do you mean? Like I want to come home? If it were still like that, I'd want to come home."

"No, that's not what I meant. You don't feel they still ridicule the way you talk, do you?"

"No, that's no problem now," Yonosuke said, laughing. Whereupon another young girl came into the room. She was short and a bit plump, but her face was round and white like a doll's. "Sorry to interrupt," she said.

3

Once the girl was in the room and saw how small it was, she looked a bit abashed.

"Oh, I beg your pardon," she said. "There was a rowdy customer next door, and I ran away. I shouldn't have come into such a tiny room."

"Nah, no problem." Ippei was in a buoyant mood. "Bunshirō, squeeze over this way a little more," he said. "And your name is?"

"Tora," she said. "Pleased to meet you."

"O-Tora? That's a nice name."

"That's what everyone says," O-Tora replied with a perfectly straight face. Compared to the quiet, thin-faced O-Kimi, O-Tora turned out to be a talker. Casting flirtatious glances all around the room, she poured for everyone.

"Then, how come it's no problem?" Ippei said, resuming their conversation.

"You mean my speaking in dialect? Well, it was about half-a-year after I enrolled in the Kasai Academy. There was a group reading the *Mencius*. I asked to join them, and they let me."

"My!" With Bunshirō and Ippei gazing fixedly at him, Yonosuke looked a little embarrassed but went on.

"By that time, I'd grown quite accustomed to Edo dialect, but in the reading circle I didn't use Edo dialect. I went at them full force in our own dialect, and I demolished some of their strange interpretations."

Semishigure

"Because we've studied the *Mencius* quite intensively here," Bunshirō said. Yonosuke nodded in agreement.

"That's right! I felt I had nothing to fear from the Kasai Academy. I even pounced on the interpretations of some of the senior students. But strange to say, I was able to make my point in those discussions in our local talk."

"Really? And they accepted that?"

"They accepted it." Yonosuke was again looking a bit self-conscious, and held out his cup to O-Tora. "And ever since that group reading, they've regarded me differently. At least, they've stopped poking fun at the way I talk."

"Yes, it's just as they say: these cute little fellows—you have to send them travelling," Ippei said in a loud voice. "Right, Bunshirō?"

"Who's the cute little fellow?" O-Tora, the talkative girl, asked Yonosuke.

"That's me," Yonosuke said.

"But he's a little too grown up now," Bunshirō chimed in and the whole room swirled with laughter.

Talk then moved on from Yonosuke's life in Edo to Ippei's search for a bride, something they'd already mentioned on their way here, and then to Bunshirō's rise to number five at the dojo.

"Number five? That's astonishing!" Yonosuke gazed at Bunshirō, his bleary eyes wide. All three of them were quite drunk by now. "I somehow sensed an air of distinction you didn't have before. My! Number five?"

"But on the other hand, I've been neglecting my studies with Ikoma Sensei."

"That can't be helped. 'Both military and academic' they say, but it's difficult for anyone to excel in both." Yonosuke then turned to Ippei. "Ippei, what's your rank?"

"Me? Number fifteen."

"What? I had a letter from Bunshirō a long time ago, in which he said you'd just been promoted to number fifteen."

"That's right! I'm the permanent number fifteen." Ippei purposely made a joke of it then called to the little serving girl. "Oi, O-Kimi. You've only been pouring for Bunshirō, haven't you? Give me some saké, too."

"Aren't I supposed to be pouring over here?" said O-Tora, holding out the saké jug and snuggling up to him

Ippei brushed her off and said, "I prefer O-Kimi."

"Oh, that's nasty." O-Tora gave Ippei a hard whack on the back, which made him choke on his saké and threw the little room into an uproar.

But once the disturbance had quietened down, it was decided, without anyone saying so, that it was time to leave. The three of them got out their money and paid the bill. As they were leaving, the woman with the thick makeup appeared again. They asked her what time it was. She told them it was past the Fourth Hour (10 p.m.).

The three of them stepped out into the street. The lamps under the eaves of the shops on either side lit the street that ran through Somekawa-chō as brightly as ever, but the number of people walking the street had diminished noticeably.

Bunshirō was a bit unsteady on his feet. He could feel himself swaying. This wasn't the first time he had drunk saké, so it must be because he had relaxed and gone on drinking so long, he thought. The three came to the midpoint of the street and stopped at the intersection.

"Well, where shall we go?" Ippei asked. Ippei, too, had been swaying slightly all the way there. "This way there's the Akebono Rō, Tsunohira, Daikokuya, Kazusaya; and that way there's the Wakamatsuya, Tsubakiya, Tokiwaya, Benten Rō …"

Semishigure

"That'll do." Ippei was about to continue, but Bunshirō silenced him. "You and Yonosuke go ahead. I'll leave you here and go home."

"What? Come on now, Bunshirō." Ippei lurched toward Bunshirō as if to grab him. "You're going to show your back to the enemy?"

"Uh huh. It might not go down too well, if I were to go to a brothel."

"I'll leave, too," Yonosuke said. "I'm here officially, in Randō Sensei's entourage. It could reflect badly upon him if I were to step out of line."

"You're just pitiful, you two," Ippei shouted. "You say this and say that; but the truth is you're afraid of women. I can see right through you."

"I have no fear at all of women," Bunshirō said. "All I'm saying is that the time is not right. Even you can understand that much, can't you?"

"Me?" Ippei looked bleary-eyed at Bunshirō. "Of course I understand. You say you're on restriction. That much I understand."

"Then tonight you go alone. You can enjoy our share of the girls' cuddles for us."

"That'll be just fine," Yonosuke added and then chuckled.

"Hopeless! And I was going to teach the genius about women tonight."

"I'll ask you to do that some other time," Yonosuke said. Whereupon Ippei stumbled away from the two and headed down the side street. The beginning of the side street was dark, but beyond there the glow of lamps could be seen.

"Hey, you two!" Ippei shouted as he looked back at his friends who were seeing him off. "You're just gutless. Keep that up and you'll never be a real man."

By now they could only hear his voice; Ippei's large body was no longer visible. They turned their backs on his voice and headed for the entrance to Somekawa-chō.

"Not a real man?" Yonosuke sniggered. "Well, maybe so."

"But even Ippei must be finding it difficult to become a real man," Bunshirō said. They both burst out laughing, which startled a woman who had just slid open the latticed door of a small eating place and stepped into the street, causing her to stop and stare at them.

"Incidentally," Yonosuke said suddenly, "there's a woman, O-Fuku-sama, His Lordship's new concubine, but ... I've heard she's the daughter of your next-door neighbor."

"That's right. You know all about it?"

"They said her father was Koyanagi Jinbei in the Defense Works Unit, so it couldn't be anyone else. In any case, she's been the talk of the Edo mansion."

"Really?"

"Anyhow ... I didn't know anything about her, but weren't you two rather fond of each other?"

"Nonsense!" Bunshirō, taken aback, looked hard at Yonosuke. "Who said that?"

"It was Ippei."

"What an irresponsible guy," Bunshirō said. It made him rather angry with Ippei. "He's said such things before, but now he's broadcasting that nonsense your way, too."

"Nonsense, is it? Hmm," Yonosuke said gruffly, as if he were somehow doubtful. "As they say, no smoke where there's no fire. Was there nothing at all of the sort Ippei spoke of?"

"Nothing. Nothing at all. But shall we sit for a while?" Bunshirō asked Yonosuke. The two of them left the quarter and went to the bridge across the stream that runs alongside Somekawa-chō.

Semishigure

4

The stream could hardly even be called a rivulet, but the bridge that spanned it, probably because of the location, was beautifully built, low railed but broad. The two of them sat down on the rail, from which they could see the brightly lit main street of Somekawa-chō, stretching out before them.

Traffic on the street had diminished, but the lamps hadn't dimmed a bit. As they watched they saw a girl, whom they took to be a waitress, run across the bright thoroughfare. Then, after they had observed the scene for a while, Bunshirō turned to Yonosuke.

"You too must have some memory of O-Fuku. Her mother …" he began, and then it occurred to him that he shouldn't refer to a favorite of His Lordship so familiarly. "But I don't know what else to call her," he muttered. "Her mother often asked me to take her to the Night Festival at the Kumano Shrine."

"Now that you mention it, I do remember that faintly," Yonosuke said. "She was a pale-complected little girl."

"That's right." Bunshirō recalled Fuku hiding behind his back while she licked her lollipop, the emotion of the memory blending with his tipsiness. "It must be because he saw something of that sort that Ippei says there was something between us. But that's just my guess."

"Oh?"

"Well, think about it. O-Fuku—or whatever I should call her—was thirteen when she went to Edo. Still a child. Not old enough to feel affection for me, or anything like it."

"Yes, true enough, when you put it like that." Yonosuke spoke as if at last he could agree with Bunshirō. Then he crossed his long legs.

In Somekawa-chō, the music of a shamisen continued without a lull. And while they listened, four or five samurai suddenly appeared on the street, singing loudly in slurred voices as they staggered toward the intersection. After watching them for a while, Yonosuke looked back toward Bunshirō.

"So that's how it was? Then I don't suppose you're much interested in how O-Fuku-sama is getting on now?"

"What do you mean by that?"

"Well, if you'd care to hear how she is, I'll tell you what I've happened to hear, but …"

For a time, Bunshirō remained silent. Then he asked, "Good news or bad news?"

"Bad news, I suppose."

"Then I'd better hear it. Tell me about it."

"This I heard just before I came here—that O-Fuku-sama seems to have lost a child. A miscarriage."

Bunshirō suddenly felt as if he had been cut by the dull blade of an axe or the like. The pain slowly spread through his body and entered his breast.

Really? But if His Lordship has laid hands upon her, this was only to be expected. She would have given birth to His Lordship's child. But could Fuku, still only fifteen, ever have wished to bear their lord's child?

"Hey, what's the matter?"

With Yonosuke staring at him, Bunshirō came to his senses and looked up.

"How is it that she had a miscarriage? Was she unwell?"

"Well, that is a bit difficult to explain in simple terms." Yonosuke lowered his voice. "You've heard of O-Fune-sama?"

"The mother of Matsunojō-sama? I've heard the name. She's very powerful, they say. Right?"

Semishigure

"Precisely," Yonosuke said. "And rumor has it that O-Fune-sama was the cause of O-Fuku-sama's miscarriage. Which is to say she desired that there be no more children by His Lordship. That's what the person who told me said."

"Hmm."

"O-Fuku-sama is the sole object of His Lordship's affection, and she's become pregnant again straightaway. The O-Fuku-san that you know apparently is detested by O-Fune-sama. O-Fuku-sama is living in the lower mansion now. But His Lordship finds it difficult to see her there, and thus, rumor has it, he may send her back to the domain."

"He'll dismiss her?"

"Not at all. It would only be because she'd be safer in the domain than in Edo," Yonosuke said. "But then, even here in the domain, there's O-Man-sama. O-Man-sama is the only one of his concubines here, and she rules the women's wing of the castle. I'm not so sure O-Fuku-sama would be happy even if she did come back here." Yonosuke looked over at Bunshirō. "But on a different subject: does this girl O-Fuku-sama monopolize His Lordship's favor because she's such a great beauty?"

But Yonosuke's casual question only exacerbated Bunshirō's sense of pain and never reached his ears.

"Yonosuke, will you stay here with me a bit longer?" As he spoke, Bunshirō stood. Yonosuke stood, too, and stretched.

"Stay for what? Saké? Women?"

"Saké."

"Hmm? You haven't had enough to drink?"

"I want to talk to you some more," Bunshirō said. Yonosuke looked hard at Bunshirō, then nodded.

"All right. You have enough money? I've only a little left."

"That's fine. I have enough."

The two of them headed back into Somekawa-chō. It would soon be halfway through the Fourth Hour (11 p.m.), they thought, but the streets were still brightly lit, the shamisen were still playing, and as they walked they could hear bursts of laughter coming from a crowd of men somewhere nearby.

"Well, I'm going to drink my fill tonight," Bunshirō said.

Yonosuke silently grinned. "That's just fine—but why?"

"You'll know soon."

When they came back, they were welcomed with surprised faces at Kinutaya.

"Well, well! I guess you didn't get enough to drink," the woman with the thick makeup laughed.

"Anything will do to go with it. Just give us some saké."

"That we shall do. But the other fellow, Owada-sama—what's become of him?"

"Ah! He went home ahead of us," said Bunshirō.

The customers had thinned out at Kinutaya. There were three men at the tables, each of them sitting alone. And only two of the rooms were lit.

"The same room will do?" The woman with the thick makeup led them to the room where they had been drinking before.

5

When they entered the room, Bunshirō felt as if he were returning to a familiar old place. The soiled walls, the scuffed tatami mats, the holes in the corner of the sliding panel.

So that's it! Now he knew why he felt such a sense of nostalgia the first time he was here. It was because this room so resembled the houses in the Defense Works quarter. Bunshirō's house, the Koyanagi's house, the Yamagishi's house—all of them were run down; their tatami mats always scuffed; their sliding panels, though repaired, soon punctured again. If you lack something, you borrow it. If you're given something, you share it. While these memories of his life, and the lives of Fuku and her little sisters, were crisscrossing his mind, the two serving girls, O-Tora and O-Kimi, brought them their saké.

"Ah! Delightful! You've come back to us." O-Tora greeted them with an exaggerated expression of joy. And Yonosuke replied in a manner quite unbecoming of a scholar of the teachings of Confucius and Mencius.

"That's right! We just had to see your faces again." Then, spontaneously, they paired up, O-Tora pouring for Yonosuke and O-Kimi for Bunshirō.

O-Kimi was younger than O-Tora, and looked to be only thirteen or fourteen. As she poured for Bunshirō, she looked a bit sleepy. For a time the two drank in silence. Finally Bunshirō spoke.

"There was no mutual fondness or affection," he said. "That is a fact. It was just as I told you. Never once did either of us speak of our feelings, nor did we exchange vows of any sort."

"If that's what you say, then I'll believe you. I don't know about Ippei, though," Yonosuke said. "So fine, this was not a case of mutual affection. But what is it you want to tell me?"

"It was the year before last when she went to Edo. Autumn of the year before last." Having said which, Bunshirō grabbed his cup and said, "Let's have a little more to drink."

The girls poured for them, and O-Tora asked Yonosuke, "Who is it you're talking about?"

"You girls needn't worry about that," he said. "Instead why don't you sing us a song?" Whereupon O-Tora immediately started clapping her hands rhythmically and began singing an old folk song. Quite unexpectedly, she had a beautiful voice, which captured the attention of both Bunshirō and Yonosuke, and they too began clapping in time with her.

When she had finished her song, Bunshirō and Yonosuke offered O-Tora their cups, and little O-Tora gulped them both dry, livening up the room a bit more. The saké cups made one round, then another, and even the silent O-Kimi emptied hers and choked it down. Then O-Tora began singing again, and the four of them clapped in time with her.

"I'm drunk tonight, aren't I, O-Kimi-chan?" O-Tora proclaimed in a merry voice when she had finished singing. O-Tora seemed the sort who only grew more lively the more she drank.

"Come on now, O-Samurai-san! Drink a little more, you boys!"

"All right, let's drink."

"I'll go and get some more saké," O-Tora said, as she stood to leave the room, but in that instant she teetered and fell directly on top of Yonosuke. Having already made a good start, she had quickly drunk even more and that had rapidly taken effect.

"Wow! This is great!" Yonosuke exclaimed with pleasure as he embraced her.

"I'll get the saké," O-Kimi said, and then left the room. Bunshirō turned to face Yonosuke.

"Going back to what I was saying before: It was in the autumn of the year before last that she went to Edo. But the day before she left for Edo, she came to see me."

"Who was it came?" Yonosuke asked, pushing his head out from under O-Tora's arms. And then finally, when he managed to roll O-Tora's body off to the side, he said, "Oh, I see, it was her that came."

"Yes. To say goodbye, don't you suppose?"

"Probably so, I'd say."

Semishigure

Bunshirō shook the jug, and then tipped the saké that remained into Yonosuke's cup.

"At the time, though, I wasn't there to meet her." Bunshirō went on and told Yonosuke all the circumstances of that occasion: how Ōhashi Ichinoshin had subjected him to severe "training," how he had arrived home later than usual, how O-Fuku had already left by the time he got back from the dojo, and everything else.

"I said before that there was no bond of mutual affection between us, and those words are in no way false. But what happened then, even now weighs heavily on my mind."

Yonosuke, holding his saké cup in his hand, looked silently at Bunshirō.

"O-Fuku was thirteen at the time. I can't imagine she would have understood what affection between men and women was all about."

When Bunshirō said that, O-Tora, still leaning on Yonosuke, looked up at him and asked, "Who is O-Fuku?"

"Just be quiet now," Yonosuke said and patted her gently on the head. Then Bunshirō went on.

"I think it must have been of her own free will, though, that O-Fuku came to see me that day. To say goodbye. But I just missed her, and I can tell you that I still regret that. Of course, I wouldn't have known much either, at that time, about affection between men and women. But if I had been there to meet Fuku, I'm sure I would have said something. What I might have said, I have no idea, even now. But probably I'd have said something serious. I didn't realize that at the time, though; only much later. Only this year, when I heard what had become of her."

"Bunshirō, have some more to drink." This time Yonosuke looked about for the jug that still contained some saké and poured for Bunshirō.

"It's possible, of course, that I'm just imagining all of this." Bunshirō sipped what little saké remained in his cup. "And if I am imagining it, that would save me from all this, but …"

"No, you're not imagining it, I'm sure." As Yonosuke spoke, O-Kimi came back into the room bearing saké and a large plate of pickles.

"The pickles are a present from the mistress," O-Kimi said. "We won't let you pay for them, she said."

"That's very kind of you," Bunshirō said. Then suddenly it occurred to him: "But won't you be closing soon?"

"Oh, that's all right. Don't worry about it," O-Tora said. "If it gets late, you can sleep here and go home in the morning, can't you? Do stay! We'll all crowd in here and sleep together. I've grown quite fond of you two, O-Samurai-san."

"O-Tora is saying she likes us and we should stay here tonight," Bunshirō said.

"Hold on now. That's a hair-raising thought," Yonosuke replied.

The two men burst out laughing in unison, which irked O-Tora, and she whacked Yonosuke on the back. O-Tora and O-Kimi then poured warmed saké for them both. It had been warm for an autumn evening, but it was cooling as it grew late, and the warm saké tasted good.

"That's what I wanted to tell you," Bunshirō said. "Ours was not a relationship of mutual affection, and of course we were not pledged to each other. But in our childish way we may have shared feelings of that sort for each other. Whether that is of any importance or not, I don't know. I just wanted to tell you that that's the way it was. If I hadn't, I'd have felt I had lied to you."

"Did you tell Ippei?"

"No." Bunshirō shook his head.

"I see," said Yonosuke. "It must have been painful for you;

Semishigure

what I was saying before." His face wore a drunken mien, but Yonosuke's dark eyes stared hard at Bunshirō. "Well, have a drink," Yonosuke said, grasping the saké jug.

"You mustn't mention this to anyone, what I've said tonight."

"Of course not. Not a word to anyone," Yonosuke said, and then, in a soft voice, not very ably but distinctly, he sang a snatch of what sounded like a popular song of old:

"This girl of whom I know naught, neither her birth nor her upbringing; What karma could have caused me to become so fond of her? Bunshirō, drink! Didn't you say you were going to drink yourself senseless tonight?" Yonosuke said, pouring another cup of saké for Bunshirō.

The next morning Bunshirō awoke with splitting headache. Then he realized that the night before he had been so drunk he had fallen asleep in the rear room of Kinutaya. He felt something soft alongside him. It was O-Kimi's body. He threw back the coverlet and sat up. At his feet, in the pale bluish light from a skylight, Bunshirō could see a human form under a coverlet. Peeping out from beneath it were O-Tora's hair and Yonosuke's long legs.

Did I drink myself unconscious in a place like this just because O-Fuku miscarried another man's child? A dim sense of sadness, wan like the morning light, filled his breast.

A Single Blow, Heaven-sent

1

About ten days after Shimazaki Yonosuke returned to Edo with his mentor, the day of the offertory tournament at the Kumano Shrine arrived. On that day, Bunshirō finished his midday meal early, and when he heard the bell of the temple Shōenji toll the Ninth Hour (12 noon), he left the house.

On the evening when the family stipend had been restored, Inspector General Ogata, had said that in the autumn he would be moved from the barracks where they were now living to the residential quarter of the district commissioners, but there had been no notification of that as yet. Bunshirō was still living in the painfully cramped, old place in Fukiya-chō that had so astonished Yonosuke.

He took up his bamboo practice sword, still in its case, tucked the parcel under his arm containing the practice gear his mother had washed for him as well as his sleeve cord and headband, and then left the house. Bunshirō, partly out of habit, cast a glance toward the Yada house.

It was one of those splendidly clear days, of the sort that seemed a brief holiday prior to the gloom of winter that was soon to come. Apart from three puffs of cloud floating at the edge of the hills that stretched across the upper reaches of the Goken River, the sky was as blue as if spread with indigo from corner to corner. The bright sunlight that poured down had by now lost the intensity of summer, but there was only the slightest hint of chill in the air.

The sun's rays shone into every bit of the broad expanse between those two old barrack blocks that once housed the domain's bird catchers, illuminating the withered weeds and the yellow chrysanthemums blooming along their edges. But the door to the Yada house, as always, was shut tight. With only a glimpse that way, Bunshirō traversed the expanse, and emerged from the hedge into the street.

That family: what's to become of them? The thought always left Bunshirō feeling downcast. Ever since the incident that summer evening that had so alarmed the residents of the barracks, Yada's widow almost never came out of the house. Occasionally she would rush out, probably to buy the necessities of their daily lives, but even then she would hurry back as quickly as she could. And for her other daily purchases, she would call the peddlers of vegetables and fish into the earthen-floored entryway and buy what she needed there. The widow seemed to avoid showing her face before other residents of the barracks as much as possible.

Only natural, I suppose, Bunshirō thought. Uninhibited though she had seemed, after an incident of that sort she could not be so thick-skinned as to act as if all were still normal—at least Bunshirō found a strange sense of relief in thinking that to be so; for he could not but pity the widow whenever he thought of the situation she now found herself in.

She has no place to run to. So long as the possibility remained of adopting another husband for her, she obviously couldn't leave the Yada family. And though she might no longer wish to meet anyone else in the barracks, the place she now lived had been decreed by the domain. There was nowhere else she could go. Such, he could see, was where the widow now stood.

At the base of Bunshirō's pity for Yada's widow was his fellow feeling for someone who had suffered the same fate as himself. That scandal, clearly, had cast them both into their present state of misfortune, which aroused in him a sense of rapport with her.

And yet, there is more to it than just that, Bunshirō was thinking. Since that recent incident, the widow had been wasting away. And to him that made her only the more beautiful. The widow's face had thinned and her cheekbones now stood out more prominently. But her skin had grown so pale as to seem almost transparent, her eyes harbored a hint of sorrow, and her beauty had taken on a startling new allure. It seemed somehow out of character in a widow – a needlessly dangerous sort of beauty. And Bunshirō was quite consciously aware that he was secretly attracted to the widow's beauty.

"Maki-san!" He was surprised to hear a voice call out to him. He looked up and saw Fusé Tsurunosuke coming out of a side street. Ishikawa Sōroku was with him. "So it's about to begin?" Fusé said as he came up alongside him. Ishikawa only nodded in greeting. Ishikawa Sōroku was two or three years older than Bunshirō and Fusé, and a man of few words.

"Thank you for your help recently," Bunshirō said. Since he had first met Fusé in Fukiya-chō, Bunshirō had visited him three times at the Ono Dojo, the last time being only a few days ago.

"What do you think?" Fusé's face wore a look of concern as he turned to Bunshirō, walking side by side with him. He spoke more politely than usual. "Have you formed any plans yet?"

Semishigure

"No, I still can't say ..." Bunshirō replied.

"I don't suppose you can, until you face off with him." Fusé was of course referring to the techniques of swordplay Bunshirō's opponent Okitsu Shinnojō would use in their match that day.

When Okitsu had fought a three-point match with Fusé, he had allowed him one hit out of three, and Ishikawa Sōroku had not scored a single hit in his match. In quick succession, Okitsu had struck him on the torso and on a gauntlet. His sword had whipped up from below and Ishikawa had been unable either to block or deflect it.

The techniques he had used against Fusé were clearly discernable. One point had been scored with a hit on the shoulder, beginning with his sword poised in mid-position. Another was a blow to the forehead, beginning with his sword held high. Fusé remembered well Okitsu's movements in scoring those points. But his movements in the match with Ishikawa, neither Ishikawa himself nor the observing Fusé could explain. What they did know, however, was that Okitsu had not begun with his sword poised in the lower position. Yet when he attacked, his sword appeared to rebound from the lower position. He had then been able to strike either torso or gauntlet, and neither Ishikawa's hands nor his feet had been able to respond. Ishikawa Sōroku had demonstrated just how it felt when that had happened.

Bunshirō had attempted to formulate a plan of defense, based upon what his friends had told him, but the feeling remained that he had not grasped thoroughly Okitsu's method of attack. Fusé told him the same.

"After all, I've only ever had that one match with Okitsu," Fusé said, a bit apprehensively. It seemed to exasperate him that he could not describe adequately the techniques of swordplay used by Okitsu Shinnojō. "If I'm mistaken, it could be disastrous."

"You mustn't worry so. I have a general idea what to expect."

"But he's been spying on you at your dojo, has he not?" Fusé said. And that was true.

The day after Shimazaki Yonosuke had returned to Edo, Bunshirō was at the dojo having a serious practice match with Sugiuchi Michizō. In preparation for his match with Okitsu Shinnojō at the offertory tournament, he had instructed Michizō in the various ways he was to attack him, in the course of which Bunshirō became uncomfortably aware that he was the object of intense observation. He signaled to Michizō to hold off and looked all around the dojo, but no one there was taking any notice of them. Then he caught sight of a pair of eyes peering in from outside the bars on the window behind him. That's it, he thought. Even when Bunshirō looked directly at them, those eyes remained calm, but slowly looked away, and then suddenly the face disappeared from the window. When he approached the window and looked out, the back of a tall young man wearing only trousers over his robe, in the style of someone still living with his parents, was moving into the distance. Though he could not see his face, Bunshirō knew at a glance that the man was Okitsu Shinnojō.

"He came to spy on me, but I've gone to you to learn Okitsu's techniques. That makes us even." When Bunshirō said that, Ishikawa Sōroku, who until now had said nothing, spoke.

"This is only a rumor," he said, "but I've heard that if he wins this year's match, Okitsu may be offered a position by the domain."

"Oh?" Bunshirō said, thinking that was a thoughtless remark to make to someone just before a tournament.

"But I can't hold back just because of that," he said bluntly.

Ishikawa Sōroku realized he had spoken out of turn, and his

face flushed as he looked at Bunshirō. "I didn't mean to say that," he said, "nor would Okitsu himself wish you to hold back, I'm sure."

"After all, O-Yumi-chō is full of fine old families," Fusé Tsurunosuke said, as if to smooth over the difference between the two. "There'll be opportunities aplenty for him."

As Fusé spoke, the gateway to the Kumano Shrine came into view. Around it clustered a crowd of samurai, come to see today's offertory tournament. Among them were some who recognized Bunshirō and were whispering softly to each other.

2

Bunshirō felt the eyes of several men focused upon him. He could hear some of them whispering "Maki" or "Bunshirō," but he pretended not to hear, and with his two friends from the Ono Dojo, passed through the gateway to the shrine.

Then from behind him boomed a loud voice. "Is that Maki? Those Maki are the troublemakers in this domain!"

"Shhh," someone said, and Bunshirō became aware of an awkward silence that pervaded the crowd. He could tell, too, that Fusé Tsurunosuke was staring at him with a perturbed look on his face. But Bunshirō moved on, looking straight ahead, his face expressionless.

Say whatever you like, Bunshirō thought. This wasn't the first time he had experienced contempt of this sort. It had befallen him time and again in the past, both behind his back and openly. At first he had been unable to prevent himself blanching, both visibly and mentally. But now, whatever he might be thinking, his face showed no sign whatsoever of his anger. Bunshirō did not look back at the speaker, but walked along calmly.

Inwardly, though, he was thinking he *must* not be defeated in today's match. For it required no deep thought to realize that whoever had just insulted the Maki family and Bunshirō himself would be hoping that his opponent Okitsu Shinnojō would be the winner.

In the very heart of Shinmei-chō, there was a great grove of old cedars, in the midst of which stood the Kumano Shrine. The buildings of the shrine were not particularly grand, but they were old and stately, and the grounds were extensive. The matches would be held within a corner of these precincts surrounded by large white curtains.

When he arrived at the site of the matches, the spectators appeared already to have crowded within the curtains, and the hum of their whispers that leaked out sounded like rolling waves. Bunshirō parted with Fusé and Ishikawa Sōroku outside the curtains and entered the curtained waiting area at the rear of the site.

"A little late, aren't you? It's about to begin." When Bunshirō entered the Ishiguri Dojo waiting area within the curtains, Satake Kinjūrō took him to task as if he had been waiting for him.

Satake was not participating in the matches himself. He appeared to be there in order to supervise the entrants from the Ishiguri Dojo. Ishiguri Yazaemon was nowhere to be seen. He may already have arrived and taken his proper seat, but the master had been unwell of late, and it was possible that something had come up that prevented him from attending the offertory tournament today. In any case, the master's assistant from the Ishiguro Dojo, Satake Kinjūrō, was there to take responsibility for the progress of the matches.

"I'm sorry I'm late," Bunshirō apologized. "I'll prepare immediately." He knew, however, that plenty of time remained before the matches were to begin. First, there would be the presentation of gifts from the domain to the Ishiguri Dojo and the Matsukawa Dojo. Then there would be a few ceremonial preliminaries. The matches would begin at the Eighth Hour (2 p.m.).

While Bunshirō was preparing himself, Inukai Hyōma came over to him.

"Have you made your plans for the match with Okitsu?" he asked. Inukai's face wore a smile that seemed almost a sneer, yet his eyes stared hard and cold at Bunshirō. "If you're afraid, I could take your place."

"We're this busy, and you have time to joke?" Bunshirō snapped back at him as he went on changing. "Instead of meddling with others, why don't you just mind your own business?"

Hyōma's smile broadened. Then he looked away and stalked off. The exchange between the two had taken place quickly, in subdued tones. No one else seemed to notice.

Maruoka Shunsaku sat on his assigned stool, his bamboo sword lying sideways across his knees, his eyes tightly shut. Ōhashi Ichinoshin stood in a corner flexing his knees and bending his torso to the rear. And Tsukahara Jinnosuke was kneeling before Satake, who was sitting on his stool warning him in great detail about something. Everyone had already tied their sleeves back and donned their headbands. Bunshirō realized that Satake had not been wrong to chasten him for being late.

Bunshirō finally finished preparing himself. He pulled his headband tight and sat on an empty stool. He then saw that Inukai Hyōma had gone to the corner opposite Ōhashi and was slowly flourishing his weapon there. As always, the combative one, Bunshirō thought. Why did he have to make those arrogant remarks before?

In today's matches, Hyōma would be the first to fight. Bunshirō would be fourth. The reason he had superseded his superiors, Tsukahara and Ōhashi, and would be competing as second in rank, was, needless to say, because he had been matched with Okitsu Shinnojō. It may well have been resentment of this that caused Hyōma to speak with such malice.

But he'll be the first ... He'd better win convincingly, Bunshirō thought as he watched Hyōma wield his sword.

Hyōma had superseded the sixth-ranked Noda Yasuke to become a competitor in the matches; singled out just as Bunshirō had been the previous year. Their master, Yazaemon, would have discussed this with his assistant, Satake, and the second-ranking Maruoka. Bunshirō had no complaint, but Hyōma did seem a bit overconfident for having been chosen in preference to Noda. He had caught a glimpse of that in his manner of speaking a moment ago, Bunshirō thought. Overconfidence, too, is dangerous. Bunshirō could not but feel apprehensive.

Hyōma's opponent was a young man named Arakawa Shōzaburō. He, too, was participating in these matches for the first time. Bunshirō only knew his name because of this pairing.

And how about you? Have you made any plans? Bunshirō wished he could ask Hyōma.

3

Despite the personal interests bound up in this offertory tournament—the chance of a position in the Corps of Vassals for Okitsu, talk of Bunshirō being taught secret techniques—ultimately this event was a struggle for reputation between the Ishiguri and Matsukawa dojos. Both felt they must win at least one more match than their opponents. In that sense, the performance of the first of their five entrants, Inukai Hyōma, was of great importance. If Hyōma were to lose to Arakawa, a newcomer like himself, then the next entrant, Tsukahara Jinnosuke, who was very skilled technically but lacking in grim persistence, might become discouraged and lose his match.

"Inukai!" Maruoka Shunsaku, who until then had kept his eyes shut tight, looked up and called out to Hyōma. "Can't you calm down a bit?"

Hyōma, accosted by Maruoka, ceased his practice strokes, whereupon the bell of the temple Shōenji echoed in the distance as it tolled the Eighth Hour (2 p.m.). Immediately thereafter, the beat of the drum sounded at the site of the matches.

The ceremonies were conducted and the participants introduced. It was all very simply done, and when it was over, Satake Kinjūrō returned. Then the drum sounded again and a voice summoned Inukai Hyōma and Arakawa Shōzaburō.

"All right, here I go!" With a shout, Hyōma came forward. His face was a bit pale, and drawn with tension.

"So even Hyōma feels the strain?" Maruoka smiled and looked over at Satake. Satake, too, smiled.

"This is his first time. That's why," Satake said, and then turned his gaze upon Bunshirō, Ōhashi, and Tsukahara, one after the other. "But the rest of you—this isn't *your* first time. So give it your all."

But Satake's hopes seem to have been unfounded. Inukai Hyōma won, but Tsukahara and Ōhashi, who followed him, both lost. In this year's match, Tsukahara was defeated by Yamane Seijirō, who had lost to Bunshirō the previous year. Perhaps Yamane had roused himself to new efforts and sharpened his skills.

"Ready? You *can't* lose!" There was a savage look in Satake's eyes as he sent Bunshirō into the fray. "Get out there and win! Even if it kills you!"

Get out there and win, even if it kills you? A ridiculous thing to say, isn't it? Bunshirō still had the leeway to think that.

Bunshirō was led to the site of the match by Sugiuchi Michizō, who today had been relegated to the role of a lackey. The white glow of the ground, illumined by the sun, struck his eyes. The afternoon sun shone calmly over the tips of the old cedars and from there cast its clear light upon the surface of the earth.

In the seats at the front sat a row of grave, black-garbed figures in surcoats and formal trousers who appeared to be domain officials, while elsewhere other men of the Corps of Vassals surrounded the site on three sides. Some wore surcoats; some did not. Some sat on reed mats spread on the ground; some stood at the rear.

Bunshirō looked from where he stood toward the place where he would meet his opponent. Another man stood there, his sleeves tied back, his headband fastened, his bamboo practice sword suspended in his left hand. It was Okitsu Shinnojō, a tall man with slightly sunken cheeks. He was said to be the fourth son of the Okitsu family, mounted samurai from Yamabuki-chō. This was the first time Bunshirō had seen his face.

But he had seen him from behind, looking out from the barred window of the dojo. Okitsu would have been two or three years older than Bunshirō. He had sprung to his feet and now stood, his eyes unblinking and fixed upon Bunshirō.

The referee, from the middle of the ground, called the two together. The referee was Ono Kigen, master of the Mugai school of swordsmanship at the Ono Dojo. He was a small, older man, his hair graying, with a long beard on the chin of his florid face, but the glare of his eyes seemed sharp enough to pierce a man. The two opponents, in obedience to Ono's orders, turned to the seats at the front and bowed. That, of course, would be where the ranking officials of the domain had gathered.

Semishigure

As he bowed, Bunshirō caught sight of his master, Ishiguri Yazaemon, sitting amongst those at the front. Yazaemon was discussing something with a dark-complected man at his side whose pate was unshaven. He was not looking toward Bunshirō. The man with the unshaven pate appeared to be in his fifties and was wearing a sleeveless garment rather than a surcoat. Bunshirō's momentary impression was of a man whose face resembled that of a bird-beaked demon.

At the referee's signal, Bunshirō and Okitsu bowed to each other, slid smoothly back into position, and poised their swords. The people who until then had been whispering softly, suddenly hushed as their swords raised.

So they should, Bunshirō thought as he fixed his gaze upon Okitsu, poised there beyond the tip of his sword. Okitsu held firm in the mid-position; not the slightest gap could be detected his defenses. His stance and the disposition of his arms appeared to mask both suppleness and limitless flexibility; he could shift into either offense or defense depending upon the situation. That much was clear.

Attack—that's all I can do, Bunshirō thought. Okitsu seemed to be waiting for Bunshirō to make a move, to which he would then respond. If Bunshirō did not make a move, that, too, would suffice. He could hold them deadlocked until Bunshirō fell into the trap of making a sudden move. That is what Okitsu's posture seemed to say.

Bunshirō slowly inched his left foot forward and gently raised his sword into the figure eight position. In that posture, his enemy's attack would be drawn toward his left side, and he would be in position to attack with a single deadly blow. Holding to that position, he began little by little circling to the right.

The distance between them was about eight yards. But at the

Ishiguri Dojo, in an attack, that distance could be closed in an instant. Okitsu Shinnojō, as if to say he was well aware of that, kept his piercing eyes fixed upon Bunshirō as he rotated his body to the right. His sword in mid-position, not the slightest gap in his defenses.

But advantage now lay with the one who moved. Bunshirō was moving in a circle with Okitsu at the center, and when he had almost come full circle, a gap opened in Okitsu's defenses.

4

Every one of the pebbles had been cleared from the site, after which fine sand was spread over the surface, leveling it as if with an iron. The two men stood barefoot on this surface.

But perhaps a pebble that had been missed still stood out from the earth. For when Okitsu moved, his footing trembled ever so slightly, and he replaced his foot in the same position. Had Bunshirō failed to notice, it would have been but an instant's miss, but he pushed off with full force and struck at that gap with his weapon.

But Okitsu's sword, as he fought back against Bunshirō's attack, was wielded with frighteningly phenomenal speed. In countering Bunshirō's blow, Okitsu had advanced a step, and the two men's swords struck each other almost simultaneously. Bunshirō's sword struck Okitsu's left shoulder. Okitsu's sword struck Bunshirō' torso.

"Hit!" Ono Kigen lifted his white fan high, then pointed it at Bunshirō. It appeared to be a draw, but Ono saw that Bunshirō's sword had struck Okitsu's shoulder an instant earlier. Bunshirō knew that this was so, and Okitsu Shinnojō, too, appeared to know. There must have been between 150 and 200 spectators

Semishigure

present, but when Ono rendered his decision, an indescribable gasp pervaded the site.

"Second Round!" Ono's voice rose above the buzz of the crowd, and Bunshirō and Okitsu quickly slid back and took their places at the proper distance from each other. Again, no one so much as coughed, and silence returned to the shrine.

Bunshirō once more raised his sword to the figure eight position. And then waited, motionless. This time Okitsu would probably attack, he thought. If, in his impatience after taking a hit, he should launch a careless attack, Bunshirō was prepared to thwart it with a single blow. With this in mind, Bunshirō calmly observed Okitsu.

But to his surprise, Okitsu did not move. The tip of his sword, poised in mid-position, rose and fell slightly, and he once lightly repositioned his feet, but his stance was defensive and he showed not the slightest sign that he might attack. Behind that sword poised in mid-position, Bunshirō could see the sunken cheeks of Okitsu's face and his broad shoulders. His eyes remained fixed upon Bunshirō, but no expression whatever appeared on Okitsu's face.

Time passed. Bunshirō moved his feet forward, bit by bit. If Okitsu was not inclined to attack, he thought, then he himself would have to make a move. Okitsu's defense was impregnable; but it was not that he had no idea how to break through it.

Bunshirō again inched forward. Whereupon Okitsu, too, made his first move forward. He was now showing a willingness to join battle. Like a spider on the surface of the water, Okitsu approached silently, his movements swift and smooth.

Little by little, both sides advanced until the distance between them closed to almost six yards, whereupon Bunshirō slipped first to the right, and then back to the left, and left again.

At the Ishiguri Dojo, this sort of footwork was called the plover's hop.

The plover's hop was used against an opponent who maintained a firm defense. It was an active measure, meant to shake the enemy's defense, in the course of which one might spot a gap and attack it. To the right, and then to the left, Bunshirō lurched lightly, all the while searching intently for an opening.

But Okitsu Shinnojō showed no sign of change in response to Bunshirō's movements. When Bunshirō moved right, Okitsu would swivel his body to the left. When Bunshirō moved left, Okitsu would swivel right, as naturally as if he were being blown by a breeze, yet never varying his stance even slightly, his sword still poised in mid-position. And then, Okitsu began gradually to slide his feet forward. He did it of his own accord, his first change of stance.

At that first sign of movement, Bunshirō gave a sharp cry and attacked. It was not that Okitsu's change of stance left him unguarded. But there did appear just a hair's breadth of a gap in his hitherto impregnable defense. Bunshirō's attack was meant to widen that opening. Strangely, however, Okitsu's defense overwhelmed Bunshirō. Just as he was shifting to the attack, he felt an uneasy sense that he was falling into Okitsu's trap. Yet to break through this tenacious defense, he did have to search for an opening and attack it.

Okitsu deflected Bunshirō's attack without dodging it. Their two swords clashed, and in the next instant the two men shot past each other so close they could feel each other's breath.

The moment he turned about, Bunshirō raised his sword to the figure eight position. Whereupon he saw Okitsu dashing back across the eight yards or so that separated them. Bunshirō's attack had not simply expanded a gap in Okitsu's defense, it seemed to have drawn him into an attack.

Semishigure

Or was it that his defense was just a pretense, and that attack was Okitsu's true specialty. The determined speed with which he covered the distance between them certainly suggested as much, as did the ease with which he raised his sword to the upper position as he ran.

From the very start it was battle he had desired. Bunshirō promptly prepared to defend himself against Okitsu's attack. He evaded Okitsu's sword as the blow came down directly in front of him. Okitsu being a tall man, added to which he came on at alarming speed, meant there was ferocious force in his attack.

Bunshirō hopped half a step back at an angle, and in that way escaped the full force of the attack. As he moved, he raised his sword to the figure eight position and prepared to strike at the path Okitsu's body would take, but then Okitsu's sword struck a hard blow to his body on the side he himself was poised to strike from.

"Hit!" This time Ono Kigen's white fan pointed straight at Okitsu Shinnojō. Seeing this, Bunshirō and Shinnojō, as if by mutual agreement, swiftly retreated. About twelve yards separated them. There they halted and awaited the referee's call.

His bamboo practice sword suspended in his left hand, Bunshirō stared at Okitsu. The pain in his side did not trouble him, but an empty feeling remained as if all the blood had drained from his head.

Was that it? He wondered. It was exactly as Ishikawa had said: Okitsu's sword had rebounded from ground level.

<u>5</u>

Bunshirō's body still trembled with tension, for he feared he could not fathom fully the technique Okitsu had used to defeat him. Bunshirō had seen with perfect clarity both Okitsu's body as he came rushing at him and the first blow of his attack.

When he hopped back half a step in order to evade that blow, Bunshirō felt he had made the move with ease. To evade Okitsu's attack, it had been enough to hop just half a step back. He kept the distance short because he meant it not as a means of flight, but an aid to mounting a counterattack. Bunshirō was totally focused, both physically and mentally, upon one aim: if Okitsu's body were to stray from its course even the least little bit, in that instant Bunshirō would be in position to strike a blow that could not fail to stop him.

But Okitsu had stopped dead in his tracks. Then his dark form loomed to fill Bunshirō's field of vision, and in that instant Okitsu's weapon rebounded from below, so rapidly his eyes could not follow it, and struck his torso. That was all that Bunshirō could remember. Perhaps in that instant after Bunshirō sidestepped him, Okitsu had swiveled back, rotating his wrist whilst his weapon was still in flight, and sent it slicing upward in the opposite direction, but Bunshirō failed to understand the technique that enabled him to do that.

"Third Round!" Ono Kigen's voice resounded. Bunshirō returned to himself and took his position. At first he poised his sword in mid-position, then slowly began moving forward until he reckoned the distance between them to be about ten yards. There he halted, calmly raised his sword to the figure eight position, and stared hard at Okitsu's posture.

Okitsu, for the third time, was poised in mid-position. He showed not a trace of his previous stormy aggression but took a firm defensive stance. His cold eyes glared at Bunshirō.

Bunshirō stood motionless. Okitsu, too, remained motionless. Time passed. In the interim the sun had sunk a bit lower, and the tips of the cedars were now shaded. Sunlight still shone brilliantly upon half the grounds of the shrine, but the long shadows of the two men had disappeared. Abandoning himself to the flow of time as he held himself in the figure eight position and searched for a gap in his opponent's defense, Bunshirō at last managed to abandon all concern for his opponent's technique.

All right then—once more! Come on! he thought. Bunshirō now saw how he had done it. It was the same as what Ishikawa Sōroku had described, of that he was certain. And that was all he needed to know. Whether Okitsu would try the same trick again, he did not know, but it now occurred to him that if he did try it again, there were ways he could contrive a response.

Bunshirō checked his stance, sword still poised in the figure eight, consciously relaxed his arms and legs then prepared himself to wait, his mind cleared, for Okitsu to make a move. He could then choose whatever response might be required.

In that state of clarity, Bunshirō registered every minute movement of Okitsu's body. Okitsu shifted the position of his feet. His eyes sharp, all expression wiped away, the hue of the blood in his face seemed to change. And just as Bunshirō realized this, Okitsu came at him with ferocious speed. His sword was raised to the upper position, almost resting upon his right shoulder.

Bunshirō, too, pushed off and ran forward. His sword bent back over his right shoulder like a reed bending in a strong wind. In an instant, the two covered the distance of ten yards, and their swords clashed at almost the very middle of the site. At first they flew apart as if they had collided with something sizzling, and when they met again, Okitsu's movements were slightly quicker.

As he charged in, Okitsu struck at Bunshirō's shoulder. Bunshirō evaded the blow and knocked the weapon aside. But this time, Bunshirō saw Okitsu's sword, which he had knocked down, bend like whip and bound back from below. Okitsu's feet were already turned, his toes pointing toward Bunshirō.

So that's how? A shiver ran down Bunshirō's backbone. Okitsu had aimed a blow at his shoulder and then reversed his sword so that he could strike from below, either at his gauntlet or at his torso. Bunshirō now realized that this technique of Okitsu's was not a series of separate moves but a single strategy. The emphasis of the attack was on the second blow. The first blow, aimed at his shoulder, was only a feint. The real point of the attack was the slash from below. That was why his sword flew with almost supernatural speed on the rebound.

Bunshirō, without an instant's hesitation, struck Okitsu's gauntlet as it came into view. The two men simultaneously gave a cry of attack as they struck out and rushed past each other.

Was that fast enough? With that hair-raising thought, Bunshirō halted and turned to the rear. Did I hit him? Or did Okitsu's sword hit me on the rebound? It was so close, he himself did not know.

When Bunshirō looked back, he could see that the referee Ono Kigen's white fan was pointed toward him. And when Ono signaled his victory, Bunshirō saw Okitsu Shinnojō, who was facing his way, quietly drop his bamboo sword. A great sigh of admiration—"Ooh"—arose from the spectators, and like a rolling wave spread throughout the shrine. Surrounded by the buzz of voices, Okitsu, moving with utter listlessness, bent to pick up his sword.

At this point, Bunshirō could feel his entire body streaming with hot sweat. His face was bathed in sweat; his breast was soaked. As he wiped his face with the sleeve of his practice gear, he waited for Okitsu to retrieve his sword and turn his way.

Semishigure

How did I happen to see that? Bunshirō wondered. That reversal of the wrist that enabled him to strike on the rebound. The tips of Okitsu's toes pointed toward Bunshirō, betraying his intent to attack. Bunshirō had no memory of striking that single blow to Okitsu's gauntlet. It was as if it were guided by the gods.

The two men bowed to each other. Bunshirō bowed also to his master, Ishiguri Yazaemon, in his seat at the front and then left the curtained area. Sugiuchi Michizō, his face glowing with excitement, grasped Bunshirō's hand, apparently too thrilled even to speak. When he emerged from the enclosure, Satake and Maruoka, unusually for them, greeted him with smiles.

Cloudburst

1

As he entered Bunshirō's room but before sitting down, Owada Ippei said, "Hey, congratulate me!" Hearing which, and looking up at his face, Bunshirō knew exactly what Ippei wanted to tell him. At last, it seemed, that day had come

"Don't say another word, Ippei." Bunshirō held up his hand and silenced him before he could speak. There wasn't another man as open as Ippei, Bunshirō thought, his feelings of affection for him welling up anew.

"First let me say it."

"All right then, say it," said Ippei, suppressing a smile as he looked at Bunshirō. Looking back, Bunshirō, too, could not but smile.

"It must be that now, at last, a bride has been found for you."

"You got it!"

"Well, first of all, my congratulations." Bunshirō offered Ippei—who at last had seated himself, a great smile coving his face—his best wishes. "And who is the young lady?"

"She's the daughter of Ikeuchi, the Financial Inspector."

"The Ikeuchi who live in Urushibara-chō?"

"That's right. It's always darkest at the base of the lamp."

"Really? Right in your own neighborhood?"

The Ikeuchi, if he remembered rightly, were enfeoffed at about seventy koku. It was somehow just like Ippei, Bunshirō thought, that he should search high and low, and then end up marrying a girl from his own neighborhood.

"I suppose, then, you'll have seen the girl's face. What's she like? A beauty?"

"Well, actually …" Unusually for Ippei, he looked perplexed. "I don't really know what she looks like. I may have seen her when we were children, but I've no memory of it."

"That's too bad."

"But Bunshirō …" Ippei lowered his voice and drew his face nearer. "The girl's name seems to be Kotoyo, and once every ten days she goes to a nun in the temple Jōrakuin for calligraphy lessons. I want to get a peek at her then. Will you come with me?"

"Don't do it, Ippei," Bunshirō said. "If word should get out that you've done something like that, and the engagement you've been at such pains to arrange should be broken off, that would be dreadful."

"True enough, but …"

"And consider your present standing." Bunshirō purposely lectured him in an officious manner. It was not as though he had never before wished to lecture Ippei for remaining such an incorrigible naughty boy. Ippei was past the age when he could be forgiven such pranks, Bunshirō had thought for some time now. "Neither you nor I derive our standing from our parents. We're both the heads of our own families now. No one else is going to look after us. The time has come when everything we want done we must do for ourselves."

"Speaking of which, you should be moving out of here before

long …" As he spoke, Ippei looked all around the tiny room. "You'll be moving to the district commissioners' quarter, they say. Will that be more spacious than here?"

"Quite a bit more. It will be a house."

"So when will you be moving?"

"About ten days from now. A lot later than I expected."

"I'll come and help you."

"I appreciate that, but I don't really need any help. We've decided to ask the servants from my brother's house." Then Bunshirō continued. "Besides, the head of the Owada house mustn't be so frivolous as to hide his face in a headscarf and come help us move house."

"What a stiff and formal fellow you've become."

"That's right. I fully intended to be stiff and formal," Bunshirō said. "There is no need for you to help us move. And you're not to go spying on Kotoyo-san. You'd best save that pleasure for your wedding day."

"Aw, you're no fun," Ippei muttered. Then suddenly he added: "We're finished; that's what you mean to say, isn't it? That our days of foolishness are finished?"

"That's right, Ippei."

"When we could fight with Yamane and Emori, those were our days of glory. We can't fight any more."

"Well, yes," Bunshirō agreed. And Ippei, too, nodded in assent.

"I'm now officially serving in the Corps of Pages, and you're going to be serving under the district commissioners. When will you start?"

"About a year from now."

"Hmm." Ippei sighed. "So that's it, then? We're finished?"

"We can't be children forever. But when is your wedding?"

"Next spring, they say."

Semishigure

"Sooner than I expected. You'll invite me won't you?"

"Of course. If I can, I'd like to invite Yonosuke from Edo, too." Ippei smiled as he spoke, and then lowered his voice again. "But Bunshirō. I don't need you to tell me that once I'm married, that will be the end of my escapades."

"Yes, I suppose it will."

"But before then, come with me once more to Somekawa-chō. That's a grown-up's entertainment," Ippei said exuberantly. "You and Yonosuke ran out on me along the way. Cowards, both of you. This time don't you run out on me."

"All right, I'll do it," Bunshirō said.

2

Bunshirō was to go to the dojo after dinner that evening. The master had summoned him. If it seemed Ippei's conversation might go on too long, he would have to concoct a plausible excuse to send him home, Bunshirō thought, but he needn't have worried. Ippei went on to tell how the offertory tournament five days earlier was still the talk everywhere in the castle, and that apparently was the last of what he had to say. When he saw the window darkening, he hastened to leave.

There may have been more to tell about how his engagement had been arranged, but it appeared he was so happy that he just couldn't stick to that subject.

Bunshirō had told his mother that he would be going to the dojo, so she had served dinner early, and as soon as he had finished, he prepared to leave. After stepping down to the earthen-floored vestibule, he turned to his mother, who had come to see him off.

"I understand a marriage has been arranged for Ippei."

"Well, that's splendid," his mother said. "Whose daughter is the bride?"

"He says she's the daughter of the Ikeuchi, of Urushibara-chō."

"My! But doesn't Ikeuchi-sama live in Ippei's neighborhood?" Toyo covered her mouth with her hand as she smiled, for until then, she had heard nothing but reports that no one would marry Ippei.

"As he himself said, it's always darkest at the base of the lamp."

"Even so ... My, that's wonderful." Toyo looked up at Bunshirō; then glancing down said, "You, too, will have to start looking for a bride before long."

Bunshirō left the house. The faint chill of the night air enveloped his body. As was his habit, Bunshirō glanced over at the Yada house in the other building but saw only the usual light in the window. He headed out through the gateway in the hedge.

After we move, what will become of them? Bunshirō wondered. He had heard the talk of an adoption, but the Yada family had gone on month after month with no word from the domain. They were allotted a dilapidated old barracks and paid barely enough to survive on. The domain was treating the Yada family no better now than when they had first moved them to Fukiya-chō. Their treatment differed outrageously from that of Bunshirō's family, whose stipend had been restored and who had been allotted a new place to move to. Bunshirō failed to understand what the reason for that difference might be. At times, Bunshirō suspected that the domain meant only to support Yada Sakunojō's mother as long as she remained alive. Even then, though, he could not imagine what the significance might be of sparing the House of Yada while barely sustaining the mother.

But what were they to do after he moved? He wondered because he knew that since he had been restored to his former stipend, his mother had sometimes taken rice and kimonos to the Yada. Just thinking about the Yada family depressed him.

Bunshirō shook his head, trying to banish the thoughts of Yada's extraordinarily beautiful widow to which he was so prone. The scrutiny of the domain the Yada family were subjected to; the hand that had grasped Bunshirō's arm and the fragrance of her makeup; her sharp voice in standing up for that man and reproving her younger brother. When he tried to ponder any one of these matters, however slightly, it was more than the eighteen-year-old Bunshirō could handle.

I try to understand. But actually I hardly understand any of it at all, Bunshirō thought. The truth lay shrouded in haze beyond a bank of mist. He crossed a bridge to the west over the Goken River, thinking he might better ponder Ippei's engagement than this.

Bunshirō carrying his lantern was the only person walking that road along the riverbank. There was no one else in sight. In the present season, as autumn deepened, sunset and nightfall came early. The hour was not late, but it felt like he was walking through town far into the night. From somewhere he could hear the fading cry of an insect.

It's good that Ippei is so open, Bunshirō thought. He was remembering Ippei's face, and how he was unable to conceal his joy. Compared to Ippei, I myself could not be called open, he thought. But tonight he was to meet the master, Ishiguri Yazaemon, to discuss the transmission of a secret technique of sword fighting. It could be that his instruction would begin straightaway. Having been told to come prepared for that, Bunshirō had changed clothes completely. Though of course he could tell no one else what he was doing.

Bunshirō turned off the riverbank road into the street that

passed through Kaji-machi and before long arrived at the Ishiguri Dojo. He entered the gate and made his way around to the master's quarters, just as he had been told. When he announced himself, the middle-aged maidservant who looked after the house came out and led Bunshirō to the room where his master was.

"Yes, he was saying he wanted to see you tonight," Yazaemon said suddenly as he waited for Bunshirō to be seated. Bunshirō understood that Yazaemon was referring to the only other recipient of the secret at the Ishiguri Dojo. He was the man who would transmit the secret techniques of Cloudburst to Bunshirō, rather than the master himself. What made the announcement sound so abrupt was that Yazaemon hadn't yet mentioned the man's name.

"I see," said Bunshirō. "Am I to meet him here?"

"No, he says you're to come to his mansion."

His mansion? Bunshirō looked speechless into his master's face.

"The man who is to transmit the secret to you is Kaji Oribe-dono."

"Kaji-sama? You mean *the* Kaji-sama?"

Bunshirō, despite himself, stared dumbstruck at Yazaemon. Kaji Oribe-no-Shō was an uncle of the lord of the domain and previously had been an eminent elder. He was head of the greatest of all great families in the domain.

"Actually Oribe-dono, too, saw your match. You must have noticed him there." Yazaemon smiled. "He praised you repeatedly. We decided the matter of the transmission on our way back."

So that was him, then, Bunshirō thought. Sitting at the front, discussing something with Yazaemon. The dark-complected man, his pate unshaven. That must have been Kaji Oribe-no-Shō.

Semishigure

Bunshirō knew very little about Kaji Oribe-no-Shō. He had heard the name. But only because Ikoma Reisuke, between lectures at the school, had told them what a great elder he had been, establishing various enterprises within the domain, encouraging the spread of learning, governing wisely. Oribe-no-Shō had also been serving as chief elder when the domain academy, the Sanseikan, was founded.

But Kaji Oribe-no-Shō, when still a young man in his thirties, having demonstrated his abilities as governor of the domain for several years, suddenly retired. The mansion of Oribe-no-Shō was toward the rear of Daikan-chō. It was a large building, surrounded by stone walls and a dark, dense grove. From the outside, only the tiles of a tall roof could be seen. As the youngest brother of the previous lord, when he had succeeded as head of his well-born mother's family, the Kaji, Oribe-no-Shō had been granted this mansion, known as the Cedar Grove Mansion.

Having withdrawn from government, Oribe-no-Shō secluded himself in this mansion and was no longer to be seen in the company of others. Neither did he ever come to the castle. The change in him was extreme, and at the time people whispered that there must be suspicious circumstances behind the reclusion of Oribe-no-Shō.

All of this took place fifteen years ago, when Bunshirō was still a child. Yazaemon's expression as he spoke suggested that it was only proper that this figure, shrouded in mystery of some sort, should be the one to teach Bunshirō the secret techniques.

Bunshirō finally regained his composure. If this man had learnt the art under Yazaemon, and had been vouchsafed the secret techniques by him, Bunshirō now realized, Kaji Oribe-no-Shō was not likely to be a demon or a serpent of any sort.

"Well then, should I be off straightaway?"

"I suppose so. You could set out soon," Yazaemon said. "But Oribe-dono doesn't sleep nights. There's no need to rush," he added, somewhat ominously.

<u>3</u>

Yazaemon took Bunshirō into the instruction hall and chose a hardwood practice sword for him to take to the mansion. Grasping the sword, enclosing it in a sheath, and suspending a lantern before him, Bunshirō again set out through the dark streets.

From Kaji-machi to Daikan-chō was not a great distance, and between the two there was a commercial district. As Bunshirō cut across the main street of that district, he could see lanterns scattered here and there along it. Then he entered Daikan-chō. Along this row of mansions surrounded by dark planked fences, only rarely did a glimmer of light leak out. The glow of Bunshirō's lantern seemed to illumine only lacquer-black darkness before it. Yet perhaps because the hour was not yet late, sounds from within a house somewhere reached him, and then at one corner the sonorous chanting of Noh.

But as he penetrated further into the quarter, fewer and fewer glimmers of light and snatches of sound reached him from houses along the way. Then, just as he was becoming aware of that peculiar stillness that permeates a cluster of great mansions in the night, Bunshirō sensed the presence of some great object bearing down upon him from ahead. This, he could tell even in the night, was a dark grove of trees. The night sky spread out above him was only slightly lighter than this grove. And at the very base of that great dark mass he could just make out a point of light from a lamp at the gate.

Soon, however, he was standing before a gatehouse so grand

he had to gaze upward to take it all in. Bunshirō knocked on the wicket, announced his name, and requested admission, whereupon a light appeared at a barred window to the right and he could see the movements of a man within. Before long the wicket opened. It was a short, old man, perhaps in his sixties, who opened the door. Bunshirō stated his name again and, with greater grace than he expected, was shown into the grounds of the mansion. It appeared the man had been informed that Bunshirō would be coming tonight.

They walked for a time through the tall trees. Then, when finally they entered the vestibule of the building that appeared to be the main house, Bunshirō was asked to wait there. But immediately a young samurai appeared to guide him. The old man left, and Bunshirō was shown within.

It was a large building. As they walked, they passed through any number of rooms, some of them lit, some dark. The interior of the house was calm and quiet. Only once, from the end of a long corridor, did the movement of a bright light and the cheery voices of women escape. That may have been the kitchen that he saw.

Bunshirō and the samurai guiding him proceeded still further into the recesses, then, where the hallway took a turn, they came to well-lighted shoji. This was Oribe-no-Shō's sitting room. Once the young samurai had shown Bunshirō in, he left. Oribe-no-Shō, who had been sitting on a high-backed, heavily decorated chair at a round, long-legged desk such as Bunshirō had never before seen, rose and approached him. Oribe-no-Shō was indeed the man Bunshirō had seen at the tournament: his pate unshaven, his hair graying, the well-formed nose on his slightly dark-complected face giving a bird-like impression.

"Unusual, is it?" Oribe-no-Shō said, glancing toward the desk and chair in the corner as he sat down at the far side of the low table. He must have noticed the expression on Bunshirō's face when he entered the room. "When I was young, I saw a foreigner using one, so I had these made for my own use. They're good when you're reading a book."

Oribe-no-Shō's words helped to relax the tension of their first meeting. When Bunshirō introduced himself formally, Oribe-no-Shō nodded in acknowledgment and told him to relax. What he said next was unexpected.

"In last year's political upheaval …" Oribe-no-Shō began, "a number of people died, and some families ceased to exist; but your family survived. I think your family stipend was restored later, too. Do you know why?"

"No, I have no idea," Bunshirō said; and his heart began beating wildly. Does this man know, and is he going to solve the mystery for me? he wondered. "But I did think it strange."

"That figures. Satomura handled the matter clumsily." Oribe-no-Shō was speaking of the man who, after the scandal, rose to become the chief elder. "And have you heard that the upheaval had to do with the succession?"

"Yes, I have heard a bit about that."

"O-Fune …" Oribe-no-Shō spoke of the favored concubine of the lord of the domain without the slightest hint of respect. "O-Fune does want her son to succeed as the next lord of the domain, and she is doing her best to eliminate Shima-no-Kami. Such nonsensical endeavors are indeed underway, but that was not what the upheaval was all about. The fact is, though, it was a leadership struggle, with each faction trying to lead the other about by the nose. The question of the succession was nothing but a front for that."

In the one faction, Oribe-no-Shō told him, were the former

junior elder, Inagaki Chūbei and the present chief elder, Satomura Sanai; and in the other faction were the second-ranking elder, Yokoyama Matasuke, and the former elder, Hirata Tatewaki.

"In the course of the struggle, the Inagaki faction expelled the Kanematsu clan from the domain and forced Hirata to commit seppuku. Their pretext was that Kanematsu and Hirata were supporters of Shima-no-Kami and were attempting to eliminate Matsunojō and O-Fune. They were able to punish them that severely on such a pretext because His Lordship did not get on well with Shima-no-Kami and was fond of Matsunojō. Besides which, there was some truth to the claim that Kanematsu and Hirata were working to eliminate Matsunojō, and they had obtained proof of it. Yet the opposing faction, too, had assembled evidence that Inagaki and Satomura were working to unseat Shima-no-Kami as heir. But the Inagaki faction struck first. That's how it happened."

Bunshirō, his body rigid, listened intently to Oribe-no-Shō's words.

"The Inagaki faction ended up the winners. But they, too, slipped up. They failed to catch the biggest fish. Do you know who that was?"

"Would that be Yokoyama-sama?"

"Right! It's Matasuke." A faint smile arose on Oribe-no-Shō's face. Then suddenly he looked up and laughed derisively. "Yokoyama Matasuke is even more of a trickster than Inagaki or Satomura. Satomura and the others searched until their eyes were bloodshot, trying to find some lapse, but they couldn't find proof of a single offense they could pin on Matasuke. Matasuke was indeed the central figure and leader of the opposing faction, but the Inagaki faction were unable to lay a finger on the man. And so, at a single stroke, they forced Matasuke's twelve cohorts to commit seppuku and beheaded one foot soldier, Soné Seihachi. That was how they wrenched off Yokoyama Matasuke's arms and legs and prevented him making any further mischief."

4

Bunshirō felt as if the mist had cleared, that all that had been concealed from him about the incident two years earlier was now revealed. He felt a strong sense of gratitude to Oribe-no-Shō for this first convincing explanation of that mystery. Yet at the same time it left him wondering about this man. Might he not be mistaken to take someone who grasped this clearly all the complexities of the domain's inner workings for a recluse who had turned his back upon the world? Just as he was thinking that Oribe-no-Shō must still be in close contact with someone high up in the domain, Oribe-no-Shō nodded, as if in agreement, to Bunshirō.

"Now let me tell you how it was that your family was restored to your former stipend."

"Yes."

"When your father, Sukezaemon; Hitotsuyanagi Yaichirō of the Corps of Pages; Yada Sakunojō, the personal attendant; Sekiguchi Shinsaku, an inspector of soldiers—valuable men, all of them—were forced to commit seppuku, Yokoyama did not lift a hand or make a move. Inagaki and his ilk charged them with treason and, quite as if they had the backing of His Lordship, went ahead with their scheme. Yokoyama Matasuke, reckoning that with one false move he, too, could be caught out, never so much as left his house. Yokoyama read the situation rightly," Oribe-no-Shō said. "At the time, the Inagaki faction were ready and waiting. If Yokoyama had shown the slightest sign of resistance, they would have dragged him before the investigators.

"It was only after the affair had quietened down a bit and the board of investigators had been disbanded that Yokoyama counterattacked. At a meeting of the Governing Council, they say, he held forth for an entire hour criticizing the opposition. But in his speech, he never criticized directly the Inagaki faction's handling of the matter. He merely delivered a scathing rebuke of the excess of a sentence that caused the death of so many talented men. It seems to have been a brilliant speech that appealed to the feelings of everyone who heard it. Throughout that entire hour in the Swan Room, the only voice to be heard was Yokoyama's. No one else so much as coughed, they say. And after Yokoyama's speech, there arose such a swell of sympathy for the surviving families, especially amongst the highest ranking officialdom, that the Inagaki faction now found themselves in a tight spot. For when he spoke, Yokoyama actually produced a letter from the villages of Kanai and Aohata in the Onuma District begging that the life of Maki Sukezaemon be spared."

Bunshirō stared wide-eyed at Oribe-no-Shō. This was extraordinary.

"Some years earlier, the waters of the Goken River had risen, flooding the streets of the town. On that night, when the Defense Works Unit cut through the embankment upstream so as to lower the waters, Sukezaemon demanded that the location of the cut be changed and that seems to have saved ten chō of rice land."

"I remember that night," Bunshirō said. "I was there."

"Oh?" Oribe-no-Shō exclaimed, gazing at Bunshirō's face. Then he continued, unhurriedly, to speak.

"Well the people of Kanai and Aohata were grateful for this, and never forgot what Sukezaemon had done for them."

"Tonight is the first I've heard of this," Bunshirō said.

"This, ultimately, is what governing is all about," Oribe-no-Shō said. "Sympathy with the feelings of the governed. So remember what your father did. The peasants in those two villages took their entreaty to the mansion of Inspector General Ogata. That was illegal but since this was a matter of urgency, Ogata accepted it and took it to Satomura's place. But Satomura ignored it, and Ogata took it to Yokoyama's mansion; and that, apparently, was how it came into Yokoyama's possession.

"The Inagaki faction were intending to watch for an opportune moment and then abolish the families of everyone they had forced to commit seppuku; but Matasuke's speech made that impossible. Not only that, they had to think of some way to perpetuate those families. And so in families where there was a legitimate heir, they cut their stipend to a third of what it had been and let them go on. If they hadn't, the mood then was such that things might not have calmed down.

"Your family in particular was restored to your full former stipend thanks to the letter of entreaty I mentioned a moment ago, but you needn't thank Yokoyama for that." A cynical smile crossed Oribe-no-Shō's face. "Yokoyama wasn't thinking of your family when he produced the letter at that meeting. He did it to protect himself. The letter was nothing but a means of drawing attention to the faults of the Inagaki faction and arousing sympathy for his own faction. But having done so, and having himself become the second-ranking elder a short while ago, he is now in much the same situation as he was before. A strange man, that. But do you grasp all the details?"

"I've listened humbly and gratefully to all that you've said." Bunshirō expressed his thanks with bowed head. "Having heard what you just told me, my questions about these past years have now vanished."

Semishigure

"Mmm," Oribe-no-Shō nodded. "But that doesn't mean you can now rest easy. As I said before, it was the intention of the Inagaki faction to abolish the families of everyone they forced to commit seppuku. That, too, was for their own protection. As they see it, allowing you to survive does them more harm than good. But be that as it may, I understand you've met Satomura?"

"Yes, when it was announced that our stipend would be restored, I called just that once at his mansion."

"I don't know what Satomura Sanai told you on that occasion, but you may be sure that he still means to abolish your house if he can catch you off guard. So don't let your guard down."

Bunshirō felt as if cold water had been poured down his back. He recalled that he had been told the same thing before, when he met District Commissioner Kashimura Yasuke.

"This may all be a bit complicated, but …" said Oribe-no-Shō, "I thought it best that you know this much before we begin your initiation."

5

It's just as this gentleman says, Bunshirō thought. Before he had come to the Kaji mansion, he had thought of his initiation in the secret teachings as simply a matter of technique. It was not that he had felt no joy or fear in acquiring the secrets of a technique unknown to others, but he had never thought of it as anything beyond that.

Yet having heard the whole story of the incident from Oribe-no-Shō, he realized that the affair was far from finished and that the malice directed toward himself and his family was still very much alive; hearing which, he now thought of it all very differently. It was not that he had never had vague premonitions, but even though Oribe-no-Shō had assured him that the danger was real, he still had no idea when disaster might strike.

This initiation into the secret technique ... Bunshirō was now thinking. This might be what would uphold his spirit, protect his mother from whatever disaster might come, and preserve the good name of his family.

"Well then, shall we go to the dojo?" Oribe-no-Shō said.

"Yes, please," Bunshirō replied with bowed head.

"I'll have someone guide you, so first you will bathe. Garments have been prepared for you. Once you've changed, you'll come to the instruction hall." Having said this, Oribe-no-Shō picked up the bell atop the table and rang it. It echoed for some time.

Led by the young samurai who had shown him to the sitting room, Bunshirō proceeded to the bath. The cypress-scented bathtub was brimming with cold water. As he poured bucket after bucket of water over himself, his body first chilled as if it would freeze, but then he could feel his mind clear, sharp as a blade.

When he emerged from the bath, he found a white kimono and white trousers laid out for him. Once he had finished drying his body and donning his garments, the young samurai, who seemed to have been waiting for him, reappeared and again led the way for Bunshirō. The two of them at first left the building, walked a short way along a path of stepping stones through the garden, and entered a different building. His guide left Bunshirō at the doorway and, having perhaps been ordered to do so, departed without a word. Carrying his hardwood sword, he entered the building. This was the instruction hall. On the altar to the gods at the head of the room stood a lamp, and beneath it, sat Oribe-no-Shō, who had of course changed into white. In addition to the lamp, only a single candle was burning. The hall was dark, but the highly polished floor glowed in the lamplight.

Semishigure

"Come here." Oribe-no-Shō called to Bunshirō. And when Bunshirō sat before him, he first made him swear never to tell another person about this secret technique. Thereafter he told him that his initiation could take place only at night and would require about seven nights. "Tonight I'll show you only the basic movements."

The two stood and bowed to the altar and then went to the center of the hall. Oribe-no-Shō placed Bunshirō with his sword poised in mid-position. Then, after calming his breath for a time, he slowly moved into the first position of that secret of swordplay, Cloudburst.

A shockwave ran through Bunshirō's breast, for Oribe-no-Shō's stance was beyond imagination. The hardwood sword in Oribe-no-Shō's right hand was held high in the figure eight position, but his left arm he extended lightly to the front, looking as if this were a position in some dance.

Early Spring

1

On the banks of the Goken River, the green of the grasses was growing deeper day by day. Spring was clearly on the way, but still there were whole days when the sun would be hidden behind gray clouds and a chill north wind would blow through every quarter of the castle town as if suddenly it had cut short the round of the seasons.

On such days, frigid ripples would rise on the waters of the Goken River as it flowed through town, giving people the impression that winter was returning. In the afternoon of one of those cold days, with no prior notice, Fusé Tsurunosuke came to call at Bunshirō's home on the edge of Tenjin-chō.

"You did well to find this place," Bunshirō said as he invited him in.

"I did search a bit," Fusé said. Perhaps because of the cold, Fusé Tsurunosuke's face was pale white, as if drained of blood. "This is much larger than your previous place," he said, as Bunshirō showed him into the sitting room. This was of course the first time he had come to the Rural Affairs Unit's quarter. Fusé seemed to be thinking of the barracks in Fukiya-chō where his head might bump against the ceiling; he had called there two or three times.

"At last a place that feels human." Bunshirō pushed the charcoal brazier toward Fusé.

"When did you move?"

"The end of last year," Bunshirō said. "It was cold." Not until the twenty-fourth of the Twelfth Month, when only a few days of the year remained, had the domain notified him that he was to move here before year's end. And no sooner had he completed the move, with the help of people from his elder brother's household, than Bunshirō had to run busily about greeting the family of his superior Kashimura and the other residents of the quarter.

"It was such a hectic time, what with moving and all, that I wasn't able to take proper leave of your sister. How is she? Still well?" When Bunshirō said this, Fusé looked away.

"You haven't heard about my sister?" Fusé had a strange air about him.

"What's the matter?" Bunshirō suddenly sensed something ominous, and his voice turned sharp. "Did something happen to her?"

"She's dead," Fusé said. Then he looked back, but with his face turned deeply downward.

"She passed away, you say? When?"

"I heard the day before yesterday." Fusé finally looked up. For some reason he tried weakly to smile at Bunshirō, who was himself in a daze. "She was a foolish girl, my sister."

"Could you tell me about it?"

"Of course. That's why I came, because I want to tell you what happened."

It was five days earlier that the Fusé family were informed

that their daughter, Yada's widow, had gone missing. Fusé had no idea what might have happened. So he ran straightaway to the Nosé family. As it happened, it was exactly as he had thought. Ikunoshin had gone out the previous day and had not returned that evening. Come morning, they still had no idea where he might be. The Nosé family had sent people out searching for him and were in an uproar trying to find where he might have gone.

In the meantime, Ikunoshin's friends with whom he served at the castle discovered that Ikunoshin had been given a checkpoint pass for himself and his wife. Their destination was to be the hot springs at Momogase in the neighboring province. It was plain to see, now, that Fusé Tsurunosuke's sister, Yoshie, had run away from the castle town with Ikunoshin.

Both families recalled the people they had sent out in search of them. Tsurunosuke's elder brother and Ikunoshin's uncle, in great secrecy, applied for a pass to leave the province and set out for Momogase. When they arrived in Momogase, however, Ikunoshin and Yoshie were not there, and purely on a hunch, the two of them searched the outskirts of the hot springs. There, in a corner at the foot of a mountain, some distance from the village, they found a couple who had died together.

"Imagine! Just over that one mountain; there was very little snow there, so I suppose the sunlight must have been stronger there than here," Tsurunosuke said. He was talking about the neighboring province. "They say the bodies lay a little way apart on a sunny slope where the witch hazel was in bloom. It was a love suicide, they said, but ..." Tsurunosuke looked away again, in the opposite direction. He appeared to be suppressing a violent outburst of emotion. "But Kōta told me, after he returned ... Sorry—Kōta is the servant my brother took with him. Kōta said it was no love suicide. It looked like my sister had stabbed Nosé and then used the knife to kill herself. Nosé hadn't even drawn his sword."

"That's probably so," Bunshirō said. "Your sister was a strong-willed person." Contrary to what one might expect, it must have been Yada's widow who proposed that they run away, he thought. She must have grown totally weary of the domain's hopeless dithering as to what they would do with her and when, and so she herself would decide the fate of the Yada house; she would abscond and take Ikunoshin with her. Wasn't that it? "If you stop now and think about it, the way the domain treated the Yada family was neither to kill them nor to let them live. For a woman, that may well have been unbearable."

"But that was no reason to run away with a man like Nosé," Tsurunosuke said. His eyes were red as he looked at Bunshirō. "There must have been a better way to do it."

"There must be feelings that a woman knows but we men just don't understand." Bunshirō smiled faintly. He did not want to blame Yada's widow. In retrospect, she seemed a woman stricken by grave misfortune that she could never have anticipated. "Nosé Ikunoshin seems to have worshipped your sister. You can't say he was a bad companion for her on the road to death."

"I suppose you could think of it that way." Tsurunosuke looked over at Bunshirō. His face, so pale until a moment ago, was now beginning to show a bit of color. "Actually, though, my father was furious," Tsurunosuke said. "The Nosé family seem to have arranged to have Ikunoshin's body brought home. But my father says, 'Have her cremated straightaway.' It's enough just to bring home her bones, he thinks. Kōta went back yesterday to Momogase, where my brother is. They must be having my sister cremated about now."

"Really? Just her bones?" Bunshirō mumbled. It's cold here, but just over those mountains, their peaks hidden in clouds, the spring sun may be shining brightly—that, at least, was what Bunshirō wanted to think.

"Yes, my sister will come back as bones," said Tsurunosuke. "It can't be helped. And my father says he'll have her bones consigned to the grave of the unknown dead at our family temple."

"Grave of the unknown dead?" Bunshirō looked at Tsurunosuke in shock. Tsurunosuke nodded in agreement.

"She can't be buried in the grave of the Yada family, of course. But she can't be buried in the grave of her own family either. That could never be justified to our forebears, they say, and then there may be a bit of reticence from the Nosé family as well ..."

"But that's just too pitiful for the deceased, is it not?" Bunshirō said. "Your sister didn't bring this misfortune upon herself. And the way she was treated afterward by the domain was merciless. That's something everyone knows. No, I think your sister had abandoned all hope for her own future, and she chose this way of dying as a protest against those who had driven her to that extreme. No one can criticize or blame her for that."

"You are truly so good as to think that?"

"Of course I do. I lived right next to her under the same circumstances. I saw it all, so I knew very well what it was like. And it seemed to me your sister was beset by those same feelings."

"There's something that I regret," Tsurunosuke said in a troubled voice. "It concerns Nosé. At the time, I felt I just couldn't ignore what he was doing, and I even drew my sword, but knowing what I know now, I can't help thinking I should have pretended not to know. What I did may have been one thing that drove my sister to her death."

"Surely there's no need to probe that deeply into it," Bunshirō said. "From what you tell me, this was a bit different from something planned by them both as a love suicide. Your sister was a beautiful woman of high pride. Isn't it enough to think, as I said before, that she set out on a journey with a man who worshipped her at her side? I can't imagine that even Nosé objected very strongly to that."

"Yes, I'm really glad I came here. Thanks to you, I'm feeling a little better about this." At last, Tsurunosuke showed a slight smile. "Because I can't talk about this with anyone else," he said. "I hope my brother and I can at least persuade father to bury her bones in a corner of our family grave." Then Tsurunosuke left.

2

When he returned to his room after seeing Tsurunosuke off, Bunshirō went back to his reading stand but couldn't get interested in reading a book just then. As he gazed absently at the shoji, he felt all manner of memories of Yada's widow swirling about within his head.

Her smooth cheeks; her spirited eyes, turned up at their tips; her bright but unaffected manner of speaking; the fragrance of her makeup, always the same; her delicate arms with which she had embraced him in the dusk. And amidst these recollections, there was Tsurunosuke's voice, bubbling up like foam upon the water, saying they must now be cremating her, and Bunshirō imagining himself watching the smoke of her pyre rising into the pure blue of the spring heavens.

This world we live in … so fragile … Bunshirō thought. Deep emotion of this sort was not something he had experienced at age sixteen when faced with the death of his father. *This* deep emotion held an element of anger not present at his father's death.

When his father, Sukezaemon, died, he and his mother, the two survivors, were preoccupied with preserving the House of Maki. Day after day passed as if they had forgotten how to feel sad or angry. But now, those who robbed Yada's widow of her life were clearly to be seen.

The crime lies with the domain, Bunshirō thought. Unable to endure the domain's treatment, which had driven her to the brink of death, Yada's widow had hastened the end of her own life. Taking Nosé with her, as he had said to Tsurunosuke, must have been her feeble attempt to get back at those warrior class rules that bound her to the Yada house.

Bunshirō reached out, removed a letter from his letter box, and spread it out on his desk. It was a letter from Shimazaki Yonosuke in Edo that had come about a month earlier. He skipped over Yonosuke's description of what he himself was doing, unrolled the scroll to the point where he began writing about Fuku, and stopped there. Yonosuke always spoke of Fuku with the utmost respect, as "O-Fuku-sama." For some reason, he said, O-Fuku-sama continued to be held in ill repute in the Edo mansion. It might be that people around O-Fune-sama were intentionally maligning her, he thought, but it was also rumored that His Lordship's regard for her had dwindled. The situation was unclear. In any case, Yonosuke concluded, O-Fuku-sama was now surrounded by enemies. There was even speculation in the Edo mansion that she might be removed from her position as a concubine. Fuku, too … she could hardly be deemed fortunate, Bunshirō thought as he rolled up the letter and replaced it.

Yada's widow. Fuku. The misfortune of these women weighed heavily upon Bunshirō's feelings. And in the depths of that sinking feeling there stirred, as ever, a sense of anger.

Shall I step outside? The thought was prompted by a weak

Semishigure

ray of sunshine that appeared unexpectedly on the shoji before him, and even as he watched, it turned a bright, burning red. A cloud in the western sky may have parted just as sunset was approaching.

Bunshirō shut his book, stood, and re-arranged his clothes. In any case, he was no longer interested in reading the book. Taking only his short sword, he left the room. From the sitting room, he could hear the voice of a visitor. She was a relative of his mother, apparently the wife of the Uehara family. She spoke in a peculiarly high-pitched voice. Bunshirō hadn't even noticed when she arrived. He thought he ought to greet her, but when he turned to go that way, he heard Uehara's wife speak.

"That's right, Fukui-sama from Naitō-chō," she said. "They're enfeoffed at seventy-five koku, quite a bit more than yourselves. But both the parents and the young lady are unassuming and friendly people, not a family that are overly sensitive to income, you know. This proposal, Toyo-sama, why don't you give it some serious thought?"

His mother's voice was much softer when she replied and did not reach Bunshirō's ears.

"Yes. Yes. Of course," Uehara's wife said, apparently nodding repeatedly in response to something his mother had said. "She's pretty, she's tall, she's gentle natured. As a bride for a mother-and-son family, I'd say she's quite the perfect young lady."

"But in a marriage, after all, there is the matter of parity …" When his mother's voice finally reached Bunshirō, he heard that much, and then he walked away from the sitting room toward the interior of the house. He took care not to let his footsteps be heard.

Their property was not very large, only about twenty-five feet long, but the house was self-standing, and on the east and south sides, a narrow path ran past just outside the rooms. Bunshirō went back through the room where he had been and into the guest room beyond it, from where he descended to the stepping stone and left the house.

The Rural Affairs Unit's residential quarter was divided between two locations, both in the midst of commoners' houses. Shimazaki Yonosuke's home was in Somemono-chō, where the waters of the Goken River first overflowed when the river flooded. The quarter where Bunshirō lived was at the rear of Himono-chō. Both were fairly close to the castle, and the groves and stone ramparts of the castle could be seen when you stepped out to the main street.

Bunshirō made his way out to the alleyway that ran alongside the quarter and from there onward to the main street. There were shops here as well, and a great many homes of the cypress craftsmen lined the street. Just as the scent of indigo wafted through the air whenever he went to visit Yonosuke, in Bunshirō's own neighborhood it was the fragrance of cypress that permeated everything. There were few people out walking. The neighborhood was bathed in the red of the afternoon sun.

The sky, when he looked, was half-cleared, and in the west the sun was about to set, its rays slanting down into the town from a corner of the castle groves. On one side of the main street, pale dusk already lurked beneath the eaves, while on the other side, in sharp contrast, the low roofs, the dark weathered siding boards, and the gray shoji seemed about to burst into flame in the red rays of the sun that shone upon them. As he walked down the street, he could smell the fragrance of the wood and hear the sounds of the cypress craftsmen as they worked.

A marriage proposal? Bunshirō recalled the high-pitched voice of Uehara's wife. She must have been the bearer of a marriage proposal for Bunshirō. Bunshirō was nineteen. Next spring, it was decided, he was to begin work in the Rural Affairs Unit. There was nothing wrong with anyone bringing him offers of marriage.

But Bunshirō could not bring himself to take any genuine pleasure in this. There was Fuku and what he had just heard about Yada's widow. All this had left him feeling deeply depressed. But it was not just that, Bunshirō recalled that when the Maki family were living in wretched poverty in that barracks in Fukiya-chō, apart from his immediate family, none of their kinsmen had ever once called upon them or invited them to any of their celebrations. It was only after they had moved to their present quarters and the domain's decree was beyond doubt, that anyone came either to call or to invite them to their gatherings, whether in celebration or mourning. Prior to that, the Maki house had been regarded as a nuisance to the clan—"the god not to be approached lest he do you harm." More cold-hearted to the Maki family, they were, than to total strangers.

Even the Uehara … the same as all the others. Just as that thought occurred to Bunshirō, a samurai in formal linens came walking toward him. Coming down this street, it must be someone from his own quarter, he thought. As the man drew nearer, he turned out to be a rural inspector named Kusaka, a man of about forty. Bunshirō imagined that Kusaka could not be unaware of his situation, but he only cast a disapproving glance at Bunshirō, probably for being out and about with only a short sword. Bunshirō stepped to the side of the street and bowed, but the man only nodded and passed on without so much as a word.

When he came to the three-way intersection that abutted the riverbank, Bunshirō turned back on the street along which he had come. Now that he could view the whole length of the neighborhood he had just traversed, it looked quite different from when he had first left the house. The rays of the sun still struck the roofs of the houses, but their glow had suddenly dwindled, and in the street, the pale light of dusk had already begun to gather.

That trail of pale gray light somehow called to Bunshirō's mind the smoke from the cremation of Yada's widow. Would her bones return tonight? Or would it be tomorrow? he wondered as he walked. Whereupon from behind, Bunshirō heard heavy footsteps, and then someone called his name. When he turned about, it was Owada Ippei.

3

"You're wandering about dressed like that?" Bunshirō said. Ippei must just have left the castle and was still wearing formal linens.

"Why not? It's all right." Ippei had come running when he saw Bunshirō, his face was red and he was out of breath. After wiping his face with one of his hands, he asked, "Out for a walk?"

"Mmm. I was tired of reading."

"Well, you have a good life, don't you?" Ippei said in an envious tone. Then he narrowed his eyes, looked all about, and lowered his voice. "How about it? Shall we go to Somekawa-chō tonight? You must be bored, and there's nothing to worry about. Luckily the wind has let up. It's not that cold."

"Oh, I've no problem with the cold," said Bunshirō. "What I was thinking about is something different. You know, Yada-san's wife is dead."

"What's that you say?" Ippei was of course astonished. "When did it happen?"

Semishigure

"Two or three days ago, apparently."

"Was she ill?"

"It was a love suicide."

"Love suicide? She was brave to do that." Ippei narrowed his eyes. "Who was the man?"

"I can't be the one to tell you that."

"Oh, come off it! Who do you think I am?"

"Before long, everyone will know. I just don't want to be the one to say it."

"Hmmph!" Ippei stared hard at Bunshirō. "Well, if that's how you feel, all right. But what's up? Are you in mourning because Yada's wife has died? Are you saying you can't go drinking?"

"That's how I feel."

"Was there something between you and her?"

"Now you're talking nonsense! We were thrown into the same dismal situation. We lived in the same barracks. She was no stranger to me. That's all."

"Well then, Bunshirō, that is a very different matter," Ippei said. "Tonight you *drink*, really drink. Poor woman! How old was she?"

"I don't really know."

"An ill-fated beauty, she was. So tonight we really drink—and in that way mourn her death. Right?"

"But I'll only drink. I won't go to the brothel."

"I understand. That's all right." Ippei again glared suspiciously around the whole area. "We'll meet just after the Sixth Hour (6 p.m.) at that corner," he said, pointing to the three-way intersection. As he parted with Ippei and began to walk away, Bunshirō realized that saké would be the very thing for the way he felt tonight.

4

That evening, about halfway through the Fifth Hour (9 p.m.), Bunshirō woke up in a room of the Wakamatsuya, a brothel in Somekawa-chō. Beside him lay a woman. She was a large, plump woman, about ten years older than himself, breathing softly as she slept.

Bunshirō rolled over and gazed up at the ceiling. The glow of the night lamp reached the walls, but only a faint reflection shone on the dark ceiling.

Drank too much at the Kinutaya, Bunshirō recalled. He had intended to go straight home after that. It must have been because he was so drunk that he had let Ippei lure him here so easily. But Bunshirō didn't really regret that he had come to a brothel and slept with a woman. He had once thought that sleeping with a woman would be something more special, more mysterious and bewildering than this. Yet having thought that, the actual act had turned out to be unexpectedly ordinary. He couldn't say that he grasped all the details, but he found it a very human activity, one that one could easily grow accustomed to. But that feeling may have come from the fact that this woman so closely resembled Bunshirō's nursemaid.

Shortly after he had been born, Bunshirō had been entrusted to the care of relatives of their servant, Kahei, in a nearby village. There was a woman there who produced a great deal of breast milk, and she had suckled Bunshirō. Clear memories were now returning to Bunshirō of that deep valley in the woman's chest; those large, soft breasts, rounded like mounds of New Year's rice cake, the feeling when he would touch the tawny but warm, soft skin of the nursemaid who had raised him until he was three. Then, too, there was the pleasure he felt when he would sit on his nursemaid's lap and grasp her large breasts. This time hadn't seemed so very different to him. Like his nursemaid, this woman, too, was quiet and had a gentle way about her.

Bunshirō had no regrets, but there was one point that still pained him. The reason he had come with Ippei to the brothel was not just because he was drunk, it must also be, he thought, because of his anger at the injustice of the way this world worked, which did not diminish even when he was drunk. But that was no excuse, he felt, for coming to the brothel on the evening he had heard of the death of someone he had been attracted to, even if only slightly.

I really should have gone home from Kinutaya—Bunshirō could feel a faint sense of guilt toward the dead woman rising from the depths of his emotions, as he lay there stock-still. The warmth of the woman beside him only accentuated that feeling.

When Bunshirō arose, the woman, who had been breathing so softly, opened her eyes and looked at him.

"Are you leaving?" she asked, in a voice that sounded as if she had been awake for some time.

"I'll be leaving."

The woman got up and began helping Bunshirō prepare himself.

"I can do this myself," he said, but the woman, silently and skillfully, helped Bunshirō don his kimono.

When he left the room, Bunshirō went to the adjacent room and called from outside the sliding panel.

"Ippei, I'm leaving now."

"Mm. Mm."

"Did you hear me?"

"I heard you. I'll leave, too," Ippei said in a quick, clear voice. "Wait for me downstairs."

Bunshirō descended the stairs. The woman came to see him off.

"It's cold. You'd better go back," he said. But the woman pulled her collar tight and waited with him for Ippei.

"Do come again," she said, as if she had just thought of it, and then she smiled shyly.

Bunshirō did not reply, but her shy smile, with her hand covering her mouth, left him with a good impression of her.

What time was it now? A light still shone brightly from the room next to the doorway where the reception desk stood, and the glow through the shoji revealed two people standing in the wooden-floored room.

What sort of woman is she? Bunshirō wondered, as he gazed aimlessly at the plain, even ugly, face that shone in the lamplight.

When his father, Sukezaemon, was still alive, he told his mother one evening how ten peasant families had fled in the night from one of the villages. Bunshirō could hear how infuriated he was as he told the tale. And that anger in the voice of his normally calm and taciturn father still lingered in his memory.

About ten years earlier, the domain had been stricken by a series of cold summers. In village after village, Bunshirō knew, poor yields and high taxes had ruined several peasant families. Even those who had not gone so far as to flee in the night were suffering under the weight of heavy taxes so that in order to survive they had to sell their children into other provinces and themselves become servants in the town; as a result of which the villages were utterly impoverished. Perhaps this woman before his eyes had been one of those villagers sold by her parents or husband at the time, Bunshirō thought. Her age, and the fact that she had never lost her natural simplicity, only strengthened his suspicion.

Before long I'll be seeing the lives of these villagers with my own eyes. As Bunshirō was thinking this, Ippei came tramping down the stairs.

Semishigure

"I'll be back! Take care you don't catch cold!" As he spoke, Ippei grasped the hand of the woman who was seeing him off, perhaps intending to show how accustomed he was to such escapades. She was a short, slender woman.

The bill had been settled in advance, and so the two of them left the brothel, seen off by their women. There was no wind, but the night air was quite cold.

"Cold!" Ippei muttered, drawing his head down. "Shall we go back to Kinutaya for one last light one?"

"What's the time?"

"Still a bit before Four (10 p.m.)," said Ippei. The pleasure quarter was as brightly lit as before, lanterns at all the eaves, the streets still filled with people.

"Hey!" Ippei turned and faced Bunshirō. His voice betrayed a faint smile. "How was it? Your first time in a brothel?"

"It wasn't bad. Quite different from what I'd imagined," Bunshirō said. He didn't mention the regrets that had beset him while he lay in bed with the woman. There was no point in talking about that with Ippei.

"Of course not. I wouldn't encourage you to do anything bad," Ippei said, a bit boastfully. "Next time we'll take Yonosuke."

"Ah yes, Yonosuke …" Bunshirō was recalling his letter. "After another year, he was saying. That would mean next year about this time. He'll be coming back then, he says."

"His studies complete?"

"Apparently so. When he returns he'll be working as librarian at the Sanseikan, he wrote."

"So at last he's embarked upon the Way of Confucius? But …" Ippei looked at Bunshirō, "Yonosuke has worked hard, too. That fellow will become a scholar good enough to succeed Shibahara-san."

"Could be."

"And you're now one of the best swordsmen in the domain. But I'm the worst of us all. Swordsmanship, scholarship—I'm no good at either."

"Swordsmanship, scholarship—we all have our strengths and weaknesses. That's nothing to get upset about," Bunshirō said. "But quite apart from those things, you have strong points of your own. There's a lot that I can learn from you."

"Like brothels, hey?" said Ippei. "I've taught you about saké and brothels. That's about it, isn't it?" Ippei's spirits had been restored. "But this month is my wedding. No more playing around for the time being."

"Yes, best to avoid that," Bunshirō said. And just then he became aware of someone standing in front of him, blocking his way. It was Yamane Seijirō and the gang that hung around with him. They were drunk and headed for the brothels. All of them reeked of saké.

"A night out at the brothels?" When the two of them stopped, Yamane called out to them in a mocking tone of voice. "Is it all right for the miscreant to be frequenting the brothels?"

"And is it all right for us to let you talk that way?" Ippei shouted back at them. "If you mean to start a fight, I'll lend a hand in that!"

"Never mind them," Bunshirō said. "Let 'em say whatever they like." Disporting himself in a brothel might be overlooked, but he was certain that a fight in the pleasure quarter would not be ignored by the domain. It was a fact, too, that Yamane now seemed strangely insignificant to him.

Once he had urged Ippei on past the gang, the men at their rear laughed derisively.

Flowing Waters

1

A year or so had passed, in the course of which major events had taken place in the domain. Lord Kamezaburō—having been granted the title of "Shima-no-Kami," the heir apparent—had been retired on the pretext of him being a sickly child. Then Lord Matsunojō, his younger half-brother, had succeeded him and been received in audience by the Shogun; whereupon he was formally named the new heir apparent to the domain and officially inherited the title of Shima-no-Kami.

At the same time, hidden inconspicuously in the shadow of these events that so shocked the domain, a lesser but related event took place. O-Fuku, the youngest of the concubines, who was once rumored to have monopolized the affections of His Lordship, was suddenly dismissed and placed in the custody of the Yashiro, the house of a bannerman related to the lord of the domain.

Those ignorant of internal affairs in the domain had no idea what the significance of these events might be; neither, perhaps, did they imagine that the two events might be connected. But those familiar with the long whispered-about succession dispute, as well as the contention between the Inagaki and Yokoyama factions, must have realized from these two events that the concubine O-Fune had succeeded in regaining the affections of His Lordship; whilst back home, the Inagaki faction had totally subdued the Yokoyama faction and at last seized power over the domain.

Maki Bunshirō was one of those who drew this conclusion from these two events. Bunshirō heard details of the succession in the course of his work at the Office of the District Deputy, which he had begun this year. Fuku's loss of favor and dismissal, he learnt of from a letter from Shimazaki Yonosuke in Edo.

Bunshirō's life had changed greatly over the past year. In the first place, his visit to the brothel in Somekawa-chō with Owada Ippei had passed unremarked, and he was commanded to report for duty at the castle from the first of the year.

He was designated a rural inspector in training. Eventually, he would be making the rounds of rice land, uplands, and forests; and in the appropriate season, he would be assigned to assist in the all-important evaluation of the rice crop. For the time being, however, while in training, he would report to the Office of the District Deputy in the third perimeter, where he would learn to compose various documents related to rural affairs and to conduct the preliminary investigation of claims lodged with the department. And from time to time, he would make the inspection round of villages and mountains in the company of his immediate superior, District Commissioner Kashimura Yasuke.

One more change in his life was that, in the Second Month, he had been married. This had been arranged in the autumn of the previous year. And in the Second Month, his superior officer; Fujii Munezō, his eboshi-oya who had capped him at the celebration of his majority; Owada Ippei; and Sugiuchi Michizō, along with various of his relatives, had held a simple ceremony.

Semishigure

Bunshirō's wife was the second daughter of Okazaki Kameji, who was in charge of the hemp and linen warehouse. She was a bit dark complected, an ordinary looking girl who would not stand out in a crowd. But Toyo was pleased to hear that she was quiet and solicitous of her parents. Of the many proposals that Uehara's wife had brought, this was the first she had shown any interest in.

Thereafter she asked Bunshirō's brother's wife to go and see the girl. And after a few details were settled, she accepted the proposal readily. Bunshirō expressed no opinion of his own. If this was a bride that would please his mother, then he had no objection. As the time approached when Bunshirō would begin work in the castle, his mother had begun to show slight signs of aging, in both speech and movement. He had to make life easier for her now. Okazaki was on a stipend of twenty-five koku per year; they were well-matched in rank, too.

In the early days of his service in the castle, Bunshirō took care to remain constantly alert. Although permitted to begin work in the castle, he could not forget the warnings of his superior officer Kashimura and Kaji Oribe-no-Shō: that the future of those families punished in the previous incident was by no means secure; that the Inagaki-Satomura faction, who held the key to life or death, were now the sole power within the domain; that Bunshirō's own position was both isolated and defenseless.

Yet despite this, his days were not filled, one after the other, with tension. As time passed, his colleagues and superiors in the Office of the District Deputy, who at first did not hide the fact that they regarded him with suspicion, softened their gaze, and within two or three months no one any longer looked upon Bunshirō as in any way out of the ordinary.

There were those who would strike up a conversation with

him completely at their ease; those who would invite him to go drinking; and none who kept their distance from Bunshirō in the course of their work. This was the atmosphere in which Bunshirō gradually grew accustomed to his work in the castle. But in the evening, when at last he was free to leave the castle, he could not deny that he did so with a sense of relief.

2

On an evening midway through the Fourth Month, when every quarter of town that one passed through was filled with the fragrance of flowers, Setsu told Bunshirō, who had just returned from the castle, that a visitor had come. She had tried to address Bunshirō as "Danna-sama," as a proper wife should, but as always her voice just faded away before the words were out of her mouth. Bunshirō pretended not to notice, but it made Setsu blush.

"A visitor? Who is it?"

"Shimazaki-sama, he says."

"Oh?" Bunshirō smiled faintly. "Has he come in?"

"Yes, I did as mother told me and showed him into the guest room."

"That's good." Bunshirō looked into the sitting room and greeted his mother, then went to his own room, shed just his formal linens, and hurried on to the guest room. There, still in his travel gear, was Yonosuke, reading a book he had taken out of his luggage. He put the book down and turned to Bunshirō.

"Ah! Sorry to drop in so suddenly," Yonosuke said. He was as thin and bony as ever but deeply tanned from his travels and looking in the best of health. The two of them exchanged the greetings usual for people who hadn't seen each other in a long while.

Semishigure

"But haven't you gone home yet?" Bunshirō said, looking at Yonosuke's travel garb.

"I came straight here," Yonosuke said. "At home, once I change out of my travel gear, I'll immediately have to go hither and thither greeting everyone. Before that I wanted to see you."

"I'm glad you came."

"Besides that, there's a little something I want to talk about." As Yonosuke said that, the panel slid open and Setsu came in carrying tea. Looking up at Setsu as she greeted them, Bunshirō told Yonosuke that she was his wife.

"I didn't write to tell you, but we were married in the Second Month."

"Isn't that the sort of thing you should report straightaway? It's quite a shock, you know, to come home, only to be welcomed unexpectedly by this beautiful new lady of the house!" Yonosuke's amiable response was quite uncharacteristic of a scholar, but perhaps this new charm was something he had learnt in Edo. And when Setsu left the room, Yonosuke lowered his voice and said, "She's quite gentle and very pleasant, isn't she?"

Bunshirō only mumbled, "Mm, mm." He was still too shy to discuss his new wife, for even to speak of "husband" and "wife" still sounded like playing house to him. Marriage did not yet seem quite real. Instead, Bunshirō himself began asking the questions.

"I thought you'd be coming back a bit sooner. Isn't this later than you'd expected?"

"Yes, I'd taken on various duties at the academy, and it took a while to arrange the handover."

"So will you start immediately at the domain academy?"

"Shibahara-sama is urging me to. I'll be calling on him tonight, after I leave here. It will be decided then what I do next. But it's looking like I won't have a great deal of free time."

"At last you'll be a teacher in the Sanseikan? I've been talking about you with Ippei. You've really worked hard, Yonosuke. Ikoma Sensei must be very pleased."

"Once I've received my instructions from Shibahara-sama, I plan to go immediately to Sensei and report to him," Yonosuke said. "But how are things with you?"

"Since New Year's I've spent all my time at the castle at the Office of the District Deputy, I'm still in training."

"So what's it like?" Yonosuke said. "Tell me about it."

Bunshirō described his work in a general way. And he told him, with no evasion, how at first his colleagues had regarded him with suspicion.

"But there's none of that any more. I'm already fairly accustomed to drafting documents. So now I'll be making the round of the villages more often."

"You and Ippei—you're both established now. I'm the slowest of us all," Yonosuke said regretfully. Whereupon Bunshirō recalled that Yonosuke had said he had something to talk about.

"You said there was something you want to talk about. What is it?"

"Yes, that." Yonosuke folded his arms, looked away from Bunshirō, then started talking as if to himself. "Shall I tell you? Or shall I not? To tell the truth, I've had a hard time making up my mind about that."

"What? What's all the mystery about? If you came here intending to tell me, you can tell me."

"All right, then, I'll tell you." Yonosuke unfolded his arms and slapped his knees, then cast a quick glance at the door to the room. "I couldn't very well discuss this in front of your wife ... but O-Fuku-sama has returned to the domain. Did you know that?"

Semishigure

Bunshirō was at a loss for words. This unexpected news came as a shock to him. But finally he shook his head.

"No," he said. "This is the first I've heard of it. Or rather, I should say, no one here has even mentioned such a thing."

"No, they wouldn't." Yonosuke nodded. "It seems to have been done in the very strictest secrecy."

"Then, O-Fuku-sama …" Bunshirō said, "has she returned to her family?"

"No, by no means." Yonosuke shook his head, then lowered his voice even further. "You know the Zelkova Mansion?"

"Mmm. That's His Lordship's villa near the village of Kanai."

At the western edge of the village of Kanai, a long, gently sloping hill came to an end where it protruded into the level plain, and there stood a villa belonging to the family of the lord of the domain. The lower reaches of the hill were covered by a dense grove of large zelkova trees, and since the villa was surrounded by these trees, it was called the Zelkova Mansion. But the building itself was the simplest of structures, hardly of the scale one would normally describe as a mansion. Yet the beauties of the four seasons that surrounded this villa, in contrast to the castle, would have been replete with a slightly rustic charm. From spring until summer there were the fresh new leaves and the flowering shrubs that colored the hill at the rear; in summer, the depths of the grove were cool; in autumn, the plume grass was in bloom along the banks of the stream that flowed past the villa. And His Lordship, being particularly fond of viewing the moon as it rose over the mountains on the border due east of there, would visit this villa from time to time whenever he returned to his domain.

Now, according to the bizarre tale that Yonosuke was telling, O-Fuku-sama was being looked after in this mansion.

"She's not with her family?" Bunshirō looked doubtfully at Yonosuke. "Not with her family, but in the Zelkova Mansion because ..."

"That's right. And that is because her relationship with His Lordship still persists. Yes, I, too, was shocked when I heard this."

Since that time two years earlier, when he had returned in the company of his teacher and lectured at the Sanseikan, Yonosuke's status had changed. From that time forward the domain had undertaken to pay the costs of his education, which implied that once he had completed his studies, he would return to the domain and become a professor at the domain academy. The domain had recognized Yonosuke's talent as a scholar.

In that connection, Yonosuke had been visiting the Edo mansion far more often than before, and among those he had come to know there was an old master gardener from the domain, whose daughter, too, was employed in the kitchens at the lower mansion.

Out of concern for her aging father, who lived all alone in a room he had been allotted in the barracks, the daughter would sometimes come to the upper mansion to tidy up his quarters there, and sometimes make something nice for him to eat before she returned. And Yonosuke, who found that father and daughter were from Somemono-chō, where he himself had lived, had been clever enough to get himself invited to their room for dinner. It was from Yoné, the daughter, that he heard about O-Fuku-sama, Yonosuke said.

"In my letter I said that O-Fuku-sama had been dismissed and placed in the custody of the Yashiro house, but according to O-Yoné, the facts of the matter seem to have been quite different."

Previously, when O-Fuku miscarried, it was rumored that O-Fune, the mother of Shima-no-Kami, who was then named Matsunojō, had been the cause of it; but since the spring of this past year, there had been several more mysterious incidents involving O-Fuku. The hallway in front of O-Fuku's room in the lower mansion was strangely slippery, and O-Fuku nearly stumbled and fell. And when she was about to take a bath, the water in the tub turned out to be almost boiling. And when she was walking in the garden at the rear of the mansion, she was attacked by a wild dog. And thereafter the food-testing maids had collapsed not just once but three times.

O-Fuku's food was of course prepared in the kitchens of the lower mansion, and when O-Yoné and her colleagues heard what had happened, they were stricken with terror. The poisoned food had not been prepared by O-Yoné or her close friends, but the fact that such a frightening thing had happened made her realize that the perpetrator must be very close at hand, most likely a member of her own group.

At that time, His Lordship had been avoiding the lower mansion. There were those who said that his affection for O-Fuku had dwindled; but there were also those who reckoned this was related to the recent horrors that had afflicted O-Fuku, that His Lordship was staying away purposely in order to quell the jealousy of O-Fune-sama. This was how the gardener's daughter O-Yoné saw it.

It had shocked those serving in the upper mansion to hear that His Highness had dismissed O-Fuku and placed her in the custody of his close kin, the Yashiro house; but even then O-Yoné and a few of the others did not alter their opinion. These women had proof that they were right.

"What proof?" Bunshirō looked at Yonosuke, and Yonosuke nodded.

"Don't mention this to anyone else," he said. "If this is true, it has to be kept a secret here in the domain. But she says that O-Fuku-sama is pregnant."

"With the lord's child?"

"Of course it's the lord's child." Yonosuke looked at Bunshirō as if to say "Don't even ask such a stupid question."

The hairs on Bunshirō's body stood on end. The domain was now under the control of the Inagaki-Satomura faction, who were in direct contact with the concubine O-Fune. If word of this should leak out, wouldn't O-Fuku's life be in danger?

"Is that a fact?"

"There are maids in attendance on O-Fuku-sama." Those maids, who were close friends of O-Yoné, were sent with O-Fuku when she was placed in the custody of the Yashiro house. And there they heard people in the Yashiro house saying that O-Fuku was pregnant, and so should be treated with special care. The maids could hardly believe their ears.

"O-Yoné also believes that it was His Lordship who decreed that O-Fuku be sent from the Yashiro house back to the domain."

"That's only what those women would have told her," Bunshirō said. "It's a bit difficult to believe coming out of the blue."

"But women like O-Yoné do often grasp the facts of a matter. Even so, though, I, too, find it impossible to dismiss my doubts …" As he spoke, Yonosuke stuffed his book back into its oilpaper packet and knotted the twine. "Sooner or later we'll know whether it's true or not."

"I suppose so."

"Confucius stood by the river and said, 'So it is with all things. The flow never ceases, night or day.' I like to think there's a lesson to be learnt from those words," Yonosuke said. "Confucius bewails his knowledge that all things pass away, never ceasing, night or day. We can only throw up our hands. With us, too, much has changed."

"I quite agree," Bunshirō said. But before he cared to join

Yonosuke in his sudden burst of emotion, there was something he wished to verify. "It seems to have been some time before now that His Lordship decided to send O-Fuku back to the domain. But was he aware then of the situation here within the domain?"

" I have no idea. But what does that signify?" Yonosuke's reply was useless. So Bunshirō told him in simple terms of the present situation in which the Inagaki-Satomura faction, in league with the concubine O-Fune, had monopolized power over the domain.

"Nothing could be more dangerous than to come back to such a place and give birth to the lord's child. The Inagaki faction, quite as much as O-Fune-sama, has no desire to see another child to be born to our lord."

"I see." Yonosuke frowned. "There's a danger both mother and child might be assassinated."

"If worst comes to worst."

"But I've only spoken to you since I returned from Edo. Here in the domain, surely no one knows about O-Fuku-sama."

"If what you say is true, sooner or later they'll know."

Yonosuke said nothing, and again, he frowned. But then the old optimism returned to his voice.

"This year, before long, His Lordship will be returning. When he learns what the situation is here in the domain, he'll surely take appropriate steps. There's nothing much to worry about."

When he returned to his room after seeing Yonosuke off, Bunshirō sank deep into thought. If what Yonosuke told him was true, O-Fuku's fate was nothing one could view with any optimism. The Inagaki-Satomura faction would sooner or later get wind of the fact that O-Fuku was hiding in the Zelkova Mansion. Here in the domain, O-Man-sama ruled over the women's wing of the castle. O-Fuku's home town was no longer a place where she could live in safety.

For O-Fuku all the more so ... Wouldn't it have been safer if she had returned to her family? Bunshirō thought.

3

About half a month later, when a day came that he was off duty, Bunshirō decided to do something he had long been considering. He donned his travel breeches, knotted his straw sandals, secured his broad-brimmed sedge hat, and left the house. He told his wife and his mother he would be making an inspection round of the villages. He was not lying. But it was the village of Kanai he was bound for.

Out beyond the town, the road led through rice fields that had just been planted. He strode swiftly, looking down at the lonely little sprouts in the fields, their limp tips quivering in the gentle breeze. In the distance, he could now see villagers still at work in fields that had not yet been planted.

The liveliest and busiest time, when even the old folks and children are at work, had passed; but the sprouts did not all mature at the same time, and there were slight differences in the pace at which the several peasant families prepared their fields. And so the planting was not yet complete. Upon close observation, there were still a few people to be seen, here and there, planting their fields.

The village of Kanai lay beyond these rice fields, spread out along the base of a hill where the new leaves were sparkling in the sunlight. Kanai was about a league and a half distant from the castle town, close enough that if one fixed one's eyes firmly upon it, one could make out the roofs of houses and the groves surrounding them. But in the vicinity of the Zelkova Mansion, the glistening new leaves were only the more striking, and there was no sign of anything resembling a building.

As he hurried along the winding road, a small hamlet came into view on his left, then receded into the distance. It was one of the settlements in the village of Aohata, which adjoins the village of Kanai, just across the Goken River. Before this little hamlet, called Kazato, a bend in river glistened like a pond, casting back the rays of the sun. Here the banks of the Goken River were so overgrown with deep clumps of reeds that the main stream was not even visible.

He walked on, gazing at the wild growth in bloom at the roadside; or at a waterbird of some sort flitting across one of the newly planted fields, then hiding in the tufts of grass on the border. At last he came to a small stream. This was the stream that flowed past the Zelkova Mansion and emptied into the Goken River.

Bunshirō crossed the small wooden bridge. There he stopped, removed his sedge hat, and looked down the way ahead of him. Having come this far, he could clearly see the central sweep of the village as it stretched out along the foot of the hill. The roofs of the houses; the groves planted as windbreaks between the houses; the bridge at the edge of the village; a column of white smoke rising, apparently, from something being burnt within the village. Nor were there only rice fields. This side of the village he could also see peasants at work in the upland fields.

Walking still further, he arrived at the entrance to the village. There at the crossroads stood a tall Kōshin monument and a road sign. The sign stated that straight ahead the road led to the village of Hokari in Onuma District; to the right was Kanai; and to the left Aohata. Bunshirō walked on down the road, which here ran through vegetable fields on either side, and entered the village of Kanai proper. Kanai and Aohata were known as prosperous villages. From the documents he was handling, Bunshirō had learnt that the number of households there and the taxes that they paid were considerable. And when he entered the village, the houses were indeed conspicuous for their size.

So this is the village that begged the domain to spare my father's life, Bunshirō thought. The emotion of visiting that village for the first time all but overwhelmed him. But within the village, the sight of Bunshirō, his sedge hat tilted upward, looking here and there as he walked, must have stood out as if he were a confused traveler from another province; for the villagers who passed by, after bowing politely, would glance back at him, their eyes filled with a curiosity they could not suppress.

Bunshirō made his way slowly through the village and finally came to the path that skirted the hill. There a stand of zelkovas at the foot of the hill, their new leaves even fresher than all the others, came into view. Bunshirō could feel his heart begin to beat just a bit faster. As he walked along this path, he had the feeling that O-Fuku might be standing in front of the villa.

But of course that was impossible. At the covered gate, so austere for a villa of the lord's family, far from any sign of habitation, it was still as if no one at all were there. A small stream flowed around the grounds of the villa, to enter which one had to cross a sturdy wooden bridge that stood before the gate.

Bunshirō passed quietly by that bridge. He could not see what lay at the rear of the villa, but at the front there was a coarse hedge that incorporated some of the huge zelkovas. As he passed, he glanced through a gap in the hedge, but all he could see was a bit of the building and a flash of sunlight that shot into the grounds like an arrow. There was nothing more to be seen. Neither could the least sound of a human voice be heard, nor did any hint of movement reach him.

Semishigure

Bunshirō walked to the corner of the property, now doubting whether what Yonosuke told him could be true; and there he turned left. The villa appeared to be uninhabited.

Even after he had turned, there was no change in the appearance of the property. The little stream followed around, now flowing to the west until it came up against the hill at the rear where it made a wide turn back toward the fields. Perhaps it was the season, but the stream was so full that the flowing water made no sound, which made Bunshirō realize that it also served as a moat around the villa. And on the far bank, the hedge, coarse though it was, made it difficult to peer within. At the side, too, there was a small bridge and a covered gate, somewhat smaller than the one at the front. Yet for a gate that small, it displayed a strength sufficient to discourage anyone from approaching it.

Having inspected the site thus far, Bunshirō turned back. And when he reached the corner of the property, he sensed for the first time hints of movement behind him. He whirled about swiftly, and next to the bridge he had just seen stood a man. He was a samurai armed with two swords. And just around the corner, another samurai appeared and approached him slowly. This man was a middle-aged samurai, whose posture revealed not the slightest gap in his defenses.

"Have you business of some sort at this place?" The man who accosted him spoke in Edo dialect, like Inukai Hyōma. His words were gentle, but his eyes looked sharply at Bunshirō. Bunshirō removed his sedge hat.

"I am on an inspection round of the rice fields for the Rural Affairs Unit. There is no cause for alarm." As he replied, Bunshirō felt a sense of relief. It was now certain, he felt, that O-Fuku was in this villa; but guarded as she was, she would be safe.

Bunshirō did not know whether they believed what he had

said. The young samurai who had appeared at the bridge behind him closed in on Bunshirō from the rear, and from their position in which they could attack him from both sides, they put two or three more stern questions to him; but Bunshirō seemed to persuade them that he meant no harm.

"You may go," the middle-aged samurai told him, and then added: "We would be grateful if you would not mention to anyone what has happened here today. May we ask that of you?"

"Concerning you two gentlemen?"

"Concerning everything that has happened," the young samurai at the rear said brusquely. When Bunshirō turned about, the young man glared at him with a clear urge to kill in his eyes. Had it been nighttime, they might have attacked, Bunshirō thought. Both men were prepared to fight at a moment's notice, for neither of them wore a surcoat. Most likely they had observed Bunshirō from within the villa, thought it suspicious that a man should be loitering about there, and come out.

"Agreed," Bunshirō replied. The expression of the middle aged samurai softened, and he cleared the way. But when Bunshirō passed in front of him and was about to turn the corner of the property, he called out to him again. The two men stood shoulder to shoulder glaring at Bunshirō. Perhaps something about Bunshirō's appearance from the rear made them sense that it was not simply the inspection of rice fields that he had in mind.

"Just for the record, let me inquire of you once more," the middle-aged samurai said. "Your office and your name?"

"I am Maki Bunshirō, Rural Affairs Inspector." When Bunshirō stated his name, the samurai nodded, and gestured with his hand, as if to say that Bunshirō was now free to go.

My name ... Will those men tell O-Fuku? Bunshirō wondered. The thought did not make his heart beat any faster.

Semishigure

Whether they told her or not was of no concern to Bunshirō. He could envision O-Fuku, carrying the child of the lord of the domain, secluded in his villa, as if wrapped in a cocoon. But to Bunshirō this woman was no longer the same Fuku that he remembered. This was the first time he had experienced that feeling.

Yonosuke's voice, telling him what Confucius had said when he stood by the river, resounded in Bunshirō's ears. Like the flowing waters, night and day, the lives of all things move on and change. Where is there anything that does not change? Bunshirō thought.

His father's death. The death of Yada Yoshie. The secrets of swordsmanship. His new work. His marriage. Bunshirō's world had changed dramatically over these past several years. And he had not remained fixated on Fuku throughout it all. At times he had forgotten her. Fuku, too, had lived through extraordinary changes. To hear the name Maki Bunshirō might no longer arouse any nostalgia in her either.

But O-Fuku the concubine was not all alone and helpless. The lord of the domain had taken the trouble to assign a guard detail to protect her. There was nothing for me to worry about, Bunshirō was thinking, when he stopped at the edge of village and looked back toward the Zelkova Mansion.

An Invitation

1

Ever since the rice fields surrounding the castle town had turned totally green, Bunshirō had been going on inspection rounds of the villages in the company of District Commissioner Kashimura or other colleagues. Sometimes their rounds would take them as far out as the borders of the domain, in which case they would stay at the headquarters of the deputy resident in that region and return on the evening of the following day. And even when they were away only for the day, they would rarely return to town while it was still light. Bunshirō was finding the work of the Rural Affairs Unit rather demanding.

"If you can't take the walking, you'll never survive the village inspections," a colleague named Kitano, a man of forty-plus, had told him. "When I was young, I walked and I walked—so much that the hair on my legs had no time to grow."

Village after village they inspected; but half of what Kashimura and the others were doing, Bunshirō could not comprehend. Kashimura, together with a man from the village, would wade out into the paddy to inspect the new shoots and check the color of their leaves. And in a certain season, when there was danger of an outbreak of leafhoppers, they would be on guard against that in their round of inspections.

This year, the spring rains had been long, a chill east wind had been blowing, and the rice had not flourished. Some of the fields, it was feared, might be stricken with disease or suffer damage from the cold. But once the rain clouds drifted off into the distance, the sun turned hot. Suddenly it was as hot as midsummer, and everyone found that so unbearable that complaints about the heat became the standard daily greeting. But the rice fields returned to life. The leaves grew with new vigor, and by the time of the Kumano Shrine Night Festival at summer's end, the heads of the rice plants had slowly begun to swell.

Bunshirō had never known the half of what agriculture was all about, but now even he could appreciate the beauty of a rice plant beginning to grow a head. For he himself had witnessed the determination with which Kashimura, his colleagues, and all the villagers looked after the growth of the rice crop. Nor was it only the rice, he realized. All agriculture was like a battle with bare blades, in which no mistakes could ever be undone. And it was a battle that took place only once in every year.

That was why only after all was in readiness and all preparations had been made could the seeds be sown and the seedlings planted. And even after planting, if the crop was not tended as it grew, the harvest would not mature. That meant, for instance, that the villagers had to crawl about under the blazing sun weeding their fields. For the first time, Bunshirō realized that every corner of level land in the domain would be picked smooth three times by hand: first weeding, second weeding, third weeding. As a child, when he had gazed out at the broad expanse of rice fields across the little stream at the rear of their house, he never dreamt that all this was going on. Now, at last, Bunshirō felt he could understand what had made his father insist that they change the place of their cut in the riverbank in order to save ten chō of rice. And that Aiba Sōroku, too, had understood when he agreed to do it.

Then one night, just when the heads were beginning to color, a dreadful gale swept through the domain and flattened the rice. Bunshirō and his colleagues split up into groups and went from village to village to assess the damage. They made their rounds in teams of two, and Bunshirō was paired with his colleague Aoki Magozō. Aoki was in his mid-thirties, his face dark and pockmarked, and a man of few words.

Although they were to check the damage, Bunshirō and his colleagues did not go directly to inspect the damaged crops. That initial inspection had been made immediately by people from the offices of the five regional deputies. Bunshirō and the others would go first to the headquarters of the local deputy, where one of the officials would explain the details of the situation; after which they would take those documents and make their own round of all the villages within that jurisdiction.

Their main task in those villages was first to consult the estimate of damage to the harvest already made by the regional deputy's people, and then, with those figures before them, to meet directly with the village officials and ask the village's own estimate of the damage. When there was a discrepancy between the two estimates, the final figure would be decided later in a meeting of the district deputy, the regional deputy, and the village officials. What Bunshirō and his colleagues had to do was, in villages where discrepancies arose, listen to the explanation of the villagers, ask what they would wish, record all this in their notebooks, and bring the information back with them.

In the past, the main duties of the district commissioners, the "kōri bugyō," had been to manage the domain's timberlands, handle the inspection and repair of river embankments, and also to adjudicate any legal proceedings involving the rural regions and to prosecute criminals. But he did not participate in the inspection of the rice crop or the assessment of damage in the fields; those tasks came entirely under the jurisdiction of the regional deputies, the "daikansho." The strengthening of the authority of the district deputy, the "gundai," in recent years, allowing him, for one thing, to oversee the work of the regional deputies, was said to have been a change introduced by that renowned elder, Kaji Oribe-no-Shō.

Perhaps there had been cases of corruption among the regional deputies during the administration of Oribe-no-Shō, and so he changed the system to prevent a recurrence of such abuses. Or perhaps this was not the case, and Oribe-no-Shō simply wished to prevent those officials dealing with agricultural matters from exercising arbitrary authority over this most crucial element of domain governance. Whatever the cause, those under the command of the district commissioners now set to work straightaway.

But the damage caused by this recent gale was greatest in the north of the domain. In the villages to the south, where Bunshirō was inspecting, the damage had been relatively light, and so the inspection round proceeded smoothly. But wherever there was damage, it was standard procedure to go out to the field and have the situation explained to them. And so they would leave at the break of day; and by the time they returned to the castle town, the sun would already be sinking in the west.

"Well, let's do one more village." As they approached the entrance to the village of Kanai, Aoki cast an anxious glance up at the sun, which was nearing the ridge of the hill. "I'd like to finish while there's still daylight."

"If nothing goes wrong, we should be able to," Bunshirō agreed.

Aoki Magozō was still striding along, full of vigor, but Bunshirō was so exhausted he could hardly lift his feet. Yet although the two were a team, Bunshirō was only observing the way Aoki did his work, so he hardly dared mention that he was tired. All he could say was that he would like to return to town as soon as possible.

Aoki was a man of few words, but Bunshirō could see that he was a capable official. He put no useless questions to the village officials, and his manner when inspecting was brisk and energetic. He was just as observant as if he were inspecting the familiar terrain of his own garden.

If only I can become as good as that, Bunshirō thought to himself. It pleased him that today he had been paired with Aoki Magozō. This being his first real job, Bunshirō would at times become flustered and write the wrong number by mistake; but the taciturn Aoki hardly ever mentioned it. He himself would correct Bunshirō's mistakes and only afterward point them out to him.

Even on the road, he seldom spoke, which at times made Bunshirō feel a bit uncomfortable, but for the most part he felt at ease with him. Aoki was not a bad partner to have as a day's travelling companion. The two of them entered the village of Kanai.

2

As they entered the village, Aoki turned suddenly to Bunshirō.

"The man we're going to visit now is Tōjirō, the village official, but ..." Aoki fell silent there; and then, for some reason, inquired searchingly of Bunshirō. "Does the name Tōjirō mean anything to you?"

"No." Bunshirō shook his head. He had no idea why Aoki should ask that. Aoki turned back, looked straight ahead, and for a time walked on saying nothing. When they came to the crossroads and turned the corner, he again spoke.

"When your honored father was forced to commit seppuku, this village and the neighboring village of Aohata jointly submitted a plea to the domain that his life be spared. Tōjirō is the man who organized the entreaty at that time; you should remember that."

"Did he? I had no idea." In a corner of his mind, Bunshirō had long wondered about that. "So he's the one who composed it?"

"That's right. Tōjirō is a sharp-witted man. Eventually, they say, he'll become the head of the village." Aoki looked back at Bunshirō's face. "Did you know about that entreaty?"

"Yes, I heard about it from someone."

"And that someone, as you call him, was Yokoyama-sama?"

"No, someone else."

"You can't say who?"

"No, I can't. I'm sorry, but …" His connection with Kaji Oribe-no-Shō was something Bunshirō had to conceal.

Bunshirō had refused to state the name, but whether this had angered Aoki he could not tell just looking at the man's pockmarked face. Aoki Magozō walked on, looking straight ahead, his face expressionless. Finally he stopped in front of a house with a well-tended hedge.

"Here it is," said Aoki. Crossing the broad front garden, the two men stood before a huge farmhouse with a roof so tall that, although thatched, it was overwhelming. Aoki entered the vestibule alone, and when he announced himself, a voice answered immediately and someone seemed to come out from within the house. But from the garden where Bunshirō stood, in the glare of the evening sun that shone down just then, the interior of the vestibule was dark and he could not see either Aoki or the person who had come out. The two appeared to converse in low tones. Aoki did not emerge for some time.

Bunshirō looked away toward a tall persimmon tree standing in a corner of the garden. The fruit, just beginning to show color, glowed in the sunlight. He could detect the scent of a horse coming from somewhere, and then he saw a young man, bearing a rack piled high with a mountain of hay, come around a corner of the house and disappear beyond the wall of a shed.

Finally, Aoki Magozō came out. With him was a man in his mid-forties with a long, dignified face. Aoki beckoned Bunshirō with his hand, and when Bunshirō went to him, he introduced the man.

"This is Tōjirō-dono." And then turning to Tōjirō, he said, "I've spoken of him before, but this is the son of Maki Sukezaemon."

"Ah, well then!" As the man spoke, he looked intently at Bunshirō. And then Bunshirō and the man exchanged greetings.

Bunshirō thanked him respectfully for composing the plea to spare his father's life; and Tōjirō waved his hand and said he had only done what was proper for the village to do, then smiled softly at Bunshirō.

"I understand you're finding this village work tiring. But how goes it? The walking must be exhausting."

"I am a bit weary today." Bunshirō answered him frankly, whereupon Tōjirō turned to Aoki.

"How about it? Shall we take a break for tea before we make the rounds of the fields?"

"But the sun is about to set." Aoki glanced up at the evening sun above the ridge of the roof of the house next door. "If we take a break, won't it get dark?"

"That shouldn't be a problem," Tōjirō said. "The rice was only flattened in one place, Furukuchida. And there's no great disparity between there and the deputy's estimate. We should finish in no time," said Tōjirō. "Yes, let's do that. And while we're having tea, I'll send a messenger to Chōnosuke and Isaku and have them come here. That will be the fastest way."

"Will it, then?" To resist so warm an invitation any further would be rude, Aoki thought, and he nodded with greater willingness than he felt. "In that case, shall we accept your kind offer of a cup of tea?" he said, and with no further ado walked toward the veranda.

Aoki and Bunshirō sat down on the veranda just outside the sitting room, and Tōjirō went into the house. They could hear what they thought must be people talking within the house, and then Tōjirō appeared in the sitting room and sat down with the two of them.

"I've just sent a messenger," he said, "so both men should be coming soon." "Chōnosuke is another village official who will be our witness," Aoki explained to Bunshirō, "and Isaku is the owner of the fields we'll be going to inspect." Aoki and Tōjirō then began discussing the overall situation in the villages of Kanai and Aohata.

"When the rains dragged on, we were worried, but then things improved and it appeared the harvest would turn out much the same as in normal years. We won't know until the inspection is complete, but …"

"What did that wind do?"

"The wind came from behind the hill; so strange to say …"

Bunshirō listened intently to their conversation. The gale

blew over the top of the village, then down to the banks of the Goken River; and from there it followed the path of the river north, Tōjirō said. That was why the only place the rice was flattened in the village of Kanai was that stretch on this side of the river called Furukuchida. But on the far side of the river, in the village of Aohata, a vast area was damage-stricken.

"Because the wind blew down from Gongen-sama?" Aoki asked.

"That's right," said Tōjirō. "If the wind had blown in from the sea, this whole village would have been hit."

Gongen-sama was the mountain that towered above the village hill. It was called that because on its peak there was a temple dedicated to Zaō Gongen; but its original name was Komaki Yama. Whenever the wind blew from the southeast, Komaki Yama served to block it; and that, they said, protected the village of Kanai from any excessive damage.

While Aoki and Tōjirō, in the most knowing manner, were discussing the strength of the wind and its direction, a young woman brought them tea and sweets and peeled pears, greeted them tersely, then left.

"Please, do have a pear," Tōjirō said, offering them to Aoki and Bunshirō. "They're a bit early, but their flavor is good," he added. Bunshirō bit into one, and it was juicy and sweet. When he sat down on the veranda, Bunshirō's weary and burning legs relaxed a bit, and this cool, sweet pear quite revived him.

"This pear is just delicious!" Bunshirō said to Tōjirō.

"Is it?" Tōjirō smiled as he sipped his tea. Then suddenly he said, "Your father, too, was fond of these pears."

"My father?" Bunshirō raised his face from the pear he was eating. His father, Sukezaemon, had been in the Defense Works Unit, but was he also in some way involved with the villages?

Semishigure

"Did he sometimes come here in connection with river works?"

"Yes, there was that, but …" Tōjirō said evasively, whereupon Aoki cleared his throat, and took over the conversation.

"Seven or eight years ago, the two bridges to Aohata were rebuilt. Isn't that the time you were talking about?"

"Yes, that may well have been the time. Because the men in the construction crew used to have their midday meal in this house." Then Tōjirō went on to ask whether Bunshirō was married, whether he had any children yet, and other such things. And when Bunshirō answered him he said, "If Sukezaemon-sama were alive now, I'm sure he would be delighted."

Just then, two men entered the garden. The tall, plump, round-faced man was Chōnosuke, and the short, thin old man was Isaku. Aoki and Bunshirō stepped down from the veranda and exchanged greetings with the two men, and together with Tōjirō, who then came outside, the five men set out.

The flattened fields, as Tōjirō had said, were close by, just at the edge of the village. Once they left the village and walked a little way down the path, the banks of the Goken River came into view, and the fields this side of it looked as if they had been swept by a single stroke of a giant hand, leaving every bit of rice lying flat.

The five men mounted the embankment, which afforded them a good view. From there they could see the flattened rice, extending from Isaku's fields, on across the river into Aohata, and far into the distance downstream. The sun was now hidden in the shadow of the hill, but they could still see the houses of Aohata illumined by it. The sky was clear, and there was no obstacle to continuing their inspection.

Aoki and the three men from Kanai were pointing their fingers at the fields, peering into their notebooks, all the while deep in discussion with each other. Bunshirō, while bending an ear to their conversation, turned his eyes toward the edge of the hill that he could see behind the village. That sector where the Zelkova Mansion would be was now shrouded in the depths of dusk, but not yet so dark that the light of any lamps could be seen.

Has her child already been born? Bunshirō had lately made an effort not to think about O-Fuku, but still he could not dismiss her entirely from his thoughts. Perhaps because somewhere within him there lurked the feeling that he was still, in some way, the guardian of O-Fuku.

He had heard rumors that the lord of the domain, who had returned in the Fifth Month, seemed to be making occasional clandestine visits to the Zelkova Mansion. But strange to say, the name of O-Fuku was never mentioned in those rumors. His Lordship must have had the power to conceal that fact, Bunshirō thought, and so the presence of O-Fuku had not yet leaked out to the public. But surely the truth must leak out sooner or later, and that could prove dangerous next year after the lord returns to Edo. But just as Bunshirō was pondering this, Aoki and the others descended from the embankment into the fields, and Bunshirō hastened to follow them.

Aoki and the three men from the village plucked the heads from the fallen rice, and in the palms of their hands peeled the hulls from the grains; then, in an exchange of short phrases that Bunshirō did not understand, nodded in assent to each other. And that seemed to be the end of the inspection.

"The village estimates ..." Aoki turned to Bunshirō, who held notebook and brush in his hands, and spoke as if he were dictating. "It is estimated that the yield of Furukuchida will be ten percent. In our opinion, then, the overall ratio should probably be set at eighty percent."

Semishigure

"At eighty percent, we will have no objection." When Tōjirō spoke, the other two men nodded. They waited until Bunshirō had written this down, and then following the ridge between the fields, the five men returned to the path and on into the village. At the crossroads, Bunshirō and Aoki parted with the other three men.

By the time they had left the village of Kanai and come to the wooden bridge across the rivulet, the sun had sunk below the edge of the hill. At the far end of the field, a pale mist had begun to rise. Before long, their way would be dark, but already they could see the castle town ahead of them. Perhaps owing to this, Aoki now slowed his pace, and Bunshirō did likewise.

"A very hurried round, that ..." Aoki looked straight ahead as he spoke. "You must be tired."

"Yes, but that aside, I'm ashamed I was of so little use in today's inspection. I must have been more of a nuisance."

"Not at all. You'll soon get used to the work." As he spoke, Aoki slowed his pace even more, and Bunshirō followed his lead. Still looking straight ahead, as was his wont, he went on.

"There's something I've been wanting to talk to you about for some time, but I've had no chance and kept putting it off. Today, luckily, there are just the two of us. I've been waiting for a moment like this."

"Something in my work that you need to warn me about?" Bunshirō spoke fearfully, but Aoki shook his head, stopped walking, then turned toward Bunshirō and stared sharply at him.

"You know, don't you, that the domain is split in two?"

"Yes."

"And that Sukezaemon-dono was working for the Yokoyama faction?"

"I've heard about that in a general way."

"Then I can come right to the point." Quite unexpectedly, Aoki Magozō broke out in a smile, so broad that he showed the white of his teeth. "I don't know who you heard about this from, but I suppose these things just naturally get passed around. So let me ask you now how you feel about this. Don't you feel you would like to join Elder Yokoyama?"

Bunshirō said nothing.

"How about it?" Aoki asked softly. "If you're aware that the domain is divided, it's unlikely you haven't heard that Inagaki and Satomura are backing the new Shima-no-Kami and attempting to monopolize control of the domain. If you say you haven't heard, I could show you several examples, right here and now; but today's round of inspections is the handiest.

"Didn't you notice something unusual on this round? The discrepancies between the estimates of the regional deputy and the villages were far too great," Aoki told him. "In the past that never happened. The two estimates were always much closer. We know now why this has happened: because Satomura has given the deputies in each of the regions secret orders to minimize their estimates of the damage. In the past, excesses of this sort were impossible. Most of the village officials belonged to the Yokoyama faction. They could subtly resist the attempts of the Inagaki-Satomura faction to squeeze the villages. But there was always the worry that if they pushed too hard and aroused opposition within the domain, then it might just be possible for the Yokoyama faction to charge them with misgovernment and seize control from them.

"A while ago, Tōjirō mentioned Sukezaemon-dono, but that had nothing to do with the construction of bridges. That was when Sukezaemon-dono was under secret orders from Yokoyama, to go into the villages and do his best to build up the Yokoyama faction."

Semishigure

"This is the first I've ever heard of that," Bunshirō said. "Does that mean that the entreaty to spare his life, submitted by the two villages, had nothing to do with cutting the embankment?"

"No. There was that, too, of course," Aoki said. "That had a great deal to do with it, but that wasn't all there was to it. Since long before that, Sukezaemon-dono had known the officials in many other villages of the region, not just those two. And they trusted him.

"But support for Yokoyama in the villages remained strong only until that power struggle. Thereafter, they gave up their resistance, and as the Inagaki-Satomura faction strengthened their grasp on authority in the domain, one after another, the villages slid over to them. The village of Kanai is now the only one that still secretly supports the Yokoyama faction," Aoki told him.

Aoki spoke with great eloquence, almost as if he had prepared his talk in advance for just such an occasion.

"Inagaki and Satomura are growing more confident now, that even if they increase the pressure a bit, there is no danger it will do any damage to their system. You saw the evidence of that today, in the discrepancies between the estimates.

"The only people in Rural Affairs who view this pressure with any concern are Kashimura-sama and District Deputy Seno'o-sama. All the others do just as Chief Elder Satomura wishes them to do. Yokoyama-sama is greatly distressed by this state of affairs. He's decided he'll run the risk of secretly recruiting those of like mind, because he simply cannot abide what Inagaki and Satomura are doing.

"Our elder now wants every single ally he can find. The time will come, eventually, when there'll be a direct confrontation with the Inagaki-Satomura faction; and he is preparing for that day. So how about it?" Aoki peered into Bunshirō's face.

"The Yokoyama faction was once dominant and then was destroyed. To rebuild it will be no easy task. If we make the wrong move, we could be demolished immediately. That is the sort of group we are. But won't you join us and lend your strength to our cause?"

"I understand perfectly what you are saying," Bunshirō replied. He knew very well what the situation was, and he was impressed by Aoki's passion; but the fact was that he felt little enthusiasm. "But I really can't give you an answer here and now."

"You're saying you'll have to think about it? I see." Aoki shut his mouth, and when he opened it again, he spoke a bit curtly. "Father will be father, but son will be son. That's one way of looking at it."

"No, that's not what I mean to say. I am the son of Maki Sukezaemon."

Aoki stared at Bunshirō with his mouth shut tight, as if he had returned to his old silent self.

"But for too long I was forced to eat cold rice, and only this year have I finally returned to living a normal life. It just won't do to place myself thoughtlessly in a position of such danger." As he said this, Bunshirō noticed a samurai on a path through the fields that ran off at an angle ahead of them. He was a tall man and sturdily built, wearing travelling breeches and carrying his surcoat in his hand.

3

The samurai had probably noticed Bunshirō and Aoki before this. As he neared the road, he was looking toward the two of them. But a distance of perhaps twenty yards still separated them, and in the gathering dusk, it was impossible to distinguish clearly his face or age.

Semishigure

At first Bunshirō thought he might be one of the guards at the Zelkova Mansion. But only because this man, who appeared suddenly on a path through the rice fields, was coming from the direction of the Zelkova Mansion. He was not one of the guards, however. His garb and the aura about him were those of a proper member of the domain's Corps of Vassals. While gazing suspiciously at this samurai who had appeared on the path in the dusk, Bunshirō went on talking.

"Give me a few days time, please, to think about this."

"You were married just this spring, if I remember rightly?"

"Yes."

"It's not that I don't understand the importance of preserving your family name and your family life, but ..." Aoki lowered his voice. It must have been just then that he noticed the samurai as he came out of the path through the fields onto the road that led to the castle town. His eyes were fastened upon the man ahead of them. "Those things are but the pleasures of the moment. So long as the Inagaki-Satomura faction hold the domain in their grasp, you'd best resign yourself to the fact that those are pleasures of the moment that may be wrested from you at any time. They were the survivors in that struggle for power, so we mustn't yet take our eyes off them." When Aoki said that, the samurai who had turned onto the road ahead, turned back toward them, as if he had heard Aoki's whispers.

"Aha!" As he approached them, the samurai called out in a strong, forceful voice. "I thought I recognized your face. You're Aoki Magozō, the rural inspector, are you not?"

Aoki removed his sedge hat, and, saying nothing, bowed. Bunshirō did likewise. But the samurai did not bow back. He stared at Aoki with sharp eyes as he spoke.

"I understand it was you who arranged that recent gathering

at the temple Taisenji. It seems to have gone very well, but there had better not be another."

Bunshirō, under cover of his sedge hat, released the catch on the sheath of his sword. He could sense murderous intent in the man. Bunshirō turned toward Aoki. Aoki stood up to the man, his chest thrust out, but even in the gathering dusk, Bunshirō could see that his face was deathly pale, drained of color. He had likely been intimidated by the man's urge to kill.

"Those in command are saying that if that happens again, it will be regarded as treason against the domain. I'll say it again." The tall samurai spoke even more forcefully and stepped menacingly forward. "That must not happen a second time. So watch your step!"

The man then moved closer still, as if to threaten Aoki. Seeing this, Bunshirō took a step forward in a stance that would allow him to protect Aoki; whereupon the man looked at Bunshirō for the first time. In the next instant, the man casually turned to face Bunshirō, and slowly retreated. Then, after he had put ample space between them, he spoke.

"You're Aoki's colleague?"

"A rural inspector in training."

"Your name?"

"I am Maki Bunshirō."

"Well, well!" the man said.

Bunshirō could not make out clearly the man's expression, but his stern mien seemed to crumble just slightly.

"Maki Bunshirō of the Kūdon school? I had the privilege to see your match with Okitsu a while back. I, too, would like to challenge you to a match sometime."

"And your name, sir?"

"Me? I won't mention my name just now, but you'll know

Semishigure

soon enough." Having said that, the man suddenly broke out in a loud, mocking laugh and turned his back. Then slipping into the surcoat that he held in his hand, he strode away, and his broad back soon dwindled into the distance.

When Bunshirō looked back, Aoki Magozō had taken the towel that hung at his waist and was wiping the sweat from his face. The air was chilly, but the sweat seemed not to stop flowing. Aoki then opened his collars wide and wiped the sweat from his neck and chest.

"Who was that?"

"Murakami Shichirōemon-dono," Aoki said. He still seemed quite tense, and his voice was deep and hoarse. But that name struck Bunshirō a heavy blow.

Unconsciously he looked off at the now tiny figure of the man walking away. Murakami Shichirōemon was the man who had severed his father's head when Sukezaemon had been forced to commit seppuku. Later he learnt that Murakami had once been a high-ranking disciple at the Matsukawa Dojo, but this was the first time he had met him.

"Just so I know," Bunshirō said, "would he be the Murakami of the Bodyguard?"

"No, he's in the Horse Guards now," Aoki told him. Aoki had finally regained his composure. "Shall we go now?" he suggested. Then he laughed lightly. "Faced with someone like that, my hands and my feet refuse to move."

For his own part, Bunshirō was pondering why Murakami should have come from the direction of the Zelkova Mansion.

4

When he and Aoki returned to the Office of the District Deputy in the third perimeter, Bunshirō notified the man on night duty in the now empty building; then, leaving Aoki to put their documents in order, he left the castle.

The castle stood on a slight rise—not really a hill—surrounded by stone ramparts. And thus when one emerged from the gate, the road sloped gently downward. The sun was fully set when Bunshirō descended the slope, and he could see the light of lanterns out in the town. Brighter than all the rest was Aoyagi-chō, the main commercial district. The air was clear, which perhaps was why the lights looked so much brighter than usual. There was no wind, but none of the heat of summer remained in the night air, which felt crisp and refreshing.

He didn't look down on me for that, did he? Bunshirō wondered, as his thoughts turned back to Aoki, who had remained behind and would now be starting to grind ink at his desk.

Ever since the death of his father, Bunshirō had been bound by the ironclad duty to defend the good name of the Maki family. Even in his child's mind, he could see the danger to the House of Maki so clearly that he felt compelled to make that his mission. Besides which, Bunshirō had become head of the Maki house as an adopted heir. Low in rank though they were, their lineage traced back to the founding of the domain. For such a house to be abolished because of a blunder on his part would never do. This he felt strongly.

Looking back, Bunshirō could not but regret that the days of his youth, which should have been so free, had to be spent in a state of constant apprehension. He had endured the cold stares of the world directed at a family of traitors. He had suppressed himself and devoted his all to preserving a family name left hanging as if from a single strand of slender thread. His one and only escape from these dismal feelings had been his training and practice at the Ishiguri Dojo. Were it not for the Kūdon school of swordsmanship, he could not have borne it.

And now, Bunshirō felt, those long years of perseverance were being rewarded. His stipend, and thus the means to live a normal life, had been restored; he had been given employment; he had a wife. As the months and years passed, children might be born, and if he were to work hard, without slacking, he might even hope to advance slightly at some point. At last he was able to imagine a future of that sort. And all, he thought, because even in the very depths of misfortune, he had never given vent to any grievance; he had never quarreled with anyone; he had kept to himself and put his energy into swordsmanship and study. He did not want to lose this security.

Then Bunshirō thought again of the words Murakami Shichirōemon had flung at Aoki Magozō on that dark road, that he would be considered a traitor. That may just have been Murakami's own threat. But if ever Bunshirō were to join the Yokoyama faction, he must understand that a day might come when the son would follow his father in being branded a traitor to the domain. He did not care to run that risk.

Bunshirō crossed the bridge. But … he thought, Aoki is a good man. He had worked in the same room with Aoki in the Office of the District Deputy, and at times they had gone together on the inspection round of the district, with District Commissioner Kashimura Yasuke as their leader. Aoki had always been a silent and inobtrusive man. Bunshirō respected his seniority but had never taken any special notice of him.

But on this first round of the villages with only the two of them working together, Bunshirō was struck by how precise Aoki's knowledge of the land and the crops was and how considerate in his dealings with all the people they met. In particular, it lingered in Bunshirō's memory how Aoki would never flaunt the authority of his office the way other rural inspectors seemed sometimes to do. In his discussions with the villagers, Aoki was cordial and never overbearing; he would say what had to be said and leave it to them to digest it.

Bunshirō recalled how Aoki had criticized the policy of the Inagaki-Satomura faction, noting how pleased they were to be squeezing the villages, and pointing out how forcible their control of agriculture had become of late.

If this was the way things were, Bunshirō thought, he too would eventually be cast in the role of the cruel official coercing the villagers. And that, he realized, he would not be able to bear; whereupon Aoki's words echoed in his mind—about those pleasures of the moment that might be taken from him at any time.

When he returned to his home in the Rural Affairs quarter, Setsu came out to greet him.

"Welcome back," she said. "You must be tired." More than half a year had passed since they were married, and Setsu seemed to have grown accustomed to speaking like a wife. Bunshirō handed her his sword, sat down on the step to the threshold, and began washing in the water she had prepared. Setsu had thoughtfully added some hot water, and the tepid liquid refreshed his weary feet. Pleasures of the moment. The words again arose in Bunshirō's mind.

After he greeted his mother, Setsu followed him into the couple's own room and helped him change. A messenger from the house of Owada Ippei had come, she said.

"It's been born, then?" Bunshirō said. Half a month earlier, he had, unusually, encountered him in the castle. Ippei had told him, he recalled, that his child would soon be born.

Semishigure

"Yes, it was a boy, they say."

"That's even better."

"He also said to remind you again to be sure to attend the Seventh Night."

So then. Ippei is finally a father? And with that thought, it suddenly occurred to Bunshirō to wonder how O-Fuku and her child were faring. Quickly he banished that thought. Setsu, who was unaware of it, spoke.

"When I told Mother about it, she seemed terribly envious." It was just like her to be envious. And when Setsu had finished helping him change, she softly pressed her cheek to Bunshirō's back. He felt guilty to be remembering Fuku while he was alone with his wife, and he pretended not to notice her gesture, so like that of a new wife.

"I will go to the Seventh Night. But then, what sort of a gift would be appropriate? Could you discuss that with Mother and prepare something?" Bunshirō said.

That night, in the darkness of his bed, however, it was not Ippei's new son, or his new wife's affectionate gesture that came back to Bunshirō's mind. It was the words of Aoki Magozō's invitation on the road back.

Father … It's possible he might be pleased if I were to join the Yokoyama faction. After long thought, this was where Bunshirō had arrived. But then, he must be prepared to abandon the pleasures of the life he had at last regained after enduring all that humiliation. He was not finding it easy to decide.

In the darkness, the scent of Setsu's hair pervaded the room. Until only a moment ago it had lain upon his breast; her fragrance now seemed the last vestige of their damp moments together. Pleasures of the moment. Those words again flickered through Bunshirō's mind.

The next day I'm off duty ... shall I go to the dojo? The thought had come to Bunshirō suddenly. And then a way forward seemed to open up. In the past, whenever he was at a loss what to do, he would go to the dojo, take up his bamboo sword, and flail with all his might. Bunshirō closed his eyes. Now he would be able to sleep.

5

The day after the Seventh Night celebration for Ippei's son, Bunshirō was off duty. He set out for the dojo.

After greeting Master Ishiguri Yazaemon in his private quarters, Bunshirō went on to the training hall. The moment he passed through the entrance the tumultuous cries of attack struck his ears, and the sweaty enthusiasm of those young bodies enveloped him with nostalgia. For a time, Bunshirō just stood on the hard earthen floor at the entrance and watched the twenty-some students at their practice. At the far end of the hall, he saw Maruoka Shunsaku; then he removed his sandals and stepped up to the wooden floor.

As Bunshirō walked toward the rear, Sugiuchi Michizō, who was practicing with a youth of thirteen or fourteen, raised his hand, ceased fighting, and ran over to Bunshirō. Since he had last seen Michizō some time ago, he had grown into a stalwart young man.

"It's been a long time!" Michizō greeted him with a smile. "This is unusual. Are you off duty today?"

"Yeah."

"Has it been half a year?"

"Surely not. I came once in the Sixth Month." As he spoke, Bunshirō was looking at Michizō's forehead, which was dripping with sweat. "We'll talk later. Go back to your practice now."

After sending Michizō back to his practice match, Bunshirō moved closer to Maruoka, who was instructing a youth of fourteen or fifteen. Maruoka didn't notice and had taken hold of the boy's hand to teach him. This was typical of Maruoka to explain things so carefully. Bunshirō waited for a break, then called out to Maruoka.

"Yo!" Maruoka turned and smiled. He gave instructions to his young student and then came over to Bunshirō.

"Have you been to see the master?"

"Yes, just a moment ago, in his quarters."

"He's aged, hasn't he?" Maruoka said.

Bunshirō nodded. Their master, Yazaemon, was up and about, but his hands were trembling, and in the short time Bunshirō had been with him, he had twice spilt tea on his knees.

"The dojo has changed." Maruoka led Bunshirō over to a corner and was casting his eyes about at the practicing students as he spoke. "Satake-san resigned as the master's assistant this summer. He's been assigned additional duties, he says, and can't come to the dojo."

"So now it's you, Maruoka-san?"

"Well, everyone was urging me, so that's what happened." The mild-mannered Maruoka had an embarrassed look on his face as he spoke. "Ōhashi, too, has quit." As Maruoka went on, he seemed to be searching for someone; and then, when he spotted Inukai Hyōma teaching someone at the far end of the hall, he gave Bunshirō a significant look. "He claimed it was because he was to become an adoptive heir. But that wasn't the real reason. He was defeated in a match with Hyōma, and it was a humiliating defeat. He seems to have felt he had to leave."

"Because it was Hyōma …" As he spoke, Bunshirō, too, was watching Hyōma, off in the distance, giving a harsh lesson to a student. It filled him with a sense of loathing. What was it about Hyōma, he wondered, that makes one feel so violent? "Was it that he ran roughshod over Ōhashi-san?"

"That was it." Maruoka answered tersely. "Satake-san left. Ōhashi quit. You're still enrolled, but your duties keep you away. Master, as you've seen, has become an old man. The dojo is a lonely place now."

"And Yada-san is dead." Bunshirō was overcome with nostalgia as he spoke. The floors of this training hall must have absorbed a great deal of his sweat. He longed for the days when the severe-natured Satake Kinjūrō and the mild but incisive Maruoka and Yada controlled the dojo.

"That's right," Maruoka said. "Things have really changed."

"What are the rankings like now?"

"Tsukahara has improved. He ranks second now," Maruoka said. "At one point he was surpassed by Hyōma, but he fought his way back up."

"So now Hyōma ranks after him?"

"That's right. Then Noda and Sugiuchi, in that order."

And then, as if he had overheard their conversation, Inukai Hyōma could be seen pushing his way through the crowd toward them.

"Hey." As he approached, Hyōma raised a hand and called out. He greeted them as if they were senior colleagues. Bunshirō said nothing but nodded, and Hyōma smirked.

"How's the round of the rice fields?"

"It's certainly worth doing."

"Worth doing?" The grin on Hyōma's face grew broader. "'The inspector grabs up all the shit.' Isn't that what they say? That you wade out into the paddy and grab all the shit that's been spread there?"

Semishigure

"Well now, I've never heard anything about that." When Bunshirō said that, Hyōma wiped the grin from his face.

"It's been a while now; so could you give me a lesson?"

Bunshirō looked cautiously into Hyōma's face. As always, Hyōma's face was slender and pale, but his eyes were uneasy and his lips were twisted when he smiled. This was not the way he had looked before. Compared to what he had been in the past, he looked ever so slightly more vulgar. What could that signify, Bunshirō wondered as he spoke.

"I haven't held a bamboo practice sword for some time now, but …"

"Please! Just this one lesson."

"Your opponent may not be up to you." But as he said this, Bunshirō was thinking how he would beat Hyōma to a pulp. Hyōma, unaware of this, smiled again.

"This is such a rare chance. Don't say that, please." Hyōma spoke in the most insistent and demanding tones.

"Well then," Bunshirō said. "But let's not just practice; let's have a proper match. Will that be all right, Maruoka-san?" When Bunshirō said that, Hyōma stared back at him with fury in his eyes, as if something had just dawned upon him.

The two of them tied back their sleeves, tightened their headbands, and with Maruoka as their referee, proceeded to the center of the training hall. Everyone else retreated to the paneled wall and sat down there to watch the match.

But the match took a disappointing turn. First of all, Bunshirō hit Hyōma on the shoulder, easily winning the first round. Hyōma, although he had taken a blow so harsh that it must have made his shoulder swell, charged back ferociously for the second round. His face had turned bright red, making him look like a demon. The second round was a violent exchange, but

Bunshirō still had reserves. He watched for his chance, then using his secret technique, Cloudburst, he put an end to the match. As Bunshirō slid across the floor on one knee and shifted into a counterattack defensive posture, Hyōma, stricken hard on the side of his torso, lurched some six feet to the rear, and lay there, unconscious.

Far from feeling refreshed at having thrashed Hyōma, it was with an unpleasant aftertaste that Bunshirō left the dojo. But before he reached the riverbank, Sugiuchi Michizō came running up after him.

"Hyōma has changed," Bunshirō said. "What happened?"

"Ever since he was beaten by Okitsu in the autumn tournament last year, he's been dreadfully violent." And immediately thereafter, as if that were not what he had come to talk about, Michizō demanded: "What was that stroke you used on Inukai-san just now?"

Hidden Strife

1

The year's end was almost upon them, and the days were growing steadily shorter. Bunshirō and his colleagues were drafting their documents by lamplight, when the panel at the door to their room slid open and Owada Ippei stuck his head in and cast a glance at Bunshirō.

"Working late?" Bunshirō came out into the corridor, and Ippei thrust his chin toward their room as he spoke.

"No, we'll be finished soon."

"That's good. There's something I want to talk to you about; so let's get together in Somekawa-chō tonight," Ippei said, and he added, "It'll be my treat."

"No, you don't have to treat me, but what is it you want to talk about?"

"I can't mention that here." Ippei quickly signaled with his eyes in the dim corridor of the district deputy's office, lit only by the lamplight that streamed out from the room. "Shall we meet at Kinutaya at the Fifth Hour (8 p.m.)?"

"That'll be fine. But saké only today; no brothels."

"It makes no difference to me, but we mustn't make your wife angry with you," Ippei said. "I'll go home first." He turned and left.

Talk about what? Bunshirō wondered. The doubt lingered, but he hadn't seen Ippei or Yonosuke for such a long time, he had no objection to going drinking.

That night, when Bunshirō went to Kinutaya in Somekawa-chō, Ippei had already arrived and was busy making the serving girls laugh.

"O-Tora, isn't it about time you were getting married? Mustn't let yourself become unsold leftovers. That'd be tragic."

"I know. I'm not leftover because I like it that way. It's just there's no one who'll have me. Right, O-Yoshi-san?" Plump little O-Tora spoke to another serving girl, as the two of them poured saké for Bunshirō and Ippei. And then to Bunshirō she said, "This is your first time with O-Yoshi-san, isn't it?" Which seemed to suggest that Ippei, despite being married and having a child, was something of a regular at Kinutaya.

"O-Kimi, who you were so fond of ..." O-Tora flicked the tip of her sleeve at Bunshirō as she spoke. "She was married just before summer. We were just talking about her."

"It wasn't that I was particularly fond of her ..." Bunshirō said with a wry smile. "That's wonderful. Who'd she marry?"

"He's a craftsman. A cabinetmaker ..."

"A master cabinetmaker? That's not bad."

"I hear he's a very handsome craftsman," Ippei said. Then he slapped his knee and said, "Now—we've got something private to talk about, so would you girls leave us alone for a little while? We'll call you back later." The two girls left the room obediently.

"Well now," Ippei said, "shall we drink as we talk?"

"So it's that sort of talk?"

"No, it's rather serious talk," Ippei said, "but then it's cold, so

Semishigure

we'd better take care lest our voices get too loud." The two of them poured for each other and then began picking at some stewed codfish heads in jellied broth.

"Have you seen Yonosuke recently?" Ippei asked, without looking up from his fish head.

"No, I've been so busy I haven't seen anyone. How about you?"

"I haven't seen him either, but I've heard rumors," Ippei said. "He seems to be held in very high regard. I never went to the domain academy, but is an assistant professor there someone important?

"That's important indeed. If he's been made an assistant professor, he's one of the top scholars in the domain."

"Well!"

"Has Yonosuke become an assistant professor?"

"So I hear."

"Well that's a great leap forward. But the domain must have been intending that from the start, when they undertook to finance his studies."

For a time, the two of them went on talking about Shimazaki Yonosuke. Their hands lifted their cups to their lips ever faster, and their faces turned red.

Then Ippei looked at Bunshirō and asked, "Do you know the cotton merchant, Shinobuya, in Aoyagi-chō?"

"I know of it. It's a big shop."

"Well, I hear that this summer there were some suspicious customers there. There was a man and a woman. The woman did the shopping, and the man was a samurai. He came into the shop, but just stood in a corner and kept his eyes on the woman until she was finished. In short, the man was her companion, and he carried the goods she had bought, but he was not *simply* her companion. He gave the impression that he was guarding her."

"Really?" Bunshirō said; but he had an idea who this man and woman might have been. Given the impression they made in the shop, these two probably were not locals. Mightn't they have come from the Zelkova Mansion? "Wouldn't the woman have been from a samurai family?"

"The people at Shinobuya seemed not to know. The woman's hair and clothes were in the style of townspeople, but she spoke in Edo dialect, they say."

"Then what did she buy?"

"Two bolts of bleached muslin." Ippei emptied his saké cup and then filled it again himself. "But that's only the start. We don't know who they were, but there's someone who saw them leave the town. And where do you suppose they went from there?"

"Well ..."

"To the Zelkova Mansion." Having said this, Ippei for a while sat silently picking away with his chopsticks. And when he had finished eating his codfish head, he heaved a sigh, lay down his chopsticks, poured himself another cup of saké, and downed it. Then he looked up at Bunshirō.

"Now I'll tell you about our lord ... Since his return this year, His Lordship has gone several times to the Zelkova Mansion. In secret, of course. He leaves on the spur of the moment, on horseback, with only one attendant."

"And then?"

"Needless to say, he is not going to view the scenery. No matter what the rustic charms of a place may be, once you visit it two or three times, you'll have seen enough. So the question then becomes, who are the people he most favors? For there must be a woman in the Zelkova Mansion of whom he is very fond."

Semishigure

"Do you know who?"

"No, that I do not know. The man who accompanies him is named Kurisu, a member of the Bodyguard, but he's a man who keeps his mouth shut as tight as an oyster. I've tried to trick him into telling, but he won't say a single word."

"Hmm."

"But lately there have been those who say that O-Fuku-sama, the woman he banished from his presence in Edo, may be the one who is now in the Zelkova Mansion. That's only a rumor, of course. There's no proof … But that rumor is tied to what I told you before about the customers at Shinobuya. It's like this." Ippei put down the empty saké cup he was holding and stared at Bunshirō. "They say that those two are looking after O-Fuku-sama at the Zelkova Mansion and that they bought those two bolts of bleached muslin because she had just given birth to a child."

"Shhh!" Bunshirō said. There was the clatter of wooden clogs as someone passed the room the two of them were in. It seemed to have been a serving girl. After he had heard the footsteps move on to the front of the shop, Ippei continued.

"The man never said a word, but we can assume that if he had spoken they would have recognized it as Edo dialect. Which is to say, it makes sense to think that the favorite of His Lordship in the Zelkova Mansion has come here from Edo. As for proof of the conjecture that this person may be O-Fuku-sama …" Ippei again stared hard into Bunshirō's face. "O-Fuku-san, of whom you were so fond …"

"Hey, now! Watch your language."

"Oops, sorry. O-Fuku-*sama*, I've heard, previously miscarried a child of His Lordship. And there are those who say that the mother of Shima-no-Kami was responsible for this. Have you heard of this?"

"I've heard."

"Hmm." Ippei slowly poured more saké into his cup. "That's probably why rumor has it that His Lordship is so secretive about the person in the Zelkova Mansion—because she is O-Fuku-sama." Ippei broke off there. But then suddenly he said, "Have you already heard all of this?"

"Yes, I've heard." If these rumors were already the talk of the castle, there was no reason for Bunshirō to keep his knowledge a secret from Ippei.

"No, I mean all that I've just told you." Ippei again stared into Bunshirō's face. "I mean, did you hear about all of this long ago?"

"Yes, I heard about it long ago."

"From whom?"

"From Yonosuke."

"And you told me nothing?"

"There was nothing certain to tell," Bunshirō said. "And it was strictly confidential. It wasn't that I didn't trust you. It's just that if you tell one person, it's not impossible the secret could leak out."

"I am not one to chatter irresponsibly."

"I know that." Bunshirō poured more saké into Ippei's cup. "But if *they* were to find out that O-Fuku-sama were there, and that she had given birth to a child of His Lordship, that would not be the end of it."

"Meaning the Satomura faction?" Ippei looked deep in thought. But then he turned his eyes back on Bunshirō. "Surely, though, they wouldn't assassinate a woman and her child?"

"We don't know that. And it was because I thought there was good reason to fear it that I said nothing to you. Don't think ill of me, please."

"But, Bunshirō!" Ippei emptied his saké cup and spoke in an

Semishigure

agitated voice. "If that is so, isn't it dangerous with all these rumors flying about?"

"Of course it's dangerous. But for the moment, we shouldn't have to worry. His Lordship will be in the castle until next spring. And besides, there are the guards you mentioned previously." Bunshirō then told him what he had heard from Yonosuke after he returned and what he had seen when he went to investigate the Zelkova Mansion. "There were two men, both of whom appeared to be very skilled swordsmen. They spoke in Edo dialect. One of them must have been the man in Shinobuya."

"Really? You went to investigate the place?" Ippei passed a saké cup to Bunshirō and poured for him. "So of course, you're still worried for O-Fuku-san's safety."

"Of course I am." Bunshirō could tell that he was drunker than usual. "I can't ignore the danger."

"Rascal! Now you're spewing out what you really feel!" Ippei must have learnt that expression from someone who had just returned from Edo. It wasn't the way one expected to hear him speak. Then suddenly, with a stunned look in his eyes, he turned to Bunshirō. "But it's still nothing more than conjecture to say that O-Fuku-san is out there. No one has actually seen her."

"No, no one has seen her," Bunshirō said. Probably even Murakami Shichirōemon had not seen O-Fuku, he thought, recalling Murakami's sudden appearance at sundown on that path through the fields. But now Bunshirō felt more firmly convinced than ever that O-Fuku was indeed in that building and that she must have borne their lord's child this summer. His reason was those two bolts of bleached muslin bought by the woman who spoke in Edo dialect. Those two had rushed to Shinobuya, had they not, despite knowing that their identity would be suspect, because the birth threatened to take place before all their preparations were complete.

2

"There's no more saké," Ippei muttered. He turned the flask upside down over his cup and shook it, but not a single drop of saké fell from it. He put the flask back on the tray and clapped his hands. The man came to take their order, and before long O-Tora came back carrying more hot saké.

"Shall I pour for you?" she asked with a welcoming smile, but Ippei told her they weren't finished talking yet and sent her away.

"There's this fellow named Endō. Endō Saburōta." As he spoke, Ippei, with busy hands, filled both Bunshirō's cup and his own with saké. "He's a long-time member of the Bodyguard, and he's related by blood to Inagaki-sama. So he's known to be a regular visitor at Chief Elder Satomura's mansion."

"Oh?"

"Actually, he's nothing but a messenger boy for the bigwigs, but that's not what he thinks. He wears his connections with the upper crust on his hat and speaks in a very arrogant manner. Nobody likes him."

"Shhh! You're a bit loud," Bunshirō cautioned him. They stopped talking and pricked up their ears but heard only indistinct singing on the other side of the wall and from a distant room the talk and laughter of several men.

Bunshirō poured for Ippei. "So what about this Endō?"

"At midday today, when we were all eating our lunches in the duty room, suddenly he stands up and starts making a speech."

"What sort of speech?"

"It was perfectly stupid." Ippei drained his cup in one gulp. "He said that recently in the domain an opposing faction had been formed and was inviting people to join them and that no one in the Bodyguard had better be fooled by them. Basically, it

Semishigure

was a rant against the Yokoyama faction, but the way he spoke was so overbearing. I found it sickening, so I told him: 'You're ruining the taste of my lunch, so would you please shut up.'"

"That must have made him mad!"

"He was furious. He threatened me, saying, 'If you won't listen to advice, you'll regret it later.' So I shot back at him: 'Whether I listen or don't listen is my choice. But that aside, when did you become commander of the Bodyguard?'"

"Was it wise to say that?"

"Why not? I don't care. What he did overstepped the mark. So I went at him again. 'I'd like to hear that from our commander,' I said. And there were others in the room who agreed with me; so the rat shut up. What a brazen-faced fellow!" Ippei looked straight at Bunshirō. "The way Endō tells it, only the Yokoyama faction is inviting others to join them, but that's not so. Ever since they noticed this, the Satomura faction, too, has been recruiting, so as to tighten their grip. But that's not going so well, I hear. Actually, I was invited once, but refused straight off."

"Did you?"

"I did indeed. I think they're afraid they could lose out to the Yokoyama faction and their new recruits, and that's why they had Endō make that speech. Because the way things stand now, Yokoyama-sama is looking like the shrewder man."

Bunshirō was recalling what Kaji Oribe-no-Shō had said—that Yokoyama had lately been restoring some balance to the situation and that he was a strangely clever man.

"Have you been invited by either of them?" Ippei asked.

"I have," Bunshirō told him. Whereupon Ippei raised his face, now red from saké.

"Of course. Which one?"

"The Yokoyama faction."

"That figures. And you'll have signed up. Your father was a member of the Yokoyama faction."

"No, it's not that simple." Bunshirō told him honestly how his fellow rural inspector had invited him to join and how he understood all the reasons he should join, but just couldn't bring himself to take that one last step. And once he had told Ippei, that pain deep in his breast that had afflicted him for so long felt a little lighter.

In hushed voices, the two men went on, deep in conversation over what might transpire in the power struggle within the domain, until finally, in a drunken voice, Ippei said, "If you do sign up, be sure to let me know. I wouldn't want the two of us to end up on opposite sides."

When they left Kinutaya, it was a little before mid-Fourth Hour (11 p.m.). They didn't see another customer in the place. They were the last two.

"Take care on your way home," the woman with high cheekbones and thick makeup said as she saw them off. "It's cold out there." She was the mistress of the owner, and it was she who managed Kinutaya, Bunshirō had recently learnt.

3

As the woman said, it was cold outside. There was no wind, but the night air was bitterly cold and it pierced their skin, now aglow from drunkenness.

"Looks like it could snow." Bunshirō looked up at the sky, but it was dark; neither the moon nor the stars could be seen. The clouds were thick and low, but there was no sign that anything would fall. It was just cold.

There remained a few lanterns hanging from the eaves along

the way, but of course fewer than before; and as cold as it was, there was no one to be seen on the street.

"Is your child well?" Bunshirō asked. Ippei's son had been placed in the care of a farm family in the village of Aohata.

"Yes. Just a little while ago, his nursemaid brought him to us, and he seems to be healthy and growing.

"That's good to know."

"And you're still waiting?" Just as Ippei spoke, at the exit of the quarter, which they could see up ahead of them, several men suddenly appeared. They were samurai dressed in dark garb. These men were running, and as they passed the exit, left to right, there was a sudden clash, and two men fell. Neither Bunshirō nor Ippei had any idea what was going on. As the men ran off after the skirmish, there was a flash of blades reflecting the light of distant lamps.

"Hurry, Ippei!" As he called out, Bunshirō raced ahead. Being drunk, breathing quickly became painful, but his legs did not weaken as he ran. To his rear, the heavy footfall of Ippei followed.

When they reached the exit, two men lay fallen. They were of course samurai, as they had seen from afar. The others seemed already to have fled, for there was no sign of them anywhere to be seen.

Bunshirō crouched and examined the wounds of the one. He was a young samurai, just over thirty, but no one he knew. He put his hand under the man's head so he could examine his face, and when he lifted it, he let out a gasp. He could see at a glance that there was no saving the young man's life. The blow that had felled him cut from the inner edge of his shoulder across his chest, even severing some of his ribs. The blood that gushed from the wound soaked his chest and his back, and spread across the ground, looking black to the eye in the night.

Bunshirō softly lowered the man's head to the ground, moved over, and crouched by the side of the other man. The man's head had been split, and he was dead. But when he stretched out his hand to examine the man's face, the light of a distant lantern shone obliquely upon him and his face suddenly came clearly into view.

"What's the matter? Do you know him?" Ippei, who was crouching next to him, let out a sharp breath as he spoke. He could sense that Bunshirō was taken aback.

"It's Aoki-san, the rural inspector." Bunshirō gently took the sword Aoki was holding and replaced it in its sheath. Now, for the first time, it occurred to him to wonder who might have done this.

A Trap

1

Shortly after seeing off the lord of the domain on his return to Edo, on a night early in the Fifth Month, someone called at the home of Bunshirō. He was a messenger from Chief Elder Satomura—a young man, apparently a retainer of the elder—and he asked that Bunshirō accompany him to the elder's mansion in connection with some urgent business. Bunshirō changed into trousers and surcoat and left the house.

"Do you know what this matter might be?"

Along the way, Bunshirō tried to sound out the young samurai, but he said only, "Hmm …" and cocked his head to one side. The man looked to be younger than twenty. His face, red with acne, and illumined by the glow of his lantern, gave the impression of innocence. It did not appear that he knew but was hiding something.

Even so, Bunshirō told himself, he must take care. He recalled how a few years earlier he had been summoned to Satomura's mansion. On that occasion, he had been overjoyed to be told, quite unexpectedly, that his family stipend was to be restored and that he was commanded to serve under the district commissioner. But that was no guarantee that such good news awaited him this time at the elder's mansion. It was rather a sense of foreboding that found its way into his thoughts.

Even then it could have gone either way: the House of Maki might have been abolished, or we might in some fashion have been formally pardoned, Bunshirō thought. Whichever way it had turned out would not have seemed strange. That his stipend had been restored and he had been allotted a house in the Rural Affairs Unit's residential quarter could only be called a stroke of good fortune. That he now clearly understood.

In his ignorance of the current state of affairs, however, he remained uneasy as he entered the mansion of the chief elder in Babasaki. It was the same room to which he had been shown before, the elder's sitting room. And just as before, there were two men there. One was the elder, Satomura, and the other was a man Bunshirō had never seen before. It was not Inspector General Ogata.

"I'm sorry to summon you in the night." Satomura spoke softly, which calmed Bunshirō a bit. Bunshirō raised his head, and Satomura said, "I doubt you know this gentleman. This is Inagaki-sama." Bunshirō bowed low again. This was the first time he had seen the former junior elder, who was reputed to be the power behind the scenes in the governance of the domain. When he raised his head, Inagaki was smiling at Bunshirō.

Inagaki's hair was graying, his face tanned, and his body strongly built. He appeared to be slightly younger than Satomura, but there was dignity in the smile he turned toward Bunshirō. Bunshirō felt himself shrink back from him.

"Maki—I understand you've been certified by the Ishiguri Dojo."

Where would Elder Satomura have heard about that?

"Yes."

"Who is the stronger? You or Inukai's son, Hyōma?"

"I'd say we're well matched."

"Now on an entirely different matter …" Satomura seemed determined to move on to his main subject straightaway. "What do you make of this outbreak of night attacks we've been having lately?"

"Yes." Bunshirō answered with strict formality. "I think they are deplorable."

It had begun toward the end of the previous year with the assassination of Aoki Magozō and Sugai Jinpachi of the Horse Guards, and after the New Year a man from the Satomura faction was killed. That was Yamazaki, a member of the Bodyguard. Then, in the Third Month, another member of the Yokoyama faction was killed; and just before His Lordship set out for Edo, at the end of the Fourth Month, another man died. This time one of the Satomura faction. In every case, these men were killed in the dark of night.

"Suspicion gives rise to fear, and their fear has deluded them. They speak of the Satomura faction and the Yokoyama faction, but in fact nothing of the sort even exists. Yet in their delusion, they go on repeating this game of retaliation."

Even if there were a grain of truth in what Satomura was saying, in the main it was a bald-faced lie. There could be no doubt whatsoever that the Satomura faction and the Yokoyama faction actually existed. Bunshirō had only to recall the deathly pallor of Aoki Magozō's face to know this. Still, it mystified him, why Satomura should summon him and tell him such things.

"I've summoned a number of these men and urged them to put a stop to this futile fighting. They always agree with me and say they will comply, but behind the scenes nothing changes.

They continue killing each other as fanatically as ever. It's a dreadful state of affairs." The elder sighed.

Bunshirō averted his eyes from the extravagant dramatics of the elder and looked over at Inagaki. And Inagaki looked back at Bunshirō. Or rather, the former junior elder had kept his eyes fixed upon Bunshirō from the very start, smiling all the while.

"We can't let this continue. Inagaki-sama and I have just been discussing it tonight. If the Shogunate should learn that there is trouble of this sort in the domain, they will not ignore it. And His Lordship is very worried about this. He commanded us to put a stop to it just before he left for Edo." Satomura then affected a deep sigh. "But His Lordship does not perceive the true cause of the trouble."

Another retainer—not the young samurai who previously had guided Bunshirō but a middle-aged samurai—brought tea, and then served the elder and Inagaki, as well as Bunshirō. Inagaki sipped his tea noisily.

"Did you know that His Lordship has a concubine, named O-Fuku?" Satomura asked, sipping his tea silently. His large Adam's apple moved visibly, as if it were dancing. Then he replaced his cup on the table.

"Yes, I know." When Bunshirō replied, Satomura nodded.

"Well, this O-Fuku-sama has secretly returned to the domain and has given birth to a child of His Lordship at the Zelkova Mansion. Have you heard of this?"

"No," Bunshirō said. So, what Yonosuke told me, and Ippei surmised, is actually true! he thought.

"You don't know?" Satomura stared hard at Bunshirō. He felt the stare lasted a little too long, but then Satomura looked away from Bunshirō. "Well, if you don't know, then I'll tell you. This child was born last summer. And since the mother is a concubine of whom he is very fond, His Lordship seems to have been overjoyed. But in fact, this child is the cause of our present problems. A new heir, Shima-no-Kami, has been installed, and now there is no cause for anxiety about the future of the domain. But a certain group within the domain, which now knows that another son has been born to His Lordship, seems to be using this child to upset the stability of the regime centered upon Shima-no-Kami. This plot is at the root of the recent spate of assassinations."

Knowing that what he was hearing was not true, Bunshirō lowered his face and listened to what the elder was saying. He still could not grasp Satomura's motive in telling him this. Bit by bit, Bunshirō was beginning to feel an oppressive sense of intimidation in the elder's tale.

"You understand what I've told you so far?"

"Yes." When Bunshirō replied, Satomura placed his elbows on the desk and leant forward on one knee. His dark, long, gourd-shaped face looked very little different from before but was now more wrinkled. Countless wrinkles traversed the upper part of the elder's face, and his pure white hair was looking a bit yellowed, as if it were soiled.

"Now then, the reason we called you here tonight …" Bunshirō pricked up his ears. "But you're not to breathe a word of this to anyone else."

"I understand."

"You are to make off with the child in the Zelkova Mansion and bring it here." Bunshirō looked toward Inagaki, who was still smiling at him. He said not a word. Bunshirō straightened his back and spoke to Satomura.

"Although I realize that this is an order, I think the task lies beyond my abilities."

"Perhaps I spoke too abruptly." Satomura opened his mouth and smiled. It was a weak smile, in the midst of which an audible breath escaped him. His mouth was red and one could see that some of his teeth were missing. "The situation is this. We've had a highly confidential report, just this evening, that members of the faction that opposes us will soon launch a secret attack on the Zelkova Mansion and abduct His Lordship's son. This would create a useless disturbance, but we know why they're doing it: they intend to trap us.

"Even His Lordship knows that we were not pleased by the birth of his child at the Zelkova Mansion. And so, they will abduct the child, then tell His Lordship they've heard that the Inagaki faction has evil intentions toward the child, but they have rescued it. If His Lordship believes this, they may then urge that he displace the present heir and name the infant his new successor. Or even worse, they may quietly do away with the child and make it look as if we were the ones who did it.

"Therefore, we have decided to strike first—for our own protection. There is nothing that need worry you. All preparations are in order, so that the child you bring here can be nursed with the greatest care until the situation settles down."

Bunshirō looked straight back at Satomura.

"But why me?"

Satomura raised himself up from the table upon which his elbows were resting and looked at Bunshirō.

"We understand that O-Fuku-sama, of whom His Lordship is so enamored, is an old friend of yours. She is the daughter of a family that lived next door to you, is she not? We don't want any blood to be spilt in bringing the child here. This must be done discreetly. And so the task has fallen to you. There are those who advise us that if you are the one to go, you will surely be able

Semishigure

to persuade O-Fuku-sama, take the infant into your care, and bring it here."

"Although she was an old friend, that was a long time ago. I doubt I would be able to persuade O-Fuku-sama now." As he spoke, Bunshirō suddenly felt his heart begin to beat violently. He realized that, whatever the outcome, if he were to comply with this command, he would at long last see O-Fuku again.

"But rather than a total stranger, you are the better choice." Satomura looked at Bunshirō with great caution in his eyes. "There are apparently two or three men in the mansion guarding O-Fuku-sama. When you state your name, those men, too, may be willing to open the gate."

"There is someone better able to do this than I am."

"Who would that be?"

"Koyanagi Jinbei-dono."

"Jinbei is useless!" Satomura snapped. "Given the circumstances we've just told you about, we don't have the leisure to ponder these matters. The moment has come when that child must be placed in our hands, even if rough measures are required to do so. That is why we've chosen you." Satomura spoke in an irate voice, as if he were at last revealing his true nature. Bunshirō's mention of Jinbei's name seemed to touch a sore spot.

"The selection process is complete. It is decided that you are the person best suited to this task. This is an order on the authority of the domain. Or do you intend to defy an order?"

"No, by no means!"

"Of course not; you're indebted to us," Satomura said. "There were many who said that, according to domain law, the House of Maki should be abolished. At the time, though, Inagaki-sama—who is here right now—held out a helping hand to you. You could hardly fail to realize how risky that was for him."

So the elder did indeed feel he was treating me too generously, but was planning at some point to cash in that debt, Bunshirō thought.

Bunshirō bowed low, humbly undertaking to do as he was commanded. When he raised his head, he looked toward Inagaki. Inagaki was still smiling at Bunshirō.

2

Bunshirō told Satomura he would need two more men to assist him and two more days to prepare. Once those requests were granted, he left the elder's mansion.

A half-moon, invisible when he had come here, now hung in the sky. The large houses that composed the residential quarter at Babasaki stood out in its pale light, but not a single person was to be seen on the street.

What Elder Satomura told me—that was nonsense, Bunshirō was thinking. He could not believe that the Yokoyama faction had the slightest interest in the child O-Fuku had borne. But even supposing they did, and they were to abduct the child, if His Lordship did not believe the story Satomura said they would tell him, that would be the end of it. Their attack on the Zelkova Mansion and their abduction of the child would still remain, and that alone would suffice to discredit the Yokoyama faction.

Much less could Bunshirō imagine that the Yokoyama faction—which from all that he had heard was now in the ascendent—would have any reason to do anything so dangerous as to kill the child and blame it on the Inagaki-Satomura faction. In that story, the benefit to the Yokoyama faction would be too slight and the risk too great.

Semishigure

On the other hand, Bunshirō was thinking, from the standpoint of the Inagaki-Satomura faction, even if such a scheme did involve some risk, the benefits could make it worth their while. Satomura might well be planning to have Bunshirō make off with the child and then wring its neck with his own hands. The son, who in future could expect to be doted upon by the lord of the domain, would be disposed of in secret, which would serve not only the interests of O-Fune and Shima-no-Kami, but those of the Inagaki-Satomura faction as well. It was possible, even, that they were already under orders to that effect from O-Fune in Edo.

Of course, if it were known that they themselves had done this, there would be no escaping the wrath of His Lordship. And however great the power that they boasted, and however lightly they regarded their lord, that was a risk even they feared.

So they use me as their tool—and to that end tell me bald-faced lies. They make me do it ... and then what? Bunshirō went on, turning these questions and conjectures over in his mind. One could imagine them eliminating both baby and Bunshirō, and then spreading it about that this had been instigated by the Yokoyama faction. In order to bring us down, Satomura would say, the Yokoyama faction had this done, and so we have cut down the criminal who killed the baby.

But would anyone believe this? Inasmuch as the criminal was the son of Maki Sukezaemon, a member of the Yokoyama faction, there would likely be some who believed this story, or at least half-believed it. There would be two generations of traitors to the domain, father and son. And if the lord of the domain should believe it, the status of Shima-no-Kami would be assured, and the Yokoyama faction would be stripped of their strength. In a single stroke, the Inagaki-Satomura faction could kill two birds with one stone.

Anger roiled within Bunshirō's breast. *Am I to tolerate being toyed with, just as they please?* But then an image arose in his mind of Elder Satomura, and of Inagaki Chūbei, who sat there with him, never saying a word but staring at him all the while with that mysterious smile on his face. And when he wondered what that smile might mean, Bunshirō felt not only anger but also a chill running down his spine.

A brilliant plan, but who do we get to do it? That's the problem, Inagaki might have said.

To which, Satomura would have replied, *Maki Bunshirō is just the man. Remember—there were strong objections to sparing the Maki house. Sooner or later he's bound to turn against us. So let's use him now and then dispose of him.*

It was a frightening thought, but entirely plausible. Bunshirō felt a vaguely ominous sense that he had just come in touch with the cold will of those in power.

At the end of it all, Bunshirō recalled, when he was leaving his seat, Satomura had called to him from the far side of his desk: "Do a good job and we'll promote you." That too would be a lie. Inagaki's smile was ominous, but the elder's lies were equally ominous.

Just as Bunshirō was thinking this, he realized that he had just passed the house of Owada Ippei. He turned back and entered the gate, then knocked on the door and announced himself.

3

"Hey! What's up?" When the old servant withdrew, Ippei came out.

"Sorry to call so late at night, but there's something I need to talk to you about."

Semishigure

"Come in! Come in!" Ippei said. "Yonosuke is here, but that's all right isn't it? He went to your house, but you were out so he came here, he says."

"That's fine. A good thing, actually," Bunshirō said.

Ippei showed Bunshirō into the guest room at the rear. Now that Ippei was married and had a family, he couldn't just barge into the sitting room the way he used to. Shimazaki Yonosuke was already there in the guest room.

"You were summoned by the elder, they said."

"I've just come from there."

"What did he want?"

"That's what I've come to talk about."

"You don't mind if I'm here?"

"Of course not. I want to borrow your brain. I've just told Ippei it's good that you're here."

Ippei, who had gone to the sitting room for a moment, had come back now, so Bunshirō told them everything that had happened that night at the elder's mansion. And finally he asked, "What do you think?"

Both Ippei's face and Yonosuke's face wore an air of doubt and consternation. After a long silence, Ippei spoke.

"It's a trap."

"Wait now. We can't jump to conclusions," Yonosuke said. "The elder did say that if it went well, he would promote him."

"That's just a bluff," Ippei said. "Don't believe it."

"But wait. Before we make up our minds, let me think whether Bunshirō could escape unscathed—even if it is a blow to the Yokoyama faction." Yonosuke folded his arms, sunk in thought, but in the end he looked up and shook his head.

"It's no good. Once Bunshirō makes off with the child, no matter what he does thereafter, things will go badly for him. There's no escaping it. If the Yokoyama faction really were scheming to do what Elder Satomura says they are, it would be a different matter. But it's just as Ippei says, that's not a story to be trusted."

"Ninety-nine percent certain," Bunshirō said. "I cannot imagine that Elder Yokoyama would do anything so outrageous."

Ippei voiced his agreement. "It's a trap. I don't know what they're up to, but they're trying to catch Bunshirō in a trap.

"I have a rough idea what they're up to," Bunshirō said. "I'll tell you what I make of it." He went on to tell them what he had been thinking on the way back from Elder Satomura's mansion. "Given the circumstances, I'd say they're trying to kill two birds with one stone."

"And the reason Bunshirō is the chosen one …" Yonosuke said. "That would be because they see him as connected with the Yokoyama faction."

"There are other advantages in using me, too," Bunshirō said. "For one, O-Fuku-sama and I are old friends. If they were to make good use of that relationship, the Satomura faction would leave no trace whatsoever of their own involvement. They also presume that that will make it possible for me to take the child away. Then, too, I possess some skill with the sword, so they could count on me to handle any rough business that might arise. And lastly, I cannot refuse their orders."

"You can't refuse?" Yonosuke looked hard at Bunshirō. "Why? Even if it's an order issued by the domain, you can at least protest if you find it disagreeable."

"Bunshirō can't do that," Ippei said. He had been sitting there all along and was quick to grasp that point. "If he refuses, they'll threaten to abolish his family."

"I've already been threatened," Bunshirō said. "There's no way out. For what if I did refuse, even knowing full well that that would be the end of my family name? The Satomura faction would attack the Zelkova Mansion themselves, I fear. Then, of course, there would be no saving the child, or O-Fuku-sama either."

"But if *you* do it, then they kill you," said Ippei. "So what are you going to do?"

"Well, I have no intention of falling into their trap," Bunshirō said.

Ippei and Yonosuke looked at Bunshirō, saying nothing. Bunshirō nodded back at them. "When I take the child from O-Fuku-sama, I'll rush straightaway to the mansion of Yokoyama-sama and tell him everything that has happened."

"You will?" they both exclaimed at once.

"His Lordship's child will be unshakeable proof. Surely the elder will believe what I say. This means I will throw my lot in with the Yokoyama faction; but there is no other way to save them."

"That's a brilliant plan!"

"There's no other way." Ippei and Yonosuke spoke one after the other.

"I've been given two days to prepare," Bunshirō said. "I'll be taking the child there rather suddenly; which may come as a surprise to Yokoyama-sama. But if I can, I'd like to get in touch with him sometime within those two days. I'll probably be watched, so it will be impossible for me to go anywhere near Yokoyama's mansion."

"Wait!" Yonosuke said. "It's three nights from tonight that you're to do it?"

"That's right."

"Well, Yokoyama will be going to Kitaura tomorrow. He'll be attending the Shinto rites at our branch school there."

Kitaura was a busy commercial harbor. The domain had a manor house there, and the Sanseikan had a branch school.

"When will he be back?"

"On the evening of the day after tomorrow, I should think."

Bunshirō breathed a sigh of relief. He would be back in time for the night of the action. "But it will be impossible to get in touch with him beforehand."

"Isn't it better that way?" Ippei said. "If they see you're in touch with the Yokoyama faction, that'll be the end of it."

"Right! I'll do it cold," Bunshirō said. Then he raised the question of who his two assistants should be. Yonosuke squirmed.

"I'd be of no use. Leave me out of it."

"Shall I go?" Ippei asked.

"But I can't do that to you. It's too great an imposition."

"And yet ... if you take someone who doesn't know the situation, he'll be useless."

"That's true, but ..."

"Do any of them seem dangerous?"

"Only the one. There's one fellow there seems no point in talking to; but if we discuss it with the others, it should be all right."

"So, it seems my life would be in no danger, doesn't it? Good! I'll go!"

"Thanks."

"Who will your other man be?" Ippei spoke as if he were enjoying it all.

"If I tell Fusé Tsurunosuke all about it, he may be willing to go along," Bunshirō said.

Reversal

1

The night sky was clouded, with not a star in sight. It was past the Fifth Hour (8 p.m.) when the three men arrived at the Zelkova Mansion on the outskirts of the village of Kanai. When they crossed the bridge, Fusé Tsurunosuke, who was carrying the lantern, dropped back a step while Bunshirō and Ippei moved on ahead.

"Halloo, in there!" The two of them called out at the gate, one after the other; but that seemed insufficient.

"We're sorry to call in the night, but we've come on urgent business. Kindly admit us." They called out in loud voices, but it remained pitch dark on the far side of the gate and not a sound could be heard.

Bunshirō gave a push at the gate, but the oaken door was thick and felt solid to the touch. It didn't budge the slightest bit.

"Let me try." When the voices of the other's tired, Fusé Tsurunosuke spoke up and came forward. "We have urgent business and would appreciate a chance to discuss it with someone." Perhaps his voice had carried better. There were sounds within the gate, and finally a faint ray of light streamed out above the door.

As the light came closer and closer it illumined the branches of the trees within the gate, and then footsteps could be heard. Then the footsteps halted and they heard a voice from within the gate.

"This is not a place where visitors are welcome. What is your urgent business?"

The voice was one Bunshirō remembered hearing. It was the middle-aged samurai he had met beside the stream. He spoke in Edo dialect, but even now his voice was soft and he gave no impression of nervousness.

"We ask that you convey a message to O-Fuku-sama, that Maki Bunshirō has come to see her concerning a matter of great urgency."

"Maki Bunshirō …?" the voice within the gate said and then suddenly fell silent. "But apparently you are not alone."

"Two of my friends have come with me. The name of one of them, Owada Ippei, will most likely be known to O-Fuku-sama."

"But have you any proof that you are Maki Bunshirō?"

"Last year, at about this time, I met you outside this mansion. On that occasion, I believe, I identified myself as Maki Bunshirō, a rural inspector … You remember that, do you not? If you will be so kind as to describe me to O-Fuku-sama as you saw me then, you should know whether I am the real Maki or not."

"Please wait a moment," the voice within said, then the lamplight and the footsteps faded into the distance. The light and the sounds were gone, and the interior of the property again fell silent.

"I wonder if they'll open up," Ippei said. And then, as if suddenly stricken with fear, "Well if they don't open up, they don't open up. And if they do refuse, everything will be fine. You'll be safe, too."

Semishigure

"You've come this far. Don't talk like a weakling," Bunshirō said.

On the far side of the gate, the glow of light and the sound of footsteps drew nearer, and finally there was the sound of a lock being opened. His Lordship's villa seemed firmly secured.

The door creaked open and the middle-aged samurai Bunshirō had once met stood before the three of them. A step behind him, holding a lantern, was the same younger samurai he had seen before. The middle-aged man took the lantern from the younger, held it up, and after examining Bunshirō's face, bowed and invited him to come in.

"O-Fuku-sama says she will meet you." Bunshirō signaled to the two men behind him, and they passed within the gate. The middle-aged samurai, holding the lantern, went ahead, and the younger samurai remained behind to lock the door.

The path from the gate, about two yards wide, led within at an angle. To the left and right stood the thick trunks of zelkovas. As they walked, the bark of the zelkovas reflected the light of the lantern back at them. Straight ahead, the bright glow of a lamp came into view. That would be the interior of the villa.

Within the building, bright lamps were alight, and every window glowed yellow. Bunshirō felt a sudden tumult arise within his breast.

Has it been five years? he thought. Fuku had become O-Fuku-sama; how different would she be now? What set his heart racing was the joy that now, without a doubt, they would meet again. Yet somewhere within his feelings, Bunshirō feared that Fuku might have changed.

When they entered the spacious vestibule, a woman, who looked a little over twenty, came out to greet them holding a portable candle stand. She appeared not to be a samurai woman but of the town, and judging from her polished appearance, Bunshirō thought she must be the woman who had come to the Shinobuya in Aoyagi-chō. Bunshirō and his companions, led by the middle-aged samurai and the woman, proceeded into the interior of the building.

When their guides came to a room from which a ray of lamplight leaked out, they knelt before the sliding panels and announced themselves to those within. A faint voice from within the room answered, whereupon Bunshirō and his companions were invited into a brilliantly lit room.

"Bunshirō-dono, please, raise your face." The voice came from the seat directly before him. It was a soft, hesitant voice, but he heard the words clearly. The voice was an adult's, but of course it was the voice of Fuku. She continued speaking.

"It's been such a long time."

"Is Your Ladyship as well as ever?" Bunshirō raised his face, and there sat Fuku. Fuku was not wearing a gorgeous flowing robe such as he had imagined she would. She was dressed plainly, in the style of a samurai wife. Her cheeks were sunken, and perhaps because of her makeup, or because of all she had suffered, she looked like a different person, her face not the least bit seductive. And yet when he looked closely at her narrow, dark eyes and her small mouth, this was unmistakably Fuku. Something hot welled up in Bunshirō's breast and felt as if it could stifle him.

"Nothing pleases me more than to see you in good health."

"Let's cease this excessive formality, shall we?" Fuku said. Her voice was soft and sounded as if she were smiling. Bunshirō could sense that Fuku was more at ease than he was. Although in appearance this was the Fuku of old, Bunshirō had to warn himself—he mustn't forget that the woman before him was now the mother of a child, and she was O-Fuku-sama as well.

Semishigure

"Is your mother well?"

"Yes, she has aged a bit, but she is still healthy."

"Does she know you'd be seeing me?"

"No, my mission tonight is secret. I couldn't tell Mother."

"And the same for O-Setsu-sama?" To which she rapidly added, "I understand you've no children yet, have you?" But when Bunshirō's faced contorted with confusion, she smiled weakly, then banished the smile and resumed her slightly formal tone of voice.

"Well then, may we inquire what your secret mission might be?"

"I have a slightly unusual request to make. I hope you'll not be shocked." Bunshirō then told her why he had called at the Zelkova Mansion. Nor did he omit to say that he strongly suspected this was a plot of the Inagaki-Satomura faction and that he intended to rush them straight to Yokoyama's mansion.

"So may I ask you to trust me and my companions, Owada and Fusé, and place your child in our care?" Bunshirō could see the blood draining from O-Fuku's face. "You'll of course be shocked by this," he said, "and if you say it is out of the question, we'll have no choice but to leave without another word. But if we do, it's likely they will attack this mansion in force. Which is why, in my humble opinion, I think it would be safest for you to entrust yourselves to our care, but …"

"Isogai, what shall we do?" O-Fuku looked at the middle-aged samurai as she spoke. He bowed to her and then turned to Bunshirō and told him he was Isogai Kazue and was stationed permanently in Edo.

"Do you have any evidence for thinking that, if we refuse, Satomura may mobilize his men and attack us?"

"No," Bunshirō said, "I have no evidence. But we are all agreed in assuming this."

"Hmm." Isogai, his hands still on his knees, stared at Bunshirō, then heaved a single sigh and spoke. "Normally, if troubled by someone bearing a groundless rumor, we would ask him, firmly, to leave, but …" Isogai, still staring at Bunshirō, went on. "Our lord, too, has warned us to beware of Satomura."

"Then His Lordship, too, suspects these people?"

"That's right. And that is precisely why Kitamura and I are here to guard this mansion. Even so," Isogai said, "we find it hard to place our trust entirely in you. But if, for example, either I or O-Michi-dono here …" Isogai said, turning to the woman at his side. "If one or the other of us were to accompany the child to the Yokoyama mansion, it would be a different story."

"There could be no objection to that."

Isogai then turned to face O-Fuku. "As we've reported previously, this mansion has from time to time been under surveillance. That is a fact."

"So I've heard."

"That being the case, we had best believe what these men tell us, that this mansion is in danger. Given which, rather than be attacked while only lightly defended, this opportunity to take your honored child …"

Isogai had said only that much when suddenly a loud noise came from outside, as if something very heavy had fallen over. Thereafter arose sharp shouts, and with these voices was mixed the unmistakable clangor of swords clashing. At these sounds, all of the men rose to their knees, leaving the two women in place. Outside the room there came the sound of someone running, and then a man—probably Kitamura—shouted.

"Isogai-dono! Be on guard! The mansion has been invaded by a band of ruffians. Those men inside, too …" At that, his voice cut out, and again the sharp clash of swords resounded. Then the footsteps retreated, and Kitamura again shouted. "Those men in there are probably with them. On guard!"

Hearing this, Isogai grabbed his sword and stood. Everyone else in the room stood, too, but Bunshirō raised his hand to restrain Isogai.

"We are on the side of O-Fuku-sama. That you must never doubt."

"Isogai," O-Fuku said, "it's just as Bunshirō-dono says."

"Then what shall we do?" When Isogai said this, there came the distant sound of things being battered back in the vestibule. The attackers apparently had entered the building.

"In the village of Kanai, there's the home of a man named Tōjirō." Bunshirō hurriedly instructed Ippei. "Take O-Fuku-sama, her baby, and O-Michi-dono there. He'll hide them. I'll come later." Bunshirō then wheeled about to Isogai. "I'd like you to let these four out the rear gate. Until you do, we'll hold off the rabble."

"Who is it attacking us?"

"I don't know. But hurry!" As Bunshirō spoke, he heard someone scream in the vestibule, following which came the sound of footsteps in the corridor.

2

The footsteps of a throng of men were coming closer. Bunshirō kept watch until Ippei and Isogai, guarding the two women, had disappeared into the interior; then he removed the cord from the sheath of his sword and quickly tied back his sleeves.

"Well, here they come!" Bunshirō called out to Fusé Tsurunosuke, who likewise was tying back his sleeves. "Let's stay calm. This will be an indoor battle; if we panic we'll be in trouble."

"Any idea who they are?" Fusé asked. Fusé's eyes were wide with anger; but his voice was calm. "The Yokoyama faction, perhaps?"

"If it's the Yokoyama faction, we should be able to talk with them." As Bunshirō spoke, the approaching invaders, sliding open the panels to room after room, finally burst into the room where the two of them stood.

Their faces were masked with cloth. There were five men. All of them carried drawn swords in their right hands, one of which was dripping blood. He had cut down Kitamura or one of the servants. The scent of blood now pervaded the room.

"Where's his mistress?" one of them asked. "I doubt we can expect you to lead us to her. But don't stand in our way." Bunshirō remembered the voice of the tall man who said that. It was the voice of the man who told Aoki Magozō he considered him a traitor. It was Murakami Shichirōemon.

"Watch out!" Bunshirō warned Fuse. He was so tense every hair on his body stood on end. They had come to eliminate not just the child and Bunshirō. He could see now that Satomura must have planned from the start to kill everyone. He would send Bunshirō into the Zelkova Mansion, then attack and kill everyone there. Then he could pin the crime entirely on Bunshirō and later insinuate that the Yokoyama faction must have put him up to it. The Yokoyama faction, he would tell them, in order to incriminate his own faction, had sent Bunshirō to abduct the child, but he had fought with the guards and they ended up killing each other.

Satomura had been notified by Bunshirō that he would be accompanied by Owada Ippei and Fusé Tsurunosuke, but apparently he was not inclined to change his plans on that account. For Owada Ippei had publicly refused an invitation to join the

Satomura faction, and Fusé, for his part, was related to Yada Sakunojō of the Yokoyama faction.

"No chance to talk it over now."

"Right," Fusé said. He seemed to understand from the way Bunshirō spoke that their opponents were not from the Yokoyama faction but the Satomura faction. This fired his desire to fight, and Fusé drew his sword. Seeing this, a man standing beside Murakami Shichirōemon suddenly attacked Fusé. His movements were agile but a bit cramped as he struck from the figure eight position. Fusé Tsurunosuke parried the blow smartly, whereupon the other masked men took this clash of steel as the signal for them all to attack.

The room was large, but they were nonetheless indoors. Their movements were cramped, and their swords failed to reach their opponents bodies. All of the men Murakami brought with him seemed highly skilled swordsmen. But for a time, both sides fought as if groping in the dark. Murakami, irritated, perhaps because this halted their advance to the interior, stepped back into the corridor and quickly kicked out one of the storm doors.

"Outside, now! Move!" he bellowed, as if the command were meant for both his own men and their enemy. Murakami himself leapt swiftly out of doors. His men followed, then Bunshirō and Fusé, too, leapt out.

When Bunshirō first realized that they had come intending to kill everyone, his whole body burned with anger, but now that the anger had subsided, he was attempting to assess their situation coolly. Until Isogai Kazue returned from the rear gate, it was essential that he contain these men standing before him. Not one of them must be allowed to follow Fuku and her child.

But are these the only men? Are there no other attackers? As he was thinking this, Bunshirō looked into the distance, over the heads of the group whose swords were pointed at the two of them. There, in the direction of the gate, he could see the flickering light of lanterns. Kitamura, the younger samurai, must already have been cut down, as there was no sound of swords clashing. The lights he could see at the gate probably were those of a group Murakami had left there to secure their route of retreat.

But to go into the village ... you have to take the same road that passes in front of the gate. Isogai would have known that. Just as that thought crossed his mind, Bunshirō heard someone scream in the distance, and the light of the lanterns near the gate began swaying about violently. Something unexpected had happened.

Both Bunshirō and the men facing him seemed to realize this. Exchanging sharp, whispered comments, they began shifting about to the right and left; then one, then two of them attacked. The incident at the gate seemed to be something they hadn't anticipated. Their uneasiness apparently spurred them to action, but their swords as they attacked were a little unsteady.

Bunshirō turned to face a man who was attacking him head on. He twisted his body to penetrate the man's defenses, then, slipping past him, he landed a sharp diagonal blow to the man's shoulder. The black figure staggered, fell across a sliver of light shining out from within the house, and crumpled into the dark shadows. He must have suffered a deep wound on the shoulder.

Murakami came quickly around to the fore, poised his sword to restrain Bunshirō, then shouted. "Don't panic! There's only two of them!" But as Murakami spoke, the chaotic sound of footsteps resounded behind him, and the shadows of more men came into view.

Semishigure

3

In the light shining out from within the mansion there appeared a group of masked men gripping bare blades. Bunshirō had just ascertained that there were perhaps three of them, when from behind them, Isogai Kazue appeared. Carrying a bare sword in one hand, Isogai walked slowly into the garden. Without looking back, Murakami, too, seemed to read the current state of affairs. He raised his sword smoothly to the upper position and lunged forward. He must have meant to put a sudden end to all of this.

Murakami's attack came with the force of a violent gust. The tip of his sword drove sharply toward Bunshirō's side. Though assailed by what felt like a searing blast of wind, Bunshirō deflected Murakami's sword as he flew past. Then he turned back, and in their second clash, Bunshirō's figure eight stroke was just slightly the swifter, and thus the victor. Murakami dodged, but his upper arm was cut deeply and he faltered.

Just then Bunshirō noticed that the men driven from the front gate by Isogai were silently moving into position to attack him—and at the same time, that Fusé Tsurunosuke had failed to evade the attack of his opponent and had totally lost his equilibrium.

Facing Fusé, who was favoring one knee, was a man who swiftly raised his sword to the figure eight position. In that instant Bunshirō recognized who it was that was attacking Fusé. The man behind the black mask was Inukai Hyōma. It was no wonder Fusé was overwhelmed.

"I'll take over, Fusé!" Bunshirō shouted. And when the man, who was attacking from the right, thrust his sword upward, Bunshirō nimbly slipped between him and Fusé.

So Fusé's opponent was indeed Hyōma! When Bunshirō

faced him, he swiftly fell back and adjusted his stance. Hyōma, in the figure eight posture, held his sword slightly higher than was the custom at the Ishiguri Dojo. In the same moment that he poised himself, Hyōma ripped the fabric from his face. Then he came running.

The distance between them closed in an instant. The two advanced on each other, and their swords clashed. Hyōma's sword was slightly the quicker. He must have felt certain he would cut down Bunshirō, for his mouth contorted in a smile. But then, his eyes still wide with astonishment, he fell to his knees, and then fully forward. Bunshirō's sword had cut deep into the side of his torso.

It was the defensive tactic known as "One Inch in the Dark of Night," one of the secret Cloudburst techniques, that had allowed Bunshirō to evade Hyōma's sword. It enabled him to see that gap of one inch that saved his life, even with his eyes shut tight. Yet although he did succeed in defending himself, Hyōma came within half an inch of closing that gap. That extension of the reach of his sword, he achieved because he was so uncommonly skilled. And Bunshirō's defeat of Hyōma must be attributed to those instincts inherent in a master swordsman. Bunshirō's entire body sensed the danger he was in, that he must kill or be killed.

They probably saw Hyōma cut down. Two new enemies rushed to attack Bunshirō. He dodged the sword of the one and wrested the sword of the other from him. Then he quickly fell back to survey the battle. Fusé was briskly moving against a large opponent. And Isogai Kazue was calmly wielding his sword against two enemies, easily evading their swords as they attacked him, crossing swords with them and deflecting their blows, then counterattacking and wounding them. Having been dealt with so expertly, the two men facing Isogai were unnerved.

"That's all!" Suddenly Murakami's booming voice resounded. Murakami was standing slightly apart from the fight, pressing his hand against his arm. He was protecting the wound inflicted upon him by Bunshirō. "We're withdrawing. Watch out!"

Hearing Murakami's voice, the two men threatening Bunshirō pulled in their swords. With Murakami Shichirōemon bringing up the rear, these men, helping their wounded comrades along, disappeared down the path through the zelkovas.

Only the smell of blood and the bodies of two fallen men remained. Bunshirō knelt and quickly checked their breath. Hyōma and the other man were no longer breathing.

"At the front gate ..." Isogai spoke to Bunshirō, who now stood up. "There should be one more dead man there."

"Which makes nine men in all." But doubts remained which somehow troubled Bunshirō. He seemed to feel that this number was incomplete. Or should he think of them as a group of eight led by Murakami Shichirōemon?

"Well, so long as they are not in pursuit of O-Fuku-sama ..." Bunshirō said as he began walking toward the front gate. "Will you be coming with us?" Bunshirō said to Isogai, who followed along with Fusé.

"Of course," Isogai said, casting a glance back at the dark vestibule, and then moving on. "I'll have to come back to put things in order, but first we must find out whether O-Fuku-sama and her child are safe." They understood that Isogai was referring to Kitamura and the servant, who might now be dead.

Bunshirō, Fusé, and Isogai hurried out the gate, crossed the bridge, and left the villa.

"At the rear gate ..." Bunshirō had to check with Isogai, "there were none of the enemy on guard there?" His suspicion that previously had crossed his mind, about the number of the enemy, returned. Why would there be only nine? Wouldn't there have been ten?

"There was no one," Isogai said. "But when I went around to the front gate, there were three or four men there, so I drove them back into the property. In the meantime, O-Fuku-sama was hurrying off toward the village."

As they followed the rivulet, the dark grove at the entrance to the village came dimly into view. The three of them halted to make sure there were none of the enemy lying in ambush.

4

There was no sign of the enemy. They could feel only the rather moist night air that enveloped the village. Three of the enemy were dead. The others, at least three of whom would be wounded, may just have given up and withdrawn to the castle town. And if they did just withdraw, then the path through the fields to the north, in the opposite direction from the village, would have been their shortest route.

With Bunshirō leading the way, the three of them, still in a line and maintaining a safe space between themselves, entered the village, and with no trouble found their way to the home of Tōjirō.

The door to Tōjirō's house was shut tight. From the outside, it looked as if everyone must be asleep. But when Bunshirō announced himself, the door opened immediately, and bright lamplight shone out from within. O-Fuku had arrived safely; and when Ippei and Tōjirō heard Bunshirō's voice, they came out to the earthen-floored entrance.

"What's become of those guys?" Ippei asked.

After he had thanked Tōjirō, Bunshirō told Ippei that for the time being they had chased them away.

"No one's wounded?"

"Fusé and I are unwounded. But from here on in, it's going to be terrible." Bunshirō went on to tell them briefly what he had been thinking on the way there.

"It wasn't a bad idea to ask Tōjirō's help. But if our enemy catches on, and they send a second striking force, it could be horrific. We can't cause Tōjirō any further trouble. So somehow we've got to sneak back into town tonight, and get O-Fuku-sama and her child to a safe place."

"And the safe place?" Ippei asked. "The mansion of Elder Yokoyama?"

"Right." Bunshirō nodded. "We have to assume, though, that they'll have blocked every one of the roads from the village to the town."

"*That* is a problem." Ippei scowled. And when Bunshirō turned about, Fusé, too, was wearing a dark look.

Bunshirō understood perfectly well how the two of them felt. Both men had responded to Bunshirō's request for help, and in the end Fusé had even fought against the masked enemy, but that was only because it had been forced upon him. To mount an attack against forces of the domain defending the entrance to the castle town far exceeded anything Bunshirō had asked of them. That amounted to total confrontation with the domain, a step both of them feared to take.

Which was only natural, Bunshirō thought. That turn of events could implicate their families and cause them to be branded traitors to the domain.

"But," Isogai said softly, "if there is no other way, we have no choice but to fight our way through."

"No," Bunshirō said, "that's a bit too difficult." Bunshirō then explained the position of Ippei and Fusé to Isogai. "If we have to break though by force, then you and I must do it by ourselves. Even then, it would be a bit much to take the women and the child with us."

"Well then," Isogai said. "We've no way to turn."

And Owada Ippei, looking totally perplexed, said, "Oh, no! Never mind Fusé—he's still living at home. But I'm all right. I'll go with you."

"No! I appreciate the thought, but that won't do." Bunshirō, shaking his head, refused him flatly.

At that point, Tōjirō, who until then had said nothing, put in a word.

"If you could avoid the entrances to the town, would that help?"

"It would, but …"

"In that case, what if you were to go by boat? At the edge of the village there's a bridge across the Goken River. It's the Chōhei Bridge that joins the village of Kanai with the neighboring village, Aohata. But under the bridge, there's a boat," Tōjirō explained. "The boatman is a man named Gonroku who lives in Kanai. Gonroku uses his boat to transport vegetables to town, to collect gravel from the river and such. It's not a passenger boat, but it could probably carry two or three people. Of course, I'd have to ask Gonroku, but …"

"That's an excellent idea," Bunshirō said. "Might we trouble you to ask Gonroku, or whomever?" He felt as if a ray of light now shone where once they thought their way forward had been blocked.

Leaving Ippei, Fusé, and O-Fuku's maidservant O-Michi behind, Bunshirō, Isogai, O-Fuku, and her child, together with

Tōjirō left the house and headed for Gonroku's place. Ippei and Fusé decided that, after a while, they would go to the castle town entrance. If they were able to enter, they would hide out somewhere in town, and if security were too strict, they would take no chances; they would simply return to Tōjirō's house and await the dawn there.

Gonroku the boatman was already asleep, but when he was roused by Tōjirō, he came out immediately. He was a big man, and even at night one could tell he was very strong. Gonroku readily agreed to take the passengers. But he could carry only two adults, and so in the end, Bunshirō alone would accompany O-Fuku and her child.

Moored under the bridge was a long, narrow, flat-bottomed gravel boat. When Bunshirō and O-Fuku holding her child boarded along with Gonroku, the boat rolled forlornly. Bunshirō sat in the bow holding a lantern, and when they waved goodbye to Tōjirō and Isogai, who had escorted them there, Gonroku, deftly wielding his pole, pushed the boat off into the middle of the river.

As the Goken River flows downstream, it becomes more than twenty yards wide, not at all as small a river as its name—"ten yards"—implies. But at the village of Kanai, it was quite narrow, and despite the amount of water that flows through it, here and there sandbars showed their heads above the water. But Gonroku effortlessly guided his boat through the deepest water.

"Do you sometimes run the river at night?" Bunshirō asked.

"I've several times taken people into town who've suddenly fallen ill. But I've been running up and down this river for years now. I could navigate these currents with my eyes shut."

"Ah! So that's how."

"But, sir," Gonroku said, "once we round Willow Bend, I

wouldn't mind if you were to put out your lantern." Tōjirō had probably told him quietly what was going on. Gonroku, too, appeared to know where there would be danger.

That danger came into view only a moment after Bunshirō, trusting in Gonroku's judgment, had extinguished his lantern. He could now see bonfires burning bright red. On the left there were two fires, and on the right one. Judging from their position, it was clear that they were blocking the roads from the villages of Kanai and Aohata into the castle town.

After they passed Willow Bend, the current slowed and the river turned to the northwest as the boat neared the town. Gonroku let the boat go where the current carried it. An occasional plash of his pole was all that was needed to keep it on the right heading. The bonfire at the edge of the village seemed to serve as a good guide to Gonroku. But before long, as they came closer and closer, the light of that fire reached out and began dimly to illumine the boat.

"Lie down," Bunshirō warned O-Fuku. He, too, rounded his back and lay low. Gonroku worked his pole rapidly. When Bunshirō looked up, the boat was in the shadow of the bushes along the bank. Gonroku kept the boat on that course.

Now they could hear human voices, like people shouting in the distance. But then the boat passed under a bridge and into the town, and the voices gradually grew fainter.

"Do you know the Ayame Bridge?" Bunshirō raised up as he spoke. If they were to go ashore near the Ayame Bridge, it would be but a short run to the Yokoyama mansion.

"Yes, I know it," Gonroku replied.

"Could you let us off at the landing there?" As he spoke, Bunshirō gazed off into the darkness on both sides of the river. Along the riverbank road, there were no lanterns alight, and all seemed quietened down. It had all gone very well, he thought. But just then, on the left bank, where he was intending to alight, a pinpoint of lantern light appeared.

"Shhh!" he cautioned Gonroku and peered at the light. The lantern was hurrying along the street, and then it turned at the corner. It was a samurai carrying the lantern, one of a group of three men. The corner where they turned was just next to the Ayame Bridge, where Bunshirō had intended to alight.

Looks like I was a little too optimistic, he thought. Bunshirō bit his lip. The street the three men had turned into led to the Yokoyama mansion. He should have assumed that Yokoyama would be under surveillance. But just as he was wondering whether he had been foiled once again, the memory of some words he had once heard suddenly flashed across his mind. "He doesn't sleep at night, so there's no need for us to hurry." It was his master, Ishiguri Yazaemon, who had said that.

5

They went two bridges further downstream from the Ayame Bridge, and there Bunshirō told Gonroku to put in at the landing. Bunshirō and O-Fuku, carrying her baby, stepped onto the stone paving and then mounted the steep stone stairway to the riverbank. Gonroku held his boat still and stood looking intently at them. But when Bunshirō, after helping O-Fuku up to the riverbank road, turned back toward Gonroku's boat, it was slowly slipping away from the shore and soon melted into the midstream darkness.

Gonroku would have turned his boat to head back upstream, but tonight he would probably tie up at one of the landings and spend the night ashore, Bunshirō thought. The Goken River was a gentle stream, but there were three rapid stretches between here and the village of Kanai that might be difficult to negotiate heading upstream at night.

Bunshirō checked the riverbank road with great care, and having ascertained that there was no one about, he took O-Fuku by the hand and crossed over the embankment. The narrow street the two of them entered was one that led to Daikan-machi, where the mansion of Kaji Oribe-no-Shō stood.

Now that we've come this far, we should be safe. Bunshirō heaved a sigh of relief.

"I'll carry your baby now." Bunshirō stopped and took the child from O-Fuku. The child was so small and soft that he felt he might drop it if he did not take care. When they boarded the boat it had been awake and whimpering, but now it was sound asleep.

This is Fuku's child, Bunshirō was thinking. The fact that the blood of His Lordship flowed through the child in his arms did not much concern him. The warmth of the child's body he thought of as the warmth of O-Fuku's blood.

"Have you heard the name of Kaji Oribe-no-Shō?"

"No." They spoke in low voices as they hurriedly turned into the next lane. "Who might he be?"

"He's an uncle of His Lordship. I expect that gentleman will be willing to hide you. You've heard of the Cedar Grove Mansion?"

"Yes, but only the name."

"That's where we're going now." O-Fuku seemed to be looking all about the place.

"Is this neighborhood Daikan-machi?"

"That's right. We've just entered it."

The two made their way through a row of mansions where not a single light could be seen. Then they emerged on a rather

Semishigure

broad street where, far ahead of them, a dense grove of trees appeared. Then suddenly the door to a mansion on their right rattled open. A bright light from the garden shone out over a hedge into the street. The two of them passed by the side of the mansion with muffled footsteps. From their rear came the sound of someone clearing his throat. O-Fuku clung to Bunshirō's hand.

Then the street was dark again and there were no more sounds, but O-Fuku did not release the hand she clung to. Bunshirō recalled the Fuku of long ago, when he brought his father's body back from the temple Ryūkōji and she came running to help him pull the cart. The strength that, beneath her gentle exterior, she concealed within herself seemed to reveal itself again on this dark street.

That time, too, Bunshirō thought, as he recalled how O-Fuku had come to their barracks in Fukiya-chō the night before she left for Edo. That was something no girl who was merely gentle and weak could do. It made Bunshirō's feelings burn to think how O-Fuku, despite all the strength she possessed, had been swept along so helplessly over the months and years.

Bunshirō had let go of O-Fuku's hand, but she took hold of him again of her own accord. O-Fuku's hand was slim and damp with perspiration. Led by Bunshirō, O-Fuku huddled up to him as they walked, and the scent of her body wafted up to him.

"Bunshirō-san." It was as if she could no longer bear this long silence when she called his name. Bunshirō felt he could tell what it was she was trying to say in her weak, trembling voice. O-Fuku probably wanted him to hear all about those horrendous months and years she had endured.

But just as O-Fuku called out to him in that desperate voice, Bunshirō heard a faint sound of something behind them—something slipping along against the wall … Bunshirō stopped, then turned and put his arm around O-Fuku's back and drew her close. The almost stifling scent of her skin and her heavy breathing enveloped him. O-Fuku was trembling in his embrace. Holding the child in one arm and drawing her close with the other, Bunshirō did not move his head but searched the street behind them with his eyes alone. Finally, at the base of the wall on his left, he spotted a dark, crouching object. It was as motionless as a rock, but it was human.

So—there was a tenth man after all, Bunshirō thought. The figure crouching in the darkness must be a spy Murakami Shichirōemon had left behind. He would have followed them to Tōjirō's place and on down to the bridge, where he would have watched them board the boat and then ran along the riverbank in pursuit. Taking this precaution was what enabled Murakami to leave while he still had men to spare, was it not?

I can't let him live, he thought. Staring at this motionless black object, Bunshirō reckoned he must be someone experienced at surveillance. Seeing Bunshirō embracing O-Fuku, he would watch for the two of them to enter the Cedar Grove Mansion. There was nothing for it but to cut him down and silence him.

"We're being followed," Bunshirō whispered to O-Fuku. Her trembling ceased and her body stiffened. She tried to release herself from Bunshirō, but he held her tightly. "Stay where you are. I'm going to pass your baby back to you. Take hold of him," Bunshirō murmured in O-Fuku's ear. In the eyes of the man crouching at the foot of the wall, they would have looked like two lovers in an illicit affair whispering to each other.

Bunshirō ran with his body low to the ground. But an instant before that, the man at the foot of the wall had sprung up like a bird taking flight and began running down the street. He must indeed have been experienced at surveillance. He had the instincts of an animal and ran as fast as one.

But about twenty yards further on, Bunshirō caught up with him. In a single instant, just as he was about to overtake him, Bunshirō drew his sword and struck. The blow knocked the man's body forward and he fell, sliding noisily along the dark surface of the street until he stopped. When Bunshirō came back to him, the man was still breathing, but already his breath was growing weaker. His shoulder must have been deeply split. A thick odor of blood arose.

The man had uttered no sound of pain, and Bunshirō could tell now that his breath had gradually dwindled and ceased. He probed the man's neck with his hand. An artery had been severed. He could not have let a man live who had seen him embracing O-Fuku.

When Bunshirō returned, O-Fuku stood holding her child with her head hanging low, but when she saw him, she quickly raised her face.

"I've taken care of him." Bunshirō said nothing more. He took the child again and began walking, leading O-Fuku by the hand. O-Fuku did not refuse his hand, but she did not huddle up to him as she had before. But by then, they could see the tall gate of the Cedar Grove mansion towering before them in the darkness.

Once Bunshirō met Kaji Oribe-no-Shō, it was a simple matter to explain the situation and request his help. He readily agreed.

"Very well. I'll hide her. Leave it to me."

"I beg your kind assistance," O-Fuku said. She was calm again. Her gentle bow and her soft but firm voice conveyed a sense of dignity. O-Fuku did not fear Oribe-no-Shō. No vestige remained of the O-Fuku who was so breathless out on the dark streets. She had returned to being a concubine beloved of the lord of the domain, Bunshirō felt. He turned to the two of them and took his leave.

"You'll be going to your home?"

"Yes."

"That's good. I'll send a messenger to Yokoyama."

"I'm very grateful that you will arrange that."

"Take care not to do anything rash. And stay put until you hear from Yokoyama." Kaji Oribe-no-Shō spoke with an air of apprehension in his voice. Bunshirō understood the significance of those words after he left the mansion and had walked a short way down the dark street.

6

The corpse of the man he cut down had already been removed. Having heard what Bunshirō told him, Oribe-no-Shō had ordered men from his mansion to take it away. But the heavy stench of blood lingered.

As he passed this place, his anger at Elder Satomura came rushing back. He actually laid a trap for me! When he recalled all those words Satomura had spun out in order to send him to his death and the faint smile of Inagaki who had listened, never saying a word, Bunshirō's feelings boiled over with anger.

And then there were those who had died needlessly. Inukai Hyōma, two more of the attackers, the man who had just been trailing them, and Kitamura, a guardian of the mansion, were all dead.

No, they're not the only ones. The deaths of Aoki Magozō and Yada's widow—in the final analysis, they, too, had to be seen as sacrificial victims of Satomura's orders. And when he thought this deeply into the matter, Bunshirō found himself

Semishigure

fairly panting with the urge to unleash the rage that for years had been pent up in his breast. His eyes blinded with anger, Bunshirō felt the time had come to speak his mind to Elder Satomura.

It was then that Bunshirō understood Oribe-no-Shō's warning that he "do nothing rash," but his feelings could no longer be suppressed. He headed not for the riverbank road, but from Yamabuki-chō he cut past the edge of the castle moat and hurried along the street that led to Babasaki.

On a night like this, when the elder would be dispatching people hither and yon, Bunshirō did not imagine that his mansion would be completely undefended, and he could see that if he went there he was in danger of clashing with Satomura's guards. But at that moment, Bunshirō was in a mood simply to trample and crush those defenses. Like a wounded beast seething with anger, Bunshirō marched through the dark streets of the town.

As it happened, the main gate of Satomura's mansion was wide open, and within the gate it was lit with fire. Here and there men with their sleeves tied back and wearing headbands were moving about, and the light of the fire reached out into the street.

For a moment, Bunshirō surveyed this scene from outside the gate. Then, releasing the catch on the sheath of his sword, he quietly entered. Next to the fire stood about ten men in headbands and tied sleeves. He had the impression that Satomura, being the sort of man he was, had fully prepared himself to do battle with the Yokoyama faction. Three of the men were sitting on kegs eating rice balls. And at first none of those who saw Bunshirō said anything. Only when he went past the men and approached the vestibule did anyone speak to him.

"Where are you going?"

"I've come to see the elder."

"Just wait a moment!"

The voice accosted him again, and when Bunshirō turned around, one of the men exclaimed, "Hey! It's Maki!" At that, all of the men came rushing toward him. Bunshirō held up a hand to restrain them.

"Calm down, please. I bear no resentment toward any of you, and I don't want to injure anyone." Still the men kept inching closer. "I only want to talk to the elder. I'll do nothing violent. So please, just wait where you are." But the looks on their faces grew only the more severe.

Then one of the men ran around to the rear of Bunshirō and tried to block his path. When Bunshirō wheeled and stood in his way, the man, who seemed small and nimble, suddenly drew his sword and attacked. But in that same instant, Bunshirō, too, drew; the man's body went flying, as if flicked off his feet, into the shrubbery beside the vestibule.

"I haven't cut him." Bunshirō restored his sword to its sheath and pointed to the fallen man. "Help him up." The other men stood as stiff as poles, their hands still on the hafts of their swords, apparently in dread of Bunshirō's all but invisible swordplay. Bunshirō turned his back on them and entered the vestibule. No one followed.

But in the vestibule, another retainer, a middle-aged samurai, barred his way. He had been watching the action out front and now stood on the step up to the entry hall, both arms extended, as if he were an actor on the stage.

"You may not enter here," he said. "His Honor the Elder will not see you."

Bunshirō, saying nothing, removed the straw travelling sandals Tōjirō had given him and cast them aside. When he mounted the step and the samurai came to seize him, Bunshirō drove

Semishigure

his fist into the man's solar plexus and knocked him out. Then, having lain the falling man down peacefully, he headed for Satomura's sitting room in the interior, the location of which he knew.

With no one to stop him, Bunshirō made his way easily to the room. Along the way he heard only the laugh of a woman somewhere in the distance. Otherwise the mansion was silent.

When he slid the panel open, Satomura, sitting at his desk, raised his head and looked at Bunshirō. If anyone else had been there it would have been troublesome, he thought, but the elder was alone. He seemed to be examining some complex documents. Satomura was wearing spectacles, but now he removed them. Bunshirō slid the panel shut, strode in, and sat down about six yards from the desk that Satomura faced.

"You despised us, treated us as inferiors."

Satomura looked at Bunshirō, saying nothing. When he saw Bunshirō, he must have realized that tonight's scheme had gone wrong, but he showed no sign of disappointment on his face. He just fastened his expressionless eyes on Bunshirō.

"People have died for nothing." Bunshirō went on in a low voice. "I, too, had to fight for my life. Because of you, our honored elder—your profit, your greed—people died."

"Not so!" Satomura spoke up for the first time. "They died for the good of the domain!"

"Shut up!" Bunshirō snapped. Cut the man down! he thought to himself, so strong was his urge to kill the elder before his eyes. "I'm sick of hearing that sort of talk. You don't seem to understand what it feels like for someone who's about to die. Well, for someone who's about to die …"

Bunshirō slid forward swiftly on his knees. His hand was already gripping the haft of his sword. He raised up on one knee and poised his sword in the figure eight position. Satomura would have seen only a white glint of steel flash before his eyes. And then two legs fell away from his desk; the documents on the desktop crashed to the tatami mats.

"*That's* what it feels like," Bunshirō said as he re-sheathed his sword.

Satomura must have felt that he was being killed. He made no attempt to flee, but his face had turned earthen-hued.

"I beg your pardon for my rudeness." Bunshirō bowed and then stood. Then at the entrance to the room, he turned back to the elder. "Having been insulted when I too am a warrior, I found that difficult to suffer in silence, and thus resorted to such behavior. But if this angers you, please, feel free to send someone to punish me at any time. I shall gladly engage him in a fair fight."

"Wait!" Satomura spoke at last. "You'll be going to Yokoyama's mansion from here?"

"No, I'm going home," Bunshirō said. "But I expect Yokoyama-sama has already heard the details of tonight's events from another source." It felt good to deliver that parting shot.

Bunshirō shut the panel and stepped into the corridor. There was no one about, and he made his way undisturbed out the dark hallway to the vestibule. Along the way he heard only the same woman laughing at something a man had said. Satomura seemed not to have called out to summon anyone.

Bunshirō raised up the still fallen samurai and resuscitated him; and when this man who had attempted to grapple with him had regained consciousness, he pushed him aside and went outside. The men gathered around the fire talking about something all stared at Bunshirō. And when Bunshirō passed silently by them, three of them hurried away to the vestibule.

He went on to the gate with no interference, but there, as it happened, he encountered another man who was just coming

Semishigure

in. "Hey, there!" the man said. His wounded arm was in a sling suspended from his neck. It was Murakami Shichirōemon, supported by another man. "What are you doing in this place?"

"I'm doing nothing, so don't worry. But you'd better hurry and have that wound treated. If you wait too long it could prove fatal." With that retort, Bunshirō left. No one followed him.

Yes, I've behaved very rashly, Bunshirō thought, but he had no regrets. He felt as if he had given vent to the bitterness of Yada's widow, Aoki, and all those who had died this night.

When he went home, a guest was waiting.

7

"He is an emissary from Elder Yokoyama, the gentleman says." When Setsu went out to meet him and told him that, Bunshirō peered hard at the man who stood up from the entry step.

"I'm very sorry to come so late at night ..." He spoke politely and asked Bunshirō to accompany him to the mansion of Elder Yokoyama. That was fast, Bunshirō thought. He's already heard from Kaji Oribe-no-Shō.

Bunshirō agreed and went into the house to change clothes. While he was doing that, he told Setsu something of what had happened that night.

"Because of that, someone may come to attack me here. So keep a careful lookout."

"I understand."

"But if anyone does come, you mustn't fight back. Just tell them that Maki will deal with them when he returns." Having told her all this, Bunshirō left the house with the messenger.

Elder Yokoyama was not alone. Inspector General Ogata Kumaki was with him.

"I've heard in a general way what happened from Kaji-sama, but I'd like you to tell me all the details," Yokoyama said. This was the first time Bunshirō had seen Yokoyama up close. He was a fat man of about fifty. His cheeks and his shoulders were rounded and his stomach quite prominent. But his hair was still black, and despite the late hour—it was already halfway through the Fourth Hour (11 p.m.)—his skin sparkled and he seemed full of vigor.

"But first …" Bunshirō began, "I wonder if I might tell you about the time I was summoned by Satomura-sama and the former junior elder, Inagaki-sama?"

"Oh? Inagaki, too? That's interesting." Yokoyama smiled, and the wrinkles at the corners of his eyes grew deep.

"When I was summoned to Elder Satomura's mansion at Babasaki, Inagaki-sama was there."

"And that is related to tonight's events?"

"That's correct."

"Then tell us. We want to hear everything."

Bunshirō told them what Satomura had said to him that night, and every detail of what had happened just tonight. As he spoke, Yokoyama and Ogata Kumaki occasionally exchanged glances and nodded to each other.

"In the course of all this, I had intended to come here and ask your assistance, but in the end I had to ask Kaji-sama."

"What is your connection with Oribe-no-Shō-sama?"

"Didn't you know? They are both disciples of the Ishiguri Dojo." Ogata Kumaki answered his question before Bunshirō could.

"Hmm." Yokoyama nodded, and turned slowly to look at Ogata. "Well, Satomura seems to have dug his own grave. He'll have no excuse for this. Our situation now seems to be reversed."

Ogata nodded, and Yokoyama Matasuke smiled. Then his smile grew and finally burst into laughter.

The Assassin

1

It was about three months after Elder Yokoyama had laughed at learning that the opposing faction had destroyed itself, when autumn winds had begun to blow, that the punishments of the Inagaki-Satomura faction were announced.

But perhaps Yokoyama Matasuke, into whose hands governance of the domain now fell, was reluctant to have those punishments perceived as factional revenge, for they were surprisingly limited in scope, and no one was put to death, as in the incident some years earlier.

Apart from Inagaki and Satomura themselves, Tada Samon, their junior elder, was sentenced to one hundred days of domiciliary confinement, and ten of the men who had waited upon them hand and foot were sentenced variously, ranging from fifty days of domiciliary confinement to mere restraint or demotion. Even Murakami Shichirōemon, who clearly bore responsibility for the attack on the Zelkova Mansion, got off with only fifty days of domiciliary confinement and reduction of his enfeoffment by half.

On the other hand, however, the former elder Satomura

Sanai was banished from the domain forever. He left, taking his family with him. Inagaki Chūbei was sentenced to rural confinement. Henceforward he was to live under house arrest in the isolated village of Ishikurazawa, a place, it was said, that even birds never visit. These men were considered the instigators of those long years of unrest.

Yokoyama, who had become the new chief elder and surrounded himself with men of his own faction, seemed confident that it would suffice if he were to punish only Inagaki and Satomura severely. His lenient treatment of the others, many thought, was meant to eliminate factionalism and was well received throughout the domain.

At about the same time that the Inagaki-Satomura faction was dealt with, the concubine O-Fuku, too, experienced a major change in her position. O-Man-sama, who until then had ruled the women's wing of the castle, was retired, and O-Fuku entered the castle in her place. This was done at the command of His Lordship in Edo. For Bunshirō, this meant that O-Fuku was once again a woman beyond his reach.

While all of this was underway, Bunshirō continued to make frequent rounds of the villages with District Commissioner Kashimura Yasuke. Then, in the autumn, he was assigned the task of making the rounds of every river in the domain, checking for any changes in their course or any breach in their embankments, and making a record thereof. There were times when he would hear of a break caused by heavy wind and rain, and he would ride several leagues on horseback to reach the scene; and there were times when he would climb to the source of a river where hardly any humans lived to investigate mudslides from the surrounding hills. Kashimura taught him the basics of the job, and the rest he learnt on his own.

Semishigure

And once he had digested all there was to know about rivers, they told him, he would go out into the forests and inspect the trees. There were no regional deputies involved in this work with forests and rivers; it was unique in being entirely under the jurisdiction of the district commissioner.

And the work was endless, Kashimura told him. Bunshirō steadily grew more and more interested in the job he had been assigned, but making the rounds of the rivers of the domain was more stressful than making the rounds of the fields. One usually had the help of a village official when inspecting the rice, but there was constant danger that one small oversight could cause a river to flood.

Bunshirō was dead tired when he returned home, only to find Owada Ippei there.

"Well! Haven't you turned dark!" When Bunshirō had changed and sat down with him, Ippei seemed quite impressed with what he saw. "You must be an old hand at the village round by now."

"Sunburnt but only half-trained, as they say. I've heard that once you master the job your face looks like a peasant." Bunshirō smiled wryly. "That's far in the future I suppose; but the village rounds are tiring."

"Tiring, are they?" From the look on Ippei's face, he seemed to agree. "Me—I get tired just walking back and forth between home and the castle."

"Have you seen Yonosuke lately?"

"Yes, that's why I've come here." He had gone to the domain academy on orders from Elder Yokoyama, Ippei said, and he had seen Yonosuke there. "Now that he's an assistant professor, he gets a room of his own there."

"Really? Did you see it?"

"I went and had a look. It's a mess; piled high with books. Yonosuke's becoming a real scholar. He made tea for me in his room and we talked for a while …" Ippei suddenly lowered his voice. "That was when Yonosuke said something that you mustn't ignore …" Bunshirō said nothing but looked Ippei straight in the face. Ippei nodded, and then spoke in an even lower voice. "Don't be shocked. It looks as if an assassin has been sent to get you."

"An assassin?" Bunshirō quietly asked. "Who would do such a thing?"

"Satomura, apparently. He's been banished, but before he and his family left their mansion, he summoned someone and arranged with him to do it. That seems to be the story … Do you know a fellow named Ishikura Shunzō; an assistant professor at the academy, like Yonosuke?"

"I've heard the name."

"He was a hard and fast adherent of the Satomura faction, they say. Yonosuke overheard this Ishikura and someone from the outside talking about it. 'Looks as if …' I said, because these two happened to notice Yonosuke while in the midst of their tête-à-tête. They stopped immediately, he says, so he never heard clearly all that they had to say …"

"Well, if it is Satomura—I wouldn't put it past him." As he spoke, Bunshirō was recalling how Satomura's face had blanched when he faced the tip of his drawn sword. That alone would have been more humiliating than the man could bear. But it was Bunshirō's failure to do as Satomura had intended him to do that in the end brought on the decisive defeat of his faction—and that, for Satomura, could only have been mortifying. Of course, from Bunshirō's point of view the man's anger was misplaced, but he could nonetheless understand how he felt.

"So who is this assassin?" Bunshirō asked.

Semishigure

"That, he says, he doesn't know."

"When did Yonosuke hear this?"

"Four or five days ago, he said." Yonosuke had intended to talk to Bunshirō that same day and warn him. But that evening, when he was preparing to leave, Ishikura came to Yonosuke's room. "'You overheard us talking today, didn't you?' Ishikura asked him. Of course Yonosuke denied it. Whereupon Ishikura told him that if the story should get out, they would assume Yonosuke had leaked it. 'So kindly understand that,' he said, threatening him in the politest possible terms."

"What?"

"Yonosuke still intended to tell you, but when he left someone followed him. He's a bit of a coward, you know. And that set him trembling. He was still fretting about it when I happened to see him." Ippei stopped talking and stared at Bunshirō. "You haven't noticed anything unusual lately?"

"No, nothing." Bunshirō shook his head; and Ippei, with a stern look on his face, went on.

"Why not report it to the inspector general? Rather than leave it to chance."

"I don't know about that," Bunshirō said. "With only that story to go on, I doubt Ogata-sama would take up the matter. Ishikura could insist he never said any such thing, that there must be some mistake—and that would be the end of it. Besides which ... if the story is true, and I report it to the inspector general, that puts Yonosuke in danger."

Ippei clicked his tongue. "Then what will you do?"

"I'll keep a sharp lookout. There's nothing else I can do." Bunshirō offered Ippei the plate of rice crackers that Setsu had brought earlier. They were a gift from Setsu's family, made by the confectioner Komakiya in town. The crackers were large, crisp, and uneven in shape, but the superb soya flavor that permeated them made them very popular. "If I know what's up, it shouldn't be easy to spring a surprise attack on me. If you see Yonosuke, be sure to thank him for me."

"On your rounds of the villages, you're often alone aren't you?" Ippei said, chewing noisily on a rice cracker. "That's when you could be attacked by two or three men. And since they'll be assassins, he'll choose the most skilled men he can find."

"Two or three men ..." Bunshirō nodded. "So it might not be just one."

"No, wait. Yonosuke did say 'an assassin,' so yes, that's just one. And if there's only one, then who?" Ippei said, cocking his head to one side. But any deeper deliberation seemed more than he could manage. Ippei went back to crunching the rice cracker he had begun. "But that elder, as he once was, has done some dirty work."

"Yeah, if it's Satomura-sama, you can be sure he won't be satisfied just to kill me. Not that I don't understand how he feels ..."

"Just because that trap he laid was a failure? That's outrageous!" Ippei was visibly angry. "If he had had his way, even I could have ended up dead."

"Gentlemen of that sort, seem to consider underlings of our sort, as nothing more than their pawns." Bunshirō was recalling when Satomura told him he was indebted to them. "And because his pawn failed to do as he intended it to do, he was banished, and *that* he finds intolerable. If you ask me, that's a self-serving excuse, but that would be how he feels, wouldn't it?"

"He should be blaming himself," Ippei said. "Before the investigators, neither Satomura nor Inagaki had a single word to offer in their defense, did they? But then, it was His Lordship's favorite concubine ..." Ippei flashed a quick glance at Bunshirō. "They try to eliminate both her and her child, which seems to have made His Lordship furious, too. And then, as if that were not vile enough, they try to get even by leaving an assassin behind when they depart."

Ippei, infuriated, reached out for another rice cracker, but then a look came over his face as if there were something he had just remembered, and he withdrew his hand.

"Did you hear that Asai Heizaburō has been appointed city magistrate?"

"No."

In his duty room, Bunshirō had heard that the Yokoyama faction would be holding "evaluation and rewards meetings" following the disposition of the Inagaki-Satomura faction, but he was often away overnight on inspection rounds of the rivers of the domain and thus was unfamiliar with developments of that sort in the castle. Bunshirō had heard none of the details of the evaluation and rewards.

"In one leap, his enfeoffment rose a hundred koku when he became city magistrate."

"Because this man Asai has been a member of the Yokoyama faction since years past—or so I hear. This was only to be expected, was it not?"

"What do you suppose they'll do for us?" Again, Ippei lowered his voice. "After all that we did and then being called before the investigators to give evidence. That was no small contribution to this changeover, it seems to me. Right?"

"I feel the same," Bunshirō said, "but that's nothing we ourselves can say to them."

As well as the matter of the assassin, Ippei also wanted to talk about rewards, but when he heard Bunshirō's unsympathetic response, he began preparing to leave.

2

About a month had passed, during which the assassin never appeared, nor did any word of rewards come from Elder Yokoyama, as Ippei had been expecting. It was now late autumn.

At that time, on a day when he was off duty, Bunshirō called at the Ono Dojo of the Mugai school. It had been a long time since he had seen Fusé Tsurunosuke and he wanted to know how he was getting on. Bunshirō felt a secret sense of indebtedness to Fusé. He had no connection with either the Yokoyama or the Satomura factions, and he was still living at home. Bunshirō thought himself deeply culpable for having involved him in a swordfight; a single blunder could have ended in a disaster he could never justify to the Fusé family.

Once the incident had settled down, Bunshirō invited Ippei and Fusé Tsurunosuke to the Kinutaya in Somekawa-chō to thank them for their efforts; but Ippei aside, he didn't think that was sufficient recompense for Fusé.

The Ono Dojo was on a backstreet in Aoyagi-chō. It was a bright, refreshing day, and thus the main street of Aoyagi-chō was thronged with people. Bunshirō made his way through the crowds for a while, then turned into an alleyway that took him around to the backstreet. There, too, the autumn sun was streaming down, but from the row of low-eaved houses, there came only the occasional sounds of the book makers' wooden mallets and the tearing of paper. Compared to the din of the main street, this backstreet was so quiet it seemed dead.

"That's what Ippei says, but …" Bunshirō was thinking. Ippei himself had done nothing very dangerous that night. By comparison, Fusé Tsurunosuke had drawn his sword and fought against the enemy. If rewards were to be forthcoming, Fusé should be given something before Ippei.

Semishigure

As he walked down the empty street, turning these thoughts over in his mind, the sharp shouts of attack began to reach him. Midway along that street, where the afternoon sun cast deep shadows beneath the eaves, there was a slightly recessed area in which stood the Ono Dojo. This had once been the place where the Aoyagi-chō festival float had been stored. The building was a bit small for the Ono Dojo; but the roof was tall, and it at least appeared large compared to the houses that surrounded it. The shouts issued from a barred window in the building.

Bunshirō entered the dojo from a rear entrance that he knew. Whereupon two men engaged in a match caught his eye. Everyone else had retreated to the walls, either sitting or kneeling on one knee as they watched the match.

Again the shouts of attack resounded, and the two bamboo swords clashed. But in the next instant, the two quickly stepped back and opened a gap between them. Bunshirō then glimpsed the face of the tall swordsman facing his way.

Well! This is unusual, he thought. The man was Okitsu Shinnojō. But just as he was wondering who his opponent might be, Fusé Tsurunosuke appeared before eyes.

"Well, well! This is a rare visit!" Fusé said. And then he learnt that Okitsu's opponent was Ishikawa Sōroku.

"Sōroku has improved, hasn't he?" Bunshirō said. Fuse smiled and turned to watch the match.

"Definitely. I have to keep on my toes with him now."

"Does that other fellow come here from time to time?" Bunshirō's eyes indicated Okitsu, and Fusé nodded.

"Lately he's come quite often."

"Since when?" His question was prompted by a certain suspicion. When Ippei mentioned the word "assassin," Bunshirō almost instinctively envisioned the face of Okitsu Shinnojō.

Bunshirō had no idea how much Satomura knew about his own skill with the sword. But if his knowledge was at all accurate, even if only through hearsay, Satomura would not likely have hired a mediocre swordsman as his assassin. He would have sought out someone as skilled as Bunshirō, or even more skilled. In which case, the lineup of candidates would have been limited, and Okitsu Shinnojō would ultimately have stood out as the best choice.

"Well, it would have been toward the end of summer or possibly the beginning of autumn. In any case, not all that long ago … Why do you ask?" Fusé asked. But Bunshirō gave him an evasive answer.

Toward the end of summer he says. Wouldn't that be just before Satomura and the others were sentenced? Isn't there some significance in that? Bunshirō was thinking to himself, when Fusé again said something.

"What?" Bunshirō said.

"No, I just asked if you were going to practice today …"

"Yes, yes. I plan to go around to Kaji-machi afterward, but there is something I want to talk with you about first.

"What's that?"

"The Yokoyama faction seem to be holding evaluation and rewards meetings, and Owada Ippei was saying we too should be receiving something."

"We're to receive something?"

"No, that's just it." Bunshirō looked down. "I was expecting a little something, too. But rather than me, I think you should be rewarded in some way. Don't some of your friends ever say that?"

"A few do."

"Of course, they would." Bunshirō raised his face and looked at Fusé. Fusé Tsurunosuke always looked very manly, his face

Semishigure

firm and fixed. "But a month or so has passed now since deliberations over rewards began, and still we've heard not a word, which makes me wonder whether in fact we haven't a hope … whether we've fought for nothing. I'm sorry about that, but you'd better resign yourself."

As Bunshirō spoke, Ishikawa Sōroku gave a violent shout and rushed in to attack. In defense, Okitsu Shinnojō raised his bamboo sword, and their bodies intertwined with dazzling speed as they exchanged blows, which resounded now like the whack of someone beating a wet rag.

"That will do." The voice came from a man who rose from amongst the students. It was the master's assistant, Miyake Tōemon. Miyake approached the two, and Okitsu Shinnojō slid to the rear. Ishikawa Sōroku was standing dazed, but eventually he, too, retreated, and the two bowed to each other.

Having watched all this, Fusé Tsurunosuke turned about toward Bunshirō, a carefree smile on his face.

"Don't trouble yourself too much. It doesn't worry me a bit."

"And yet—you'll have fought for nothing. So I still feel that I've done something inexcusable."

"What? We didn't go looking for a battle. And we accomplished something very worthwhile."

As Fusé spoke, a short, slightly plump man came and stood next to the two of them. It was Miyake, the master's assistant. Miyake returned Bunshirō's greeting with a cheerful smile then turned toward the center of the instruction hall. Okitsu Shinnojō was there holding his bamboo practice sword, looking at Bunshirō.

"That fellow is saying he'd like to have a match with you …" Miyake said. He was a man in his mid-thirties, beginning to lose the hair at his temples, who spoke with a distinctive softness.

Miyake served as an official in the rice stores. Nor was it just his speech; his movements, too, were very soft. If you hadn't been told that he was a fleet-footed master of the Mugai school of swordsmanship, you would never guess it. Miyake went on:

"Just one round will do, he says. How about it? Won't you do it as a demonstration for our students?"

"A match?" Bunshirō hesitated. Even in a practice match, crossing swords with Okitsu Shinnojō was not something he had expected to do. That alone was an imposition; but he was also deterred by his feelings. If Okitsu was indeed the assassin, he had no desire to fight a match with him. But while he was vacillating, Fusé put in a word.

"It's exactly as the assistant says. A match between the likes of you and Okitsu-san is something students rarely get to see. I do hope you'll give them a demonstration."

Having been told that, there was no way he could escape. Bunshirō borrowed a bamboo sword and went to the center of the floor. He had come here any number of times, so the students at the Ono Dojo knew Bunshirō by name. And knowing what was about to begin, the students were buzzing with excitement, but the buzz quickly quietened down and gave way to the silence of expectation.

"Just a moment," Bunshirō called out to Okitsu. But Okitsu did not respond to Bunshirō's greeting. Instead only a threatening smile spread over his sunken cheeks and drained face.

"I thought you were going to run away, but you've changed your mind, it seems," Okitsu said. That was his greeting. Bunshirō was irked, and he spoke out powerfully.

"I never run away! Ready to go?"

"Good!" Okitsu replied; and the two of them cautiously opened the distance between them. They were about ten yards apart.

Semishigure

Okitsu Shinnojō poised his sword in the mid-position. Bunshirō noticed, though, that the tip of the weapon was just a bit higher than he had seen him hold it previously. Perhaps this meant he had some particular plan in mind?

Bunshirō, holding his own sword in the figure eight position, moved forward slowly. With each step he checked the position of Okitsu's bamboo sword, but it remained just a bit high and did not move even slightly. Okitsu, too, was moving forward little by little.

They were about six yards apart, he reckoned, when the tip of Okitsu's sword swiftly fell, and he came sliding forward at a run. It was a firm, fast run, and in an instant he was within striking distance. His sword rose smoothly to the upper position. Then shouting, Okitsu almost casually lowered his sword as he came.

It'll be his second stroke, Bunshirō thought. He recalled that previously it had been Okitsu's practice to place greatest emphasis not his first blow but on the one that followed it. Bunshirō deflected Okitsu's sword with an upward stroke.

But then Okitsu's tall body suddenly dropped. He pulled his feet back from where he had attacked, and from a stance in which he was almost crouched on the floor, he launched his second blow. By the time Bunshirō noticed, he had been struck on the torso. His instantaneous attempt to block the blow was too late. Bunshirō's body gave off the sound of a wet rag being struck, and he gasped.

"I'm hit!" Bunshirō shouted and quickly fell back.

"That will do," Miyake Tōemon called out. Okitsu relaxed his defensive posture and stood up. He was looking at Bunshirō, his face expressionless. Bunshirō, for his part, while watching Fusé Tsurunosuke challenge Okitsu to a match, took his leave of Miyake and headed for the door. Miyake saw him out.

When Bunshirō had put on his sandals and again taken his leave, Miyake suddenly spoke.

"You didn't use Cloudburst, did you? If you had, you wouldn't have been hit."

Bunshirō was shocked and looked up. Miyake, his head balding, a broad, friendly smile on his round face, nodded to Bunshirō, turned, and left.

When he stepped outside, the glaring sun shone down on Bunshirō. The astonishment that he felt persisted, and he walked away from the Ono Dojo more rapidly than he realized. It didn't trouble him greatly that he had been hit by Okitsu. Next time I won't be hit, he told himself. His astonishment was caused by what Miyake had said.

3

The secret techniques of swordplay, Cloudburst ... Bunshirō was puzzling over whom Miyake Tōemon could have heard that from. Bunshirō himself knew he had never mentioned it to anyone. The only others who knew the name would have to be Master Ishiguri Yazaemon and Kaji Oribe-no-Shō. If the secret had leaked out, perhaps it was from his master?

He had heard from Maruoka, the assistant, that Ishiguri Yazaemon's decline in old age had been rather pronounced of late. Even Bunshirō himself had noticed, although he seldom went to the dojo now. Yazaemon no longer went out to the instruction hall; he would sit the whole day through next to the brazier in his sitting room. Nor did ageing affect only Yazaemon's body. His mind, too, had begun to deteriorate.

Occasionally Yazaemon would have visitors from the outside. Most of the time Yazaemon would sit facing his guest, saying

Semishigure

nothing, listening to the other man talk. But rarely, they say, there were times when he would break out in smiles and become quite talkative, as if a fire had been lit in him. That, Bunshirō recalled Maruoka saying, would usually be when his guest, for some reason, would touch upon some event in Yazaemon's past.

There was no proof that the name of Cloudburst hadn't slipped out on just such an occasion, Bunshirō thought. But even so, it was unthinkable that details of those secrets could have leaked out. Still, Miyake's brief comment had sown the seeds of anxiety in Bunshirō's breast.

When he crossed the bridge into Kaji-machi, however, Bunshirō's thoughts moved away from Miyake Tōemon's words and returned to his match with Okitsu Shinnojō.

He really is powerful. Bunshirō was recalling his feelings when that sword, that should have gone astray when he deflected it, far from losing force only gained in speed as it returned to strike his torso. That was a technique that only the most exceptional swordsman could master.

If Okitsu were the assassin that Ippei mentioned, this could be difficult, Bunshirō thought. In their match, Okitsu Shinnojō had shown no sign of any urge to kill, but that was no proof that Okitsu was not the assassin. If he were an intelligent swordsman, he would do nothing so careless as to reveal the urge to kill to his opponent.

When he arrived at the Ishiguri Dojo, he was at a loss what to do, but in the end he decided to go around to the instruction hall entrance, rather than stop at his master's rooms. He felt no inclination to meet with his ageing master, though not without a certain sense of guilt. It depressed him to think that he and his master were slowly drifting apart.

As he stepped over the threshold of the instruction hall, the din of the shouts and the stamping of feet assaulted his ears. But compared to the days when the master's eyes sparkled with attention and his assistant, Satake Kinjūrō, walked about the hall bamboo sword in hand, shouting abuse, the place somehow lacked spirit. He noticed, too, that the number of people practicing was actually very small.

As he stood in the earthen entryway, Sugiuchi Michizō noticed Bunshirō, stopped practicing, and came over.

"It's been a long time. Won't you come in?"

"I was just wondering what to do, but ..."

"Oh, don't say that. Come in and give us a lesson," Michizō said, while Bunshirō still stood on the earthen floor. But Bunshirō stood where he was and peered into the hall.

"Maruoka-san doesn't seem to be here today." If Maruoka, the assistant, were there, he wanted to ask whether anyone from the Mugai school had come to the master's quarters recently. But Maruoka was nowhere in sight.

"The assistant is off today. There's a funeral in his family, they say."

"Is that Ōhashi-san over there?" Bunshirō's eyes were fixed upon a man who was fighting vigorously in a match against Noda Yasuke at the rear of the hall. "That's strange. I'd heard from Maruoka-san that he quit the dojo ..."

"He's come back." Sugiuchi Michizō smiled wryly. "He quit in the first place because he didn't get along with Hyōma. But now that Hyōma is dead, wouldn't that be why he felt like coming back?"

The fight at the Zelkova Mansion had been kept a secret by the ranking officials of the domain, who at the time revealed only that there had been another factional clash. And so Michizō would not have known that Inukai Hyōma had been killed in a failed attempt to assassinate Bunshirō and the others.

"Then he's officially restored his name tag?"

"That's right."

"Since when?"

"I think it was sometime around early autumn …"

"Early autumn?" Bunshirō frowned. But no, Ōhashi Ichinoshin would not be the assassin. "That's a violent match, isn't it?"

"It certainly is. Neither Noda nor I can stand up to him now." Michizō again smiled wryly. And still smiling, invited him again. "How about it? Do come in."

"No, another time," Bunshirō said. He couldn't be bothered meeting Ōhashi Ichinoshin. "I'll come back again soon. Give my regards to Maruoka-san."

Just when he had given up all hope, a summons concerning rewards came from Elder Yokoyama. Autumn had ended, and only a few withered leaves still clung to the trees. It was now early winter. But of course it was only that night, after he arrived at the Yokoyama mansion by the edge of the moat, that he realized the summons concerned rewards for what they had done on behalf of the Yokoyama faction.

"I'm sorry this has taken so long," Yokoyama said, "but we've summoned you because the rewards for Maki, Owada Ippei, and Fusé Tsurunosuke have, for the most part, been decided."

4

In the inner room to which Bunshirō had been summoned, there were three or four desks lined up, all of them covered with documents and writing equipment boxes. It felt more like an office than a sitting room. In fact, ever since the change in government, Yokoyama, even after returning from the castle, night after night would gather his people, probably in this same room, and carry on busily with the work of governing the domain.

Now, too, there were three other men present, as well as the elder. There was Sakakibara Shuri, who had become the second-ranking elder; the samurai commander, Horie Kanjūrō; and one other man Bunshirō was seeing for the first time. Sakakibara and Horie were in their mid-forties, but the other man looked perhaps ten years younger.

"Well then, the rewards …" Yokoyama said. A smile appeared on his round, fleshy face as he looked at Bunshirō. "For Maki Bunshirō, a rise of thirty koku; and for Owada Ippei, a rise of five koku has been decided upon."

Bunshirō looked down, saying nothing. This was a much greater rise than he had expected. He was so dumbfounded that in that instant no words of thanks would emerge.

"In this recent changeover, your feats of arms have played an exceptionally great part. Concerning which, we have received orders from His Lordship in Edo to reward you with particular generosity. And incidentally, this is a good opportunity to introduce you. This is Tamiya Nakajirō-dono, who has come from Edo. You know the name, I'm sure."

"Yes, I do know," Bunshirō replied. Tamiya Nakajirō was His Lordship's adjutant. He was a young man, but even the elders deferred to him as the most powerful of those close to His Lordship. This was clearly to be seen in Yokoyama's manner of speaking. The adjutant, who was reputed to be a man of exceptional ability, responded to Bunshirō's bow with a polite nod, but the expression on his face was friendly.

"You may think that a rise of thirty koku is excessive,"

Yokoyama said, "but that rise includes a reward to the late Sukezaemon. So give it your best; no less so than your late father!"

"I am deeply grateful for your generosity, and I am sure my late father, too, is delighted." Bunshirō had at last calmed down sufficiently to express his thanks. Whereupon Yokoyama told Bunshirō that he had summoned him alone because there was another matter concerning which he wished to ask his opinion.

"It's the matter of Fusé Tsurunosuke. Fusé is still living at home, and there are those of the opinion that we should induct him into the Corps of Vassals and establish him in a family of his own. But what do you think?"

"In that case …" Bunshirō thought hard about this. If Fusé were to be inducted and established in a family of his own, the domain still would not grant him much of a stipendiary allowance. At most something like five koku, and certainly less than ten koku. But as a handsome young man, skilled with the sword, it was possible that, without ever saying a word, he might be adopted as the heir to a house of 100 or 150 koku.

I mustn't speak carelessly, Bunshirō was thinking, but then a thought flickered across his mind.

"What has become of the house of Yada Sakunojō since that incident?"

"It wouldn't have been abolished," Yokoyama said.

"If I'm not mistaken," Sakakibara Shuri added, "his old mother has been placed in the custody of relatives and given a meager stipend to live on."

"This is nothing but a sudden thought of mine," Bunshirō said. "But Fusé is related to kin of the Yada. I'd be grateful if you could give some thought to allowing Fusé to inherit what remains and restore the house."

"How much was Yada's original stipend?" Yokoyama asked.

Then Sakakibara and Tamiya joined in, and the whispering among them went on for some time. It wouldn't do to give him all of it; no, but half might be all right, they were saying. Then they asked Bunshirō some rather pointed questions about Fusé Tsurunosuke's character. And finally Yokoyama spoke.

"Your idea is most interesting. Of course we shall have to check with the man himself, but if Fusé desires it, we shall consider the restoration of the House of Yada."

It was past the Fourth Hour (10 p.m.) when Bunshirō left the Yokoyama mansion. It was a bright moonlit night. High in the sky the moon shone as if it were a silver platter, illumining the broad streets of this neighborhood of mansions where not another person was to be seen. The night air was cold; Bunshirō unconsciously pulled his collar tight and began walking.

Fusé—if he could inherit the Yada house, that would be good, Bunshirō was thinking. If that were possible, that sense of anxiety he felt, that feeling of desolation that had lingered so long, would vanish. In fact, he felt, it could even be salvation of a sort for the late Yada Sakunojō and his widow. For the first time in a long while, Bunshirō recalled the sorrowful death of the widow, which immersed him in bittersweet emotion.

It was probably because of those feelings that Bunshirō was slow to notice the man behind him. When he turned to face the black form, the man had closed to within a few yards of him. In his hand he held the bare blade of a drawn sword. The man walked slowly.

Though instantly he drew his own sword, Bunshirō had no choice but to retreat. The initiative in this fight was held by the other man, probably the assassin Ippei had spoken of. It was clear that one false move now could lead to a painful defeat.

About the time he sensed that the riverbank road was but

Semishigure

a short distance behind him, the man for the first time halted. Then in the next instant he attacked with the force of a wild wind. Bunshirō only barely managed to deflect his blade. But when the man pulled up, there was a scant unguarded moment. Seizing that moment, Bunshirō was able to shift into his Cloudburst defensive stance. Even so, he was wounded on the shoulder. But in the clash that followed, Bunshirō's blow was just an instant faster.

When Bunshirō tore the mask from the face of the fallen man, for a moment he just gazed at him in astonishment. The man was Miyake Tōemon of the Mugai school. As he thought back, still trembling, to the speed of Miyake's swordplay, Bunshirō felt that at long last his struggle with Satomura had come to an end.

Cicada Showers

1

Twenty-some years had passed.

As a younger man he had gone by the name of Bunshirō. Since then, he had become a district commissioner and had assumed the name of his late father. He was now Maki Sukezaemon II.

Sukezaemon rode into the courtyard of the regional deputy's headquarters in the village of Yajiri, the district of Ōura, and dismounted. It was one of those days when the glare of the midsummer sun bathed every corner of the domain. The air was so still that with every breath he could feel his lungs fill with heat.

Sukezaemon led his horse into the shade of a plum tree that stood within the hedge and tethered him there. Tokusuke, the servant, had heard the hoofbeats and came running from the house.

"Welcome back!" he said. "I wasn't expecting you until after the Eighth Hour (2 p.m.); you're back early. It was hot, I'll bet!"

"Is Kuwamura-dono in?" Sukezaemon said, asking after the deputy. Tokusuke shook his head.

"He went to the castle early this morning, said he'd be back in the evening. But what would you like for lunch? We have cold rice, but if you're not in a hurry, shall I have Granny fix you some noodles?"

When he was young, Tokusuke had served in a samurai household, but now he and his wife lived and worked out here in the deputy's headquarters.

"It's too hot to be cooking," Sukezaemon said. "Cold rice will be just fine. But before that, I'd better bathe. I've been sweating something terrible. Could you give my horse a drink, though?"

Sukezaemon went inside. The deputy's headquarters in Yajiri had not been purpose-built as an office. It was the run-down house of a once well-to-do family which had been confiscated in lieu of unpaid taxes and then refurbished a little for official use. In appearance, it was much the same farmhouse it always had been.

When he stepped into the earthen-floored entrance and took off his sandals, the deputy's assistant, Nakayama Shigejūrō, and three other lesser officials, who must have heard him talking with Tokusuke, came out and welcomed Sukezaemon.

Since the beginning of summer, Sukezaemon had been making the rounds of the forests in Ōura, inspecting the previous year's cedar plantings. For more than a month now, he had been lodging at the deputy's headquarters in Yajiri. Today he was returning after three days away in the mountain villages. He went to the room they had assigned him, laid out the undergarments he would change into, then went out to the well in the garden behind the house. There he stripped down to his loincloth and washed away the grime and sweat that clung to his body.

Another month and I should be finished, he thought. There was one more plantation on his rounds; he had to inspect the new groves out in the mountains beyond the village of Sugizawa. Once he had taken care of that, the job would be done.

Usually his subordinates would lodge in the villages and supervise the peasants. But in some places, as in the present case, Sukezaemon himself would have to stay behind. Until that work was done, he could not return to the castle town.

The rush of cool water over his sweltering body revived and refreshed him. When he changed and went out to the sitting room, Nakayama told him he had had a caller that morning.

"A caller? For me?"

"Yes, the chief clerk of the Mikuniya in Minoura brought this for you." Nakayama handed Sukezaemon a letter. It was very light, written in a faint hand, and sealed. The address read simply, "Maki Sukezaemon-sama." It was unsigned.

"Was there any other message?" Sukezaemon asked.

"No," Nakayama told him, "the man just said, 'Please give this to him,' and left. That was all."

Shaking his head in puzzlement, Sukezaemon went into his room. He sat down at his desk, broke the seal and opened the letter. As he read the brief text, he could feel the blood drain from his face. It read:

I have decided to become a nun at the temple Byakuren'in, and will cut my hair in the autumn. Yet moved by the one small regret that remains to me in this life, I have come to Minoura in the hope that we might meet again. If I could see you, nothing would give me greater pleasure, but I would not wish to ask the impossible. I send this letter, hoping against hope that I may be so fortunate.
To Bunshirō,
with respect

There was no signature, but neither was there room for any doubt. This letter could only have been sent by O-Fuku-sama.

Semishigure

Become a nun? Sukezaemon thought. Byakuren'in was a convent with connections to the house of the lord of the domain. Almost a year had passed since the death of the previous lord. O-Fuku-sama probably intends to cut her hair before the first anniversary. And yet ... What a daring thing she is doing ...

As he turned these thoughts over in his mind, Sukezaemon sat staring at two lines set apart from the main text of the letter: "I plan to return to the castle on the 20th." The twentieth; that was today. Those last two lines seemed to demand that Sukezaemon make up his mind immediately.

Sukezaemon rose and began changing clothes. Once decided, he was quick to prepare. When he emerged from his room, he called Nakayama and told him he would be going out, then he looked into the kitchen to tell Tokusuke he would not be needing anything to eat.

When he mounted his horse and set out, the midday summer heat totally enveloped Sukezaemon. Even under his broad sedge hat, the surface of the earth cast the heat back up and burnt his face. Sweat rolled down his cheeks.

As he left the village and headed out the road through the rice fields, far off to his left he could see a low hill that looked like the shell of a crawling turtle. That hill, covered with pines and cedars, jutting up from amongst the rice paddies, was where a great cache of stone arrowheads had once been found, which is what gave the village its name, Yajiri—"Arrowhead."

He rode on for two leagues or so, passing through three more villages, whereupon the road entered a stretch of gently rolling sand dunes. Then, as he emerged from a stand of black pines, their trunks bent sharply by the fierce sea winds of winter, he could smell the seashore and hear the sound of waves.

Minoura was a fishing village with a small harbor but was

better known for the ten or more hot-springs inns on its outskirts. He could see the steam rising from them now.

2

There were no very grand inns in Minoura, but with the waves breaking upon the shore, the long sandy beach, the pine groves, and of course fish fresh from the sea, it had an excellent reputation. Minoura had long been the resort where families of the Corps of Vassals came to take the waters.

But the season for taking the waters was from autumn through early spring. In midsummer the hot springs were deserted. Sukezaemon rode slowly through the village, halted at the Mikuniya, and dismounted. Whereupon a middle-aged man, who must have seen him, came running from the gate.

"You're the commissioner, sir?" the man asked.

When Sukezaemon told him that he was, the man introduced himself as Chief Clerk of the Mikuniya, who had brought the letter that morning.

"Our guest from Minoya said she would be leaving in the Eighth Hour (2 p.m.). Everyone at the inn has been worried for you. We're delighted you've arrived in time."

The chief clerk spoke excitedly. He called one of his men and told him to lead the horse around to the garden at the rear, then invited Sukezaemon to come in.

O-Fuku-sama ... she seems to have concealed her identity, Sukezaemon thought. That he could tell from what the chief clerk had just said. The Minoya was a clothier that had dealings with people in the castle. She must have taken rooms at the inn under the name of Minoya.

The chief clerk headed down a long narrow corridor, then

led Sukezaemon up to a room at the far end of the second floor. There were no guests in any of the rooms along the way. The sliding doors and the shoji were all wide open, and from the window at the end of the hall, he could see the sea.

When he entered the room, there she was, her hair already cut short, sitting with a girl of thirteen or fourteen, apparently her attendant.

"It's been a long time … O-Fuku-sama." When Sukezaemon greeted her, she smiled gently and nodded, then asked the chief clerk to bring the things he had prepared.

"But, no," she said, after the chief clerk and the girl had left. "Today I'm Fuku. Just Fuku."

Sukezaemon had not seen Fuku often since she had come to rule the women's wing of the castle. Yet neither was it that he never saw her. Occasionally over the years he had encountered her on visits to temples or shrines. And he had seen her at performances of Noh, sponsored by His Lordship when he was resident in the domain. But always from a distance. This was the first time he had seen her up close since he had escorted mother and child on their escape from the Zelkova Mansion to the mansion of Kaji Oribe-no-Shō. Since then, she had grown a bit fuller in face and figure. But her face remained strangely youthful, so much so that one would never take her for a woman over forty. Her eyes still sparkled, her mouth was dainty, the fingers on her lap white and thin. And her bearing and speech bespoke such elegance and refinement that it seemed only natural one should address her as O-Fuku-sama.

"Have you had anything to eat?" she asked.

"Not yet," Sukezaemon said. "I'd just come back from the mountains."

"Why of course. You must be hungry." Fuku spoke with

leisurely ease. "The chief clerk was saying you would be out in the mountains until today."

"So I was."

"I was worried you might not be able to come."

"Somehow I made it," Sukezaemon said. But now he understood why, when she knew he would be inspecting in the mountains, she had made no attempt to ascertain his movements, but had sent her letter at the last possible moment before returning to the castle. If he failed to arrive on time, that would be that, and there would be nothing she could do about it. Wasn't that what she was thinking?

After all, Fuku, too, must have feared meeting Sukezaemon. Whatever their present circumstances, the fact remained that she was a former concubine, still in mourning, secretly trysting with another man. Sending that letter at the last possible moment had the look of a gamble, as if she had decided to chance what their luck might be at that very last moment. Whether he arrived on time or failed to arrive on time—that would be decided by fate.

But Fuku revealed none of that fear on her face. Sukezaemon watched her expression closely as he told her of his work in the mountains.

Then they heard footsteps, and two maids came carrying trays of food and flasks of saké.

"Do have a drink," Fuku said after the women had left the room. "I'll have some, too." She picked up the flask and poured for Sukezaemon, and he, silently, filled her cup with saké.

"And please do relax," Fuku said. "We can trust the girl who was here before. She knows everything. She'll be keeping watch to make sure no one comes near this room until I call her."

"Really?" Sukezaemon emptied his cup and reached for the

flask, but Fuku stayed his hand and filled his cup herself. "When did you come here?" he asked.

"Five days ago."

So that was it, Sukezaemon thought. She came five days ago, and finally, on the morning of the day she was to return to the castle, she made up her mind to meet him.

"My, but you've been very daring."

"Yes."

"But of course. Ever since you were a child, you've had a hidden streak of daring in you."

Fuku smiled, but said nothing. Her face wore the same smile as when she was a child.

"Bunshirō-san," she said suddenly. "Since we have managed to meet, shall we talk about old times?"

"I'd like that."

"I was so attached to you, Bunshirō-san. I remember that night you took me to the festival at the Kumano Shrine. I must have been a terrible nuisance."

"No, not really."

"What's become of your friends from those days?" she asked, counting on her fingers. "Owada Ippei-sama, Shimazaki Yonosuke-sama …"

"You have a good memory."

"Owada-sama was a big man, rather frightening; Shimazaki-sama was very bright, but so slight …"

They looked at each other and smiled.

"Perhaps you've heard, but Shimazaki Yonosuke is now teaching at the domain academy; they say that in a few more years he'll be made dean. And Owada Ippei is an inspector. He has eight children."

"My! *Eight* children!" Fuku started to laugh aloud, then

checked herself and mumbled something about Bunshirō-san, too, having been a success.

"You have children, too, Bunshirō-san?

"I have two."

Sukezaemon's eldest was a boy and his younger a daughter. His son was now twenty. This year he would begin training as a member of the Bodyguard.

"I'll have to be arranging a marriage for my daughter soon, too.

"So now we've both become parents, haven't we?"

"So we have."

"But was there never any way that your children could have been my children, and my children could have been yours?" Fuku spoke precipitately, but her face remained calm, and she smiled softly, as though she were dreaming of something that might actually have been possible. Sukezaemon, too, smiled, but spoke quite directly.

"That that could never be, I shall regret as long as I live."

"Truly …? That makes me happy. But that is how it must end, isn't it? There's no one in the world who has no regrets; there's no other way …" A look of vague despair came over Fuku's pale face. Then suddenly, as Sukezaemon gazed at her, her eyes flashed back at him, now full of life.

"Do you remember that night before I went to Edo, when I came to your home?"

"I remember it well."

"I hated to go to Edo. I went to ask your mother: 'Please—marry me to Bunshirō-san …' But the words just wouldn't come out. I can never forget how I cried all the way home, along that dark road."

Fuku heaved a deep sigh—the voice of her grief that fate had driven them apart. She had been left a widow by the late lord

Semishigure

of the domain. The child she had borne him had already been adopted by a high-ranking bannerman. Her parents were no longer living. She was alone in the world.

"Do you remember this finger?" Fuku edged closer to Sukezaemon as she showed him the middle finger of her right hand. The sweet fragrance of her skin wafted up to him.

"It's the finger that snake bit," she said.

"Yes, I sucked the blood from it for you.

Fuku cast her eyes downward and sipped a bit of saké from her cup. Then she slid even closer, and threw herself upon Sukezaemon's breast. The two of them clasped each other. Sukezaemon sought her lips and Fuku responded feverishly. Sukezaemon's heart seemed almost to overflow with affection.

How long had it been? How much time had passed? Fuku gently raised herself from Sukezaemon's embrace. As she turned away to rearrange the disheveled folds of her kimono, Fuku tried to conceal her sobs. Then she raised her face, turned back to him, and smiled.

"Thank you Bunshirō-san," she said, her voice still tearful. "Now I have no more regrets."

When they descended the stairs, her conveyance was waiting. They had come for her at the appointed hour, but with a simple town litter. They would first transport Fuku to the Minoya, where she would change to her own palanquin and return to the castle.

Sukezaemon stood holding the bridle of his horse as he watched Fuku, accompanied by her attendant, bow silently, then board her litter. After she had passed through the gate, he himself nodded to the people at the inn and led his horse out. He could see her litter dwindling into the distance down the dry, bright, sandy road. As he watched, it disappeared behind a dune dotted sparsely with scrub pines and covered in morning glory vines. Sukezaemon patted his horse on the face, swung smartly up into the saddle, and rode slowly away.

Ah, if only ... he thought; if only I had never seen the white of her breast. Until that memory should fade, he felt, the pain would never cease, yet at the same time he felt a deep sense of fulfillment. He would have to consider himself fortunate that their meeting today would at least linger in his memory.

Sukezaemon headed out the road through the dunes that led back to the village of Yajiri. The image of a young girl floated into his mind, her face despondent, her eyes downcast, walking along in a kimono too short for her. Probably he would never see Fuku again.

He hadn't noticed before, but now, as he looked up into the grove of black pines, the shrilling of the cicadas fairly deafened him, now swelling, now fading, as if he were caught in a passing shower. The cicadas called to mind Yaba-machi, where they had lived as children, and the thicket there on the outskirts. Sukezaemon rode slowly through the grove, and where the road emerged from the dunes, he reined in his horse for a moment. Ahead of him he could see the parched fields, still baking under the sun, its glare undiminished despite all the time that had passed.

Then Sukezaemon pressed his heels into the flanks of his horse and galloped off into the light.

Semishigure

honfordstar.com